Also by Robin F. Gainey and Untreed Reads Publishing

Jack of Hearts

For my daughters, Erin and Sara,
the strongest women I know,
of gentle spirit and abiding love.
You are my heroes.

Acknowledgments

Contrary to popular belief, writing is not a solitary profession. Feedback is the most important part of crafting a novel. Many gave their time and skill to this story, and I wish to thank them from the bottom of my heart for their great suggestions and critical thinking along the way. Among them, in order of their time spent along the way, Jerry Sanford, Susan Wiggs, Don McQuinn, Veronica Randall, Kathryn Craft, Elsa Bowman, Tom Skerritt, Julie Tokashiki, Erin Gainey, Sara Gainey, Elizabeth Stuver, Elizabeth Evans, Tom Bruhn, Karen Langley Stephen, Mimi Benhart, Mary Sanders, Enid Gilbert, Jennifer Reibman, Jane Charles, and Caron Carlyon. A special thanks to editor, and publisher, at Untreed Reads, K.D., Sullivan and Jay Hartman, for their support, and the wonderful job they do. I appreciate you all so much.

Great things are done when men and mountains meet.

William Blake

Contents

The Outer Journey

Part One

To Conquer Death

Minutes after noon, as Aiden McBride rummaged through saddlebags for a bite of grease-soaked biscuit to welcome midday, the big bay horse beneath him startled and froze.

Aiden looked up. The snowbound Bighorn mountains watched in silence as a grizzly stormed over a downed elk. Massive paws lurched the carcass to and fro, as skilled jaws peeled skin from flesh in broad, ruby stripes. Raw wind ruffled the bear's hackles. The creature paused at the horse's nicker—and looked straight at Aiden.

Learning from a hunting guide that no wisdom came in locking eyes with the wild, Aiden looked away, mind racing. He'd been gunning for grizzly since riding the mountain. To a desk-bound Scotsman in 1888, such a kill equated to taming the Wild West. At least that's how he considered the scheme when the whole affair lay as undeclared ambition. Squared off against the beast, some thirty yards away, the aim struck him as pure death wish.

A chill rivaling the subzero air gripped him at the prospect of taking the monster alone. First impulse was to flee. A choice his to make. Behind the bear stood slab-sided Cloud Peak. Hemming them in on the left, a wide creek rushed, and smoked into the cold. Escape laid in the direction he'd come. The big bay's shoulder quivered indecision. A warning growl set everything into motion.

Knee and shoulders, Aiden aimed the big bay at his prey. Yanked off his gloves, slipped his rifle from the scabbard on his saddle, and raised its salvation. "Bear, you're the only why in Wyoming."

His horse wanted nothing to do with the venture—hooves dancing on the ground, clatter echoing off the granite floor. Aiden sat deep in the saddle to steady the animal beneath him, but the big bay fought the reins, making a clean shot impossible. He wrapped the reins around the saddle horn to free both his hands. The horse jigged. Saddlebags and gloves slipped to the earth. Aiden's heart pumped into his ears as he braced the rifle to his torso. Aimed. Horse, sidestepping, snorted steam into the biting cold.

With the commotion the grizzly lost patience, leapt over the elk, and charged.

The big bay spun toward the creek. Aiden and his rifle hit the granite hard. He leapt up, grabbing for reins still fastened to the horn—he would not try to outrun the bear on foot. He twisted one end of the tight leather once around his left wrist. Braced against the rocky bank. The frantic animal pulled back. Aiden dragged behind into the middle of the stream. His clothes sucked up the glacial water. The horse, unrelenting, stretched Aiden's arm to its limit. Aiden grabbed a hunting knife from his belt, lunging its blade in the direction of reins tight-wire taut. Missed. Leather skidded against his wrist, burning deep into his skin. Blood mixed into the ice water on his hand. Again and again he swiped the knife toward his bond to free the horse. Release them both.

Two winners in the tug-of-war.

His shoulder gave up first. Deep within the muscle came a sickening pop as Aiden sliced through the strap and on, deep into his forearm. His fingers, shocked at what his hand had done, dropped the knife into the stream. The water ran too deep and swift to grant any hope of retrieval. His two gloves, already well downstream. Aiden whirled around in searing pain, searching for the bear, his fingers limp with the dislocation of his shoulder, blood gushing from the knife wound. The big bay splashed across the water. Thundering hooves faded into the hoary storm of woods and underbrush, leaving behind the solitary whoosh of indifferent flow pushing between jagged rocks.

The moose-size grizzly reared up in Aiden's footprints along the shore and sniffed the air. Aiden dissolved into the water, chin grazing the surface, hoping to become another stone in the stream. The gash on his arm was fire.

Rifle and saddlebags lay in a useless heap at the bear's feet. The menace fell to all fours, rocking back and forth as though swaying to a moronic rhythm of some distant dirge, then pawed the saddlebags.

Biscuits.

That, and a bit of desiccated beef the hunters called "pemmican," was Aiden's only food. The demon turned its rump to the stream and defecated into the water. A wolf howled somewhere up-mountain. The bear raised his head to the sound, then moved toward the elk to protect its kill. Aiden envied that. The fiend had better things to do than eat a few meager lumps of grease-soaked dough and tired flesh. With one long groan the grizzly rumbled upstream, disappearing over a rise in the bank.

Thanks to the pardon of a dead elk, Aiden would live, though miserably. He lingered in the stream. He wouldn't share the same shore with the bear until a good distance stood between them. His body numbed. He knew he had to take action while he still could. With his horse nothing but a memory, he moved back toward the shallows to retrieve his weapon.

Strong currents battered his shoulder as he plodded one dull foot after another until he stooped on the bank, keeping his head hidden from the bear. Water rushed from his trousers and boots. His neck and head throbbed with cold. He grabbed a dripping, oversized kerchief from his pants pocket. With one end between his teeth, he pulled the cloth taut around his upper arm, and tied the ends off to stop his bleeding. He used the drenched neck scarf to wrap the knife wound, holding the arm tight against his body to lessen the excruciating pain.

God, the air was cold.

Morning had taken a razor's edge. Ice crept up the cuffs on his pants. The collar of his flannel shirt stiffened with frost. His sheepskin coat, sopped. The ungodly weight of fleece pressing on his injury. He ripped the sodden coat from his back. Nothing must slow him. Again, the wolf cried, and the bear moaned in answer. An arctic breeze slapped the drenched shirt against his skin as he reached for his rifle. The weapon, too, had found its way into the water.

He wasted no hope on thoughts of rescue. Eager to win the prize of a grizzly, he'd left the rest of the hunting party behind to sleep away the predawn and spend the final day of hunting in mountain meadows. No one knew his plan.

None knew his path.

He'd ridden up 2,000 feet short of Cloud Peak's 13,000 foot granite tip, ready to punctuate his accomplishments: conquering a mountain and killing a great bear. Warrior enough to provide meat to shepherd his sister through the brutish winter. Able to be the man she measured.

The man he wanted to be.

Aiden peered over the rise. The bear once again hunched over its prey, grumbling through its meal, protecting its quarry. The titan looked in Aiden's direction and gnashed its teeth as if to say, *watch and learn.*

Wincing, Aiden swung the saddlebags around his neck with his functional hand, and tucked the rifle under his right arm. He dragged the soggy pelt behind him a few dozen paces, his aching body faltering on the uneven soil.

Should he leave the coat?

The wool would freeze before ever drying. Slow him. No use to keep a piece of ice. He shook the idiotic idea from his mind. Even wet, the lambskin would hold some comfort—as long as his body had heat to grant.

The chill taking Aiden wasn't from the twenty-below freeze. Behind him, the crackle of bones between the grizzly's jowls peppered the mountain silence, and he knew his quest had changed.

To conquer death.

For that he must dry the clothes. Raise his body temperature.

Fire. His one hope.

When Sorrows Come

Eden Rose trudged the dingy pasture rim, she-goats bouncing along at her heels. The pair had no names. Such a thing would make them harder to eat if life came to that. Her husband had said so. And ever since Hugh had delivered Eden to the godforsaken Wyoming territory, she feared that, in time, there'd be goat on the table.

But summer had seen them lean, not fatten, along with the pock-marked land around her. Eden doubted the goats had enough flesh on them for prairie flies stalking the living, depending on death. She swept a hand through the buzzing about her head.

What in Satan's name drove people west? The struggle to be different? To understand man's limits to grief or vigor?

Homesteading was little more than hanging from an unbridled noose over a tall canyon.

The wait for doom, endless.

Though, as God stood above, she'd not let the rope tighten. She adored the little creatures. Hugh bought them as a novelty on their way West a decade ago. The pair giving them plenty of milk and cheese until the drought had turned the flow to a trickle. But to Eden they granted much more: affection, laughter—and love. Hugh's paucities.

Every detail fit for an opera.

A mournful wind soughed through cottonwoods flanking the Powder River, stirring her anger along with the dust. The warm September morning had fallen prey to a chilling breeze from the west. The temperature, a good thirty degrees below the comfort of noon, danced in an undecided fit. Eden flexed her fingers to warm them, and pulled the thick shawl around her shoulders, kneeling at a small break in the barb along an uneven fence-line. She grabbed a pair of canvas gloves from her pocket, and a short piece of wire from a leather pouch across her shoulder.

Her constant battle was to contain the mustangs. They'd broken through the rickety fence twice that week. Four mares, four foals, two weanlings, and a two-year-old colt that should have been separated last spring, but was too rank to catch, had scattered to the wind as soon as they were free. Rounding them up alone, a brutal job. The space between pronghorn antelope wanting in to eat the hay and horses wanting out to roam was her prison.

Wild things tested all boundaries.

The notion of freedom buoyed her for a moment before drowning in the sight of another fence-break.

She pushed a few strands of her hair back underneath a headscarf, and focused on the task. Winding wire around one end of the severed line, she threaded an eye at the end of the other. The link was pulled as tight as her hands allowed while she searched the back corners of her memory for the things her husband tended in preparation for winter. Eight years had been whittled away by a sharp focus to her own duties: endless canning, mending, hauling wood, and patching never-ending gaps in the walls and ceiling of the sod cabin. Eden glanced at the barn. Besides putting up hay, Hugh's primary concern was the curing of meat and repairing the stable and fences. None of which she'd accomplished to his standards. Even if she had meat to cure, she'd not paid close attention to the process. She was unsure the task could be accomplished without producing poison.

A violent cough bent Eden in two. The goats scattered. She wiped the back of her hand across the corner of her mouth, and caught her breath. The illness in her lungs since August, though waning, had sapped her strength and shortened the time left to ready for the coming snow. She massaged her upper arms, hoping to reinvigorate them. Bones at her shoulders were little more than nobs, and the muscles at the base of her neck ached. Little strength remained to lend to a bath, yet she didn't see how she could creep into bed without one. She'd not be claimed by the filth of homesteading. A warm tub kept her sane.

Barbs pressed into her palms as she finished securing a curl of wire back upon itself and twice around a post. She tugged with all her strength, knowing the mend was feeble, but it would have to do. Another load of feed waited to be hauled to pasture, and water to cart from creek to trough after fences were secured. Her fists clenched tight at the thought of splitting a section of log before nightfall. Ranch work was staggering. Though she blessed Hugh for the peace he'd given her in his absence, she damned him for being gone so long.

He had left for Southampton in the spring with the last sound group of polo ponies, determined to raise more cash for their failing claim before winter's snow. In Hugh's absence, her brother had come all the way from Glasgow to help her. His arrival, the only good thing about her husband's departure. The first time Aiden had set eyes on her in five years, his face reflected a wicked truth—she'd grown haggard and frail. Yet his twisted clown expression of surprise made her laugh. She loved him for his spark. Aiden's willing grin always improved the climate of her heart. And always been a constant savior.

Aiden, all of ten, had ventured into a raging surf to turn her spaniel pup toward shore after the dog had gone too far to fetch a stick she'd thrown. And it had been Aiden to discover an abandoned stone cottage overgrown in the dale near their home of Lilybank. The magical chanty held a tattered library, left behind as though the books had been read too many times to bother packing—their owner longing for undiscovered tales. Surrounded by the cool of stone walls, the two read to each other long into balmy summer afternoons. *Canterbury Tales*, the entire series of Waverly Novels, and Aiden's favorite, Dickens' *Nicholas Nickleby*, about a young man's family left penniless after the death of his father.

A novel written about them.

Then, her beloved Guarneri violin.

A gift from her affluent parents when she turned twelve, the centuries-old instrument had been sold in destitution to pay Aiden's first year of college tuition. Her most prized possession, gone. But Aiden's expression at learning he'd attend the University in Glasgow was ample repayment for her privation. Still, she had pined for its return. Life went monotone without her music.

And Aiden knew.

He'd used his bagpipes as collateral to save her violin from being sold again, and worked two jobs to buy the instrument back. Graduation day, his gift to Eden: a gorgeous box she suspected held flowers, instead bore her cherished music.

Dressed in finery as he stepped from the train in Sheridan two months before, Aiden was the most civilized thing she'd encountered since leaving Scotland. He played jester to her meager court, peppering their banter with Shakespeare as though he'd written the words himself. And his jig to the music of her violin, the dance of a God. He was a constant reminder—she'd once been as fine a thing as he.

Aiden to the aid.

Rescuing dogs and deserted books—or an old woman from a pond. Eden shut her eyes to the quicksilver memories of a time long buried.

Yet his face, a mother's twin.

Aiden was a darling, even though her spirit no longer found anything pure about beauty. Whether the face of her brother or the spectacular mountains beyond, both held caveats. Aiden's cheery countenance was all he had to offer. He didn't take to ranching. Raised an aristocrat, he'd never dabbled in anything less. Clueless to the threat of a destitute winter, he'd been too long behind a barrister's door in a big city, with coal for the fire on command and fine dining halls at every corner. He was game for any job, but lacked awareness. Never dealt with the wild. Yet Eden wouldn't shame him. He made her happy. And a nurtured spirit could deal with anything, even the extra labor of covertly fixing a brother's mistakes.

But double-duty left her no time to finish the canning required for winter. Bacon had run out, and with it, the fat that bathed the biscuits. She'd not asked her closest friend, Maddie, for more. The request was hard enough the first time. Maddie already had ten mouths to feed. Hugh was due to send a letter that would certainly come with money. Eden could wait.

Wind caught a stand of cottonwoods beside the pasture. Rustling leaves cackled awake a few roosting hens. Eden peered at the branches.

So, that's where they'd gotten to.

Ravening wolves had raided Aiden's poor patch of the coop. Surviving chickens scattered, leaving Eden to forage an egg or two beneath the scrub—when she could find them. They had eaten the last bird they dared, a scrawny rooster, before Aiden set off to hunt the Bighorn. Discussion over the skimpy meal centered on all the things that had gone wrong since he'd arrived.

"When sorrows come, they come not single spies, but in battalions." Aiden chewed a stringy thigh, smiling through his Shakespeare. "Act four, scene five—Hamlet."

Humor in the face of starvation.

Eden eyed the chickens. Too high to reach, the birds fluffed their feathers and gabbled laughter, as though they knew she was unarmed. Her mouth watered at the memory of meat. Henceforth, she'd bring along the rifle. A vow of desperation. Until that moment, a gun, the one thing she'd not touch. Murder might be the way of a necropolis called the West, and she'd done her share with her bare hands, but she'd not use lead. Killing that way was the work of men.

Or the way of a woman starved.

Soon, something other than dry biscuits and the occasional egg would have to appear. With the last money in the bank, she'd bought only a ten-pound sack of flour, and spent the rest on a load of grass hay. Horses were the priority, and she'd tacked up flyers all over the small, nearby town of Suggs offering them for sale. Unpredictable at best, they'd as soon take a hunk of flesh than a bite of fruit, but they were trained to ride and drive. If kept up they had some value.

Hugh would be livid if he knew. He'd not yet given up on the polo pony enterprise. She imagined him now, in a Scottish bank, begging for a loan to bolster his delusions, while she dealt with the reality of an empty stomach.

Another cool gust confirmed the determined business of approaching winter. Eden turned to the west, scanning the top of the Bighorn range. As a rule, clouds were in scant supply until autumn broke, but they billowed up over the shoulder of the eastern slope with mid-September, tall and serious, laying claim to an eastward path straight to Rose Ranch. Their beauty took her breath away until the storm brewing settled in her heart. With no word yet from Hugh, she said a silent prayer to hold the weather until her brother returned with enough game to sustain them. Aiden was young and strong, but she knew the mountains to be relentless when gripped by snow. Few dared to cross them.

A crack split the air like a bullet. At the far end of the pasture, a solitary mare raised a hind foot to the rowdy young stallion. A fine horse sure to be a good stud. Tomorrow she'd have to muster the courage to pull him from harm's way. One well-placed blow and he'd be nothing more than a gelding.

The angry mare kicked again, catching the fence instead. With a snap, the post shattered, wire coiling around the splintered wood like spun sugar. The goats fell, paralyzed in surprise. The herd of mustangs stampeded toward them.

Eden grabbed each goat by a hind leg. Pulled hard, and struggled her way under the fence, barbs snatching at her hands and skirt. Dragging the little animals to safety, her garment ripped through from waist to hem. She thrust one hand through the wire to pull her skirt from the barb, and caught her palm instead. Sticky blood trickled into the creases of her hand. She lay on the hardpan dirt behind the safety of the fence as the mustangs thundered past. Kicked-up earth hailed all around. Relieved, Eden closed her eyes to stave off frightened tears. She opened them to the goats licking a set of crimson scratches on one arm. She put a hand on each animal. Their cashmere filled in for winter. The rich feel of silken wool reminded Eden of the Scotland home she'd left behind. Woolen tartans and soft, delicate lace; a maid to bring cream tea at four.

Nothing but a dream in tatters.

She scratched their withers, reveling in a single remnant of comfort. One lifted a hind foot to its ear and scratched.

"Aye, you see? Better than a simple salt-lick, I am, even though I'm quite sure I look no better."

She sat up to examine her ruined skirt, tore a piece away, and wrapped the cloth around the deep cut on her hand. Her little friends bleated an objection as she stood.

"Oh, quit pestering yourselves. Hugh'll be bringing a trunk full of treasures when he returns. I'll have a new skirt." A goat nibbled at the base of her bloomers laid open on one side by the wire. "A few china bowls and a bolt of linen lace for the windows, too." Eden scanned the dilapidated ranch spread out in the glen below and brushed her hands together. "Finery for the hell hole."

The goats followed her to a gaping hole at the fence post. They yanked at her flagging skirt while she repaired the damage with the last few pieces of wire in her pouch. All too short for a proper fix, but light was fading. She'd mend her paltry effort come morning. She prayed the horses not test its muscle.

Dry leaves rustled, and she glanced behind her, uneasy at the sunset. Truth be told, she sensed being watched.

Ah well, who would hear a cry for help?

The fence could be mile-high iron and not keep out the one thing thriving on the hateful ranch—her fear. Dread had moved in, made itself at home, and found plenty on which to feed. Imagination was the barbwire she used to keep such devils out.

Her best hope, a soothing memory of time, long passed: her fine home across the sea, flanked by broad green meadows and jagged hills, the Firth of Clyde tossing its head beyond, between a bonnie wee island and the Glasgow shore.

And the dream of a beautiful man. One she'd seen only in her visions but was sure existed, somewhere. A loving man—a man she loved.

With one more nervous glance around, she told herself that watching eyes belonged to the chickens, and that she'd yet have her way with them. She stood tall to show herself capable, packed her tools, and walked the fence line up and over the modest rise toward her sod home. Yet trepidation laced her, tight and uncomfortable as an old undersized shoe.

Dust from a passing rider was no more than a pale swirl at the road's horizon, as she crossed the wagon-wide bridge above Crazy Woman Creek. She dropped the tools in the barn. The goats pushed through a narrow stand of willows flanking one side of her cabin to forage for their supper. A short picket fence marked the edge of grass dried to dust under the weight of a long drought. Passing three heartrendingly small graves, Eden muttered a prayer for the souls of her lost babes—dreams denied. Each inscription, sharp edged and sore, carved into her heart.

The soil, taken so much, returned so little.

Overhead, the willows arced in the breeze and Eden stopped cold at their miracle: autumn leaves speckling the trees turned to branches full of roosting chickens. She gentled her breathing, and inched her way across the hardpan yard. Keeping her eyes on the birds, Eden pushed open the door to the cabin, and reached for the shotgun. Pulled its weight through the doorway. Lifted its power to her breast. She drew the hammer back, bracing her feet the way Hugh always did. No need to fret about perfect aim, she knew the shot would scatter. Her targets blinked cold poultry eyes as though disbelieving Eden had the mettle in her to squeeze the trigger. She clenched her teeth. They couldn't fathom her driving hunger. She held her breath. Closed her eyes tight. Fired.

The blast was a mule kicking her shoulder. Back she fell, into the doorway. A fracas of chickens moved to higher limbs in a whirl of feathers and disgust. Not one took a hit for her famine.

She beat the ground with a fist and clenched her teeth. "God be damned."

Cursing came as much a surprise to Eden as the feel of the gun. Both shocked her, as though executed by someone else. Fear was capable of things overlooked by the unharmed heart.

She picked herself up to find a she-goat at the base of her cabin door. Upturned by the shock of gunfire, the wee brute's teeth clamped tight to the edge of an envelope. Eden shrieked, yanking the casing from its mouth. The goat stood again by the time Eden pushed the cabin door open and collapsed into a rocker.

Slipping the headscarf from her hair, she let her hand rest under the date on the piece of rumpled mail: twentieth of July. Two months before. She tossed her scarf on the mahogany dining table, the only piece of furniture to follow her across the Atlantic, and opened the rest of the torn envelope with care. She didn't want to damage the bank check she would find. Inside was a single sheet of flimsy paper inscribed with fine handwriting.

> *Dearest,*
>
> *I will be brief in the recounting of my journey, for what occurred is no longer of concern. I say only that the ocean passing was cruel and the landing more so. The little sorrel, Jess, could not get to his feet and died on the ship. The passage was much longer than usual due to foul weather. All were so weak from starvation they had trouble setting one foot in front of the other. I slung the roan, trying to save him, as he could not stand. Four ponies were lost in the end, dying like rotten sheep in the ship's hold. I fear a good forty-percent of the remaining horses will not live. To cap the blow, I was badly hurt, dragged by a pony during the offload. I am recovering, but the mend is slow. In hospital for near a month, I*

have been released to the mercy of the bank, where I sit writing a letter. I received a mere fifty pounds for each head surviving passage. Credit is at an end. Doctors say I should attempt no travel until spring. As my mind is set, I am afraid, even then, my injuries may prevent me from laboring at the ranch. So, with a heavy spirit, I propose the remaining stock be sold, Rose Ranch be closed up, and the funds used to join me.

Loving, Hugh

The hope of returning to Scotland took her breath away, until anger found its legs. One page. Twelve uses of *I*. Not a single word given to *her*. As ever, all about Hugh. It wasn't possible to do what he bid before winter, and she had no cash to grant her fare. The Crazy Woman held her for ransom. She had little strength to chuckle at an irony that would have had Aiden rolling on the plank floor.

She looked back across the words on the linen paper. *Dearest*—an expected salutation; the obligatory "how are you?" one expresses to an acquaintance on the street. And, *Loving*—Hugh didn't know the meaning. The word was used in hindsight.

Eden wiggled loose the simple gold band on her finger and contemplated the prudence of selling such a thing. Wind blustered through one of the open windows and she set the ring on a dresser, rushing to stop the raw air. Frayed woolen curtains billowed in the breeze, reminding her of the bolt of linen lace promised to replace them. Another pledge broken. She batted the frame hard, unmooring one of its small panes. Glass shattered on the hard oak floor. Hugh's missive fell into the shards.

A life, in pieces.

Eden picked up the letter, walked to the corner kitchen, and laid her husband's charge on the table next to another bill recently arrived. She unwrapped her bloodied hand, and reached for the last bottle of Scotch whisky in the cupboard. Using her teeth to pull the top free, she poured what remained into her stinging palm. She yanked clean linen hanging at the side of the stove to sop up the rest, examined her wound, and licked off the excess alcohol dripping from her fingers. Eden cupped the palm to her nose and inhaled the peaty scent, a dank cloud surrounding Hugh every evening, as he sipped a jigger of Scotch and peered at the fire in silence. The odor turned her stomach.

With no details of his injury offered, she questioned the severity of his condition. Had he taken a shine to the luxuries of civilization? Old habits died hard. Rounders only go round and round. The way of a career military man—falling as easily into bed with a different woman as he did a foreign war. She imagined him getting to London and attaching himself to a dollish nurse tending his wounds. How long had he contemplated leaving and not coming back? Doubtless the idea was in his mind, as one thing after another went wrong on the ranch. God knew the notion was in hers. She shook her head. Life had laid opportunity in his lap and yanked away her every option.

Eden's fist banged the table hard. The china in the adjacent cupboard rattled. Her fury fought her hunger for first place. She could take no more. If she had to do a man's work, she'd slog along without feminine trappings. She ripped remaining shreds of skirt from her waist and headed for the barn in her bloomers. The goats were curious kittens prattling along beside.

From a wall full of tools she grabbed the shovel, pulled an oilcloth coat from a hook, and headed for the overgrown garden behind the cabin. Crickets lauded the arrival of dusk as she stomped across the yard. A solitary hen clucked a muted taunt from a willow.

The garden lay picked clean, but Eden held out hope for buried fortune. She dug up the mounds of withering potato plants with the deep thrusts of a gravedigger. Three stunted russets the size of a big toe appeared in the discarded dirt. She was quick to push them into her coat pockets before the goats overtook them. Eden continued turning soil to no avail. At the end of the fourth row she quit, tears streaming at the refuse her life had become.

17

The garden, finished.

A scraping sound brought her attention to the goats. Bickering over something scavenged under a broad plant in the next row, they grunted like piglets. A squash, gold amid the ruin, disappeared in large bites. Eden screamed. One of the beggars ran, the other fainted. She leapt across the garden row, sobbing as she landed next to the disabled goat. Eden blinked through her tears. The helpless beast lay as if in rigor-mortis awaiting burial.

Without a name.

Its terrified eyes tracked her movement as Eden, thankful for her teary vision, raised the shovel above her head. She grimaced at the impulse forcing her hand as she acted to end the life of something she adored. But the circumference of her love had dwindled over the years and she'd been taken only once before by such hopelessness.

Through the veil of Eden's despair her mother struggled for breath beyond the same bars of a cage Eden had shared with duty so many years ago. She smelled the rotting flesh of the vegetables beneath her, tasting a vague and bitter truth.

Desperation—the iron fist of survival.

A Man Lost

A woman with hair of fire. In the middle of a pasture, a good distance from her shelter, and far from finished for the day. Neither here nor there.

And she didn't see him.

Hidden in the shadow of a solitary oak under the crest of a hill, he held a hand to the late afternoon sun streaming through the branches. His chest lay bare to the heat of the day, shoulders sweating under the protection of his hair, but the breeze had turned cool. He sat still, knowing his burnished skin and roan horse blended well into the arid landscape.

The woman never looked his way.

He measured distance by the slant of the sun. Starting well before light, he raced the orb westward. Weary from the ride, if he kept to the trail he'd be within reach of his goal that evening: the Face of Arrows, cliffs at the eastern base of the Bighorn where the Crazy Woman spilled onto the plains. Winter would soon be with him, the tease of snow now dappling the Bighorn piling chin-deep till spring. Yet, he did not move, drawn to the woman below as a horse is drawn home.

He'd meant to linger a few minutes. To rest his mount in the shade before continuing. But seeing her set his memory aflame. The square set of her shoulders and curve of her bosom, familiar. Not until she'd appeared without a scarf, last ray of sunset catching her copper hair, did he sit tall enough upon the horse to give himself away.

He sat still, eyes unfocused at the oak leaves overhead, sound of the nearby Powder River prattling over stones like memories. His mind retreated eight long years.

He had seen her before.

* * *

19

In the ruin of a white man's camp up-mountain, his horse had stepped unevenly, anticipating the unknown. Brittle autumn grass stood littered with metal pots and pans, mangled bedrolls. One loose sleeve of a canvas coat fluttered as if trying to command the frigid breeze. No other movement, no sound, nothing to suggest suffering.

No one remaining to whom he could offer aid.

A crumbling roll of fresh earth served as windbreak to a recent campfire of cool ash, lifting in a gust to mingle with a smattering of tiny snowflakes. Deep prints of a great bear tracked over the soft ridge, first toward the camp, then in retreat. Blood froze in the footsteps, paled by snow like the dust of time.

He had seen the immense creature that morning. Its greyish coat, thick and bright, the animal was young, yet it swayed and slipped along a mountain ridge. Thinking the beast was sick, or rabid, he'd kept well downwind. The puddles of blood revealed the truth—serious injury caused its struggle. Depending on where the animal had taken the bullet, the slug might be carried for years, and suffering endless.

He understood that breed of timeless pain.

Scanning the surrounding woods, he sharpened his hearing. An injured bear had no equal.

To one side of the camp a wooden container the size of a gun box lay abandoned. The withdrawal of the hunters must have been swift and careless. He had no need for another firearm but preferred his hand hold the weapon to that of an enemy. He swung off his mount, pulled the box upright, slipped its wide leather straps from their buckles, and opened the lid.

Inside, rested two rolls of felt. One, short and thick, the other, long and slender; each tied with a narrow black ribbon. He opened the fat roll first. An array of small, squeezable tubes secured in individual pockets lay side-by-side along the length of the fabric. A marvelous display. Labels revealed pigments he had never seen in nature's generous spectrum. The brighter of these looked untouched. Darker tubes were squeezed to near nothing. The slender roll held an assortment of brushes. He pulled one from its place and swept the tip across his cheek. Soft as mink.

He replaced the brushes and pulled a wide, leather-bound book from the foot of the box. Its paper lay thick and stiff, the surfaces rough as a canvas bedroll. After the first few pages, sharp-edged ink sketches flowed into dusky landscapes. The turn of every page suggested a somber dream filled in by a solemn dreamer, each horizon a gilded promise of dawn—or a blemished stagger at a day's end. Then, came a startle of color.

The woman with hair of fire.

Her features etched fine as a doe's. But a vacant cast to the eyes, as though trying to capture a retreating dream, was disturbing. Her body was present; her spirit seemed elsewhere. A soul neither here nor there. A plight not unlike his own.

One look at that face of beauty opened a reservoir of memories holding the loss of his own woman; a pool of tragedy he'd sworn to leave without ripples. He had given up the search for water.

He'd traced his fingers along smooth curls falling in a wreath around the woman's face, then drawn the odor of the color deep into his lungs; the earthy scent of the canyon dirt used to redden the hair. The smell of the soil beneath a buffalo hide shelter after a hard rain. A sanctuary in a native camp, long gone...long ago. A way of life, lost. The weight of loss, the burden of years, lead around his heart.

* * *

Still. Time was a sly and tenacious companion. Grief, deep and unhurried.

He arched his back and put a hand to the base of his skull. He should ride on. Fence-mending held no interest for him; he hated seeing animals confined. Yet the woman's white blouse shone so bright against the sunburned hillside as she worked. Lovely limbs swung as she crossed to her home. She shot at the leaves of a willow for no reason, and he laughed. When she raced half-clad into a barn before disappearing behind the cabin, he'd craned his neck to see her. As shadows reached long he waited for her to return, rewarded as she pulled a bucket of water from a hand pump near the creek, crossing the yard again and again, awakening his own thirst.

Crickets hailed the coming evening. He sucked a welcome drink of water from a doeskin bag. Crows drew circles in the lavender sky above, coaxing him since the Black Hills, always in his sight, baiting the direction of his travel. He considered the wisdom of approaching. The beauty of a bird hovering in the wind was best appreciated from a distance.

He waited for a sign.

From the cover of the oak canopy, he considered the vacant yard until the cool dusk nipped his skin. The chill practiced for a freeze. Clouds tumbled down the shoulders of the eastern slope. He pulled the bearskin draping his horse up over his back.

Sudden movement—horses the woman worked to keep at pasture. They pawed the dust, resolute as warriors in their desire to escape. Finally, the wayward band broke through the fence to freedom.

With that he turned his horse in their direction, bid the guiding spirit thanks, and rode down toward the woman in the shelter below, eager as a man lost in darkness seeks a light.

Only God Knew

A murder of crows circled above the creek upstream as water trickled from the barrel of Aiden's rifle. Any killing would have to wait. Sun was a smudge behind clouds. Blue sky peeking through at that altitude was not the faded stain above the prairie, but dark and clear and close enough to touch. Moisture in the air turned to tiny crystals until the landscape resembled a dream world.

Colder than dawn. He'd prepared for that, but not for the drenching.

He pushed his rifle tight along the rifle under his good arm, and accomplished a feeble sprint down the mountain under the torture of his injured shoulder. Racking pain ran from his jawbone all the way to his spine. His shoulder socket became his whole core. His feet were senseless with cold. His knees did the work, pushing him forward over granite and brown grass. Downstream several miles, he stopped in the protection of trees.

Steam rose from his exposed skin, even though his clothes stiffened with ice. But the moment he was still, the feeling in his hands retreated as his blood sought warmer harbor. He knew the respite a deadening freeze brought to his aching shoulder came with a heavy price. Frostbite. Rotting flesh. Death. He reeled under the threat of rueful memories. Scottish winters, too, offered a brutish wrath.

He managed to pull a gold watch from his vest pocket and snapped open its cover. Four in the afternoon. Darkness would soon take him. Aiden searched the sky for a promise of more clouds to insulate against a further drop in temperature.

Nothing.

He pulled the scarf from his knife wound. The bleeding had stopped but the gash was full of grit and slime. He picked some away, and bound the limb back to his body as best he could. The task was agony but allowed him to work. He scoured the forest floor for tinder, blessing the drought for providing plenty of dry pine needles and dead wood. Soon a mound of kindling and brush piled high, with a few thick, dry branches to one side that he'd managed to draw up close. Another adage from his hunting guide remembered—what seemed good enough was five times too little to last the night. His shoulder begged rest, but he pruned anything not firmly rooted. If he stopped, the cold would seize him.

Aiden's hands were too dead to fumble through the saddlebags. Grimacing against the pain, he dropped to his knees, and turned their contents out onto the barren ground. Six biscuits he'd soaked in bacon grease and wrapped in linen before leaving camp that morning fell first. A strip of pemmican followed. He shoved the dry meat in his mouth then pawed through two apples, a small pocketknife, a bottle full of useless frozen onyx, a pen, and a small leather-bound journal, before finding the tin of matches he sought.

Aiden searched the rocky, tree-strewn landscape he'd left behind for any sign of the bear. The odor of bacon was fierce even in the glacial air. He dug the earth with the miniature knife and his one good hand. He ate another biscuit, rewrapped the remainder, pushed them to the bottom of the shallow hole, and mounded the stash with dirt. He wouldn't eat them all right away, but neither would he leave them to draw predators. Under the cover of soil the scent was erased. The protection of an alabaster sky as clouds appeared moving eastward from the peak, promised the temperature would drop no more.

He flicked open the canister of matches, counted twelve heads, and pulled a single match from the case. He touched its flame to the dry needles and resinous pine sticks and blew the embers to a decent blaze. His clothes steamed in the warmth.

But he would not relax. Beyond the circle of firelight was the bear, wolves—and if hunting stories proved true—murderous natives.

The bulk of native threat was history, but darkness fed all fears. Night had pecked at him from childhood. Scottish gales whipped in from the Firth of Clyde with regularity, thrashing Lilybank as though trying to wipe his island home clean of humanity. The crash of the sea and the frightful howl of a certain storm had long ago cast a fatal blow to Aiden's ego. Calamity had challenged, he'd refused. The failure became a metaphor for his inability to be that gale, rising against any dread. The whole reason he was on the mountain. But the Bighorn had become a thousand gales, trying his courage, begging him to rally.

All that was missing was the salt air.

He raised a hand to his lips and focused his foggy breath on the tips of his fingers. Once they could move, he thrust a hand into the pocket of his damp shirt and pulled a single coin from its depths, rolling the metal over between his fingers. The silver dulled in the fading light, but the letters stood dark against its background—J.W. Hunt Club. A memento. Proof of the invitation. Holding the evidence in his hand granted Aiden a surge of pride. Being in Jack's company was a coup. Son of Boss Williams, biggest cattle baron west of the Mississippi, the name was known as far away as Scotland. Aiden had been awed by the sight of the Williams' herd. They covered the plains, one enormous dappled cowhide. Aiden rotated the coin in his hand. Substantiation to those who'd question that he had ever faced the mountains of the American West. Those last two words turned round and round in his head. He put the coin atop his saddlebags. Of little use, the only thing its cool shine fed was vanity.

He imagined the snug cabin—Eden, using her hands to articulate her soul from the cavity of a violin. Aiden, cajoling his bagpipes in reply. Sister and brother, musical notes forever entwined against the same two-staff format. Bagpipes alone never sounded as rich or meaningful as when tended by the violin. The first work he'd ever taken had been for Eden. Every penny he'd earned had gone to buying back the instrument she'd sacrificed for his education. A year after becoming a barrister, he was still paying to recover his bagpipes from a music store owner who'd rather make a penny more than be honest. But he'd succeeded. And Aiden and the pipes had come to Wyoming to Eden's rescue again, in a way. Bringing his instrument to echo the sounds of youth when his sister was near and the score of his life complete. The picture made him drunk with fatigue and longing, until the crackle of brush sobered him.

His body stiffened, gaze searching the wood. Two whitetails bounded through the trees on their way down the mountain, pale rumps flashing like a blond spaniel puppy against sea-green waves. Aiden thought about that swim to rescue Eden's dog years before. The firth had been tepid compared to the bitter mountain air chewing at his skin. He missed the sound of the rumpled ocean; the fresh-faced energy of siblings; the lightness of being that a child feels at looking into the sky. Mostly he missed Eden, not only since he'd left Rose Ranch, and not since she'd left Scotland. But the Eden his sister had left behind once she walked down the aisle with Hugh Rose. The joyful, nonsensical young woman she had been. One thing she hadn't forsaken was her obstinacy. She was bent on holding her desiccated and forlorn ground in Wyoming.

Only God knew why.

A dusting of snow slipped its way through the cover of trees and onto his nose as he speculated what had pushed the deer to rush through his camp. He wrapped the cold fingers of his right hand around the rifle and pulled back the hammer. He checked the flesh on his fingers—pink. He'd kept frostbite at bay but his clothes refused to dry. In desperation, he stripped and hung the garments from long sticks near the heat, turning them, all the time keeping his naked skin as close to the heat as flame allowed, and balancing the rifle upon his good shoulder.

Aiden weighed the option of taking a shot to discourage the lurking bear against the chance that any sound might alert nearby Indians to his presence. Even though he imagined his hunting party to still be in camp, there remained but one fool on the mountain that night. He'd not waste a bullet on silliness. He dismissed the folly as being as equally daft as the father of Eden's best friend.

In one leap, Madeline True jumped into his mind. Despite the fact that her father was addled, Aiden had a fleeting whim to court her once. A small, sturdy woman with bright eyes and a sparkle of comedy that was as seductive a feature as her flock of children were a blight. The two were hard to reconcile. While he weighed the contrast, he did nothing to discourage her from coming around. Maddie was one of the few joys in Eden's life.

He fingered the only thing left clinging to his body, a woven bracelet made of Eden's hair. His mother made herself two, one from the hair of each child. The intricate auburn braids were capped in carved gold at each end; one engraved with initials, the other, with a birthdate. Golden clasp joined them. Their mother wore them until death. He and Eden vowed to wear each other's bracelets from then on. A few frays around the edges, he noted, but, all in all, they'd held up well against the years. Far better than he was holding up. The bracelet cut deep into the swollen wrist of his bad arm.

The clothes dried in half an hour. His sheepskin coat still dripped with water. He left the fleece turned out to the fire and dressed. Clothing was a warm comfort against his skin as he fed the fire until flames turned his part of the forest to midday. Sparks aspired in the heat of the blaze before him, mingled with the falling snowflakes—a dance of fire and ice. At half past seven his throat was dry, but he wouldn't walk the dark way to the water's edge. His thirst would have to wait until morning. He checked his watch at eight thirty, dug for another biscuit and ate the nugget whole. From a pants pocket he retrieved a small linen sachet of heather he liked to keep with him as a nod to his homeland. He held the damp bundle to his nose to capture what remained of its heady scent. He took up the ink he'd thawed by the fire, penning an entry in the journal:

October's fourth morning. I have injured my left arm and shoulder. Alone of my own volition, it has proven a bad choice. I am reminded that though risk is a necessary element of success and courage alike, foolishness and stupid errors often abridge brave lives. The horse is lost, but I know the way back to camp and I am well on that course. I may yet kill the bear if he wanders my way, for if I return to the mid-mountain camp with nothing to show for the loss of my mount and a poor condition, I shall be sorely criticized all around. No matter. My pride rode the runaway horse. Eden depends on me—this alone sets my course. God as my witness, I hate America.

Aiden focused a moment on the unvarnished truth of that last sentence. The West had a way of its own, turning man to prey, setting beast or weather on his trail. He secured the ink along with the pen and book, and pushed the annals to safety under the pile of kindling.

New throbbing took his shoulder, and the slash on his forearm was a hot poker, but he preferred a willing pain to the wicked cold. Aiden clutched his rifle, placing the weapon at an angle to brace himself as he rested against its steel. He stared at the glittering fire until his eyes surrendered. With them closed, feigning a warm sleep under the sun, propped against a metal porch chair was easier. Even as the flickering light on his eyelids danced like a dozen Indians around a bright flame.

When sleep overcame his pain, Aiden dreamed of Maddie. They lay in the deep grass beside the Powder River, enjoying the slow spark of each other's hands. A warm feeling inched its way up his spine, though even in his dream, the stirring was shameful. To know a woman out of wedlock in that way was a sin—unless the pleasure came with the guarantee of marriage. And wedlock was the last thing on Aiden's mind, even in sleep. With the rise of distant laughter, the pleasure ceased, the couple soon taunted by the poking fingers of a bandy brood of children.

Aiden bolted upright, wincing at the motion. By the time he knew the heckling was real, there was no time to raise his rifle against its torment. A knife blade crossed his throat, and the ruddy face of an Indian was so close that the rancid pemmican on his breath seemed to shrink the glow of the fire.

Fear struck him colder than any darkness he'd ever known. His mind ran away with stories of treasure in white scalps and the castration of small boys.

"Odd brand of hair you got, or is the firelight making me think it's that pretty red?" The man leaned past Aiden's face, running his other hand down Aiden's backside, grabbing his hand. "Pity I ain't got no time to spend the night."

Aiden was frozen. One move, and he knew the blade would do what it did best.

"It's a piss of a fire. Makes me laugh to think you're so stupid. Too stupid to need this." The man, hunched and hungry looking, grabbed Aiden's rifle. "How about I trade you for it?"

He punctuated every sentence with a press of the blade against flesh. A slight smile mimicked the shape of the knife.

"Trade?" A drop of warm blood chilled on Aiden's neck.

"Life for the rifle."

Aiden strained to raise his chin from the threat. The gleam of a shell choker around the man's neck struck Aiden that the two might at least have one civil thing in common.

The sight of an ocean.

He struggled to steady his voice. "Take it and you may as well kill me."

"Only one you got?"

Aiden eyed the big bay standing under a pine. "I had but one weapon and one horse."

The Indian looked around, gaze settling on the dying embers. "And one fine coat. Guess I have them all, now. Lucky for that horse he found me. You won't last long enough to tend him."

Keeping the knife against Aiden's neck, he tossed the rifle toward the horse, and reached for the silver coin atop Aiden's saddlebags. He turned the disk over in his hand. "J.W. Wouldn't be Jack Williams, would it?"

"I'm not he."

"Oh, I know." The Indian sneered, raising his chin into the air. "But he's near. I can smell him."

"My hunting party isn't far."

A weak argument.

"Well then, I'll leave you be. If you live long enough, let Jack Williams know the first time he turns his back, I'll be on him. He can spend the winter with that."

"You know him?"

"Sent me to hang."

"You look alive enough to me."

"Bars can't hold a raven." He pushed the coin into a pocket.

His eyes glistened in what little light was left of the fire and, for a moment, Aiden believed the Indian might turn to feathers and flee.

"Winter'll hold them all in a tomb. I can wait for the snow— take care of them all at once. With no notice till spring." The man gazed off into the wood as though he were seeing his words played out against the inky palette of darkness.

"All who?"

"Ranchers stealing the Powder." The Indian stared at the big bay. "You can steal a man's horse, he'll get another. But stealing land—hanging's too good for a man who does that."

Ranchers like Eden.

Aiden's toes gripped inside his boots. An owl hooted from the trees and drew the Indian's attention upward. Aiden rolled away from his grasp in the direction of the rifle, over his bad shoulder, in a loud whoop of pain. The canister of matches rattled beneath him. The Indian swept up the container and got to his feet in one fluid motion. He opened the top and slid eleven remaining matches into his gloved hand, fondling them like a handful of gold nuggets.

"You'll be dead before you need all this luck." He picked out one of the matches and tossed the gift toward Aiden. "I'd say you don't have more than a night to last. One match'll do you."

The Indian slid ten of Aiden's chances into the canister and shoved them into the pocket of his buffalo coat. He aimed the rifle inches from Aiden's eyes, paused, and lowered its barrel. "I put a bullet in a grizzly two days ago and it's affected his mood. Won't throw away another bullet doing something that'll happen natural."

The man stooped above Aiden, running a hand over his hair. "Should take that red scalp. But I'd rather come when I have more time to run my fingers through it. Makes no difference to me if I use you alive or dead."

He drew the knife blade in two quick, shallow pulls across Aiden's throat. "X marks the spot. We'll give that bear a fresh scent to follow."

A trail of blood tickled Aiden's neck. For the first time, he recognized the horror of the man's choker—an array of translucent thumbnails strung on a catgut line. The man grabbed his sheepskin coat, gathered up the rifle, and walked to the big bay. He mounted and spat in his direction. A keen wind minced up the last coals of the fire, and they shone as blue sparks in the narrowed eyes of the Indian.

"Maybe I can finish him off before he decides he's hungry enough to eat the rotten flesh of a white man." He turned the horse away. "Either way, he'll die. And so will you."

Aiden considered the spittle on the dirt in front of him as the mucus froze solid. His ears rang with the report of laughter as the Indian turned Aiden's horse up the slope. The man vanished behind a curtain of thick and steady flakes. Hoofbeats fading into snowfall, a notch above silence.

Stranger at the Door

Eden emptied four large pots of hot water into the oval tin tub as though emptying the contents of her soul. She didn't recognize the woman she'd become. She rinsed her grimy hands in the full sink, its cold water adding to the chill of her bones. Complete immersion in a hot bath could retrieve the comfort she'd long abandoned—a mother's touch and tender care. Someone to scrub her back and wash her hair. The only memory of the woman she yearned to reignite. To simply flicker the notion made all the hauling and heating and pouring worth the effort, even at the end of an exhausting day. A struggle that would soon swell with the coming snows. She dreaded winter and the cold that would nest in her core. Her frailty promised to make its lair all the worse.

The wind came up and the cabin groaned like a mare in labor. Eden stood at the sink thinking about the home she'd left behind. Lilybank with its deep pond above. Summer's warmth made the tarn a joy to swim. She longed to plunge beneath its surface again; to float, feeling buoyant and without charge—free of reluctance. In winter, she and Aiden would don their skates at its first thick ice. The image of smooth, frozen water made her shiver.

Her mother's end.

Setting a kettle to simmer on the wood stove for tea later, she stripped and slid into the steamy water. As she steeped, a breeze from the broken pane of window pushed pale steam in peaks and swirls across the surface of the tub. A dance that would soon be over. No matter how quickly she filled the tub, the heat never lingered long enough to satisfy. She simply wanted time to stop.

Instead, a rush of wings. The door flung open with a thud against the cabin wall, releasing a thick puff of soil from the ceiling into the tub below. A brown spider the size of a dollar piece followed. Eden was up and out of the water, away from the spider, dripping a pool on the floor as her best friend appeared.

Maddie materialized in a flurry of dust and feathers, expression poised between panic and tranquility. She carried a knapsack under one arm and a cranky attitude in the hand over her heart. The two little she-goats followed her through the door.

"Maddie, you scared me half to death."

"Well, then remind me not to do it twice." Maddie panted as she turned to shoo the goats outside. "Git."

"Be gentle with them." Eden bit her lip. "They've had a wretch of a day."

Maddie closed the door. "Goddern hens frighten the daylights out of me, the way they perch up in them willows and swoop down on a body. Why you keep 'em so close to your door?"

"The hens or the willows?" Eden bent with caution to crush the spider in a small piece of newsprint. "I can only control the whereabouts of the ones without wings."

"Let's just shoot them goddern hens."

"Maddie, since that husband left you." Eden shook her head as she crawled back into the bathwater. "Your language." The words of a controlling husband. Eden shuddered. She wouldn't make that mistake again. Maddie was one of the few valuables she had left.

"Don't know what you need a mess of eggs fer anyways. Cain't eat but a couple a day here."

Eden didn't bother to say that they'd not been back in the coop for some time. Or, that she had tried to shoot them and failed. She didn't want to relive any of the horrid day.

After dragging a chair up to the tub, Maddie put her bag on the plank floor and sat down. "A bath before the end of the week?"

"It was a filth of a day."

Maddie shook her head. "Them ain't the kind of words I'm used to hearing you speak. You need a pick-me-up. Maybe play that fiddle a yourn after bathin'?"

Even the beloved violin Eden carried all the way from the Isle of Arran no longer soothed. Its music, as hollow as the instrument. She used to paint, as well. Fitting somehow that the box of paints and sketchbook were lost to the Bighorn on her honeymoon hunt all those years ago. Her nine-year marriage to Hugh had been marked by loss even before the union began. One dream after another.

"Not tonight. My fingers are tired to the bone."

"Come on, girl." Maddie smiled. "I been locked up with eight young'uns and not one visit from you since last month. Neither of us with a husband to fuss over. We gotta do somethin' fun."

"Fun?" Eden pulled a washcloth across her forehead. "What's that?"

Maddie stepped on a beetle before its spindly legs could scuttle through a crack in the floor's rickety planks. "Guess I know what you mean. I ain't had me real fun since before young'uns. God love 'em, seems all I do is wipe one end or the other. Just need a little break—and a night off from cookin' for the troops. Jenny can handle the commotion tonight. She's old enough."

Jenny, a mere fifteen years younger than her mother. Eden had been shocked to learn that Madeline was raised up just old enough to get herself married at fourteen to a lime quarry man who, according to Maddie, raised her to suit his notions. He had an itchy foot to move out of Carolina and into the West. She'd taken colonization as a challenge. The day the ink dried on their marriage certificate she set about populating the sparse prairie. The way she told the tale, farming life proved to be more of a trial than her first husband bargained for and he turned hard. His health gave out after child number five. One day a drifter wandered by and found him out in the field, the life gone out of him, still hanging on the traces of the plowing team standing idle. The picture painted by Maddie's words still hung in Eden's mind. Maddie had chuckled.

Grateful for both events, she married the drifter called Big and went back in the business of expanding the West. Some were old enough to stand with their mother as Bigford True rode one of their plow mules down the dirt path one day three years ago, and never came back. Eden heard the story the day after Big made his exit. Maddie didn't spite him for leaving, except for breaking up her team of red mules and leaving her with two more children and one on the way. Eden laughed at that. Maddie had a way of always making her smile. The fact of the matter was, Maddie had said he'd been more trouble than he was worth. She enjoyed the holiday from his company, but his absence harnessed her to the house more, and that fact made her irritable from time to time.

"Got somethin' for you." Maddie pulled a linen package from her knapsack, unwrapped a double-fist-sized portion of a roast pork loin and grinned. "Cookin' for two—now that's fun."

"My heavens." Eden's mouth watered. "But, really, I can't take more from you."

One of the goats bleated softly outside the door.

"Hell you can't. 'Sides, we kilt a pig last Friday. Kill another next month. Don't want good pork goin' to waste." Maddie held up the knapsack. "Brung a side of bacon, too."

Eden's pride tussled with her mother's etiquette. Her stomach growled.

"Fair enough. But just until Aiden returns. I'll pay you back in fresh game. How's that?"

Maddie brightened at Aiden's name. "Where's that pretty kin of yours?"

Eden dipped a wrist beneath the water, rinsed the dirt from the braided bracelet on her wrist and nodded in the direction of the sunset. "The Bighorn."

"Bighorn?"

"That's right. Why?"

"Cleve Hackett, that butcher from Suggs, rode down with news this mornin'. The renegade shut up in Sheridan got loose."

"So?"

"So he's that Indian that kilt the James family. The one Jack Williams spent all that time in Sheridan testifyin' against."

"What does that have to do with the Bighorn?"

"Well, Cleve says the Indian's headed into the mountains to hide."

Eden rubbed her chin with a wet hand, and leaned back into the warm water trying to unwind the prickly coil around her chest.

"Cleve's got his mind satisfied to join the posse," Maddie said. "Thinks it'll impress me. He knows I don't need no man around the farm, besides my pa. Guess it's the only thing he can think of doing that he reckons I can't."

"Maddie, Aiden is hunting with Jack Williams."

The two women were silent for a moment.

"Well, if an Indian can hole up in the mountains, so can Aiden." Maddie wore a crooked smile. "Huntin' for winter, then? Guess Aiden'll be stayin' at least till spring."

Eden knew her friend tried to turn the conversation. Maddie never featured worry, and Aiden was a favorite subject. She did her best to tempt him, even going so far as to place an indecent hand on his knee one evening in front of the fire shortly after he'd arrived. Aiden showed little interest.

"Don't you think your plate's full?" asked Eden.

"Just 'cause Cleve Hackett comes callin' ever once in a while don't mean I'm taken. Cleve could use a little competition. Good for a man's soul. Besides, he's a rib of raw beef most the time. He don't think I notice. Ain't saying I couldn't git used to the odor, but Aiden smells of that heather he keeps in his pocket."

Over fresh cornmeal cookies Eden had made and delivered to her friend last spring, Aiden opened the small pouch of heather beneath Maddie's nose. The memory made Eden smile. She had closed her eyes to inhale its sweetness, as well. Aiden's only words: That's home. For a moment, the fragrance wrapped its arms around Eden. More urgent matters remained to the day than dreaming. She wanted to keep her mind off the mountain. Little room existed for more worry. Her husband caused enough of that.

"I had word from Hugh. Letter's on the table."

"You know I cain't read." Maddie reached for an apple on the stand next to her chair.

"You've never asked why Hugh travels to Britain once a year."

"I already know enough of your personals." Maddie had helped Eden through the loss of each child. "Expect he markets them ponies." She bit into the fruit.

"He tries." Eden sat back and pulled a warm washcloth over her breasts. "But he's injured now and there's not a fool in Britain who'll loan him a penny more, no matter how many ponies he puts up. And I'll not agree to mortgage this parcel."

"So, he comes back and you trade the horses for some cattle. Start again."

"He's not coming back." The words scratched at Eden's throat. "He wants me to join him."

Maddie raised a hand to her neck and gasped. "Leave?"

"I can't. This place is all I have. I've no money. I won't ask Aiden for more."

"Darlin', worrying is prayin' for the worst. Hugh'll figure the whole thing out. He'll change his mind and be back with a fistful of silvers and all them fancy things from civilization." Maddie fingered the fine gold locket around her neck. A present from Hugh, Eden passed the gift to Maddie in gratitude for helping tend her infants' sicknesses.

"I'm afraid his affair with this country is finished. There's no passion left in him—for anything." The words brought tears to her eyes as memories swelled. She tried to call up Hugh's arms around her, tight and warm as they were in the beginning. Even if she'd never loved him, she'd learned to rely on the security of an embrace. But all she sensed was a bath gone cold. "There's little to hold us through the winter. And I've no solid plan that'll carry us to spring."

Maddie put her apple on the table. She took the cloth from Eden, and washed her back. "If I had a fine piece o' land like yourn in this holler, a fresh stream of water at my door, I'd bank on its profit. Get me a second mule and a hired man—maybe one that had a hankerin' to cook. Go back to farmin'. Maybe a field or two of beets growin' thicker than fur on a squirrel. Beets is good profit these days." Maddie grasped Eden's hand to punctuate the notion and looked through the window as if to finish the fantasy in her mind.

Eden let Maddie's hand slip free. "Well, I'd need a plow, a hired man and the start of spring now, wouldn't I. Don't suppose you can arrange all that?"

Maddie worked the tip of her shoe into a small indentation in one of the planks, voice quiet. "Things'll be easy again. You'll see."

She poured a pail of clean, warm water over Eden's head and took a bar of soap to her hair. "Love to wash the kids' hair. The smell of Castile makes my innards warm. Reminds me of Ma, the way she used to wash my head. Don't you love someone's fingers through your hair?"

Eden's throat closed at the memory of her own mother doing the same. She couldn't speak. As soon as Maddie rinsed the soap away and squeezed the water from her hair, Eden stepped from the tub. She pulled a cotton wrap around her body, tucking one end in above her bust.

"Land sakes, you're a stick doll, girl."

"Hard work, that's all. It's been a hell of a summer. I'm weary, Maddie. Make me smile."

"Now whose language needs cleanin' up?" Maddie fingered the shattered pane at the window. "Hit a high note did you on that fiddle of yours?"

Eden cracked a smile. "I was thinking of Hugh when I closed the window."

Maddie shook her head and drew the threadbare curtains closed. "So, you might say he puts work on your list without even bein' around. Guess it's effort well spent. Ma always said, rage without a target is rapture wasted."

"What?"

"She liked a good argument."

"It did feel good at the time."

"Well, I'm here all night. Think laughin' gets you closer to God. I'll have to watch not to cross you." Maddie set upon slicing the pork roast on the kitchen cutting-block. "Nothing matches a nice cut of pig. A mite bigger than the one Pa landed a couple days ago."

"I thought Cleve did your butchering."

"He does—for the most part. But you know Pa, always a rifle on his arm. Shot the ear off the old sow."

Eden gasped. "On purpose?"

"Hell, no. Everythin' he does is accident. His mind's gettin' worse by the minute. Won't stay put for nothin', no matter how harsh I be. Get him to bed and he's up again." Maddie pulled a plate from a shelf and piled the meat in the center. "Young'uns kept declarin' they heard noises in the yard all night till, near sunrise, Pa grabbed his shotgun, opened up the door to the yard, and let her go just to humor 'em. Dern if the blast didn't shut 'em all up. Figured the creature'd been kilt. Slept till noon. Gonna make the act a ritual I think, only earlier. Guess that old sow'll be the next feature on the boarding house menu in town. May as well kill her all at once, than to do it in stages."

Laughter faded into thoughts of killing. Scents of pine and sage from the mountains miles away slipped out of the Bighorn as dusk wrung the last few drops of light from day. Images of Aiden rode the evening breeze into the cabin through the broken pane. A stovetop kettle sang out. The women flinched in unison.

"It's been over a fortnight," Eden said. "Weather turned, did you feel the cold? May be an early snow on the mountain, can't tell for the clouds."

"September drifts ain't that queer."

Aiden had dealt with snows blown in from the North Atlantic. He was well acquainted with the cold. She shook off her concern. "He's convinced I can't do without the help of a man. In the end, if he's right, there'll be no living with him." Eden emptied the teakettle into the tub. "All I wanted was a couple of elk, but I know him. He's probably holding out for a grizzly, as well. Scotland has no bears."

"You said he came from the city—he may not know the difference."

"Fair enough." Eden gestured to the tub. "The water's still warm."

"Ain't had me more than a quick rinse since afore the river leaned up. I'll be clean and nowhere to go but home. Kind of a waste."

"If you're sleeping with me tonight, the gesture won't go unnoticed."

"Two days to tea. Least I'll be clean for that."

"If Aiden's still away, I'll be staying put Sunday. This place won't work itself."

"Cain't. You're the music." Maddie gave a nod to the violin case in the corner as she stripped naked. "And I know your pleasure at seein' all them fine things laid out on the table."

Eden did love the finery of tea. The lace, silver, roses on the buffet. Once a month she stepped into the world she'd been taken from, liberated from the purgatory of ranching. Even though the gathering was a gauntlet she had to endure, just as she'd suffered intimidation in the face of her husband, the land, and life itself. She'd risen up, but only in her solitude, afraid to break ranks in polite company. None had witnessed the gumption she'd seen inside herself at times. The raw fortitude in pursuit of the wild colt in the pasture beyond. The anguish at losing a newborn foal to a wolf. Not Hugh. Not Maddie. Not Aiden. None but the willows flanking the Crazy Woman. Eden never wept alone.

She peered at the tea cups on the top shelf of her cupboard and on around the room. The only finery she had was a dwindling set of English porcelain, a handsome dining table, her violin, and a few dozen hard-bound books she'd read a hundred times. All she'd brought west. As though their civility alone might tame the wild.

Maddie climbed into the tub and moaned as she sank into the cloudy water. "'Sides, we don't show, Boss Williams'll send a posse over to sniff you out. You know how he gits when he knows you're alone. With his son on the mountain, and a renegade loose, he'll be twice as nosey."

Eden knew the neighbors, though distant, kept a wide-ranging eye on her. She was one of the clan.

"Not that they'd set a foot in my house if they had an option. A pack of young'uns beats the plague in protectin' against invaders," said Maddie, her eyes closed. "But you, they fancy."

Eden pulled on a fresh pair of white cotton bloomers, a pale green blouse and wrapped a cashmere shawl around her shoulders. "All right, we'll go. And a bonnie time it'll be if you say. Boss might have news of the hunting party."

Eden thought a minute. She might pique the man's interest in the fine colt she had, as well. If she could book his mares for next summer's breeding, there'd be fees to come in this fall. And, the plan could be tested over a mouthwatering buffet of food.

Hope crept upon two fronts.

"Glad that's settled," Maddie said after sinking beneath the surface to drench her hair. "Sure like to hear some of that broke back music. Maybe practice just one tune?"

"That's Baroque, Maddie." Eden lit two kerosene lamps, then touched a sulfur match to a pile of logs in the cavernous fireplace. "Bach."

"What I said."

Horses nickered in the yard. The women turned their attention toward the door.

"Clean and lucky. At this hour, has to be baby brother." Maddie pushed herself up out of the water. "Hold him off till I can present proper."

"Our definitions of that last word differ."

Maddie drew a cloth around her torso, rubbing her legs dry. "Maybe he can play that gussied up udder in the crook, and we can us have a real party."

"It's a bagpipe."

Eden hurried to the window eager to catch a glimpse of Aiden, and stopped, spotting instead her horses. They stood in a perfect line awash in the light pouring from the cabin window. Hair stood up on the back of Eden's neck.

"What?" Maddie pulled her skirt off the table and held its umber wool to her body. "Not Aiden?"

"I…I don't know, horses and…it's too dark." Eden cursed her poor eyesight in silence.

Maddie joined Eden at the window. "Goddern."

Eden's eyes focused. A muscled, buckskin horse stepped out of the darkness into the glow coming from the cabin. A large figure under a massive fur sat high upon its back. The gentle sound of breathing of horses eased through the window's broken pane. Without a word, the rider swung off its mount, and started for the cabin door.

"Indian," said Maddie.

The two women threw on the rest of their clothes, racing around the house until dust hung in the air like morning haze.

"I git the gun." Maddie grabbed the rifle set beside the entry.

Eden made no argument. She placed her hand on the door latch, as Maddie shouldered the piece and fit foresight bead to rear sight notch in time to meet the stranger at the door.

Misery Acquaints a Man

The Indian dissolved into icy fog and snowflakes. Aiden glared at the vacant spot, disbelieving, knowing he should act. His soul was stone.

No horse. No weapon. Without a coat. Snow fell in lacy fluff erasing the man's tracks, and the fire glimmered a swan song. Every twig that might grant a fresh spark, he'd gathered—and he had but one match. Exhausted by the cold, adrenaline ebbed and fatigue advanced. His bad arm was numb. The screaming gash, silent. He closed his eyes to greet oblivion.

Better the flame die sooner than later.

But his brain continued to percolate, brewing Eden, alone in the sod house, vulnerable to a murderous renegade. Tending the ranch alone. The notion was a swift jab. Resolve kindled. Cold may have set deep into his lungs, but dawn drew pale hope on the eastern plain. Walking to camp, a good twelve-mile trek, was the day's work. He mustered strength to come to his sister's aid.

He dug up his store of biscuits and ate them, walked to the stream and drank several long pulls of water. Then, looping his saddlebags around his neck, he turned down the mountain. He would be with the rest of the men by noon—hot food and a fire. At intervals, he flapped his one good arm hard against his body for warmth, though each time he did, his shoulder shot him with the searing pain of a bullet. The logic of running teased his mind. But he was dry. Sweat, and he knew he was as good as dead in the fierce cold.

Snow piled to the thickness of a featherbed over the broad, open meadows between huddled stands of pine. Falling fast and heavy at times, its shroud left direction to a guess. But the slope beneath Aiden's feet told no lies. The way off the mountain was down.

45

As snowfall broke, he reached the first stream he had crossed the day before. Sunlight peaked from a gap in the clouds and the landscape turned to blazing light. Aiden squinted against its brilliance. Newfound determination steadied his feet as he leapt from rock to rock across the shallow creek. Snowmelt dripped from pines along the stream.

By dusk the scent of wood smoke clinging to a stand of lodgepole beckoned, and he stood for a moment breathing in the welcome. Aiden tipped his head, granting an ear to the direction of the campfire. No pots or pans rattled from the cook wagon, and nary a voice echoed across the canyon. Tracking dogs they'd brought along had quit their bay. Eerie silence but for a trifling wind soughing through the branches in the over-story.

Perhaps the men searched for him. Yet, beyond a thicket, a low fire still smoldered. Even in the snow, his companions would not leave coals unattended within reach of a dry and brittle autumn. By the time he reached the edge of camp, brambles bloodied his good hand. The iron scent repulsed him. He looked down to his bandaged arm, and below him the source of the scent was clear. A broad black stain tarnished the ground. Well protected by trees above, the spot stood bare to the snowfall. Beyond, the ice turned to scarlet. Huge rusty paw prints wrote chaos across the camp, empty but for the carcass of a blood chestnut stallion.

J.W.'s horse.

Aiden bent to wipe a finger through a small puddle of blood at his feet. The deposit was quivering black pudding, smooth and moist. Whatever happened had not been long ago. The men must not be far ahead. Aiden walked to the body of the horse. Its neck was cold, legs seized in the brief rigidity of death, withers and half of its hind flank lay ripped open. The throat mangled as though chipped away with a dull axe. The remains lay pushed up against the skeleton of a tree trunk. From its bark waved long tufts of coarse, silver hair like boney fingers in the up-mountain breeze.

The bear. The stinking wounded bear.

Nothing of the horse was eaten. With a bullet in its hide the beast wasn't hungry, it was mad—in every sense of the word.

Two crows cursed him from a tree branch, badgering him to quit their claim. Even though darkness was near full, the birds would work until they were blind before they'd leave such a treasure. Aiden gave them no fight but they continued to press him, coughing and sputtering so that he swore they issued their warnings in English.

"Away," said one crow.

"Obey," called the other.

A familiar word. "Aid-en!" The birds flapped off through the trees in a swirl of glossy coal feathers.

Aiden looked up. Fixed to a spindle branch high in a lean pine, black against the violescent twilight, sat a small man in a blue plaid shirt. The camp cook looked down, eyes bright as newly minted silver dollars against his ebony face.

"Ink! How in blazes did you land there?"

Ink's arms clasped to the tree trunk, feet dangling from either side of a limb.

His words stuttered like a new-fangled quick-firing rifle. "Bear big enough to stand on all fours, nose-to-nose with a wagon, Mister Aiden. Came to kill and did some. Unhitched the lift line when the demon jump Mister Jack. Thought he'd leave him off for the beef in the stores, but he wanted blood. Took two of us to lift all the stores into the tree to begin with to keep critters away. Seemed the safest for me to do was to follow the line, so I cut it loose, held fast, and here I am."

"How long?"

"Yesterday—long after you rode out. I'd a crawled down by now but there's no way to quit this perch and live to tell."

The rumpled sack of goods lay nearby, dug tight into the dirt by the fall, rope still attached. The bear had no interest in dried beef and long-eyed potatoes.

"I've but one good arm, but I'll try to get a rope to you. Hold on." Aiden let his saddlebags slide to the ground.

"Yessir. Be right here. Appreciate you usin' some speed, though. My feet hates being this far from dirt."

It cost Aiden a good deal of effort and pain using one hand to untie the hemp rope from its bundle. He made two large knots in the line to weight one end and made a sturdy, long toss in the direction of the man who resembled an oversized crow in the tree above. On the third try, Ink grabbed the line as it vaulted over the limb. But his balance was lost. He hung onto the hemp as though it would save his life, even as he fell toward earth, rope in tow, howling all the way. At some point the line pulled taught in both men's hands at the same instant, jerking them toward each other. Ink was a sack of prize-winning yams swinging smack into Aiden. Aiden cried out in pain, and they both let go and rolled to a stop straight into the bloodied carcass of the horse.

"Already rank." Ink crinkled his nose as he got to his feet. "I seen lots of things, Mister Aiden. Fort Pillow, holes in men the size of a Christmas ham, lost limbs feeding the steam of the Union Pacific west, but I ain't never seen something like this."

"Where are the others?" Aiden pushed to his feet, then cradled his aching arm with his good hand.

"Ran outta camp with the horses. Put so many bullets in that bear, if he's still standing, gonna be a banshee." Ink swatted the muck from his clothes with both hands.

"They just left you?"

"Everyone ran in a different direction, sir. Spent no time looking back. Knowing what they know 'bout me, I guess they figured I was well ahead."

"Fortunate for you I came by. Would have been a long season in that tree." Aiden wiped his hand across the sticky blood on his shirt.

"One night was enough. I'd sooner meet that bear than hole up at that height again." Ink looked Aiden up and down. "You missed the beast, but you still in bad shape, sir."

"Afraid I didn't miss the grizzly. Scared the daylights out of my horse. My shoulder took the brunt. The horse is yet on the mountain under some heathen Indian who has my coat and rifle, as well."

"Rode by right beneath me at dawn. Figured it weren't good news when I recognized your big bay. Reckoned the only thing he'd help me with was my black scalp. Stayed quiet as a mole rat in winter."

"Wise. I imagine he'd taken pleasure at shooting you out of the tree."

"Take everything did he?"

"Oh, no, I have my saddlebags," said Aiden as he fumbled in his pocket, trembling against the cold. "And one magic stick." He held up his match with a crooked smile.

"By Jim, that's the only one we have between us. Those was in the wagon, and the wagon's long gone."

The two men regarded the match, then each other, and on to the spent fire.

"Give it here," said Ink. "You got a pocket knife?"

Aiden handed him the match and his small knife. Ink laid the match on a smooth stone, held the knife tip to the middle of the wooden stick, and split it lengthwise down the middle.

Ink handed the knife and slender sticks back to Aiden. "Got two now."

A great pile of fodder lay near a canvas bloodied by the previous day's events. Ink took a handful of kindling and leaned down to blow on the grey embers. Nothing. Aiden held the half-a-match up to the light, checking the amount of sulfur at its tip. He pushed its twin back into his pocket and struck the remainder carefully against a piece of granite. Touching its flame to the tinder, Aiden laid his head next to the ashes opposite Ink, and blew great wisps of hazy breath in earnest to entice a fire.

Soon the coals burned hot, their bright, flickering light turning the horrific scene around them to a bizarre jig of blazing color. Aiden's warming shoulder throbbed, his hand a swollen plum around the braided bracelet.

"I seen a hand like that once," said Ink, "walking west across Oklahoma to join the railroad. Blizzard howled from hell and before long I was spinning in all directions, going nowhere, slow. I played the prairie dog, pushing up the snow around me to shun the gale. Last fistful of ice I took and up come a finger, a bloated purple maggot of a thing froze solid. Sat up all night wondering what kind of eyes spied its last wiggle."

Aiden winced. Seeking what comfort he could, he retrieved the bloodied canvas from the edge of camp and dragged it around his shoulders.

Ink buttoned up his coat and crossed his arms. "I can fix it."

"What?"

"That arm. Dislocated I figure. An easy fix."

Aiden narrowed his eyes, measuring the meaning of *easy*.

"Won't feel too good, but I reckon it's no worse than what you been through so far. Least you'll be able to use it a might better."

With no other option, Aiden nodded.

Ink unwrapped the long scarf used to bind the arm and told Aiden to lie flat. He placed his booted foot at Aiden's armpit and, before Aiden could question the approach, pulled the limb forward hard in one quick motion.

Aiden cried out, and was silent. When he'd caught his breath, the pain lessened in his shoulder, though the arm still lay useless.

Ink unwrapped the scarf at Aiden's forearm. He scowled, touching the wound. "Feel that?"

Aiden shook his head.

"Better cut that binding on your upper arm, sir. Get blood movin' so the swelling go down." Ink's expression was unsettling. He looked at Aiden's bracelet. "That, too."

Aiden studied the braid. "Thanks, I'll keep it." The circular braid was a strong tether to Eden, the luck he needed to see him through. He started to rewrap his forearm.

Ink's words were an epitaph, "Best let the gash enjoy the air, Mister Aiden."

Aiden wrapped the blood-crusted scarf around his neck for warmth instead.

Ink sat back down as Aiden arranged the canvas over his head. The harsh cold of the day before was turned away, leaving a drizzle of rain too light to sway a fire that did its meager best to warm them. From time to time Ink wiped away the water dripping across his forehead. Aiden scribbled in his journal from underneath the cover. He looked up once to find Ink's gaze fastened on Aiden's vest. The gold watch his father had given him peeked from his pocket. Aiden looked at Ink, measuring his intent. If the man wanted to rob him, he was an easy target. Ink shivered with cold, looking resigned to his lot.

"Hey, there." Aiden opened the canvas to invitation.

Ink sat stock-still. "Ain't never sat side-to-side with a white man."

"Well, misery acquaints a man with strange bedfellows."

Ink cocked his head.

"Shakespeare. The Tempest. Act two, scene two."

"What?"

"Shakespeare." Aiden shook his head and motioned to Ink. "For heaven's sake, man. If you need a better reason than staying dry, coming in will afford you a closer view of my watch."

They sat together, quiet and comfortable in the warming air, but Aiden knew that if the mountain changed its mind again the cold would be a deadly arrow on their trail.

Aiden outlined the future he'd prefer rather than dwell on the worst. "Think I'll be going back to Scotland when I get off this mountain. Try to convince my sister to do the same. What's in your mind to do, Mister Ink?"

"Going west. California, I 'spect." Ink pulled the canvas tight around his side. "Hear it's warm year-round by the ocean. And her creeks are lined in gold."

"You don't say?" Aiden placed a hand on his watch pocket.

"Yessir. I ain't never held a gold piece. Like to do that 'fore I die."

Aiden looked at Ink and folded his arms. "By taking it from a stream."

Ink blinked twice. "Well, yessir."

One more night. The next day would show them a way off the mountain. Once he reached Buffalo at the base of the Bighorn, he could sweet-talk the favor of a horse. Even though Eden lived a long day's ride east of town, Aiden would be as good as home.

In his tardiness, Aiden thought his sister was sure to be keeping company at Maddie's. He imagined the wood frame house packed tight with small children and humid with laughter, her irrational father, Ezra, marching guard on the porch, lips moving in silent mussitation. The image warmed Aiden even as freezing rain dripped from his nose.

The fire popped and he jerked thinking it was gunfire in the distance. An echo, Aiden prayed.

His imagination made no such pledge.

More Stirring in Person

A squeak of the door stopped him short of the shelter's threshold. The door swung halfway out to reveal a rifle. Laid out in his direction, the barrel was close enough to deliver the rotten odor of sulfur. The weapon lay cradled in the arms of a wild-eyed woman whose dark hair hung in long, wet spindles across her shoulders. She was not the woman he had watched all afternoon.

He puzzled at his mistake as the white woman he sought stepped from behind the open door. His gaze traced her silhouette, moving upward from her bare feet to the frizzy sweep of red hair sitting in a bundle atop her head. She stood taller than he guessed she would, her curves as inviting as the creek bordering the shelter.

Her face came into focus as his sight adjusted to the sudden wash of cabin light. Beneath that glorious hair her pale green eyes met him somewhere between wonder and reproach. Her features, even more delicate than those the portrait artist had bestowed. Stunning.

"I return your horses. My life is thanks enough," he said, looking at the rifle.

The short woman spoke. "Reckon we can thank you any way we like, as long as you'd be on the receiving side of this weapon. You've done a good deed. We're grateful."

She licked her thumb and wiped it across the fore sight, though the man stood close enough to do the same if he'd wished. She kept the rifle raised, her aim steady, staring into his eyes as though she were searching for something.

The taller woman's voice trembled. "Apologies for the rudeness, sir. We aren't used to seeing strangers during the day, much less after dark. I'm afraid you gave us a start. Indeed, I thank you for gathering my horses."

"You git now," the small woman insisted with a nod to the road beyond. "We got menfolk coming."

"I'll see the horses to their pasture then," he said. "I know where they broke through. I'll bind it up as best I can tonight."

The red-haired woman glanced at her companion, who kept the rifle on her shoulder, finger on the trigger.

He turned and walked into the darkness. The horses followed as the door latched behind him with the sluggish clink of an iron bolt sliding into its cradle. He opened the paddock gate and the meager herd passed through, trotting into the darkness as he secured the latch behind them. He led his horse well away from the homestead, down a short ravine to a stand of cottonwoods surrounded by tall grass. He gathered his bags from the horse and slipped off its headstall, setting the animal free for the night. He settled on the ground, into the heavy fur of the bearskin. His horse moved over the low ridge to graze. Scurrying rodents and the rhythmic breathing of horses in the nearby paddock were his only company.

His whole body, tight as a fist from the long day's ride, relaxed as he stretched out flat, his hands touching a bit of dewy grass at the edge of the bearskin. The night sky was freckled with silver. Aquila, the eagle, flew above him, wings outstretched. His mother had taught him to recognize the stars. His father had taught him their meaning. The eagle, a medicine bird with magical powers.

Cygnus floated nearby. He remembered the swan's plea to man: to spread his wings and take flight into waking dreams. Perhaps the two constellations sat eternally together because without the eagle, the swan's plea would forever go unanswered. A curious sensation crept his core at the notion. He closed his eyes as an invitation to sleep, but the movement of the steady gait across the rolling plain that day was unforgiving. He knew days would pass after his arrival home before the feeling waned.

Each year he traveled east as the leaves of the whitewood trees appeared to color on the flanks of the Bighorn. He always journeyed alone, riding hard to meet the sacred land laying beyond the Belle Fourche. The simple plea of his vision quest was to find fulfillment in his daily life. To appreciate each moment, expecting pleasure to unfold as life went on. After receiving the vision he sought, he was always eager to return to the Ten Sleep in good time. He never expected to come across the woman whose portrait he'd found so many years ago. But, as he lay listening to the low female voices in the distance, he knew finding the red-haired woman was no accident. He asked direction from the spirit to meet with pleasure along the way, and the wish was satisfied. It was all part of an unfolding, even if he was to catch sight of her just once. Pure pleasure, indeed.

A field mouse wiggled its way from underneath the hide to explore the deep side of the bearskin. Darting up and over his legs, the creature came to rest in a depression between his knees. He slowed his breath, inviting the animal, in silence, to move back onto the hide. And so it did, burrowing into the soft curve of the fur near his feet.

The trill of distant laughter was an odd comfort. He folded the bearskin across his body for warmth. The odor of dry grass mingled with mellow bear fat long since scraped from the hide. A familiar ache rose under his ribs as he resisted a memory. In denying the pain, he knew he denied as well remembering the happiness a woman could grant. Joy and sorrow; lush grass growing in the wake of a wildfire. One was not possible without the other.

His thoughts turned to a woman once his, who crossed an open field with the same grace as the one he'd seen that afternoon. Who was always laughing, even as he looked back to see her for the last time, bouncing their son in her arms. The memory dissolved into a cloud mounting from a single point on a far horizon. From it, soldiers marched across the land.

* * *

His woman had wanted to come. The two of them often rode together, hunting small game. But never in the company of others.

Women didn't ride. It was not the way of his people. He told her to return to the shelter, to wait for another time. This hunt was for men alone.

The party slipped out before dawn to catch elk off guard in the gorge before the animals climbed higher slopes with the rising sun. They hunted long and well. But the bounty came at a brutal cost. The cavalry had waited for the strong, young men to leave the village. Hours later the hunters returned to find all that they'd known in ashes. Shelters burned, corpses charred, the earth black with blood and soot. Nothing remained. Nothing.

He scoured the smoldering ground for hours. The autumn grass was tall, thick and crisp, and the flames had burned hot. Even the pottery was black, standing at loose intervals around the camp, tipped as if suspended in time. Bodies, melted into the doughy shapes of Native black-bread across a sheet of iron.

Amid the rubble a single spark of light signaled to him as he walked. When he came to its source he found the tiny, flat obsidian fragment he'd fashioned—the simple bee, symbol of union with his wife and their work together. The talisman hung at her neck on a length of woven horsehair. Their toddler loved to reach for its shiny shape nestling at her breasts.

He stooped to cup his hand through cinders that were soft snow between his fingers. He closed his hand and raised the flake of obsidian to his heart—all that remained of everything he'd ever known. Emptiness took him then, so deep that he could fall through time a thousand years and know no difference.

When he finally turned, at the crest of the hill, a single man on horseback. A Native scout. The man who had cast his people to the ruin around him, even as crystal water splashed from the Ten Sleep Canyon above. And he knew that man as well as he knew himself. He looked away to the river for a moment and when he turned back, the scout was gone.

* * *

He had seen destruction at the hands of his own people who had learned to use horses and weapons in the same cruel fashion as the whites. Little variation in the souls of most men. He quit his people's fight between liberty and confinement to walk the space between the two—alone. He closed his eyes to the ache, and sleep brought the dream. Gentle voices coax forgotten images from the shelter of his heart, at once rank and beguiling. He falls to the blood-hot soil, covered in embers. Soot clogs his throat. He turns to the river, knowing its water will cleanse his body and carry him away from the ruin, but he is the trunk of a fossilized tree, wedded to his scorched world. The solitary man on the hillside spreads his mouth in a hateful smile, raises his rifle and disappears over the crest. Vicious laughter settles into whirling ashen dust behind him.

In dreams, the dreamer can never look away.

A Wee Bit Familiar

Maddie's voice squeaked, "We best git."

Eden couldn't think above the hammering in her chest as she latched the door handle and scraped the bolt across the thick wood door into position. She turned to face Maddie whose cheeks were embers. "I'll not ride out in the dark."

"But we're fat hogs with one foot caught in the fence here." Maddie slapped a hand against her side, and shook her head. "Good news is you ain't alone. The bad news, too. Pair of scalps, not one. A mite more appealin' for one night's work, you ask me. How do we know it ain't that renegade busted outta jail?"

Maddie followed Eden as she walked to the stove. She stood, one hand on her hip, the other clenched to the tip of the rifle, its butt resting on the floor.

"Hush," Eden said, turning to add wood to the stove and reheat the teakettle. Her hands trembled and her voice cracked. "A bad Indian would have taken my horses, not returned them." She was trying to convince herself more than Maddie. The fact that a murderer was on the loose was a blade in her spine.

"What better way to get a couple of gals to open a door, I say. Only bad Indians resisted the reservations, girl. If he's so good, why don't he obey the law like the rest?"

"It's obvious he's not all Indian."

"What part you think weren't Indian, the bearskin?"

"His speech." A sign of civility. Eden reached for a pair of china cups in the cupboard, set them on the table, and filled a strainer with loose tea from a tin.

"Same as yourn, so what? You see how he looked at you? May as well seen a ghost or sumpin'. Probably admirin' that red scalp o'yours."

"Didn't it sound a wee bit familiar?"

Maddie turned to sit in a rocking chair next to the fireplace, laid the rifle across her lap, and rocked.

"So he's got a lilt...he's a half-breed. Afraid that don't grant me comfort. A silver tongue ain't no credit unless there's more honor in bein' kilt by an educated man than by one that cain't thank you for your time."

Eden set the strainer inside the china pot. "Well, if our one hope is to ride to your place in the pitch black, with a renegade possibly in the shadows, I'll be staying, thank you, with the bolt drawn dead against the door and light in the window."

Maddie stopped rocking and leaned forward. "If you'd act more adult like, I could spend more time raisin' my own children. God almighty. Guess stayin' put's the way to find out if he's good or bad. If you're right, we live. If you're not, we don't. Ain't sure I shine to them odds, but reckon I ain't got a choice. Yessir, they can put that on my headstone: she was a True friend, capital *T*." Let's hope they won't be chiselin' it out tomorrow."

Maddie sat down, working the rocker again, and shivered. Her wet hair soaked the top of her blouse. "Least it'll serve for a good story if we live to tell."

"I don't think it's a tale that needs telling, Maddie. I imagine the general reaction to not shooting him on the spot would be something on the order of yours. I need no more concern from the rest of the valley. They're skilled enough at dipping out advice in Hugh's absence. I'm sure there will be no trace of the Indian come daylight. Story over."

The kettle sang and Eden poured the hot water into the readied pot. She pulled a cotton towel and wool blanket from the bottom of the cupboard and placed them on the arm of the rocker.

Maddie unfastened the mismatched buttons of her blouse. "Guess you're right, but dern if it don't beat all. We finally git us an adventure and we cain't tell nobody. Might as well die right now if I ain't gonna get to spin this one."

"Pneumonia is more likely to kill you." Eden pulled the damp garment off of Maddie, draped it over a kitchen chair and tossed the towel over Maddie's head.

Eden rubbed Maddie's wet head with the thick towel until her hair was dry. More misery had come her way from fever and storms than from Indians, but she was ill at ease thinking the man was somewhere nearby. He wouldn't have gone far in the dark.

She and Hugh arrived in the territory well after most of the Indians had marched off to the reservations. To her, stories of the horrors they'd wrought seemed too terrible to be counted as truth. She imagined that land-seeking settlers had stretched the yarns into grotesque exaggeration as an excuse to keep the Indians incarcerated and the land unchallenged. But that's when Indians were distant. With one close at hand she was agitated enough to heed the warnings.

Eden filled the teacups.

The two women sat in silence save the creak of the rocker, drinking their tea, contemplating their differing points of view, until Eden got up to pull a nightdress from a hook by the bed. She handed another to Maddie.

"It's late. We both need sleep." Eden looked at the linen wrapped around the pork. "I'm not hungry at the moment. Shall we save the roast for later?"

"Ain't no sense in fattenin' us up for eaten. And sleep? That Indian might have a buffalo gun big enough to blow the side of this shack in—or know how to charm a bolt out of a lock. There's gonna be at least one of us awake all night. I ain't gonna be kilt without knowin' it."

"Well, I'm going to bed." Eden measured her voice trying to offer Maddie a cool head, but her heart still raced. "I shall depend on you to let me know if you think you're being killed." Eden put the roast in her root cellar, donned her nightdress, and crawled between a thick comforter and feather mattress. She drew the covers up around her ears.

"May as well be comfortable if I'm gonna die." Maddie slipped on the nightdress and took the lantern to the window.

She set the light on the sill, checking the bolt across the door before returning to the kitchen to paw through a cupboard drawer. With a ball of yarn in one hand she walked back to the door, tied one end of line to the door handle and, pulling the line tight, secured the other end to the ladder-back rocking chair.

Maddie spoke under her breath, "Might work magic on that bolt but least I'll know it."

After adding wood to the stove and to the fire in the hearth, she poured another cup of tea, wrapped herself in the blanket and nestled into the rocker.

She pulled the rifle across her lap.

Killin' Tools

Cleve Hackett panted as he removed his hat, "Missus True, I apologize, those hens took the wind outta me." He took the bowl of his pipe into one hand and rubbed the other over his head. His dull brown hair was bristle on a shoe brush.

"Glory, Mr. Hackett, you woke me out of a sound sleep. Frightened me to death. What in tarnation you doin' here this hour of the mornin'?"

Maddie rested the butt of the rifle on the floor beside her. Cleve's face reddened and he turned his back. She stood in her nightdress and a thin shawl.

"Glory." She stepped back inside the house and drew the door to a crack.

"It's near nine in the morning, ma'am. Forgive me but I expected you'd be percolatin' along with the coffee by now."

"We was up all hours talking and such. You know how it is when two lone women get together."

Cleve put his pipe between his teeth and shifted his weight. He stared at the ground. Maddie imagined he had no idea what being with two women all night was like, let alone one. Though she figured he might enjoy ruminating on that picture awhile if he were alone. His posture suggested that the prospect of thinking those thoughts was awkward.

"Well, anyhow, we had us a late night and with no men folk or young'uns to get us up for nothing, we took advantage of the situation. Ain't you supposed to be hooked onto some posse?"

Cleve took the pipe from his mouth. "No man around? Where's Mr. McBride?"

"Huntin'."

"Leaving a woman alone in this country's downright impolite."

Maddie knew Cleve figured hunting a proper reason to leave a woman alone. The jab was meant for Aiden.

"Mr. Hackett, I should think you'd be able to recognize women who can fend for themselves from women who cannot," Eden, dressed for the day, stepped from the cabin and into the yard. "My brother's concern for me is no concern of yours." She searched the edge of the ranch for any sign of last night's visitor.

"Meant no disrespect, ma'am."

"I know what you meant, Mr. Hackett." Eden glanced back to Maddie's face peeking from behind the door.

"What's your business, anyway, Cleve? You supposed to be huntin' renegades."

"Jenny told me you was here. I missed the posse. They rode out before I got to Sheridan. I come back with a wanted poster, though, for you to look at. You women shouldn't be alone, and your young'uns ought to stay close to home, too."

Maddie's voice was high and thin as she dressed, "I never saw no picture of him when he was on trial. What's he look like?"

Cleve studied the poster. "An Indian, I suppose. Scouted for the army. Rode with Crazy Horse, then switched to Custer. You know what he did at the James house. He's a bad one. Come out in leg irons but they say he's clever—won't have 'em on long. You best be on your guard till that brother of yours gets back." Cleve laid the poster out toward the crack in the door.

Maddie's heart leaped to her throat at the face on the poster. The pencil portrait bore more than a vague likeness to their visitor.

Eden squinted at the picture then took a step back, again scanning the perimeter of the property. Her voice was tense. "Tell me Mr. Hackett, did that posse follow the renegade into the Bighorn or push him?"

"Ma'am, I weren't there. I don't know."

"Well, it's a lovely coincidence, isn't it?" asked Eden.

"Ma'am?"

Maddie looked at Cleve. He was clearly fuddled.

"My brother, Mr. Hackett, is in the Bighorn with Jack Williams as we speak."

Cleve looked stricken. "Had no idea."

"I'd be surprised if you had any ideas in that empty head of yours," said Maddie. Confirmation of how little she needed a man.

"Well, ma'am, all I can do is advise you join Maddie's brood until Mr. McBride's back safe. It's not sensible, here alone."

"There's stock to care for, Mr. Hackett, and a ranch to tend," Eden said. "I've matched more than a bad Indian or two over the years."

Cleve Hackett would not understand Eden's brand of logic in the face of such a danger. Neither did Maddie, but the determination in Eden's voice told her all she needed to know. If she hadn't been scared off in the years she'd spent trying to make a go of her hovel, Eden wouldn't leave now.

"If you don't mind me saying so, you ain't no match for this one, ma'am. Maddie, you know what he did to the James's."

She knew. He'd hanged the whole family by their heels from a rafter and burned the house down around them. Jack Williams witnessed the renegade running from the blaze.

"You both best come now," Cleve called through the door. "Maddie, need those lambs you promised me last week for the railroad and I don't know which ones to cull."

Maddie emerged from the house dressed, weapon in hand. She crossed the bridge to the barn at a brisk pace in silence.

"Maddie." The pitch of Eden's voice caused Cleve to jump.

Maddie stopped short of the barn and turned.

Eden's tone was incredulous. "You're leaving?"

"More reasons to git home. God help you if yer too stubborn for your own good."

Eden softened, "Let me help you with your horse."

"Best let me do that, Missus Rose," offered Cleve.

"Eden'll do it, Cleve." Maddie wanted a few minutes alone with Eden for plain talk. "We got some personals hanging in the barn."

She stood sure that information would stop Cleve cold. He shied from the details of femininity. Maddie remembered once surprising a band of mice at the root cellar door when she retrieved a jar of peaches as an offering to Cleve. She thwarted the tiny creature's advance up her skirt, grabbing its body through the clothes and lifting her petticoat to reveal a pale knee in front of Cleve. The man turned white as a hen's egg, then scarlet, choking on a piece of information too big to swallow. The rush of embarrassment turned him tail to the next room quicker than a skunk turns a possum.

Eden joined Maddie outside the barn door and pulled the rifle from her hand.

"Ain't leavin' you," said Maddie. "But I cain't not go with Cleve. Wouldn't make sense to him that I stay here with young'uns at home in the face of danger. The picture on that poster's too close a likeness to take a chance, Eden. You git on that horse of yours and come along."

"He's gone, Maddie. I can't just leave this place alone."

"How do you know he won't double back, try to catch you off guard?"

"I've stood my ground this long, I'll not be run off."

"You might end up being buried in the ground you're defending, girl." Maddie grabbed Eden by the hand and they walked into the barn together, as Cleve, beet-faced by Maddie's frankness, remained a statue in the yard. As soon as they were inside, the two women fell into silence. Before them was a plank wall strewn with a wide array of tools hanging by nail heads. Maddie knew their order, having helped Eden more than once with her work. The missing items were obvious.

"Axe and scythe," Eden said.

Maddie's words tumbled into the air on a shaky exhale, "Killin' tools."

Some Men Shoot First

He slept well until awakened by songbirds calling both dawn and memory of the night before—the red-haired woman.

Turning on his side, he looked across to the barn in the distance. Day brought its defects to light. A few boards stood in tatters on the windward side of the building. Two planks missing from a latticework roof dared an autumn rain to mold the hay underneath. The disrepair was not for lack of intention. He'd seen the red-haired one work hard the day before, but the strength of a woman was no rival to the hard labor a homestead demanded. And a day didn't hold enough light to allow for the mending of every detail.

A spider spun a broad web between two sturdy blades of grass, living in the moment, with no thought toward spring. Surely, he measured, if it gauged the coming of a bug-sparse winter, its web would span the barn. Living in the moment was a fret-free proposition for most. A woman alone had no such luxury.

A horse snorted in the field beyond. Dewy mist cloaked the shoulders of the creek. No men were in sight as one of the women had suggested the night before. He suspected no men, period. A man wouldn't let a horse shelter break down as the barn had.

The sun broke above the low fog, setting its mind to warm the air. Another day of good weather. No reason he couldn't take the time to make a modest repair to the structure if the woman would let him. He gazed across the rolling prairie to the Bighorn. Home beckoned. Snow threatened. He gave a second thought to moving along, yet it made sense to do so. But he knew excuses to skew the reality of a thing. The pretext of a rickety barn spoke the truth: he wished to linger.

He laid the bearskin out flat to let the sun dry the dew, donned a muslin shirt from a doeskin bag, and approached the barn. The lower floor of the shelter was tidy. A broken harness hung on a long wall, along with an assortment of tools.

With the implements he needed in hand, he slipped away toward the perimeter pasture. Daylight colored up the landscape under thick clouds moving in from the west. Morning was a warm breeze on his face.

He felled a small tree and stripped it clean before splitting a pile of shakes. They'd not match the existing roof but they'd be cover enough until spring. The scythe swung with ease over the scrap of wild wheat carpeting the road to the pasture. Soon he bundled a load of fresh vegetation for the loft. Prairie chickens were plentiful and easy to catch in the sagebrush dotting the coulee. In no time three fat Sharp-tails swung by their feet at his side. He headed toward the cabin, weighed down by his efforts, against a cold breeze blowing fresh off the Bighorn. The sun melted the clouds enough to reveal the first fall of snow on the mountains. His journey home would be harder unless the weather warmed again.

As he came over the riverbank, a man and a horse stood at the door of the cabin. He dropped flat, letting his burdens fall into the dry grass, and raised his head high enough above the ridge to watch without being seen.

His presence in the midst of white women would not go unmeasured. Many of his years had been spent avoiding confrontation with settlers and he did not intend to change that. He bent low and blended into the riverbank scrub, listening for any sound that might betray the man's approach.

When no noise came he raised his head again. The man in the distance stood with his horse next to the water trough that met the gate. The women emerged from the barn with a saddled horse in tow. The friend of the red-headed woman mounted, turned and rode out the gate to the north with the man, now on horseback, by her side.

As soon as they were out of sight he gathered his bounty and stood. As he did, the lone woman looked up to see him walking in her direction through the grass. She turned and disappeared into the cabin. He continued, certain his gift of grouse and labor would coax the woman to humor. Unreasonable fear of him held no logic.

"I have something for a meal," he said through the closed door. "And, I see the horse shelter needs repair. If you'll let me, I will fix what I can before I go."

"And when will you be going?"

The muffled cock of a rifle begged he wait a moment before speaking. "Nightfall."

"Why do you want to help me?"

He looked at the barn. "Because there's need?"

The woman's footsteps echoed as she moved to the window. One pane was missing. The tip of the rifle emerged through its frame.

"You did well to be away this morning. There's concern about a man who broke jail in Sheridan—an Indian."

"I am not he." Moving to the window, he engaged the woman's eyes. Her trembling hands clutched the weapon.

The woman's voice was long in coming. "Well, some men might shoot first and ask later if you're found here. You understand that?"

"I'm alive."

The woman pulled the rifle back through the window and stared at him through the open frame, gaze moving to the small obsidian bee sewn as a button on his shirt, then up again in a wide stare.

He smiled at her beauty and the fortune of finding her. He had no business being in her company. She was right. Yet, his being there could be no accident.

The woman nodded her head, without taking her gaze from his. "Those are fine grouse. If you have a mind to share, leave them cleaned at the door and I'll cook."

A few moments stood between them as he gauged his decision the same way he'd measure the wisdom of leaping into a deep and narrow chasm. He blinked twice to clear his doubts, and carried the birds to the bank of the creek, wondering where her man had gone.

Leave or Follow

"Can't understand that gal," said Cleve. "Willing to stay alone with the news I brung."

"She's mulish," said Maddie.

Maddie and Cleve headed back to her farm. She didn't want to leave Eden, but as quick as her pa would be with a gun if threatened by an Indian, she wouldn't rest easy until she counted each and every one of her children safe. And the lambs were important business. She'd made Eden promise to keep her rifle close, bolt the door and stay put until she rode the round-trip.

"Scotsmen—a stubborn lot. The condition runs deep, I suspect," Cleve said.

He tossed her a sideways glance. She returned a cool glare. When Cleve piped up to tell the story of his morning, she knew it was an effort to change her mood.

He said he had ridden in the dark for two hours before dawn and found Maddie's daughter at first light in the road flanking the Powder River.

"Told me she was out pickin' rose hips at dawn and the dern mule threw her." He smiled. "At a distance Jenny looks like you, dark hair and all."

She knew Cleve was doing his best to charm her by the comparison.

Maddie's voice tightened, "She bent up?"

"No. She's a tough squirt. But that mule's no good. Oughta buy her a horse."

"You give me a dollar or two more for them lambs and I might."

Cleve straightened and cleared his throat. "Well, anyway, she shouldn't a been out there alone."

"You take her home?"

"Yep. Found the red mule knee deep in the Powder. That mule's a sight, covered with mud. Take Jenny the rest of the day to groom him up nice."

"Don't need no red mule to be prettied up. Reckon the mud will fall off soon enough. Jenny's got better things to do, like milkin' and washin'. She's got the reins when I'm gone."

Cleve shook his head. "Bet she didn't know nothin' about those lambs."

"Did you ask her?"

"Well, no," said Cleve.

Maddie let her fast-paced horse take the lead once Cleve stopped talking. By the time they reached her house, he trailed well behind and, before he caught up, Maddie was off her horse and in the corral with the ewes.

"The ones with the beet stains on them's the ones that go to town. Ain't no big mystify."

"I reckoned that were the case, but it coulda been the opposite, and I been chided for lesser mistakes."

Maddie shot him an irritated look. Her time wasn't wasted. "Wouldn't call murderin' my best sow lesser."

Cleve once took the wrong pig and for weeks she'd made him feel sorrow for the lives of the unborn piglets laid to rest along with the ribs and loin. Truth was, he never laid eyes on the litter, knew nothing about it until the boy who worked for him pulled one of the dead, half-term pigs from his coat pocket. But the deed was his doing just by employing the young heathen.

"I know you're aggravated at me, but I ain't sorry to bring you back to a place of better safety." He dismounted and walked into the corral.

As soon as he reached Maddie, she turned and quit the pen, closing the gate behind her. She had noses to count.

Jenny stuck her head beyond the door of the house. "I got rose hips fer yer tea."

Maddie's father sat upon a wide squat stool on the porch. As soon as Maddie climbed the steps the door swung open to deliver three squealing children onto the planks. She joined her daughter in the small kitchen. The walls were covered with newspaper illustrations Maddie cut—pictures of things she'd like to have from advertisements and such. A real ice box for river ice, a tin bathtub, wallpaper for the tiny parlor, the frivolity of a fine feathered hat. Her gaze settled on the drawing of a Confederate soldier with a baseball in his hands. How much she'd give to have the tools of that game for her children.

Maddie looked at Jenny. "I tallied four. Where's the rest?"

"Barn I 'spect. They was swinging on a rope from the hay loft a few minutes ago. Why?"

Maddie relaxed. "Just tryin' to keep track of the population."

Maddie pulled the handle of a top drawer with care as she looked for a metal tea strainer. The knob came clean away from the wood nine times out of ten. One more broken thing she hadn't had time to fix. The drawer pulled free and clean, brass intact.

"You fix this, Jen?" asked Maddie.

"Mr. Hackett."

Maddie delivered a scowl in Jenny's direction.

"The mule throwed me this morning. He gave me a ride home. Came in for some water and when I was looking for string to tie up the rose hips he noticed the broken pull. Fixed it, that's all."

"Well, we don't need no man fixing us up. Just 'cause I ain't had time to git to it, don't mean I need another pair of hands."

"Yes, Mama." Jenny knelt on a stool and put her elbows on the kitchen table. "Got a good story, too. Guess what I asked him?"

Maddie was used to the unusual leaking from her oldest child's lips. The girl gave little care to what people thought. "What's that?"

"Are you wanting to marry my mama, Mr. Hackett, I sez."

Maddie put a hand to her face. Her cheek blazed. "Lan, child."

"That's what Mr. Hackett said." Jenny made a cup around her mouth with one hand. "What's in your mind to ask such a question, sez he."

Maddie knew exactly what he had in mind, but the process was slower than a hobbled mule. Anyone smart enough to get off a train track would know why he traveled three hours once a week to gather stock for the slaughterhouse in Suggs, a rough little town sprung up with the hope of a railroad, or deliver the occasional piece of mail. In the beginning, he wanted to help out a grass widow who hadn't any other way to make means. Lending a hand had turned to grabbing one. Cleve was thinking to be a part of her life.

Maddie knew she had complicated things the minute she included a pie in one transaction. Then fresh-baked bread, then a jar of jam and put-up peaches. With the first gift of kerchiefs and socks, Cleve graduated from taking stock to town to taking stock of the situation. He always looked at her with half-closed eyes, like she was the star of a stage play he wrote in his mind.

"I sez, might only be fourteen, but any sod bustin' fool knows you don't need to ride all the way out here to fetch a meal for the rail men. Even Mama knows."

Maddie pursed her lips to let Jenny know she said too much, but she wanted to laugh. Jenny knew her mother well.

"What else?"

"Mind yourself, sis, he sez. Thirstin' for information can drive a body harder than thirstin' for water." Jenny laughed.

Cleve stepped into the kitchen. "And if you're not careful, you'll find yourself alone in the middle of a river full of answers long before you learn to swim."

Jenny tipped her chin. Maddie reckoned she was still trying to figure his words.

"I got no time for all this," said Maddie. She brushed by Cleve and walked out the door, crossing the yard to her horse. She didn't have the energy to debate the morning's events, though since she'd set her mind on him, she supposed Cleve would be walking across her thoughts all day.

Cleve had no doubt skated through to midlife without the touch of a woman. Maddie had first seen him in town, while she and Big were buying seed to sow their fields. Since then she'd grown and shrunk three times with a trio of children in as many years. When Big rode half their team of two mules down the way for the last time, she'd quit coming to town. The railroad was tracking its way east. Not easy to shrink from a challenge, she started raising stock for sale to the work camps that were certain to spring up in town.

Cleve was the town mortician then. He'd told her of the many jobs he'd had in his life, gone from blacksmith to locksmith because he knew iron and he'd been bitten on the backside one too many times while shoeing horses. The last lock he'd fashioned was for the coffin of a man whose wife wanted him to stay put. When the mortician told him what he made for bleeding out a body and filling it up again with clear fluid, Cleve changed careers. He'd read Maddie an article about an outbreak of corpse explosions in Wyoming that headed him west. She'd remembered his arrival. The work of a mortician was welcomed.

A person passed on during the hard freeze of winter was coffined and put up on ice until spring thaw. As soon as the sun became hot enough to soften the earth enough to dig, a service was held.

Given the proclivity of ranchers in the area to gift their dead with expensive boxes, and their penchant for throwing long gatherings to honor those passed, a procession of funerals popped up every spring. The better the coffin, the more airtight. As the sun shone down on the festivity and the sealed boxes, science took hold and did the rest. She'd been to more than one wake that was interrupted by the bursting of an overheated, un-embalmed corpse. Maddie had re-boxed an infant or two over the years.

With the nearing railroad crews, though, Cleve had told her more money was to be made in butchering, even if he had to drive the stores miles east to meet them. He took to carving up a different species of western settler—the steer. Maddie imagined he'd made the leap from mortician to butcher without much fuss. Tools were similar, she guessed, and a carcass was a carcass whether the face wore a smile or not. The railroad was eager to buy beef for the men on the line. That's why she'd gone into farming animals. Cleve had taken up the prospect of offering her more diverse raft of meat to the company camps. In exchange, she set an extra place at her table for Cleve when he came to call. She'd even mend a loose button or ripped glove for him from time to time, but she'd never accept more help than she needed in return.

Granted, neither mortician nor butcher was a magnetizing target of a lady's affection, she reckoned. The tangy stench of blood from one work or the other, teamed with either formaldehyde or offal, was a difficult thing to erase from hands and clothes. Maddie figured he took to the pipe in order to mask the odor with tobacco. But she had tended too many babies' breeches to be put off by the signature scent of the slaughterhouse. She wasn't afraid to brush up against his arm or sit close by on the porch after dinner, giving Cleve hope for the best. While she didn't need his help, she had to admit the attention appealed. Wooing made her feel prettier than she reckoned she was. She wagered that children had a way of diminishing the glow of a healthy woman.

Contrary to fortune for Cleve, late spring brought the arrival of Aiden McBride. Maddie had seen the suspicion on Cleve's face the first time he and Aiden met. Even Maddie noticed that the offerings she made with each shipment of stock to town trickled to a halt. Her attention was diverted to the young, handsome red-head. Cleve was miffed, she reckoned. He'd invested more time in

Maddie than Aiden ever returned her way. But Eden's brother was as fine looking a man as she'd ever seen. She was a puppy in his presence, yearning for his attention.

It hadn't yet been offered.

She shook the contemplation of another husband from her weary mind. The fancy was, in the main, fuel for a perky imagination. The smaller her house got with a crowd of children, the more she needed the solitary space of the open country against her body, not the groping hands of a hungry mate.

She'd fancy a hired man, though. Like the negro she had over the summer. Someone she could boss and pay and give a day off to and be sure he'd be out of her hair. His name was Ink. He'd come north from Cheyenne with the railroad, he'd said, sick and tired of laying rail for three squares and a dollar a day. Quit to work land instead. Maddie gave him the missing mule's stall in the barn, meals, and fifteen silver Morgans a month in return for help tending the patchwork farm, delivering lambs to town, and an occasional watching of the children—and her pa. Soon as Cleve launched his call for stock, Maddie let Ink go. A portion of regret gripped her at the memory of the black man walking down the road.

Maddie stood in front of the barn. "How many of y'alls in there?"

A choir of voices answered, "Four, Ma."

Maddie nodded, remounted, rode to the house and whistled. Cleve walked onto the porch and seven children of intermediate growth trotted in from their activities to form a rough circle around their mother.

"You all stay close to home with Papaw." Maddie turned to her father. "Pa, Cleve's got some news from town."

Maddie's father perked up and stared at her. "Where you off to, child?"

"Headin' back to Eden's. My visit weren't up yet, and besides, she took herself a chill last night with the drop in temperature."

Jenny emerged from the house with a bundle of dried vegetation. "Here's the rose hips for you, Ma. Want to take the dried up ones on to Missus Rose?"

"Might be a comfort to the fever—and fetch me my pistol, too."

"The woman looked in fine fettle to me," Cleve said. "Ain't you gonna pay no heed to my news?"

"Well go on then. The sun ain't gonna stay in the sky just fer you," said Ezra.

Ezra gave Cleve a long look up and down like he was trying to figure what flavor he was.

Cleve delivered the news of the renegade in all its detail. When he handed the poster of the wanted man to Ezra, the old man slid his youngest grandchild from his lap to the porch and walked without a word into the clapboard house. The flimsy door banged hard behind him.

Cleve had one foot on the first step of the porch. "I ain't sure to leave or follow."

Maddie could guess where her father went. The old man returned with a Springfield in hand.

"Guess you believe me," said Cleve, shifting his weight from one foot to the other in Ezra's silence. "That rifle's a relic, but I expect the old breech loader'll do. Shoots far enough."

"That it do. Red devils everywhere." Ezra looked at Maddie as she turned her horse south. "Be back before dark, ye hear?"

Maddie called behind her, "Don't fret if I ain't. You know I got me a good aim and a watchful eye. And, Pa, stay put, will you?"

Cleve stood up straight and put his hands in his pockets. "You bring that woman back with you. She's taking a big chance being alone."

"Do my best, Cleve."

Jenny returned with a pouch of rose hips and her mother's pistol.

Maddie reached down to take them, whispering under her breath, "Take care with Papaw while I'm gone. You know he ain't right. Swing wide, Jen. Understand?"

Maddie gave her a wink, pushed the gun deep into her skirt pocket and trotted the horse down the lumpy road toward Rose Ranch.

Cleve's voice rose in the dust behind the horse. "Well then."

Lucky Ones Die Fast

Aiden slept in fits and starts, dreaming the sounds of a frittering autumn—moose snorts and the patter of coyotes on the move down the mountain to kinder climes.

When he wakened, the rain no longer fell. The edges of his hair were soaked but his body was dry under the canvas. Ink snored in soft puffs as he leaned against Aiden, warming the side facing away from a withering fire. Aiden tilted his head back, checking the mood of the coming day. Midnight's drizzle dissolved into a star-quilt twinkling through the high piney branches of the lodgepoles. Cold had the mountain under its thumb again and hung heavy around the remaining embers. Aiden pushed his sluggish hand against the smooth warm surface of a facing stone near the few flames and let it rest there, soaking up a heat that he couldn't feel.

With a long breath, he was returned to his mother's bedside. The stench of rotting flesh—gas gangrene.

Aiden sat up. The camp spun. He blinked several times to focus. The flesh of his lower arm, from wrist to elbow was black as coal. He put a hand to his neck. His skin was clammy. He couldn't catch his breath. Aiden had seen the effect of shock on a body.

Mother.

He shouted, feeble and frightened, "Ink!"

Ink stood bolt upright taking the tarp with him as he ran without cause into the thicket.

Aiden called out again, his racing heart, "I need you." He tried to stand but the flutter of his breath warned against it.

Ink skulked out of the brush. "Pardon, Mister Aiden. Sounded a might like you spotted that bear. Scarified me out of dreamin' the same."

Ink walked up to Aiden, gaze targeting the source of Aiden's frightening wail. His eyes spoke the horror.

Ink's words were a textbook recitation, "Poison in flesh-rot heads north to take a heart or lung. Lucky ones die fast." His gaze met Aiden's, voice changing as though he hadn't meant to speak that last line, "Stay quiet. Try breathin' slow. I seen this plenty. Know what to do."

Aiden slumped onto the hardpan, pulled the cold stiff canvas over him as best he could and let his shoulders go limp. But his heart pummeled the air flowing in and out of his lungs as though he'd run a mile. The fire was near out, but the activity of building up the flames was out of the question.

"Fire." Aiden's eyes were leaden. "Ink, the Indian who stole my horse has some fight with Jack Williams. Has it in mind to clean out all the settlers on the Powder come the lock of winter. If I don't make it off this mountain, you must. Warn them. Warn...my sister." The words came across his lips in a slur but his worries seemed lifted at delivering the news. Ink was a good man.

Ink fed the fire then sat close by until the sun teased at the morning sky with a pale wash of silvery light. Aiden shivered, even though the flames stood tall and hot.

Through slits of half-closed eyes, a splintered moon shone above him, moving in smooth fashion across the sky each time he focused, then blinded by clouds rolling across to the east. Aiden wanted to grab one of the billows and ride it home, but his hand was the size of a small melon and the color of a prune. Skin on his forearm pulled apart by the swelling, oozing a thick mossy green. A thin, red line advanced past his elbow. He stared at Ink.

Ink's eyes glistened black gold as he rocked back and forth in the fresh morning, axe in his lap.

The Scarce Side of Detail

Maddie urged her gelding to trot the four miles back to Eden's farm. The old gent was lame on a forefoot and after a mile her head ached with the uneven cadence. Gritty dust driven by the noon breeze at her back filled her lungs and she coughed in time to the gelding's hoof beats. The worst catch in her throat was fear. She'd met with loss from Indians before. That's why her pa had without notice appeared in the hen yard one day, everything he owned strapped to the slat sides of a spotted mule.

Even then he'd been a man who used the alphabet sparingly. All he'd done was stand at the shoulder of that mule, in front of her house, and sob. The whole of a week passed before she patched a picture together of what had happened.

He told of Indians astride their horses, pickets in an endless fence skirting the top of the bluff above their homestead. How he'd stand outside, sometimes for hours, rifle ready, staring them down until they moved away. The cavalry had warned him.

The land was claimed by an Indian tribe. Her pa, too proud to heed it. He sobbed as he told her about leaving her ailing ma behind one day to make a long trip to town for linctus. When he returned, his home was in flames, his stock gone, and Maddie's mother, dead.

Maddie talked Big into taking her father into their home. After testifying to the attack, Ezra hadn't spoken for months, and then only as if he were talking to his wife alone, as though she sat beside him on the shallow steps of the long porch. His mind grew threadbare over the years. Most of the time, he sat by the door, sometimes clear as the crow of a rooster at daybreak, but most often confused and disoriented. Other times, he wandered through the cottonwoods and was hell to find. He paid little mind to his daughter's orders. He was just another child.

She never shared the truth about her mother's death with Eden. That was five years before Eden's arrival. Maddie feared the tale of murderous Indians might scare off the one close friend she'd ever had. A long time had passed since Maddie had seen an Indian loose in these parts. The story, best left buried. At present, moving at a lopsided trot down the dirt road, she wasn't sure. Maddie pushed the rumination away, but nothing denied the fear crowding her brain.

Maddie gave the old horse a kick or two to perk up his pace. Soon she passed under the split rail portal to Rose Ranch. White smoke streamed from the chimney and the front door stood ajar. Chickens littered the yard. Maddie slid off her gimpy mount and tethered it to the hitching post before stepping to the doorway. She put her ear to the door then gave it a knock. Something clattered to the floor.

Maddie stepped through and bolted the latch. Eden retrieved a metal spoon at her feet, wiped it clean with a cotton towel and stepped to the wood stove to tend a cast-iron pan. The smell of bacon fat filled the cabin, coaxing Maddie's memory. She'd not yet eaten.

"Somethin' mighty good cookin'. Pork?"

"You came a long way just for dinner."

"My business with Cleve is done. Not gonna leave you alone till I'm sure you are alone. What's cookin' smells so good?"

"Birds."

"Kilt a pullet?" Maddie walked to the table in front of the stove.

"Grouse."

Maddie scanned the small room. The rifle stood where she'd left it that morning, propped just so at the cabin door. "Fall from the sky, did they?"

Eden's refusal to look her in the eye was as good as confession.

"Where is he?"

"Mending a far piece of the pasture fence. Where the mares came through last night. He brought the birds after you left. I told him that if he cleaned them I'd cook."

"Ain't that cozy. Well, set three for dinner, 'cause I ain't leavin'."

"Maddie, I didn't invite him to dinner. I merely said I'd cook the birds. He can take his meal outside."

"Don't think he wants to fatten you up a bit 'fore he eats you?"

Eden's tone rose a scale. She kept her attention on the stove. "That's enough. Things need fixing. He's glad to do it."

Maddie walked straight to Eden and turned her around to face her. "You ain't afraid of him."

Eden grabbed Maddie's hand and pressed the palm hard against her chest. "Feel that? My heart's beating like a drummer boy at the battle of Vicksburg."

"Then why in tarnation don't you tell him to git?"

Eden let Maddie's hand fall from her own. "Because, dear lady, as anyone can see, I do need help."

"And what's he git in return?"

Eden glanced out the window. "The benefit of the doubt."

The birds sputtered in the pan. Eden removed them to rest atop a tin of biscuits in the oven. She pulled small green apples from a bin, sliced them into quarters, and tossed them in the pan that had held the grouse. When the apples were soft she added them to the birds and bread.

Eden folded her apron in a neat square and tucked a sachet into the cuff of her sleeve. Always proper. A mystery given the company the woman kept. Eden poured a jar of sun tea into two tin cups and the women stepped outside into the warmth of noon. But the heat of summer backed away. At the creek, the rabbit-ear leaves of the willow were tinged yellow, and the water was but a trickle, thirsty for the melt to follow winter.

The friends sipped their tea, standing near the safety of the front door. A few remaining birds spoke of autumn as ponies ran down from the high pasture to a fence near the barn.

"That's a fine colt you have," Maddie said.

"As good a stallion as we've ever bred, he may save the ranch."

"Stud horse?"

"There's plenty of interest around the valley. He's fresh blood from Britain, and Lord knows there's been enough inbreeding in the horses here to look for something new." Eden wiped a loose strand of hair from her eyes. "If he doesn't kill me first. He's a wild one."

The women lapsed into silence again, but Maddie's mind brimmed with questions—and advice finding its way free. "Ain't no use wasting this time being dumb. Soon enough we won't be seeing much of each other." The ride for a visit between the friends would grow longer and less frequent as soon as the deep snows arrived. "You're taking a big chance."

"Isn't that all life is?"

"What are you talkin' about?"

"I'm tired of being afraid, that's all. Afraid of the weather, the people, of dying—of living."

"Don't mean turnin' your back to danger, darlin'."

"I'm not turning my back. That's the point. I'm looking fear in the eye. And for the first time in my life, it's my decision."

Eden's decisiveness made Maddie uneasy. She drank down the rest of her tea in one gulp, wishing for a slug of moonshine to steady her nerves instead. "I know you, Eden Rose. You gotta be scared."

Eden looked long into Maddie's eyes. "That's nothing new, now is it?"

"Then, why in blazes are you doing this?"

"You know me so well, you tell me."

Maddie studied her friend for a few seconds. "It's something new you want."

The Indian appeared at the crest of the pasture, carrying a coil of wire in one hand and a hand sledge in the other. As he cleared the crest, both women stopped talking. The herd of otherwise flighty mustang mares, and the headstrong young stallion, followed him at a docile pace all the way to the gate beside the barn.

"Dern. If that don't beat all."

"Did you see a line on those mares last night, Maddie?"

She looked to the sky. "Reckon not."

The Indian closed the gate behind him while the mares lined up along the fence, hanging their heads over the top, pining after him. Maddie rubbed her cheek to make sure she wasn't dreaming.

"To say he has a way with horses is the scarce side of detail, don't you think? I've not seen anything like it. Ever. And no animal abides a wicked man."

"Glory," was all Maddie mustered.

Secrecy, the Human Dress

Maddie served herself first. She'd never been one to shy from a meal. With each child, she'd adopted a quicker pace at her food. Eden supposed that if she hadn't, by the time the interruptions were over, her meal would be cold as well water.

Eden fixed a plate of food for the Indian and crossed the yard to leave the meal at the foot of the barn entrance. A ladder angled its way to the rafters.

"Birds are cooked." Eden stretched her neck and stood on tiptoe to see the other end of the roof. The Indian was nowhere in sight.

If she left the meal on the ground the goats would clean the plate in no time. If she delivered the meal to the top of the ladder, he could eat it on the roof. She pulled her skirt up with one hand and took hold of the plate with the same, keeping the other hand free to hold the ladder as she climbed. When she was halfway up, the Indian rounded the barn below. Eden lost her balance at the shock of it, the ladder slid to one side, and at once Eden sat at the man's feet.

She found his warm hands around her waist, pulling her to her feet, and was again face to face with the bluest eyes she'd ever seen. Her cheeks burned. Not wanting to show surprise, she turned her attention to the goats as they closed in from across the yard. They were quick to clean the scrapes of food scattered about the fallen plate.

Eden reached for her ankle, which throbbed at the quick turn.

"Let me see." The man bent toward her.

The solicitation was inappropriate at best. Eden's tone, harsh. "Certainly not."

He stepped back.

"I'm sorry." Eden softened. "It's not our way to show a lady's ankle to a man other than her own. I know you were trying to help." She was sure her pounding heart was audible.

The man glanced at the goats as they finished up the scattered meal.

"And there's the dinner for your trouble." Eden looked toward the cabin.

Maddie stood in the open doorway with a pistol at her side. Eden shook her head. The man who'd brought the food and used his time in mending didn't deserve to be fed on a rooftop. "No need to eat outside anyway. Come in," Eden said.

He regarded Maddie and the weapon.

"Maddie, it's all right, now," Eden called. "'Twas an accident. The man will be coming in for his dinner."

Maddie disappeared into the cabin. When Eden and the Indian reached the door, she was already seated. Eden placed a fresh plate at the table. He sat down, taking a biscuit and strip of bacon from the pan in the center of the feast.

Maddie anchored her elbows to the table and held a Sharp-tail carcass to her lips as she looked across the table to the guest. "Got a name?"

"Intah. And you?"

"Maddie True."

"And your friend?" Intah nodded to Eden.

"You mean you ain't met formally? Or ain't that an Indian way?"

"Eden Rose," said Eden.

"Kinda Indian you, anyways?" Maddie asked.

"Solitary."

"By choice?" Eden sipped the remainder of her tea, watching him across the table with careful regard.

Intah's voice was quiet and deliberate. "Bidding of the white man."

"Don't figure you're too happy with that," Maddie said.

"Reservations hold the discontented."

Maddie sat back. "Why you ain't there?"

"I choose to be content."

"You roam by permission?" asked Eden.

"Permission?" Intah stripped the flesh off of one of the Sharp-tail breasts with his teeth.

"Ain't right, riding around these parts on your own. Law's the law. And most of the law's a pretty fair shot." Maddie put the bare bones of a grouse on her plate, and reached for a biscuit.

"Right and wrong is simple," he said. "Don't eat or drink: die. Act in hate: pay. Neither right, nor wrong—but truth."

Eden turned Intah's brief missive over in her mind a time or two. The only thing Maddie seemed to be considering was another biscuit.

Maddie tilted her head. "So I suppose you reckon there's no crime in stealin' or killin'."

"Reality lies in inspiration. Look to a cause, you find the truth."

Cause often lay buried. That was the truth. Eden marveled at the man's train of thought. High concepts for the heathen Maddie supposed him to be. His speech alone was curious. Words flowed without the normal halt of second language—and with a gentle hint of Britain she was certain.

"How did you come to speak English so well?" Eden asked.

"White women kin."

"So that's why you're willing to help me."

Intah stopped chewing and looked at Eden as though wanting to say more.

"Well-educated women, I guess," Eden said.

"My father's mother was white, taken as a child. My white mother came to my father as a young woman, a teacher, schoolbooks in hand. She passed them to me."

"Must have been quite a library. Do you have it still?" Eden expected a small range of minor works: *The Lamplighter; Ruth Hall.*

"Burned long ago."

Maddie's question dripped sarcasm. "Prairie fires?"

"Yes. The blaze of soldiers west."

"Cruelty has a human heart." Eden recited an early version of Blake's "The Divine Image" under her breath. She quoted the poem often, as elegy and condemnation, anytime thoughts of her mother arose from the grave. The quotation seemed, as well, a fitting lament for a people once brimming the land she called home.

Intah's deep blue eyes looked square into Eden's. "Jealousy, a human face."

Eden's arms tingled. No man had ever matched her knowledge of Blake. The poet was neither well known nor highly regarded, and Blake let stand this particular verse from "The Divine Image" in very few copies of his work. That she and Intah were both privy to the poem created an uncomfortable intimacy in the room. Eden lifted her napkin to her mouth to wipe beads of perspiration cooling her lip.

Intah regarded Maddie from the corner of his eye. "Terror, the human form divine. And Secrecy, the human dress."

"Fine words," Eden said.

"For an Indian." Intah wore a slight smile and wiped his hands on a square of cloth to the left of his plate.

Eden didn't intend him to think she and Maddie thought him inferior. She cleared her throat.

"Ain't no call to comment on my clothes," Maddie said.

Eden laughed. "Oh, Maddie."

"Well, there ain't." Slapping both hands on the table, Maddie pushed her chair back and stood. "And it ain't right him being here."

She thrust a hand deep into the pocket of her skirt and her sleeve caught one of the china teacups. Porcelain scattered into splinters when it hit the floor.

Eden put a hand to her mouth to stem a gasp. Tears pooled in her eyes. Grief was doltish, but it couldn't be helped. Eight teacups crossed the ocean with her. Six made the trip west in one piece. Three remained, as though they were some gauge of her tenure. When the final piece of china broke there'd be no memory left of Scotland.

"Dern, Eden, I'm sorry. You know I'm sorry." Maddie pulled her hand from her pocket and placed it on Eden's arm.

Eden wiped a tear from one eye and stood to survey the damage. Intah watched her as though he'd never before seen a woman weep. She moved to gather the broken cup.

He pushed back from the table, picked up a shard, and looked at Maddie. "True to your name, you stated the fact. This is no place for me and—"

"You'd be a boon around here until my brother returns." The words were out before Eden knew they existed.

Both Intah and Maddie stared at her with the same surprised expression.

The loss of another cup touched a barren place within Eden. For the first time she dreaded being alone. Before, solitude had a limit. But would she ever see either Hugh or Aiden again?

Her eyes focused on an ivory-colored claw hanging from a woven band of horsehair fallen from behind the man's muslin shirt. The band was unlike any she'd ever seen and adorned with an intricate pattern. The claw was as long and curved as a thumb and forefinger of a sturdy man showing the size of a minnow.

Imagining an animal big enough to grow such a talon gave Eden a chill. "If you'll stay, you can have the barn loft. You said yourself, I need the help."

Intah walked to the entry. "I must go before snow sets too deep in the mountains. I'll stay until the weather turns cold again." He paused by the leaning rifle. "Best load the rifle. You may have need of it someday."

He opened the door, and headed across the yard. His horse lumbered down off the hill, to stand by the cabin.

Maddie followed Intah as far as the door. She watched him for a moment, then let her gaze drop to the weapon by her side.

Picking up the rifle, Eden broke the piece open. "Empty."

Maddie nodded. "Dern."

Day's Shadows

"Ain't gonna spend another night. Cain't. But I'll be back early with the buckboard to take you to tea, per usual. Cain't afford not to go. All we need is witnesses to the circus you got goin' here. We'd all be cooked for sure." Maddie gathered her horse and took Eden's hand. "Guess you're right about him—still."

She didn't want to leave, yet excuses to stay were spent. Jenny was good with the youngsters at home, but she'd been minding them for the better part of two days. Pandemonium was a spring-loaded toy waiting to pounce. Besides, dealing with her grandfather and dealing with her siblings were as different as cornering a wild cat and a puppy.

Eden kissed Maddie's cheek and gave a nod to the barn. "Oh, for heaven's sake, Maddie, get on your horse and go home. I'll see you tomorrow."

Intah banged a hammer at a loose board without a look her way. She mounted her horse and turned to leave, throwing a final edict at Eden. "The mornin', at eight."

* * *

When Maddie got close enough to her house to see the porch, her pa opened the breech of his Springfield to check its load. The barrel wood shone satiny smooth in the sun from years of wear, the metal, the tarnish of autumn. He held the rifle in perfect balance, between palm and thumb. She'd held the weapon the same way many times. It was comfortable, cool bronze warming her skin—the firm hand of an old friend.

The old breechloader was the one thing left from Carolina. He let go anything that served any memory of the war, before he'd burdened a wagon and headed west, wanting to purge his soul of the conflict. Maddie guessed that banishing its artifacts was the easiest first step to that end.

He'd taken up the new Trapdoor Springfield as a last purchase on the way out of the maze called Blue Ridge. It had gotten him, his woman, and all their spotted mule could pull, as far as the territory of Wyoming. He'd told Maddie tales of how he used the rifle to hunt game, change the minds of less civil men, and even once, to start a fire. But he'd never used that particular weapon to end a human life. He'd said that as far as he was concerned, he'd shrugged off the killing he'd done as soon as he crossed the line to Kansas.

But Indians were different. Ezra counted them as the worst of thieves, not much more so than the Federals. He often said they all stood probable as not to cut a throat or hang a neck. Pocketeers he called them—murdering, mutinous, pocket robbers, trying to take every possession and the land, razing anything that kept them from that purpose.

To his mind, a government pledge to hold natives to the reservation didn't mean the danger had diminished. "There's treachery in promise," Ezra said. He'd taken the lesson from his own army as men fell before him on the field like waves against a jagged shore. It was always the next battle that would win the war. A man's word could always be shaped to proffer his own bent.

Her pa watched Cleve rustle the white lambs into a group and shepherd them down the road in a cloud of red dust. Ezra believed the man to be a certain type of treason. Only a fool would believe fat stock was the only thing bringing Cleve such a distance. Ezra had said so on more than one occasion. But his reason mattered little. Fact was Ezra understood Cleve's game as well as she did. It was no worry to her. What vexed her was the silence Ezra took to for days at a time—and the wistful way he had started to consider Jenny.

Maddie owed the interest Ezra set on her daughter to the resemblance the girl had taken to Maddie's ma over the summer. Jenny had begun to fill out, and her face had taken on the same shape as her grandmother's. Her daughter's form even gave

Maddie a start when seeing the girl milking in the distance. She had a way of sitting on the stool in the same way Maddie's ma had—a shade bent and leaned to one side, head canted to attend the squirting flow. Maddie understood why Ezra cottoned to the picture, but pity gave her a queer, uneasy feeling, even though she wagered her father was harmless enough.

Mostly, he'd sit on the porch in the braided seat of a metal rocker the blacksmith had made him, looking out to the Powder River. But the blankness in his eyes was not owed to emptiness in his head, reckoned Maddie. Most of the time, she expected he was just trying to get his mind wrapped around a riddle—the why of living and its ways.

The unraveling was something he'd worked at most of his life, in the peculiar afterglow that wartime killing leaves in the souls of some men. Used to be, he boasted a string of chatter, but as he'd aged his voice had hushed. Maddie suspected that Ezra found conversation's best partner to be silence.

Maddie's horse approached the porch as Jenny stepped from the front door with a wood bucket and set it on the planks.

Jenny called out. "Hey, ma." She pulled the door closed, and perched her hands on her hips, regarding Ezra. The Springfield lay a babe rocking in his arms. "Papaw, that thing loaded?"

The breech lay wide open at the crook of Ezra's arm. He turned his head in Jenny's direction without regard to her mother's arrival. He raised the rifle to her for an opinion.

"Well, you best be topping the breech afore you try to fire," Jenny said as she shot her mother a concerned look. "He's gonna kill someone with that thing someday who don't deserve it and that might be his own self." Grabbing the bucket, she threw it over a shoulder as she jumped down the stairs. "There's milk to pull for supper."

As Maddie dismounted and put her horse away, she questioned if the old man could even kill an Indian if one showed up. She remembered the look of shame on his face as he told her that, after finding her mother dead, he'd packed up to join his daughter and her brood under the watchful eye of a solitary Indian sitting a tall horse on the crest of a low hill. Ezra passed close enough to see the man's face, jaw set brazen in the face of morning. Yet he'd made no move to shoot him. Her pa had told her that it was simple: he had no heart left at all to kill the renegade. Not that he shouldn't have—he couldn't. He had no feeling left for anything.

Milking complete, Jenny shooed the cow from the barn. The beast ambled across the yard to the trough beneath the well pump and took a long draught of water. The girl moved from barn to house, more woman than child. Jenny drew the full pail close to Ezra as she passed, tempting him with the fresh milk.

"Indians," he said.

Ezra drew his hand through Jenny's long chestnut locks, the same shade as her grandma's, letting his palm rest in the crook of her neck.

He wasn't thinking of Jenny.

Jenny put a gentle hand on her grandfather's. Ezra gave a light tug to the girl's hair and a faint smile, then scanned the long road running out in each direction from the farm, leaving his hand engaged with Jenny's hair. The picture troubled Maddie. The absent look in her pa's eyes was there more than not. Too often, his actions didn't mirror his focus. The disconnection made her wonder how long she had before she'd have another child on her hands. Ezra spied less and less difference between truth and fiction. Evidence lay buried under the oak she'd planted in her hardpan yard. A secret Eden shared. Maddie would shoot her pa before she'd ever let him kill again.

Maddie crossed the yard and scaled the stairs to the porch, relieving Jenny of the milk pail with one hand and taking her pa's hand from her daughter's hair. She squeezed his fingers, trying to bring him to the moment, whispering, "Pa."

Ezra drew his observation of the horizon to Maddie's eyes. "I'm here, kitten."

He delivered new meaning to the term *here*. She was bound, from dawn till dusk, by the constant needs of others.

He touched his hand to Maddie's cheek. "You know I love you."

She took his hand and squeezed it, weaving flimsy words through a bush of thorns. "Love you, too, Pa—I do."

The day's shadows disappeared as the autumn sun backed down over the Bighorn. Maddie drudged her way through the cooking of another meal and called for supper. A gaggle of children were a band of chickens bound for the henhouse, flushing up the porch stairs: Harriet, Helen, Ruth, Oran, Rob, James, Fran and Jenny. She used the fragrance of fried eggs and warm soda biscuits to tempt Ezra to the table, but the old man held his place on the porch, maintaining a gentle sway of his chair, rocking the Springfield, staring out toward the Powder.

In search of Indians.

A Sturdy Brew

"Gotta take that arm, Mister Aiden. That red line's the devil looking for your heart. He finds it, take you straight to hell." Ink stoked the fire.

Aiden looked at him in horror. He hadn't aimed to lose an appendage. His mind went to the dream he'd had of Maddie by the Powder. One less hand to have slapped. He tried to cajole himself into the proposition, but his fear grew with the blaze.

"I seen men go to Hades on rotten legs. Learned how to take 'em off during the war. Axe was left behind near the stack of wood." Ink stood with tool in hand. "Sooner that festerin' comes off, longer you'll live."

"Done this before have you then?" His heart was already missing the limb.

"Nope." Ink ran his thumb up the blade's edge. "But I sharpened this blade myself before we came up the mountain. Ain't cut but a part-cord a wood since. It'll do."

Aiden eyed the tool and then Ink, gauging the man's ability to walk a straight line. "One draw."

"One draw."

"Don't suppose you have any whisky."

Ink pushed his hand between the buttons on his coat and pulled out a pewter flask. "For cookin'."

"Sure."

Ink put the warm flask to Aiden's lips and emptied the contents.

"Do you a might better than my Irish stew. Good medicine I reckon."

"The miserable have no other medicine but only hope." Aiden's faith in his survival waned with every breath.

"That Shakesbeer feller?"

"Aye." Aiden wiped the errant streams of liquor from his chin, squeezed his eyes shut, and let out a long raspy breath. "You write?"

Ink shook his head. "Not like that."

"Then like what?"

"Some."

"Then write for me." Aiden motioned toward the woodpile.

Ink pulled the journal, pen, and well from underneath the safety of the timber, opened to a page, and met Aiden's eyes.

"I find myself with no choice but to allow Ink...what is your full name?"

"Incus O'Hearn."

"O'Hearn?" Aiden thought the poison tricked his ears.

"What?" Ink squinted his eyes, drew his mouth tight and stuck out his chin.

Aiden shook his head. He imagined himself and Eden rolling on the ground at the humor of the moment. He'd normally laugh at such a thing, but he was too dizzy, his head swimming in the afternoon's fading blue cotton haze. Oh, to live to tell the tale of the Irish Negro's Axe.

He wanted to write to Eden; tell her to follow Hugh back to the green of Britain; to get out of this terrible country. But he'd didn't want her to follow Hugh anywhere. The man had withered her easy smile to hard resolve. To outlast Hugh should be her mission. With him gone, no line of story would convince her to leave Rose Ranch. Mere words would hold no charm.

Aiden cleared his throat. "I find myself with no choice but to allow Master...O'Hearn to take my venomous arm. Since the sole tool of the deed remains an axe, and I am ill-acquainted with the skill of my physician, I will depend on the mercy of God to deliver this journal to Eden Rose, Rose Ranch south of Suggs township, the vexed Territory of Wyoming."

Ink looked up. "Spell me venomous."

"Indeed." Aiden had little strength to lend education. What was left he intended to give to what might be his last correspondence with Eden. His patience, at an end. "Just use the letters you know. Or something close."

"Yessir."

Aiden's tone held the authority of a general. "What I am about to relay, Master O'Hearn, is a tale that I depend on you to keep. That is to say, the story shall go no further than this journal. Are we clear on this?"

"Yessir." Ink put the pen to paper and kept his eyes to the page.

Aiden went on in a quiet, measured tone until the sentences tied his tongue and his head nodded to his chest.

* * *

Ink tried to keep up, but some letters he'd never learned. He feared his writing would be code to all but him. No guarantee existed that even he could make out the words given the test of time.

He tried to feel the meaning of the sentences; to relay it within his limited skill. A gruesome tale. The truth of it, the heft of a dead horse on the man's chest. Certainly, the confession should go no further than the journal.

Aiden drawled out the last lines of the entry: *If I could beat this mountain and that bear, I'd be the man you believe I am. But life is disparate.*

Ink finished the last few letters. Aiden's eyes shut. Poor wretch. Plenty of ways to become a man that didn't involve beating the wild. Ink wasn't even sure such a feat was possible. The wild couldn't be beaten. Lesser men died learning the same.

Ink closed the book, tied the binding with a leather strap, and slipped it inside his clothes beside the pewter flask.

He walked to Aiden and put his palm underneath the man's nose. The air was warm and moist on Ink's skin. Alive, he reckoned. The odor of the gangrene made him gag. He wished he'd had the honey from the chow wagon. Would have killed a good part of the bacteria in the wound. Maybe stopped the rot.

He tugged the sleeve of Aiden's shirt above his hand. No budging the sweaty flannel up the arm any farther, and neither would it be pulled over the swelling. Without a good knife, he was left to take hard aim and hope the axe was as sharp as he figured it was. If he couldn't get a clean chop through the coat, the man was dead. Like enough, dead anyway. But the war taught Ink not to give a man up until life was gone.

He took off his belt, readying it as tourniquet, then he tipped Aiden over flat. When he did, the gold watch fell from Aiden's pocket. Ink retrieved the treasure and let the cold precious metal rest in his warm palm while he opened it, examining the fine detail of carving around the narrow frame of the face. He snapped the lid closed and turned it over in his hand.

McBride 1810-1831-1857

Ink lingered at the middle date. His own year. Before the war, before the railroad, before Custer. He studied Aiden's face. In sleep the man looked somehow younger, smooth-skinned and fair-haired. No doubt the easy life of a white man encouraged youth to hang back.

He let the timepiece linger in his hand until the gold warmed. God knew when his fingers would touch such a fine thing again. He slipped it back into Aiden's pocket, laid Aiden's arm out, and picked up the axe. He pushed the head into the fire thinking of a leg he'd once seen taken off with a bone saw.

Amputation was a messy thing, ripping back and forth through flesh already ravaged by war, hard to see bone for gore— and hellishly slow. He judged the edge of an axe better. Quick and clean. And the shirt, though another layer to break, would shield the initial spurt of blood he expected, and the carnage to follow. Aiden's belly rose and fell with the delirium of poison.

Whisky and gangrene—a sturdy brew.

Ink pulled the iron from the flame and, with heat rising from the metal in filmy waves, raised the axe high.

As You Think

Maddie's horse plodded down the dusty road. Eden's breath seemed to disappear along with the image of her friend. Her heart dug deep into her breast for safety. Intah shouldn't be around. His presence was dangerous for them both. Even though she could use the help in readying for winter, the risk wasn't worth the gain.

Intah climbed down the ladder and crossed the paddock full of ponies with ease. In all her time upon the prairie Eden had yet to learn to use the land and direct its creatures. She never crossed anything without her shoulders squared and her head turned to see what might come from behind. She gathered her resolve and walked to the barn. One decision to look things square in the eye, the challenge, pleasing. She would make another.

"I'll be leaving tomorrow morning for the day. I'll understand if you have to be going." She chewed her lip at the realization of not seeing him again. His presence, an odd blend of foolish pleasure. "What I mean is, I know I asked you to stay and appreciate your work, but my friends wouldn't understand your being here. I'm afraid it may be unsafe for you."

Intah replaced a couple of tools on the barn wall. "And for you."

"It's an odd lot. They're quick to judge—long to forgive."

Intah pulled a handful of nails from a leather pouch hanging on a peg, then turned to look at Eden. "Unfortunate quality in friends, don't you think?"

Eden broke his gaze, knowing that her one real friend in the valley was Maddie.

"I'd think you'd want to stay close with a fugitive on the loose." Intah took a rake and pulled saw shavings into a pile.

"Well, once a month Sundays are celebrated with the ritual of tea at a ranch up-valley. Might be news of my brother. He's overdue from the Bighorn. I'm worried for him. And I have a stallion to market for stud. People there have mares to breed."

"So it's business."

Eden thought of the music they always requested of her for the afternoon of dancing that followed tea. She and Hugh were the sole Scots in the area with such bad financial luck. Since Hugh'd been gone, she'd viewed herself as more servant than guest at the monthly gatherings.

"It's always business," she said.

A hawk yanked a sparrow from the sky above Eden without a sound. Three lone feathers rained down around her. "I'm expected to go. If I don't, curiosity will bring visitors. My neighbors come from the same tribe." Eden tried to put the concept in terms Intah would grasp. "We watch each other."

"So, you're watching them, as well."

Eden tapped her foot as she mulled over the truth. Tea was nothing more than the trading of judgments. "I guess that's right. It's habit."

"Habit-forming. A hard mold to break. But, as you think, so shall it be." Intah climbed up the ladder and hammered a last nail into the barn.

The man above her stood an ultimate contrariety—a familiar mystery. "What books did your mother leave behind?"

"Only two. Blake, and the Bible."

"You know them well."

Intah descended again, hung the hammer on the wall and turned to Eden. "And they know me."

She eyed the ivory talon peeking out at the edge of Intah's shirt as he stood before her. "And the claw?"

"Bear medicine." He touched his hand to the talisman. "Guardian in the wild."

"Where are you bound for?"

"The other side of the Bighorn."

"A long ride."

"Up the Crazy Woman canyon. Not so hard a journey."

The words took Eden's mind back to her brother. When he'd left she'd had no meat to offer that might sustain him. "There'll be bacon and biscuits for supper."

"I've eaten for the day."

"Suit yourself." She turned toward the cabin.

When Eden reached the house she closed the door behind her and pulled the heavy curtains across the two small windows. Lighting the stove, she was grateful for the bucket of water she'd brought from the well earlier. She'd not have to venture outside the cabin again that night. Dry wood cracked inside the stove, and Eden jumped. She placed a hand on her breast. Her heart thumped as though she'd just run across the pasture and she suddenly yearned for company. It was easier to feel safe when speaking to the man than when sequestered, visions of what lay beyond the door occupying her mind.

Yet.

She walked to the door and pushed the bolt into the lock knowing the effort would not keep her imagination nor the weather at bay. A wintry draft blew beneath the door, teasing goose bumps from her toes on up. She drew a shawl tight around her shoulders and transferred the pork roast that Maddie had delivered to the oven. Waited for her tea to color. The odors were comforting. At least she'd not go hungry that night.

When she'd finished her meal, the sky was full dark. Flames from the fireplace settled into ash and the room took on a tender, burnished glow that invited loneliness to gather close. She sat in the wooden rocker squeaking its own brand of conversation into the empty room.

All at once, she dreaded tomorrow's tea. A venue for gossip where feeding on the faults and miseries of others was the special of the day. Her gaze settled on Aiden's Highland bagpipes across the room. The case of her violin rested on its shoulder. Its song would never be as sweet as long ago, across a distant ocean, in the parlor at Lilybank, her brother by her side.

A presence deep within her reared its head in answer: nothing would ever be the same.

Soon the instrument was in her arms—an old friend she didn't recognize—singing in her ear. Bach bore gifts. One partita in particular, her favorite. She played the tune over and over, as though it had no end, one constant string of notes and melody until the minutes became hours, and the music, her breath. Eyes closed, she focused on Aiden. His smile lifted her spirits and in that she became lost in the genius of the song, free from care, vanished in time, touching the face of a merciful God.

Tomorrow would bring Aiden home. Bach would turn to Highlands fiddle and the odd Indian in her barn would ride off into the hills. All would be well.

She set the bow and violin into their velvet lining and leaned the case against the wall. Peeking through the curtain for a light in the barn, all she saw was darkness. Suspicion that the Indian watched the cabin chilled her hands.

Or was it dread at the notion of him leaving?

Cheat the Reaper

In his delirium Aiden had no arms at all. His rifle lay at the water's edge before him, broad bear tracks stepping a frenzied edge in the sand around its barrel. The stream clutched his neck and he was cold as ice, helpless against its current, floating in a sea of dull agony. Muffled screams mounted in the distance as the bear turned into the renegade, and the stream became a crazy woman, and Aiden all the while knowing the Indian would soon return.

Soon return.

His eyes snapped open to darkness splashed with amber firelight as a screaming echo danced through a canyon. He drew a quick shallow breath across his stinging throat. The scream was his, the pain real. The sleeve of his shirt wrapped up tight across the remaining stub, but the canvas, soaked through. Blood clotted under what was left of his arm. Steam arose from the wound. At the sight, a violent shiver took Aiden and he wretched.

Ink huddled close. "Buried it deep and well off. Won't attract no varmints. Bleeding's stopped. Some severing don't bleed much. Vessels shrink back into what's left and that cuts the flow."

"Perhaps there's little left." Aiden struggled to remain conscious. The deep ache from his dislocated shoulder crept clear across his spine and down into the fiery terminus of his other arm.

"Well, the end's still warm, and you're talking, ain't ya?"

"Aye." He looked Ink in the eyes.

Ink pushed his hand into a pocket and presented Aiden with the braided bracelet. "Saved this. Reckon it's important to ya."

"You're a good man. Will you fasten it to my wrist, please?"

Ink fiddled with the clasp until it was secure. "I cain't take you off the mountain by myself. But I can wrap you good and go for help."

"A day to Buffalo, you think?"

Ink looked at the black above strewn with dazzling stars. "A day if this weather holds. May be by nightfall tomorrow—then back."

The sky was clear, making way for colder air. Aiden quivered at the concept of being left helpless on the mountain. His skin dampened. He feared a sweat would deliver a final blow.

"Two more nights," Aiden said.

The fingers of his missing hand tapped the rock beside him and he looked to confirm the impossibility. In his mind he made the hand a fist and the tapping stopped. Fist, tight and warm, the pain set up where the arm ended. Yet with eyes closed, he judged his hand as normal as it had been yesterday, even comfortable.

Horrifying.

"Still feelin', ain't it?" Ink got up to fetch a wooden pail of water sitting at the edge of the firelight. "Lasts for months sometimes, maybe more. Lucky ain't a leg. You'd be trying to jump on out of bed every morning finding yer nose to the floorboards."

Ink stoked the fire, then moved the pile of tinder, piece by piece, closer to Aiden. "Ground's dry under this tree. Any rain won't touch you. Have to feed that fire with the hand you still got." He wrapped the canvas tarp around Aiden, and then rummaged through the sack of stores that had come free from the limbs above. "Got a side of fat back I can hold over the fire. I'll feed us both then be on my way." He pulled a long stick from the fodder and pierced the bacon through.

"No food." Sleep teased. Aiden's eyelids lay heavy and his head swam every time he blinked.

"No matter. I'll cook it up and leave it. Take a draw of water." Ink dipped a ladle into the bucket and poured a little water into Aiden's mouth.

The fire blazed up under the dripping bacon fat. Its light shone bronze on Ink's face. Aiden pulled the gold watch from his pocket by its dangling chain. Slow and sure, an agony stabbing at his shoulder with every move.

He popped open the watchcase. "Midnight."

"I'll start come dawn."

"Pass the news of that Indian on. In case you don't get back. I have a sister on the Powder. You tell them. You tell them all." Aiden's voice trailed off into the crackling of the fire.

"Lucky you ever come to. But yer strong."

"Good luck is often with the man who doesn't include it in his plans." Shakespeare seemed Aiden's best friend. He turned his head toward Ink. The slightest movement and camp spun as though he had no blood pressure left.

Ink's interest rested on the golden timepiece. "Rich, too, I guess."

"Like you said, I've been lucky."

"Seen plenty of Southerners cheat the reaper with a gold coin or two."

Aiden studied the man's face. Ink's expression was lost in memory. Odds were, none of it shined a rosy light on Aiden's pale skin. He closed his eyes, certain his fight was lost.

Not a bad way to go.

Aiden embraced the fire's heat penetrating his canvas swaddle. He dozed at times, clear through the night, trying to keep some guard up against Ink's turn in tone. Even though the man had saved his life so far, Aiden sensed a barb to the man's character giving him pause at turning a blind eye. Yet when darkness bowed to the pale of the eastern sky, he succumbed to a deep sleep.

Aiden awoke hours later to sunshine. The fire was stoked to a fine, warm blaze. Ink, gone.

Between Struggle and Comfort

Eden awakened at dawn and peered through one of the small windows. No sign of Intah. Perhaps he still slept, or was off to hunt up another raft of birds. She dressed in her work clothes and hauled fresh water to the paddock trough. Her arms ached. Late season dandelions rimmed its base, waited for wishes to be made. She picked one of the largest, blowing its stem empty to watch her hopes fly into the blue, wanting no more than to follow.

She finished the morning chores and washed her face. Dressed in her finest river-blue woolen skirt and white linen blouse, she laced up a pair of patent leather boots above her ankles. An egg, discovered under the brush near the water trough, boiled for breakfast. But she took no biscuit. She counted on plenty to eat at tea. The biscuits would keep for supper, along with the remains of the pork roast.

Maddie arrived in her wagon through a flurry of hen chatter at the appointed hour. Eden unbolted the door and handed her a cup of tea as she entered the cabin.

Maddie smiled. "Don't you look fine."

Eden continued to tidy the undersized front room. She didn't think she looked fine at all. She'd used two pins to take in the waist of her skirt. The first comment made at tea would without doubt be directed at her withering frame.

"Good God, Eden, what you so determined about makin' this place in order?" Maddie stood stock straight and looked out the window to the barn. "Ain't no one else to see it."

Order held a certain security that Maddie, living in the chaos of a large family, would never understand.

"I like things right, that's all." She moved a glass bowl of apples one way on the long kitchen table, then the other and back again, judging its place. "I haven't seen him this morning, if that's what you're asking."

Maddie's shoulders dropped as though relieved. "All this bother, makin' things prime. Seems a fair bit of worry over a small bit of bliss. Cain't you just see the finery of the apples and let the rest be?"

"I like it perfect."

Maddie picked out an apple and held it up. "Already is. Ain't nothin' more." She bit into the fruit and put her cup on the table carefully. "Had coffee. We best go before I drip anything on these duds."

Eden smiled. Dressed in her best finery, grey flannel skirt and crisp white linen blouse, Maddie managed to escape the house without a speck of child on her.

The two friends gave a long, silent look toward the barn as they clattered down the road in the direction of Williams' draw. Still no sign of the Indian, but neither spoke of him more. The subject wore thin between them.

"Don't know why I let you drag me off to these," said Maddie. "Food's good, and the music fun, but dern if those women don't gall me."

The Williams' clan were English. They'd spent centuries looking down their noses at the Scots. Hired help fashioned their manicured yards and tended the fat cattle they raised. But be they Scot or English, they were all from British Isles. In this faraway place, that made them as good as kin to Eden.

Once-a-month tea brought folks from every hollow in the settled region, from Sheridan to the sparsely settled banks of the Crazy Woman. For Eden, the long wagon ride to Williams Ranch across a low wooden bridge over the Powder River served to abate any visit from stuffy women who took pleasure in pointing out the imperfections of Rose Ranch. Blistered hands and aching muscles never afflicted gentlewomen bent on maintaining an air of aristocracy, despite the harshness of the land. The help was hired.

They passed Barber Creek as the sun approached midday. At the top of the next hill, as they turned toward the short rift leading to Williams Ranch, a straight fence with skilled railing cropped up, long and flat, a comely perimeter to the flawless house it protected. A thousand head of cattle cast a dark web over the hills beyond, confirming the wealth spread before her, a stark contrast to the barren prairie outside her own door.

The wagon rolled Eden and Maddie around a final bend and a grand, gabled home came into view. Horse-and-buggies abided at a long hitching post to one side of the wide yard. Forty-some people, with cups full of cider punch and mouths full of gossip, watched a game of polo in the field beyond.

When the buckboard stopped, the crowd on the porch turned and clapped and the noise filled the eaves. The music had arrived.

Boss Williams was the first to welcome the two women. A retired British colonel, he'd left his accent behind in England decades before, and made it clear to all that he considered himself more American than the natives who'd murdered four of his five sons over the years. "Good day, Mrs. Rose. Mrs. True."

Maddie nodded her head to mimic the rat-faced man's abbreviated greeting. He never presented her with a decent salutation. Something closed his throat short of saying "nice to see you."

Eden was sure he wasn't.

"We'd given you up," Boss said, leering at Eden. "About ready to send the cavalry, but then again, I don't suppose you'd need them."

Boss never missed the opportunity to note Eden's headstrong nature in a disapproving way. She was as certain his manner reflected frustration with her coolness toward his insipidly coy advances over the years, as she was he'd never give up. Boss wore his wealth on his sleeve, like a gold button lure.

Eden hated gold. "Sounds to me like the cavalry should be in the Bighorn."

"So, you've heard." Boss looked to the west. "Well, those hunters on the mountain know their way with a rifle. A renegade in chains is no match for six able bodies."

Maddie bristled. "Wasn't there six in the James family?"

Boss looked at Maddie. "Not six men. He killed a man, two women and some children."

"I see," Maddie said. "That's what gave him the soft underbelly in the face of a pack of men."

"He'll be found and get what he deserves, like any Indian."

"Not all Indians kill." Eden felt every gaze within range move her way.

Boss raised his eyebrows. "You haven't been in the territory as long as I, Mrs. Rose, nor seen the things I have. Before Custer, the savages were just that."

Eden drew a long breath. A week ago she would never have uttered the defense of an Indian, let alone in present company. But the inequity of his statement struck her as hard-hearted against the seemingly gentle man who'd spent the last two days working to help her, even though standing in his presence made the hair on her arms stand on end.

Boss's wife Ruth shouldered her way into the circle, voice still clinging to the vestige of a British Isle lilt. "Now, Boss, we needn't cast a cloud over the social."

Ruth slipped her arm around Eden's waist and whispered, "I know what you meant. There's a fine old squaw in town I use for my mending. Pay her next to nothing." She looked into Eden's eyes and frowned as she squeezed her fingers around Eden's waist. "Good for alterations, too."

Eden frowned at Ruth's first thorn.

Ruth turned to Maddie. "Mrs. True, how nice." She gave her customary once-over to Maddie with the pursed lips of a satisfied cat.

Maddie put a hand on one hip and cocked her head. "Missus Boss. Always a pleasure, ma'am."

Eden stifled a laugh. Ruth Williams hated to be addressed as Mrs. Boss.

She turned back to Ruth's husband. "That posse drove the renegade right into the Bighorn, Boss. Straight for your son." Ruth turned as if hearing the news for the first time. "That doesn't concern you?"

"What concerns me is having a heathen renegade on the Powder. And the mission he may have in mind—for us all."

"And you would sacrifice another son for the peace of mind that brings you," said Ruth.

Boss set his shoulders square against the background of a thousand cattle scattered along the ridge above the river. "I've sacrificed more than that for the success you see around you woman."

Ruth's round cheeks grew colorless under her salt-and-pepper curls. She threw a yearning glance at the set of crosses behind a low picket fence across the yard. Her voice softened. "Well, no more talk of the Bighorn. I expect the boys in no time. I prefer to enjoy this day worry-free. Eden, have a bite to eat before you play. You'll need your strength; we're in the mood to dance. You look half starved."

The observation, and the command that she play—this pretense—grated on Eden. As though her hands were hired and the food, a luxury. Which, of course it was, but she wouldn't complicate Ruth's impropriety by adding a refusal of either. She would, however, take her sweet time at the buffet. Even though she'd rather crack the violin against the woman's backside.

The table stood on the wide covered porch. A fine pink lace cloth presented a crystal vase of huge multicolored roses standing sentry amidst a dozen sterling trays of cured ham, biscuits, cheeses, fresh scones, and tantalizing tea sandwiches. At the far end, an ornate ceramic compote full of curried fruit. A hand-cranked ice cream maker stood ready to do the work of dessert.

Eden didn't know where to start. She set the violin on a nearby chair and picked up a small dish. She was a starved sheep on spring grass. For every item she placed on the plate, she put one in her mouth. One ear attended to Ruth's prattling: new bolts of English wool from London, a trip planned to San Francisco for spring, the nonsense of imported tangerines on their way for Christmas—the weather.

Ruth arrived with a cup of punch. Her eyes popped at the sight of food piled on Eden's plate.

Eden blurted, "There was work to do this morning. Maddie came early. No time to eat breakfast."

The expression on Ruth's face told Eden that little stock was given to her excuse. But it wasn't the food that had caused Ruth to balk.

"Where's your wedding band, dear?"

Eden looked at her ring finger. She had no memory of taking the band off. Had she lost it in the garden tussling with the goats over the last piece of squash?

She looked up at Ruth and raised her palm, fence-wound in plain sight. "I must have taken it off to tend to my hand."

Ruth's brows knit together in suspicion, but she said nothing.

Boss stomped up the stairs to the porch, pointing to the mountains. "Snow's let up. By the look of the clouds, and the shift in temperature, I'll guess rain will wash it away by tomorrow. River'll be up and the boys will be home."

The range stood tall and clear from the lie of the Williams house. Eden's gaze trailed upwards—the mountains lay under a solid sheet of white. Her appetite vanished at the sight. What must be Aiden going through to provide them food? No doubt he'd turn the tale into an entertainment. She yearned to hear it.

Eden slowed her nibbling to a gentile pace as Boss lit a pipe and scrutinized the polo field. "How's that fine young stud?"

"Near fifteen hands already." Eden looked out at a pasture full of mares adjacent the nearby barn. "Good for those runt mares of yours. I can hold some spaces for you next spring for a small fee."

Boss snorted. "Have my own stallion, you know that."

High hope deflated, Eden set her plate on a side table wishing she could do the same with her troubles.

Boss's eyes devoured her. He pulled the pipe from his mouth. "If you need money, I'm sure you and I could come to some—"

"What chukka are they playing?" Eden kept her gaze on the field, unwilling to entertain anything Boss might have a mind to suggest.

"Been at it about an hour," said Boss. "Should be the last one."

"A high-goal game, then."

Maddie sidled up to Eden. "And that means?"

"Means they play longer," said Eden.

How long would Boss continue to play?

Another clap of mallet to ball and the riders in the distance turned their horses in a short bend and headed for the opposite goal full tilt, dust mimicking a smoking prairie fire behind them.

"All it is to me is a good way to spend a pricey horse quick," Maddie said.

Eden whispered. "That's why Boss needs me, Maddie. Polo players use several ponies in a game." She turned to the man. "You'll need outcross blood to those mares eventually to keep your pony strings strong. I'd sell the colt to you at a fair price." Eden held her breath.

Selling a great stallion was not as good in the long run. More garnered in multiple years of breeding fees than in a single sale. Boss was no fool. He'd figure she was desperate.

Boss cocked his head, puffing a cloud of smoke from his pipe, an accusatory tone to his voice. "I do my business with Hugh. When does he return?"

Eden looked at Maddie, her eyes begging for her friend's silence. Boss had been their best customer early on, when he wanted to build a few strings to feed his fancy for polo.

Eden shifted her weight. "Spring."

"Don't believe I'll breed my mares next year," Boss said. "Drought's been hard on the fodder. The yearlings are still eating hay from last season. And this year's weanlings are next in the feed line for what's left. Mares will be rebred year after next—if this drought turns."

Riders trickled into the yard as the polo game was over. Laughing and slapping each other on the back, they let the ranch hands lead the spent horses to the barn for a cool bath and a walk-out.

"Enough business talk," Ruth said. "I believe we have enough of a crowd for dancing."

Eden took Ruth's cue and fetched her violin. She stood on the porch, above the crowded yard and played Highland tunes while the others danced and laughed. With her stomach full and hope of Aiden's imminent return in mind, the hour passed in comfort. When the music ceased, Eden's arm was weak and a small spot at the top of her neck burned where the instrument kissed her at the constant play.

The heat of the afternoon sun drove most of the revelry inside, except for a band of children and a toddler, all standing on chairs circling a barrel full of water. Golden apples bobbed along the surface. The youngsters giggled and screamed in delight as each took a turn to fasten their teeth to one. Eden sat on the porch steps sipping a cool peach tea from the splendor of a delicate glass.

Maddie's voice lilted from the parlor as she traded farm talk with one of the local men: the way to nurse a runt piglet on a mother's teat, how to fatten a goat on buttermilk and chicken skin, the best way to run fluids from a butchered sow. Eden closed her eyes and smiled as she pictured the ladies of the clan, mouths agape at the florid description spilling from her friend's lips.

A frantic cry pierced the vision.

One of the young boys in the yard shouted. "Molly!"

Eden's eyes snapped open. A young girl's arm reached into the barrel, clear up to the shoulder.

Molly's voice was a bell. "The baby's at the bottom. Help me."

Eden's glass fell to pieces on the porch. She was at the side of the barrel in three steps.

Tears streamed from Molly's eyes. "Was holding her up to the apples, that's all."

Flinging herself face first, deep into the barrel, Eden fished the bottom with both arms until she sensed a hand. Up came Ruth's granddaughter in Eden's arms.

As Ruth arrived to claim the child and others fawned over it, Eden faded back into remembered trauma. The wet clothing, the sputtering air—Lilybank...the night Aiden pulled their mother from the pond. The way Aiden wept so long, even after their mother was dry and warm. The understanding struck her deep, as averted tragedy sprouted panic in her bones.

The uproar moved the party back outside, Eden dripping from head to toe in front of the crowd, shaking.

Ruth turned to her, holding her howling grandchild to her breast. "My God, you're a savior."

Maddie joined Eden with a few cloth napkins from the buffet, piecing them over Eden's blouse as the group looked on. "Best take these. Now."

Eden looked down at her linen blouse. Translucent against her breasts, only a thin piece of undergarment separated truth from imagination. She held two napkins over her bodice against the attention of every eye in the yard.

Ruth handed the baby to its mother, and took Eden's hand. "Come with me. We'll get you into something dry."

Eden followed the woman through the house to a large bedroom in a back corner. Ruth opened a tall cupboard full of fine clothes and pulled a pink flowered dress from a peg.

"This will do you home, dear. I'll find a canvas for your wet things." Ruth left the room, closing the door behind her.

Eden slipped off her clothing and let it drop to the floor. Stepping out of its soaking folds, she turned to pull the fresh garment from the chair where Ruth had laid it when something moved across the room. She jumped on instinct, ducked behind the cupboard door, then peeked around its edge to an empty room. When she stepped from behind the door, the full view of a gaunt reflection in a long mirror greeted her head on. She stared, horrified at the figure staring back.

Except for snippets of her face in the small hand-mirror at home, she had not seen herself whole in years. Not since a full-length looking glass captured the image in the New York hotel room she and Hugh occupied the night before they boarded the train west. She remembered her skin pale, her tall figure full and, as Hugh used to quip, round in all the right places. That soft and vulnerable memory at odds with scant curves and scrawny limbs. Skin once smooth and creamy was the tarnished bronze of an Indian, creased by constant wind and blistering heat. Water dripped from curls streaked mustard by the sun, a corkscrew willow in a hurricane. No wonder Hugh's touch had been rare. She'd become as wild and desiccated as the land she tended. The drought, a reflection of the parched well she held within, drying ever more as tears spilled onto her cheeks. Fructification lay beyond the realm of land and soul, neither bearing fruit of a decade's labor.

Eden pressed her fingertips to the glass in disbelief. She reached for a boar bristle brush on the vanity and tried to smooth her hair, but the brushing made the strands fly outward. She gave up and pulled its thickness back in a twist, pushing a long slender hairpin of Ruth's into the center to keep the mess atop her head.

It was all too much. The horses were doomed, as scrawny and forlorn as she. There'd be no rescue at the hand of Boss Williams or in the heart of Hugh. And if any one of the clan discovered she harbored an Indian they might as well nail tight her coffin. She sat on the small stool beside the dresser and stared at the squash-yellow spread covering a brass bed next to the window. Tiny flowers specked the quilted fabric. Highland gorse. The wild scrub of Lilybank. Identical to the one she'd drawn across her mother's face at death.

They were both doomed. Without rescue. She put a hand to her throat, squeezing three fingers against her windpipe.

"What's keeping you, girl?" Maddie opened the door a crack. "Got me a bag for your wet clothes."

Eden wiped the back of her hand across her eyes, pulled on the frock belonging to the short, rotund Ruth Williams, and buttoned up the front.

Maddie pushed open the door. "Got something in your eyes from that water?"

"You never told me," Eden said, turning to face Maddie. "I'm repellent."

"What are you rantin' about? I reckon you ain't no different than me, Eden Rose. The years don't pass no one by."

Eden bolted past Maddie, out the front door, and cut a straight path through the guests as they gathered buggies to leave. Conversations faded into murmur as Eden pushed her way through the party. The abundant fabric of her borrowed dress billowed behind her as she ran, the shortened hem drawing scandalous attention to her ankles and bare feet.

The one voice behind her was the lone word of a woman somewhere in the swarm. "Lan."

She untied the horse and vaulted into the buckboard. Before Maddie could join her the barking of dogs swelled from cottonwoods flanking the river below. The crowd hushed. Eden imagined the silence triggered by her behavior until she recognized the nature of the barking: hounds.

The overdue hunters.

Dogs bounded up the hill and into the yard, tongues dripping sweat. Behind them came three horses, one with two men riding double, one carrying the mountain guide well known to all, Little Pete. The other horse held but a single freight—a body flung across its back like a bedroll.

Eden closed her eyes to the picture, petrified to see the dead man's face. The breath went out of her as she strained to listen. The lead rider, difficult to understand.

Little Pete drawled with a heavy French accent as horse hooves stopped. "Forgive me to bring you heartache, *Madame*."

Ruth's voice. "Yes?"

Eden opened her eyes ashamed to be relieved at what she knew was coming. Little Pete sat tall in the saddle, long legs resting in stirrups let out as far as they would go.

He looked into the eyes of Ruth Williams. "Disaster comes."

Ruth bolted to the horse Little Pete led, cradled her boy's head in her arms.

Boss drew up behind her to put a hand on the bloodstained back of his son. His voice trembled. "Tell me."

"Grizzly, *Monsieur*, a monster. Ravaged our camp. Nothing we could do. At least six shots in him, not one flinch. Jack stood ground, but the beast took him. Killed his horse, scattered the rest to the mountain. Took us a day to round them up. We made Buffalo last night."

Stunned silence gave way to Ruth's sobbing. Ranching cattle had been kind to the Williams family, but the West was an unforgiving ally.

"Where'd you make camp?" asked Boss.

"The other side of Powder River Pass, along West Ten Sleep Lake."

"And you left the bear alive, with the taste of a man in his mouth?"

"Perhaps," said Pete. "I did not remain to find out. Our cook is yet on the mountain, run away when the bear struck—or dead, as well."

Boss nodded as he worked the palms of his hands together. "With six bullets in him I suspect he'd be bled out by now anyway."

"Bury him while you can. Your son, *Monsieur*. He was brave." Pete looked at the mountains. "It rains on them now, but the cold, she comes again, soon."

A chill ran through Eden from head to toe. Little Pete had trapped the territory for fifty years—knew the weather as well as what he wanted for supper. The silence she'd kept out of respect could be held no longer. She stood up in the buckboard. "And what of my brother, sir?"

"Who is?" asked Little Pete.

"Aiden McBride."

"No word, *Madame*. He quit camp to hunt alone before dawn of the attack. Afraid we didn't wait for him."

Eden shrieked. "You have to go back!"

"I have hunted the Bighorn since before the beaver ran out and not seen such a creature. We made it down the mountain. Your brother has a horse and a weapon, and if he uses the brain God gave him, so will he."

Eden was incredulous. She looked at the men on horseback. "Is there not one of you who'll go back then?"

The men looked one to the other, then at Eden. No one spoke.

Eden's voice took a sharp tone of disgust. "You're a fine lot, then, aren't you?" She untied the reins of the horse pulling her wagon and climbed into the front, looking back at the bedraggled hunters. "May the devil take you all."

Maddie arrived on the edge of the yard, carrying Eden's socks and button-top shoes. She gave Ruth a parting glance. "Hell of a party."

Eden sat down and urged the horse on as Maddie hurled herself into the wagon bed. The buckboard thundered down the road toward home, somber crowd disappearing behind a veil of dust.

Maddie crawled forward onto the seat beside Eden. They rode the jostling buckboard with only the creak and squeal of the axle as background, until the sun grazed the crest of the mountains to the west and the wagon slowed to crawl up a minor incline short of Rose Ranch.

Maddie looked out at the trees passing by. "I know you're worried for your brother. I am, too. But bein' riled up ain't gonna help."

"I'm not angry with them anymore. Those men aren't worth the trouble."

"Dern, if you ain't the stubbornest. Don't mean with them, Eden Rose. I mean with yourself."

"What—"

Maddie raised her hand. "Hear me out. I lied back there in Ruth's dressin' room. You and me ain't the same in a lot of ways. You weren't never made to be in this place, a drudge working at somethin' you hate."

Eden slowed the horse to a walk to cool him, and so she could better hear her friend.

"Me, I don't know the difference between struggle and comfort, 'cept when I look at you." Maddie's eyes watered. "No matter who you met in that lookin' glass, you're still a fine thing from a glorious place I'll never know. Fine as them china cups you have left. And that's fact."

Tears bathed Eden's face.

Maddie continued. "You may think I'm foolish, and maybe I am, but I don't think myself as wore out or disgustin'. I know I'm not the girl I was, even if that girl weren't much. But I love my home and this land and my babes, even if the house is too small and the land too poor, 'cause it's my home. It's where my young'uns was borned, and I'm content to know it's like to be where I'm gonna die watchin' 'em grow. Things don't always need to be perfect to see perfection in 'em."

Eden wiped the tears from her eyes. "I never asked for this place. Four babies and most of a decade lost to it. Time to give up, I think, don't you?"

Maddie shook her head. "Who ain't lost a babe or two? Glory, your no better than a possum pup clinging to its ma. At some point you got to start looking ahead of those graves and that hardship. This country'll take you piece-by-piece if you let it. Don't. Life sure ain't gave me what I asked for. But I come to believe it's givin' me what I need. There's contentment in that."

"At least you know what you're dealing with. Hugh, now Aiden. What if my brother never comes off that mountain? Without him, I'll lose the last thing holding me together."

"Or maybe lose them both and gain the choice you crave."

Eden looked at Maddie, startled. "And that is?"

"Freedom."

Crazy Woman Rides Alone

Light took on the burnished turn of late afternoon as the buckboard rolled into Rose Ranch. The hens roosted up in the trees next to the house, and the horses tended the far side of the long pasture. The goats peeked their heads from the barn and trotted over to greet them, but the place was otherwise empty. With the Indian gone, for once Eden had gotten what she asked for. The concession made her miss her brother all the more.

Maddie quit the wagon to tie the hitched horse to the fence. The two women walked together to the barn, Intah's last few words teasing Eden: *Up the Crazy Woman Canyon. Not so hard a journey.*

"I see them thoughts churnin'. What's in your mind?"

"The Bighorn." Eden's breath shortened at the prospect.

"And?"

"Aiden wouldn't spend a night alone up there without a reason. He may be lured to hunt on his own, but darkness has vexed him since he was a boy."

"And?"

"If he's not off the mountain by now, he must be injured."

"And?" Maddie stood relentless.

"Stop. You know me. I must find him."

"You're strong, Eden. Stronger than you know. But you cain't go all the way up there alone."

Eden's mind turned with a plan.

"No. Oh, no. I see that look in your eyes, like lookin' at a man you want. Don't you be tellin' me your going with that heathen. You lost your mind?"

Maddie reached for Eden's arm. "Indians rape. Murder. Torture. And he's one of them, Eden. Ain't you afraid of him at all?"

Truth be told she was scared witless, as sure as she'd seen a Scottish water-beast, but she didn't see the benefit in admission.

She dosed out some parcel of truth instead. "I'm more frightened of not going." Eden was already through the door when she was stopped by Maddie's grasp.

Maddie's gaze traveled to the far side of the structure for confirmation. Intah's things were gone. "Too late, I reckon."

"If I can catch up to him, he's headed into the mountains."

"Only a crazy woman rides alone. And you ain't crazy."

Eden grabbed a halter and lead rope and started for a small paddock behind the building.

Maddie followed. "Eden Rose, tell me you ain't crazy. Least wait till morning. It's more'n a day's ride just makin' the base of the Bighorn. You won't git far in the daylight left."

"If I wait, he'll be that much ahead of me tomorrow." Eden pulled a halter over the head of her most dependable pony and led him back to the barn.

"How you know where he's headin' anyways?"

"He lives across the Bighorn." Eden looked off to the west, thinking on his path as she spoke, not wanting to let Maddie know that he'd told Eden exactly how he'd go. "He'll follow the Powder a while. Too many settlers on the Crazy Woman. Bypass Buffalo. Too many white men there. Crazy Woman Canyon would be the way I'd go if I were Indian."

"Which you ain't."

Eden didn't answer.

"Lord love a preacher. You chasin' a heathen."

Eden looked at Maddie. "Listen to me. I know I can't be going into the mountains on my own. I need someone who knows them. A man willing to go. A man going anyway for God's sake."

"How do you know he'll have a mind to go with you?"

"I don't."

Eden couldn't explain the hunch. Intah was kind, and principled, and for some reason wanted to help her. If a few loose boards on a barn had urged him to linger, her distress might compel him to find Aiden.

"What about the ranch? You cain't leave the critters to fend for thereselves."

"That's where you come in."

Maddie put her hands on her hips. "Ain't no way I can tend both plots."

"If the renegade's on the mountain, it's safe enough. Jenny can come." The sudden inspiration was more omen than edict. Jenny was a child.

Eden turned to study Maddie. Her daughter was young, but as strong as her mother, and raised well to look after stock. Eden owed her disquiet to the prospect of heading to the mountains— alone.

She continued into the barn. "The horses can see to themselves for a few days with the dry grass on the hillside. They're fatter now than they ever were on the range. With the flood of runoff, creek runs through at a jog of the near pasture. Put them all in there so they can take water as they please. Goats will do the same. The chickens have fended for themselves for the last month. They'll do. Everything else can wait. And if..." She swallowed hard to cure the catch in her throat. "If I come back without Aiden, there'll be no work that begs finishing before snow falls because I can't spend a winter alone."

Maddie stood on the other side of the horse. "I ain't gonna do it. Ain't gonna make it easy for you to follow that Indian. You cain't be running around the countryside with him. You heard what them folks at tea said about his kind. That posse would shoot him dead, and maybe you in the aim."

"You'll do it," said Eden as she saddled the horse. "Or *Ella May Brennan* might learn her husband didn't shoot himself after all."

Maddie looked horrified.

Ella's name hadn't been mentioned for five years, not since the widow packed her children into a wagon and headed back to Texas. Eden promised her allegiance to a secret long since buried.

"Were an accident. You know full well. Pa ain't right now, and he weren't right then."

The truth was as hard as the earthen floor of the barn. Eden was sorry for bringing up the past but she had no choice. "I need your help, Maddie. I won't leave Aiden on the mountain. He needs me—and I need you."

"Shoot." Maddie wiped her hands on her skirt, pushed a strand of hair from her brow and took the reins of the horse. "All right."

Eden carried a set of saddlebags across the bridge to the cabin. On the door latch her hand caught on a thread—hanging from the handle was the bear claw. Bear medicine, Intah had said. Guardian in the wild. Had he left the talisman for her protection?

Or did he somehow know she would come? Either way it was a sign of his goodness. Her whole being sighed in relief.

Eden lifted the horsehair braid and entered the cabin. She paused at the small mirror hanging on the wall above her dresser. Her hair had worked its way out of the twist she'd made and was a wild mass about her neck. She pulled the necklace over her head. The claw was foreign against her skin, in a way that excited her. Emboldening. No proper Scottish woman would seek the company of an Indian to guide her—not alone.

She traced a fine wrinkle at the edge of her eye. She bore little resemblance to the woman who crossed an ocean. That Eden Rose had seen enough of the Bighorn. What she had in mind reflected what she'd become. The West had made her an uncommon woman.

She dressed in a pair of Hugh's long johns, a linen shirt with a second thick flannel of Hugh's on top, and a pair of Aiden's woolen trousers, tying up excess at the waist with a length of twine. She pushed a change of similar clothes, her last biscuits, a wrapped fat slab of bacon and remainder of the roast, into the saddlebags. Adding a small knife and a tin of matches, she pulled the feather blanket from her bed and rolled it as tight as she could, binding its bulk with two lengths of twine. From the empty cradle in a corner of the room she pulled a soft blue blanket to use as a pillow.

A small pair of scissors gleamed in a slim ray of the day's final sunlight, and a spark of inspiration caught her eye. In a blink, the woman who rode that train west was lost to the shears as a pile of tarnished locks littered the floor. She stooped to touch the shearing, the hair brittle in her hands. Her head was cool and light, somehow free from the bondage of dark thoughts.

Her gaze landed on the dresser top. Her wedding band sat abandoned. Now she remembered. Taken from her hand with the idea of cashing in the troth. Eden picked it up, staring at the wide smooth gold absent inscription of endearing words. She pushed it halfway up her ring finger and stopped. No ring existed wide enough to carry the inscription she'd like to write. No hoop except the one she'd been jumping through for a decade. Another circle like homesteading's noose.

How precious was metal really? Costly, not valuable. Ruinous—not dear. Eden placed the ring on the dresser, backing away from a life she wished with every fiber of her heart to forget.

She pawed through a small cupboard near the stove until she found the tin canister. She pulled out a fistful of silver coins, her last, and pushed them deep into a pocket. Eden donned a short canvas coat, tucked the baby blanket inside for warmth, and pulled a broad brimmed hat over her head to hide her work. She'd waste no time explaining to Maddie. She gripped the rifle and returned to the barn. Eden grabbed the oilcloth coat, packed the horse, took its reins from Maddie, and walked with her friend into the timeworn yard. They both looked in the direction of the Bighorn.

"Pa'd never live long enough to set an eye on the inside of a jail. I'll have Jenny come."

"I'll be back. I promise." Eden kissed Maddie's cheek. She mounted the horse, headed down the trail, the pair of she-goats following behind.

Eden looked over her shoulder twice. She could bear the uncertainty of her actions no longer. Making use of the remaining light she urged the horse beneath her into a trot, leaving even her bleating goats behind.

Part Two

Not His to Know

Intah set his sight on the Bighorn, squeezed the barrel of his horse between his thighs, and pushed the animal through the water. Bloated by snowmelt from a day of warmer weather, the Powder ran high. Its soft hush turned to gentle roar.

He wore the bearskin down around his waist, draped low over the horse's rump. The day was not cold. The night would be mild, but a wet bearskin took time to dry in the half-hearted heat of an autumn day. So when the time came to cross the river, he hoisted the skin up around his shoulders and turned the horse into the flow. By midstream the animal's hooves were still on the river bottom, but pushing downstream with the strong current. Intah pointed the horse in a diagonal line and let it move with the course to the opposite shore, losing a quarter mile of headway before landing on the sandy bank. He slipped from the back of the horse, letting the animal shake the water from its body. He refilled his water skin before mounting and headed upriver in search of time lost.

He'd left his companion alone long enough. The old blind woman needed him, though his dalliance was sweeter than anything he'd tasted in a decade.

Intah would keep an eye open to traces of the hunting party. He was curious at their delay in light of a snow that should have driven them down. If something tragic happened, with winter on the march, he doubted a rescue to be probable, let alone prudent. Yet any woman who tended a solitary existence was strong—and strong-willed. He smiled as he considered her fiery spirit. She would cross the mountains herself if she had to. He had left the bear claw behind just in case.

Up the riverbank, the horse skipped a step and shied in the loose sand of the steep rise. Intah eased his legs into the animal for support and the horse settled, even as it reached the top of the slope and the reason for its startle. Over the rise and to one side lay the drenched, silver-tipped body of a coyote bitch, freshly dead. Intah pulled up beside her and stopped. She'd made a poor attempt at crossing the river. Her teats, still fat with milk. No doubt, a batch of pups close by would soon starve. But nothing was to be done. She'd be fodder for other more fortunate creatures; ants were already mining the details. In two days the carcass would be gone, and the pups satisfying the hunger of other beasts.

The way and the circle, complete.

The same way the woman's portrait, encountered on the mountain so many years ago, had circled back to meet that vision. He'd found pleasure at Eden's side even if he'd not shown it to her. A pleasure he'd once known, then forgotten, returned. End of the cycle. Not his to know.

Intah followed the Powder to a westward running creek and turned its way up a narrow, treed draw. He wished he'd told her what their meeting brought him, and why, but the story would have made little sense to her. Women didn't see the fixing of a barn or the shooting of a few birds as anything to do with kindling the heart. They didn't understand the ways of men: the satisfaction in providing, delight taken from an expression of appreciation. Life's promises renewed by a simple glance.

He long believed he would never again feel such promises. Fantasy at best for one who kept to the mountains. No—folly. But pleasure in it, nonetheless. And, something more—a flicker in Eden's eyes that suggested more than the novelty of being in the company of an Indian. He sensed she'd seen him as a man.

A yearning swelled as penny-colored autumn leaves fluttered to a path before him. The color of her hair. She was as beautiful a woman as he'd seen—burnished, fit and nimble as a native woman. The vision filled him as effortless breath.

Endings were also beginnings.

As he urged his horse toward the mountains his chest rose and fell a little quicker. A new cycle. He shook the notion of Eden from his mind. Spirit spoke, and he listened.

Intah put a broad hand on his horse's withers. The animal had carried him for a long time. He understood well the privilege in their relationship. On the horse's back, man returned to beast. Horse linked the enduring earth with the man's eternal spirit. The animal served as ground.

The wind shifted, carrying from the slopes the smell of fatback from somewhere upriver. The aroma of bacon reminded him again of what he'd left behind. He resisted the impulse to look back.

Creation lay in looking forward.

He guided the horse through golden cottonwoods and up onto a barren low ridge, away from the threat of a white man's camp. A waxing quarter moon was a lazy cougar eye over the peaks ahead, pale in the flicker of falling light, begging the black night to follow. Intah's gaze searched the Bighorn, picturing Eden in the soft folds of its hills, and made his way onward.

The River Laughed

Eden followed the tracks of Intah's unshod horse to the Powder where they disappeared into the muddy water. The flow was not too deep to cross.

Yet.

Though the river had risen since morning, it broke wide and calm at the place she stopped. She pushed the horse through knee-deep water, having no trouble making the other side.

In the soft silt of the opposite bank his tracks were easy to follow. Intah would cover them if he didn't want to be found. He'd kept to the low shore flanking the river, zig-zagging across the river and back to confuse the trackers, but two more hours upstream, the rising water overtook the last of the hoofprints. The sun dropped behind the Bighorn. Balmy air fell from the mountains in anticipation of nightfall. If she didn't cross to the west, the added snowmelt would demand she follow the torrent well to the south before falling enough to allow a crossing. Far from the place she was sure Intah would enter the mountains. She'd be too far behind to ever catch up.

A voice called up from the bank. "Ain't a good spot here, mister."

Eden turned with a start.

"I say, ain't a good spot." A large man sat atop a speckled mule on the ridge above Eden. The man's eyes were black under the white of a single eyebrow reaching across his brow. A ruffled screech owl with nose hooked long, he held a rifle in one arm, led another mule, and gave Eden a half grin.

"Better now than when the water rises another inch," said Eden.

"You's a woman under there? I declare."

"I'm on my way to meet someone across the river."

"Best go up a mile or two. Broadens out to paper there, an easy cross in most flows." The man wiped a tobacco-stained hand over his droopy mustache. "You alone?"

"If I wait another mile or two the dark will prevent a crossing. I can't afford the time."

"Well, drown and all whoever's meeting you'll do is wait."

"Won't be the first swim for this horse."

"Suit yourself, ma'am, but I been trappin' these parts for more years than you been drawing air. You best listen." The man spurred his mount and moved on along the ridge. The iron jaws tied to his saddle rattled all the way.

He muttered above the rush of the river. "Women. Never listen."

She sat on her horse, watching the water move north, examining the deep purple mountains to the west, a gloomy bulkhead before her, heavy against her will. Swimming was little worry. Her mount was strong and mercy lay on the opposite shoreline. But the Bighorn held no kindness for Eden. Her core quaked in consideration of climbing them alone. Catching Intah was the only way. No time to lose. Eden urged her horse into the shocking cold of the river, holding fast to its mane.

The current carried them along at mid-river, cottonwoods, coach markers on the trail, mocking the time it took her to ride along the shore. Eden kept her eye on the opposite bank. They floated around a tapered bend even as the horse struggled forward with no headway made.

Eden turned her mount in the direction of the flow. The animal grunted and gasped like a racehorse as it sank lower into the water, tiring.

Then, from behind came a slap, as hard as the back hand of a Highlands troll, and she was swept from the horse. Helpless, she tread water welling in arcs toward her as a relentless stump pushed the horse farther downstream. Waves splashed over her head and swirling current pulled at her hips sucking away the air, laying a trembling hand of death on her shoulder. The inches of dread between certain drowning and the savior of oxygen, like a map legend: miles.

The river flowed a slurry of debris and silt, tumultuous and dark. Eden lost all direction. She pulled herself through the water until the wings of a strong up-current lifted her to the surface. When she broke through, she took a breath, kicked with all her might, and swam with the flow toward shore, all the time eyeing the horse shrinking to a speck in the dingy torrent. Another bend and the animal was out of sight as Eden's feet touched solid ground.

She stood in the rushing water, breathless and dripping mud, shouting downriver. "Half a horse, you are."

The river replied a one-note rage.

Eden slogged her way out of the water and heaved herself onto the diminishing dry bank, spitting out a mouthful of slurry. She pulled her knees to her chest, hugged them, grateful for the job they'd done in delivering her to safety. She reassessed as she rested.

Darkness fell fast. She'd lost her horse, her food and her oilcloth coat—and matches for a fire to dry the clothes on her back. The river laughed along beside her, daring her to turn back. But years of wintering on the prairie taught her to wait out the worst. The trapper be damned, though he was right. That irritated her all the more.

Eden got to her feet, peeled off her soggy coat, and let a warm breeze do its work on her wet clothing. Her horse was long gone. If the animal survived the swim it would head for home. She climbed the steep bank and followed the river an hour until twilight bode her stop. Her clothes no longer dripped, but a damp and idle body would soon chill.

Tall, dry grasses flanked the river at the top of a rise over the edge of the floodplain. Eden put on her still-moist canvas jacket and made her way up the berm, using the fist-sized lizard dens as handholds to climb the eroded bank. Near the top a faint whimper rose above the noise of the river. Another leg up, and the whimpering grew louder. She put her ear to the slope side and turned her face up toward the crying.

Above her lay a broad ledge. Eden pushed herself up until her head was above the slight path, only to see a small den of wriggly, squealing coyote pups, eyes still closed, newborn naked to the closing dark.

She gasped, climbing fast above the den and trotting off away from the pups some distance before looking back. The last thing she wanted dogging her was a defensive coyote bitch. Eden walked well upriver, following the thigh-high grass in the dusk until she found a small, flat, protected patch of land under a towering cottonwood. She pulled great handfuls of long grasses from their roots until her palms were raw and she had a mounded stack of thatch.

She remembered doing the same with Aiden when they were children, ripping up tall greens and burying themselves to play hide and seek against the treeless hillsides. She'd been warm beneath those reeds and pulled faster at the recollection. When a stack heaved up as high as her knee, Eden laid down her damp coat, burrowed inside the grass, and pulled the loose vegetation overhead.

Soon she was warm if not dry, but she was famished. Tomorrow she would find food, and Intah. If she must run all the way to the Bighorn, twenty-five miles beyond, she would find him. And together they would find Aiden. She fingered the bracelet on her wrist. She believed that all she needed was rest and a full day of sunshine to dry her clothes. She slid deeper under the grass, making sure no part of her peeked through its cover. A false security. Passing antelope could traipse clean over her. A stiff breeze would reveal her. The grass shelter, a house of cards against nothing should a renegade Indian be at hand.

Eden closed her eyes against the worry, inhaled the fresh smell of just-pulled flora, and for a moment was in the Highlands, broad as the prairie around her, yet in her tiny shelter she lay blind to the exposure, secure in her ignorance of what might lie beyond. The rush of the river in the distance overcame a host of night sounds, and fatigue took her to the safety of sleep.

* * *

Sunlight shone warm from the east. Eden donned her coat, the silver coins jingling into memory. She vowed to buy a new hat and gloves in Buffalo. She unbuttoned one of the pockets in her coat, and slipped the money into her hand. She hadn't enough for a horse.

This was not how she'd dreamed the trek would go. She wanted to greet Intah as a woman independent and capable, not as a needy burden. She'd even lost her rifle, her sole protection should the wild bring out a side of Intah she had not intuited. The coins in her hand had power only among her own kind—they'd hold no attraction for him.

Eden slipped the money back into her pocket, disgusted with her own vulnerability. She'd feel a lot better after a meal. Her empty stomach warped at the inkling of food. Out of luck. She put a hand around her neck to check for the necklace. She ran her hands down the horsehair braid, pulling it up, examining its detail. She'd done some braiding over the years, but she deemed it never as fine. The surface was smooth as porcelain, the pattern woven tight—and strong. The strength of it, a portent to the fate of her day. Her life lay in the hands of Bear Medicine.

She put on the damp canvas coat and set off following the water's edge, keeping to the high berm. Her head was light with hunger and she dropped down to the river to drink, thinking to bolster her drive. The river had risen another foot or two over the course of the night, but a high watermark streaked the bank. The flow had receded. Not far from where she'd spent the night she came across the carcass of a coyote bitch, bloated and rank, flies buzzing the air above as maggots quivered the flesh beneath her skin.

The pups.

She turned tail and found the orphan den. The brood was cold, still squealing with hunger. She couldn't bear to think of them suffering starvation—a cruel and lengthy passing. She made a pouch of her shirttail and placed the four of them in the flannel, carrying them to the river. She stood at the edge of the water looking out over the tumble and flow.

Eden couldn't bring herself to toss them to the tumult. A quick end would do. She knelt by the river and, tears streaming down her face, held each to her cheek for a moment before holding them under the water until they ceased squirming. Then she laid their slick, tiny bodies side-by-side on the wet sand. The four lay across the cold earth like babes she'd lost, and for a moment she believed she'd be swallowed by heartache. No time to wallow, she reasoned. She'd have to shoulder her grief—as always.

She dug a deep hole in the bank with her hands, placed the little ones together as they had been in life, and pushed sand over a generation, as she'd done so many times before.

Life. Callous and unkind. Little joy was left in the universe when she was called to either push puppies into a watery death or leave them to cold, cruel starvation.

She climbed back up the berm and retraced her steps in the direction of the dead coyote, sobbing all the way, looking back once at a mother that never felt the pain of loss. Death was no gruesome keeper. How much easier it would have been to die in childbirth. Physical pain had nothing on sorrow.

She wiped her face with a sleeve and, with the sun high behind her, changed her direction. Bound for the mountains, she thought of no reason to revisit a carcass that was sure to be buzzing otherworldly in the sand.

Her heart bled a constant loss—she and the coyote were one.

As a Man Might Need

Aiden wasn't hungry, but only food would keep him alive long enough to see Ink again. He chewed at the bacon the man left him, even though the lump was cold grease. He reached for his journal, flipped the pages to find the final words scrawled by Ink, read them once, and closed the book.

He regarded the sun, estimated the time, then reached for his pocket watch. "Bloody sot." He struck the ground with his remaining wrist and howled in pain.

The watch was gone.

His back ached from the hardpan. He rolled onto his one arm and pushed himself up little by little, testing his shoulder. Sitting against a fat pine, head spinning, his sight went black for a moment before he found his balance. No way could he stand. He would go nowhere until help, or death, arrived.

He took a two-dip drink from the ladle in the water bucket next to him and looked at his arm. Ink had done a clean job on the stump. The watch was worth the effort he guessed, though he would have preferred the man had asked permission. He would have given it for the question.

Then it struck him: If Ink had stolen his watch, the man had no plans to return. And no plans to forward any news of the Indian threat.

Holding dark thoughts drained what little energy he had. He prayed Ink would at least tell someone that a man lay dying on the mountain. Nothing less would save him. Nothing more, expected.

Aiden turned his face to the east. Seven thousand feet below, the prairie was a rolling ocean of waves off the mountains, until becoming the calm of a summer sea at horizon's edge; that low window of memory. His mind landed on Maddie, her little board house sitting on a minor crest of land below, target of the Indian, as well. A twinge of guilt took him. Eden should be most on his mind. Yet Maddie filled him, eyes sparkling, so full of life. The idea of a house full of laughing and squabbling children, at once, seemed right. The vision, as Maddie would say, warmed his innards. Aiden closed his eyes to the notion. Like it or not, the union was as far from happening as water rising to crown the Bighorn. The odds against any chance he'd have to tell her the words forming on his tongue.

He wiped a hand over his brow and pinched his mouth. "Aye, Madeline, you're as fine a woman as a man might need."

Sunlight lay hot across his face, and twinkled rain left on trees above him. A light breeze stuttered through branches, whisking gilded leaves to the ground. The sight, stunning, even as his body throbbed and his head reeled. For a moment, that loveliness overcame the pain and whirl, and he was in the stone house again with Eden, warm and dry on a Highland hill, surrounded by other people's stories.

Tales that might end well.

Then, memories were a fire blazing across a bridge of three decades. Desperate to overcome childhood fears. Despair at the guilt-ridden loss of his mother. Forlorn at Eden's abandonment as she moved a world away. Standing among a crowd of hopefuls on the westward ship's deck at Southhampton, and he, utterly hopeless in the prospect of America. Except for the chance of redemption in the hide of a bear. Out of all the buried tombs in his head, dead thoughts crawled, moaning along with the over-story wind.

Defeat.

He drew up his journal, dipped the pen's tip in ink, and pressed it to the linen paper.

To Say the Words

The harness chains clanked in lazy rhythm. Cottonwoods standing guard by the wide river rustled in a warm late afternoon breeze, joining the song of rushing water, filling the valley with nature's churn. Roan leaves shimmered in the sun as they bid their trees farewell and fluttered to earth.

Maddie loved the autumn. Apple pies and pear crumbles, the caramel smell of jarring fruit. The sweet acid odor of canning tomatoes, even though it all promised a long, raw freeze. Soon winter would be on them. If Eden didn't beat the snow to her front door, Maddie might not see her again. She yearned to ride after her friend, or straight to Cleve and tell him what had happened. A man of his talents would know what to do. Cleve would know. For the first time she tested the need for a man.

Maddie pulled the wagon to a stop, looking back over her shoulder to the Bighorn beyond. It was Cleve in her heart. She shook her head. She hadn't intended it to happen. Aiden was a fantasy, a useful tool in making Cleve more smitten with her. A self-serving tactic to validate she was still attractive to a man.

Aiden was misplaced in her world and she'd always known it. A pretty face, no more. A creature from a far-off land, used to a country without bears, for pity's sake. She'd seen Britain's fancy ways at teas, and the finery of Eden's cabinet. Things she neither had nor craved. Maddie's needs were easy as pie. All she'd allow was a man who'd cotton to her on occasion, bring a lamb or two to town once a week for cash; one who shot a straight, sure line in order to break the monotony of meat with a prairie chicken once in a while. Cleve fit that simple bill.

Maddie knew her mind for some time without seeing it clear.

She drove on to the rickety front gate, passing through to find the children and her pa at the rim of the well. She pulled the wagon up near.

"Ya'll look like the sun's never gonna shine again. Pa, thought I told you to stay put on the porch." Maddie made a fast count. Seven. There was always one, and that one always seemed to be her youngest. If you could fall into it or from it, Oran obliged. "Where's Oran?"

The children turned in unison, but only Ezra spoke. "Untie that knot in yer breeches, girl. Know right where he is." He took a step to the well and leaned a wrinkled hand on its rim, shouting into it's cavern. "Ain't that right Cleve?"

Cleve's voice echoed. "That's enough now, Mr. Caine. You can bring us up."

Maddie leapt from the wagon and ran to the well. She looked down into the cavity to see two pair of eyes staring up. Cleve and two-year-old Oran were as still as a pair of possums in the site of a short-barreled gun, eyes wide and bright in the reflection of sunlight. Cleve stood knee deep in the water, Oran perched on his right arm holding a brown baby rabbit, one hand on a wooden bucket hanging from above.

Maddie's voice rang out. "Cleve Hackett, how'd you git yerself down there?"

"Came down to fetch little bit Oran, who come down after his rabbit. But your pa lowered me down on a one-way ticket."

"Pa, yer crazier'n a—" She'd never said it before, and stopped short. No time for name-calling. "He in one piece?"

"More than one piece," said Cleve. "Needs his drawers changed. And so will I soon if your pa won't pull me up."

Maddie grabbed the bitter end of the well rope, untied it and leaned back over the lip. "Lord sake. Put Oran in the bucket, Cleve."

Oran came up with a grin on his face. Maddie took him from the pail.

"Glory, you smell like you ain't been changed since December." Wrinkling her nose she handed the baby to Jenny, who trotted him into the house. She waved a hand over her flock. "You kids git now. Circus is on its way outta town."

The children scattered in laughter.

Ezra stood his ground, leaning an arm on the well. "Ain't answered my question."

"What the hell you talking about Ezra Caine?" Few and far between had she ever sworn at her father, let alone called him by name, but Maddie reckoned she had no time for politeness when a man with a full bladder stood in her clean drinking water. "You'll be helpin' me git Cleve outta there, now."

"Cain't do it without me half pint, and I ain't budgin' till he gives me an answer."

"Oh, for Lord's sake." Maddie bent over the rim of the well. "Answer whatever in blazes he wants to know, Cleve, or cross your legs then. There'll be no peein' in my well."

"Then you get back a far piece, Maddie. This is between me and your pa."

Maddie gave Cleve a flabbergasted look, shook her head, and backed away.

Cleve yelled. "Go on. I know you're still close by. Back to the house with you."

"Oh, for…" Maddie turned to walk across the yard and onto the porch.

Ezra leaned deep into the well. A moment later, he popped up, slapped his hands together and waved Maddie over.

"Cain't have been too complicated an answer, I guess. You satisfied to pull him up, or do you need to ponder the great effect his reply has on the universe?" Maddie stretched out her arms to punctuate her irritation.

Ezra pulled hard at the rope and soon Cleve straddled the lip of the well, dripping from the waist down, a scowl on his face.

"Between us, old man," he said.

Ezra granted him a wry smile. "'Tween us, son."

"Well, between you and me, there ain't enough room in the loony bin for you both." Maddie walked into the house and banged the door behind her. Not the scene she'd imagined after proclaiming her affection for Cleve—even if the admission was only to herself.

A knock at the door brought Cleve. "Mind if I change my britches?"

"Don't have but an old pair of Big's, but I imagine they'll do."

"I'm obliged," said Cleve.

Maddie opened a door to a small bedroom. "There. Bottom drawer."

When he emerged, Cleve wore the pants with cuffs rolled up high above his ankles, a belt taking up some of the slack left by Big.

Maddie had to chuckle. "You look like a goose egg."

Cleve pulled the belt high and tight around his middle, mocking an hourglass. "This any better?"

They both laughed.

"What you doin' back again today, Cleve? It's a long ride from Suggs for a daily visit."

"Three things. Got a letter for Missus Rose, and Little Pete rode through. Heard about the Williams boy and that crazed bear. Know Mr. McBride's on that trip."

"Was. God knows where he is now."

"Well, I thought Missus Rose might like to know that the camp cook from the huntin' party rolled into Buffalo yesterday. A man come through Suggs told me. Big news in town. Cook had quite a story to tell. Missus Rose's brother's alive, at least when the cook left him. Said he was in bad shape. He had no horse to bring him off the mountain. Cook was in town to fetch a ride and go back."

Maddie clenched her jaw hard not to spill the contents of her mind Cleve's way. "I'll ride out Eden's way first thing in the mornin'. Too late in the day to go now. She'll be mighty relieved to know."

"Don't git her hope up too much. Man's lost an arm and a fair amount of blood accordin' to the cook. My personal view's he's lost."

"Lost?"

"Cain't lie on the side of a mountain with blood in the air and expect animals to leave you alone, Maddie. You know that."

She did. Wolves smelled death a mile gone. And a bear with a taste for flesh could follow the scent blind. She wiped a palm over her forehead and held her brow. Her heart pounded against her lungs making it difficult to breathe. When she placed a hand on the back of a nearby chair, Cleve moved forward to steady her with his hands. She took the cue, fell into his arms and broke down.

"I know you cotton to that McBride feller. Don't take my words to heart so. Could be wide of the mark."

"Ain't that, Cleve." Maddie's mind was on Eden, alone with a blood-thirsty bear and an Indian of unknown intent. And Maddie, bound not to tell. She pushed Cleve away, wiped her eyes and smoothed her skirt. "He's never been nothin' more to me than a trinket." Maddie offered a weak smile.

"Oh, well I..." started Cleve. He cleared his throat twice. "Then what's this fuss all about?"

"Just clean tuckered. That's all. The news won't sit well with Eden." She had to change the subject before she burst.

She walked to the small root cellar underneath the kitchen, pulled the heavy door open from the floor, and reached in. "Cup of milk?"

She smelled the jar before pouring its contents. The thick river ice she'd packed in sawdust the spring before was down to a chip, and the cellar near room temperature.

"Thanks." Cleve took a full cup.

"So, what's number three?"

"Huh?"

"You only told me two things so far."

"Oh. Well, the posse came back without the Indian. Snowfall buried the trail. But a barn burnt up last night just outta Buffalo. People's sayin' it's him."

Maddie's arms turned to gooseflesh. "What do you say?"

"Reckon I don't know. But if I was you, think I'd turn the stock out for a while. If you did lose the barn, least it'd be empty."

Maddie walked to the kitchen window and looked across the yard. Cleve was right. Her gaze settled on the well.

"So, what were you and Pa banterin' about that kept you in that water for so long?" Cleve stood silent while he rubbed the cup with a hand several times, staring at the floor. "Well?"

Cleve cleared his throat again. "I hadn't pictured to share it with you this way."

"Yes?"

"Well...he wanted to know if my intentions was serious."

"Yer intentions? To what?"

Cleve nodded, turning as red as the apples on the tree across the yard. "You know."

Maddie put a hand to her mouth masking a smile. She did know, but she wanted him to say the words. Small price to pay for her affection.

Cleve looked up at her as he bowed his head. "If I planned to court you."

"Court me? Glory, sounds like a canning process. Is that what you been doin' all these months, Cleve Hackett? Tryin' to put me in a can?" Maddie smiled. She loved making life difficult for men who looked into their hearts with infrequence.

"I declare Madeline True, you are harder than a hare brain to get a straight answer from." Cleve shifted his weight from one leg to the other and back again. "I know things is going well enough for you. Don't need somethin' else folded in. But I think you're something more than just pretty."

Maddie was taken aback by the idea Cleve found her pretty. She pushed her hair back with one hand. "My Momma always said that if everything seems to be going along good, you must have overlooked somethin'."

Cleve frowned. "Well, is it fine with you?"

Maddie giggled. "Fine, Cleve. Just fine. You keep courtin' and we'll see how long the process takes."

"Well, then," said Cleve in a tone suggesting he'd been acquitted of a high crime. "Look Maddie, if you promise to give the news and this letter to Missus Rose, I best be getting back to town before dark." Cleve reached into his shirt pocket then handed her an envelope.

"I will." Her belly sat two-faced. Soft to Cleve on one side, and hard to the secret she kept on the other. She didn't like lying to a man she'd moments ago agreed to spark. Jenny came down the stairs with a fresh version of Oran on her hip. His nose was a rosy smidgen and his ears, bright pink, stood out from his head.

Maddie pushed Oran's hair back off his forehead. "You're a well rat."

"I'll be back at the end of the week for those pigs you want to sell. If I come by noon, I can bring a brisket out to cook for supper."

Jenny looked at Cleve. "Supper?"

The notion was a breath of spring. "Ya'll can cook?"

"Ain't got no one else to do it for me," Cleve said as he grabbed his wet pants and headed for the door.

Jenny's voice filled with wonder. "Glory, a man that cooks?"

Cleve shrugged and closed the door behind him. Jenny slipped Oran to the floor, broke two pieces of bread off a fresh loaf on the table, gave one to the baby and nibbled on the other.

Jenny raised an eyebrow to her mother. "Last time a man stayed for supper, you married him."

"What's wrong with that?" She hadn't even believed the concept possible, really, until this afternoon. A fall down a well and one cup of milk later, she had a formal courting decree from a man who cooked. The room spun.

"Ain't nothin' wrong," said Jenny. "Just don't know where you'll be sleeping him. House is full up."

"If he sleeps at all, missy, he'll sleep in my bed." Maddie felt her cheeks color up at being so frank with Jenny. But she was, after all, fourteen. Marrying age.

Jenny flushed. "Ma."

"Anyway, you'll be spending some time down at Rose Ranch. And this is our secret, missy." Maddie turned to face Jenny. "You hear?"

"Yes, ma'am."

"Mrs. Rose has gone away for some days and I promised you to watch her place. You'll ride out every day and tend the horses and chickens...goats, too, if they's there. And take the short-barrel rifle that Big left. It's under my bed."

"A gun?"

"Rifle, Jenny."

Maddie didn't want to alarm the child but she wouldn't set her off by herself, with a renegade in the country, without a weapon. Jenny had shot plenty rabbit and squirrel. She was a good aim and taught to be on her guard anytime. With the railroad moving through, all sorts of scoundrels passed through the valley.

"Yes, ma'am."

"Well, then, you can get a move on in the mornin'."

She looked down at the letter in her hands, raised the envelope to her eyes and read the only letters on its face she understood: Bank. The front wore an odd stamp she hadn't seen

160

before. She set the letter on a shelf near the basin. Jenny moved the milk back into the cool of the shallow earthen cellar and closed the door.

"Jen, was a dangerous, crazy-fool thing to leave that down-turned bucket at the edge of the well with a toddler under foot."

Jenny studied the floor. "Weren't me, ma."

"Would'a drown weren't for Cleve. A long gulp of well water into those baby lungs and he'd be gone forever."

Jenny's chin quivered. Maddie hadn't meant to paint such a vivid picture, but as she reflected, the whole near-disaster made her woozy after what happened at the Williams place. She looked out of the window. Oran raced behind two of his older siblings.

"Love to say he learned a lesson but 'spect the adventure of it all was more fun than fear to him. You know how he cottons to attention. You're gonna have to tell me who done the deed so I can give 'em a whoopin' that'll stick to memory."

Jenny rolled her tongue to her cheek. A tear rolled down her cheek. Maddie walked to Jenny and put a hand on her shoulder.

"I know you don't like tattlin', but I won't lose a child to an empty head."

Jenny looked out the window, finally saying, "Papaw. He left it there."

Only Observation

By the time Eden was halfway to Buffalo sky was pitch. She was dry and the evening, warm. Tonight would be easier than the one before. Time to look for shelter.

She walked ahead to a small stand of cottonwood and straight into the invitation of a flickering fire and the smell of bacon in the air. The fragrance was as sweet as a dozen roses. Soon she hunched behind a scrub oak, hidden from the small camp of a disheveled trapper.

The site lay strewn with the stretching of animal skins from one end to the other. Worn iron leg-traps hung from several branches of a wide bush where two mules stood tied to a picket line. A dingy white shirt and a pair of black woolen socks hung from a low limb of a scrub oak. Several cook pots lay underneath, waiting on a wash at the river.

The food spit and smoked over the fire. Eden shook with hunger and doubt. A lumpy figure sat at the fire turning the meat in an iron pan with a long fork. Eden wished she'd been quicker to order her spectacles from the east. She squinted in concentration. Poor sight did not grant a clear picture of his face, but the bushy brow above his eyes betrayed him: the man she'd met at the river.

He'd been kind enough to warn her off the flood. If she'd listened, she'd yet have her horse. She hated to admit her fault, but she couldn't deny her stomach. A dose of humility was sure to cure her hunger. She stepped from behind the thatch.

The man looked up with a start. "I declare. If it ain't the crazy woman."

"'Tis. And you were right, sir. The river was angry and swift."

The man nodded, then shook his head. "Never knew a woman to take advice from any man."

163

Eden mocked him. "Aye. And we all seem to pay for it, sooner or later now don't we?"

"Brazen one, at that. A Scot are you?"

"Aye."

"That explains your mind. Did you know that in some parts you can get arrested for dressin' like a man?"

Eden straightened. "I'm doing my best to be humble. You needn't slur me."

"No judgment given, ma'am. Only observation. And if you call that humility my name's Grover Cleveland."

"Well, in any case, I've lost my horse. My mind is to reach Buffalo for another. How far do you suppose that is?" She'd go on until she dropped before she'd beg a meal from this rub of a man.

"Another few hours, I expect—on foot. Thought you was meetin' somebody."

"I am, but that'd be past Buffalo."

"Past Buffalo there's big mountains, ma'am. Mountains with winter upon 'em is no place for a man, let alone a woman any time of the year. Snow may be melting now, but—" His voice trailed off as though he'd lost his train of thinking. He glanced in the direction of the Bighorn. "And there's a bad Indian on the roam, you know?"

"Nonetheless, I'll be going." Eden started off through the camp in a huff.

The man scratched his ear as she passed, put a fork full of bacon in his mouth and spoke as he chewed. "Lost your stores, too?"

Eden slowed her pace. "I have."

"Then come to the fire and eat, woman. Spend your rest here. There's a blanket for you if you chose. It's too dark to travel. The mountains will be there tomorrow."

Eden stopped. The invitation enticed but the man was boorish. Unwashed, unkempt, and uncivilized. Still, her legs ached from travel and her belly whimpered. She stepped to the flames and sat down on a large, flat rock.

"Name's Adam."

"Eden."

The man's gaze climbed over her as he smiled. "'Course it is."

For the first time in a long time she missed the company of a husband, if only as a buffer. The old man admired her, even though she was certain that she looked a sight.

She was in no mood for horseplay. "No, really. Eden Rose."

"Adam Finch." He stuck out a greasy hand and Eden shook it. "But mind you, that's where the coincidence is lost." Adam took a piece of bacon from the pan with a fork and handed it to Eden. "Got no apples. A bit of fatback, week-old biscuits, and coffee."

"Paradise, to me." Eden smiled and took a bite of the pork.

"You've a fine wit about you, ma'am."

"It's been a long time since the other side of the river, sir. I'm afraid my appetite has overcome my good humor. I apologize." A cough shook her.

"Nothing better for an old man than a woman's smile." Adam delivered a broad yellow grin missing half a dozen teeth. "That's a bad cough. Takin' something for it?"

"Just time."

Adam rummaged through a small pouch. He pulled a bundle of dusty looking brush from its depths. "This is the only thyme to cure it. A good strong brew."

He crumbled the herb into a tin pot, covered it with water from his canteen, and set it over the fire. The odor of its steam reminded Eden of the wild thyme that grew between the rockery at Lilybank.

When the tea was ready, he poured it in a metal cup and handed it to Eden. "Drink it down, leaves and all."

The steamy liquid seemed to evaporate away Eden's cough, and her lungs relaxed. The fire radiated in the fading daylight, flickering shadows across the strung-out skins, making them seem as a row of soldiers standing guard in the night. The two new friends sat at the fire, eating the fatback and biscuits, until Adam pulled a pipe from his pack for a smoke.

"My father had a pipe," said Eden.

"In Scotland is he?"

Eden missed her father for the first time in a long while. "Under a broad Highlands hill that overlooks a lake."

"I'll wager he'd either be proud of your bravery in the middle of nowhere, or as mad as the devil you were out alone."

"Both, I'm sure. He had a temper." Eden drew circles in the dirt with a small stick and remembered the time she'd last seen her father—lying dead on the parlor floor, destroyed by the ruin of bankruptcy...after doing his best to rebuild a fortune. She and Hugh were trying to do the same. God help them. "He was a fine man and he has a fine son."

"Your brother?"

"Yes. It's he on the mountain."

"Can't come out on his own?"

"I fear he may be injured. He was part of a hunting party that met with an irate bear. Killed a man." The words were an arrow.

"I met an irritated griz myself on the mountain once. A she-bear. Put a big bullet in her and she howled a note so deep and pure I swored it was flute song. Strange that." Adam scowled into the darkness. "Opened her up and found she'd eaten my traps as well as my catch. Maybe that's what made her sing."

"Flute song..." The phrase was an eerie refrain. Last time she was on the mountain the wind howled a yawning lazy note the night the bear came upon them.

Honeymoon turned to hell.

The scene was all too vivid in her mind, and she hated to review it with Aiden at its core. "I had my own dealings with a bear, as well. A long time ago. It's kept me from the mountains since." Eden tossed her stick into the fire. "But love for my brother's stronger."

"You're a damn fool goin' up alone, if you don't mind me sayin' so. Cain't go on foot."

"I've done some business with the blacksmith in Buffalo. He'll loan me a mount."

"You're gonna need a heavier coat and some stores. And a good rifle. Got enough for that?"

She placed a hand on her pocket to make sure the full of coins were still there. "I'll get by."

"Well, got an old buffalo gun I don't use much anymore. Nothing that big around these parts now." The man advanced to his bedroll to pick up the rifle. "Keep it by my bed in case, but in case o'what, I don't know. You take it."

"That's kind of you, but—I can't take your weapon."

"You come across that bear in those woods up yonder and you'll need it, ma'am. I ain't your pa, but I insist. And I have a temper, too." Adam walked back to Eden and placed the rifle in her hands. "I reckon you lived in these parts long enough to know how to use one." He moved to his saddlebags, pulled out a small box, and tossed it Eden's way. "Here's some shells. You best get some sleep if you're fixin' to make the Bighorn tomorrow. There's a blanket next to my saddle over there."

Eden nodded and retrieved the cover. She put the shells in her pocket, wrapped herself up near the fire, and lay on her side watching its sparks while Adam set the dirty pan next to the other used pots. He fed the fire a few more fat, round logs and crawled into his bedroll.

"Adam?"

The man grunted.

"Thank you."

"Thank me on your way back. If that gun don't see you home, I don't deserve no thanks."

Eden closed her eyes to the fire.

* * *

She slept for brief moments during the night, the dread at trekking into the mountains a constant on her mind. Dawn brought the woods to faint light. Leaving a snoring Adam behind, she made her way to the river with the buffalo gun in hand. When she reached the banks she removed her boots, dipped her toes in the water, and splashed her cheeks until the cobwebs of a sleepless night fell away. Eden sat by the water listening to its rush until the sun spread its rays across her lap. Once her back was warm she made her way back to camp to thank Adam for his kindness and be on her way.

The Bighorn heaved up in the distance as she walked and her eyes were on them when she entered the small camp. She expected the fire to be up and something to eat on its flame. But no flames burned. No mules, no saddle—no man. The skins were there, pots hung by the fire pit, and bedding still laid to one side. Eden crossed the camp to the bedroll. Adam's boots stood at its foot. No chance he'd be riding without boots. Yet his mules were gone.

"Adam?" She edged past the bedroll, through the thicket surrounding the camp. If he'd gone into the wood to relieve himself he may have fallen. The land was uneven. The man was old.

Eden pushed through the brush until a scent begged her to stop. Sweet, metallic—the faint whiff of rain on fresh hay. But not.

Blood.

She swallowed hard and pushed on. In a few steps, she found him. She clasped a hand to her mouth not wanting to betray her position. But the core of her screamed. The only mark Adam bore was a deep slash to his neck. He lay a slaughtered pig, blood puddling under his shoulders.

Adam's face still wore the surprise he must have had at the hands of his killer: brow furrowed and eyes wide, one end of his bushy white eyebrow cocked in disbelief.

Eden scanned the woods. Blood rushed in her ears offering no clues to the whereabouts of the murderer, but he couldn't be far. She'd not been an hour at the river. Even on horseback whomever killed the old man was not far away. She clutched the buffalo gun and put a hand to Adam's lukewarm cheek. If she hadn't gone to the river she'd be dead, too.

The renegade.

Her desperation was balanced by relief. If he was in the valley, he was not with Aiden on the mountain.

Eden had no tool to bury the old man. Some guilt took her for not making do with at least a pile of rocks. But her best move would be to get far away from the scene, removed from the possibility of being found a witness if the villain returned. The whinny of a distant horse sent her racing through the brush in the direction of the Bighorn. Twice her legs collapsed under her as they found uneven footing, and twice she scrambled to her feet.

She ran until she felt her lungs would burst, up a shallow draw, until she reached its head, draw coming to an end. Before her lay a steep bank of loose rock. In her fright she was halfway up the face before the stones moved beneath her. Eden stopped as the scree slid downward. By the time the motion ceased, she was thigh deep in heavy debris. The rocks were sharp through her trousers, and their weight, nails against her flesh. She wiggled her toes inside her boots. Nothing broken.

Pebbles tumbled down around her. She was no better than a fox in one of Adam's traps. Fright took the wind from her lungs. She had no water, and she'd left her coat behind. She was open to the elements, or worse.

She moved as many of the rocks as she could, but beneath the first layer of the slide they sat too heavy to lift. Something growled in the distance. A wolf or a bear. She couldn't tell which.

Maybe her empty stomach. Or an admonition. No trees buffered the hillside or crest above to shield her from the eyes of one who'd do her harm, whether human or a four-footed predator.

Without water, if she didn't free herself, she'd be done for. Two turkey buzzards already circled above, signposts in the sky. Cocking their heads, taking in the full view of the catch they'd found. Their ebony eyes flickered in the sun with every pass.

At least she had a weapon. She hugged the rifle the way she used to hug her father's neck. She might use it to pry away the granite pinning her legs, but she'd not risk bending its barrel, rendering it useless.

She banked on the mercy of anyone who wandered by—except the renegade.

A Simple Gift

Stars still dazzled the sky, but the lights of the north had flickered away. Intah was happy to trade sleep for the magnificence of their rippled dance. Though he'd seen them a hundred times before, his fascination never dulled. He didn't see them unless he pushed himself to stay awake past midnight. But when he did they always granted inspiration. By morning the sight had beckoned him beyond his obsession with the white woman and on toward his canyon home.

Intah pulled crisp air into his lungs. Once again snow was in the fickle mind of the weather. The notion was a wedge at the base of his ribs. Reach the cave at Ten Sleep before it fell, or the going would be hard.

He kicked dirt over the smoldering fire and whistled. His horse whinnied and trotted from a copse of trees below the rim of the knoll. Intah threw his bearskin around him, mounted, and dropped down to the riverside where the water receded, leaving the banks soggy and deep. The horse drank long from the stream and Intah dipped his hand for a drink as well. He pulled a piece of pemmican from a doeskin sack and nibbled at the dried meat as he turned the horse toward the Bighorn, following the broad swath of the Powder until dawn broke.

At the curve of the river, he spotted an elk resting in the sand, well away from the edge of the water. The animal made no effort to move as he approached. The hoofbeats of the horse should have roused it, even if the noise of the river denied the sound of his movements.

The bull lay dead.

He pulled up beside the beast. Well intact and without rigor. No match to the swelling torrent of the river the day before. Its fur lay long and thick, a drag to a swift crossing—but a boon to an able man with a sharp blade. His delay would be but an hour or two, and the hide, a welcome addition to a frosty cave in winter. A simple gift too good to pass up.

He slid off the horse and went to work, using all his strength to heave the bull onto its side. Taking a large hunting knife from a sheath in his boot, he sliced him along the back, head to tail. Then he repeated the same along the belly and pushed his fist between the flesh and the hide. The skin came away with ease. With one piece free, he turned the elk onto the exposed flesh and peeled away the other skin.

Intah whittled sharp stakes from thin willow branches and used them to draw the two skins tight. He pulled a flat, sharp-edged stone from his bag and fleshed out the skins until the hides were cleaned of sinew and near dry in the warm sun. He would finish the job in the sanctuary of the cave, curing the hides in front of a hot fire to leach away their damp, rank odor.

He rolled them tight to deny the air's rot of the fresh skin, then linked them with leather thong, laid them across the withers of the horse, and mounted. He left the river's course and moved up a slender draw until he reached a broad stand of cottonwoods. He pushed the horse up the hill and, with the Bighorn in his sights, continued on. When he reached the head of the draw below, his horse nickered and pranced, unsettled at the passing. Such agitation surprised him; his mount was well-traveled. Intah pushed the animal to the lip of the draw. The way to show an animal the path of courage was to face its fear and find it benign.

Intah looked over the remains of a rocky slide blocking the ravine. The source of the horse's nervous step, clear—a red-headed figure sat with legs buried beneath the heavy scree, buffalo gun aimed at the hill beyond. On the other side a sizable black bear swayed down the slope not twenty great leaps behind the figure. The animal slipped across the loose rocks with a scraping sound that raised the hair on Intah's arms.

The horse nickered again. Intah dismounted, leaving his horse on the hill as he slipped his way down the steep draw. As he approached, Intah was sure he'd found Eden's brother—until he came close enough to see fine features in profile.

"It's you."

Eden kept her eyes and gun trained on the bear.

He lowered his voice. "Are you hurt?"

She spoke as though she'd expected his arrival. "Not for the cramp in my legs."

"Lucky." He watched the bear. Without making any sound or sudden moves that might draw its ire, he crouched and pulled away rocks, one by one.

"Not sure how you reach that conclusion."

"Lucky, so far." Intah nodded to boulders perched at the top the slide above them. "Why would you go up the rift this way?"

"I was running."

Intah turned a few of the smaller stones away from the pile. "You'd do well to mind your direction."

"Suppose we could have this conversation after you free me? The bear's headed here and I'd rather not include him in our discussion."

Intah began to rethink his wish to see her again, and paused his excavation. "Perhaps you'd find his help more welcome."

Eden let out a long sigh. "I'm sorry, but I've been here since dawn. A trapper was murdered neither far off nor long ago. That's why I ran."

"How?"

She lowered the gun. "Throat slashed. Horrible thing. Took his mules but nothing more. No skins, no tools."

Intah studied the bear. It walked nose to the dirt, grumbling and growling as it weaved a slow path in their direction. Eden gasped.

"Shh," said Intah.

The animal moaned. Eden struggled against the scree.

Intah straightened and stood tall. "Always stand your ground."

"Well, I haven't a choice, have I?"

"It may not know we're here. I think it's drunk."

"Are you mad?"

Intah shook his head. "Rotten fruit's the windfall of autumn. Hard as whiskey."

The animal's head swayed back and forth as though it couldn't focus—on a path to walk right by them. Intah took the grizzly hide from his back, lifted it above his head and stood stock still, staring at the beast. The creature stopped and the two regarded each other until the beast loped down the hillside like a tumbling stone. Intah listened to the wind coming off the prairie for a moment then walked down the rocky slope.

"Where are you going?"

Intah continued without a look back. "Be still or that whole hillside will be in your lap."

"You can't be leaving me."

Without a word, he set to work looking for a long sturdy branch beneath the cottonwoods—something dry enough to have fallen, but moist enough not to crack in his hands. He picked up a suitable choice and returned to Eden.

"Your horse?"

Eden looked toward the river a few seconds with a resigned expression before she answered. "Lost in the crossing."

Her tone told him not only her feelings hurt, but her confidence suffered as well. He'd not wound her further. "Found a dead elk at dawn who tried to do the same. Lucky again, wouldn't you say?"

Eden's voice took an irritated turn. "Are you ever discouraged?"

"Would that serve me?" Intah poked the branch alongside her foot and pushed down upon its length. The rocks lifted enough to free her.

She pulled her ankles up close to rub the battered skin. "There'll be bruising."

"You're welcome."

Eden shot him a sharp look and stood. "I was going to say."

"Soon as you finished complaining."

Sheepish for the first time, she said, "Well—thank you. Do you think it was that outlaw Indian?"

"Indians aren't the only ones who kill."

"I know that. But who else do we know of at the moment who might slash the throat of an old man just to take his horse?"

To use the familiarity—and pleasure—of a knife when a bullet could do the same, the woman was right.

She looked up at him, the full force of her resolve evident. "I was hoping to find you."

"More luck." He cocked his head at the short curls framing her face. "You cut your hair."

Eden put a hand to her head although she'd forgotten. Under the cap of her fringe curls she resembled a child.

"Why did you leave?" asked Eden

"You wanted me to."

"But I hoped to speak to you when I returned. While I was at the gathering the hunting party came back with a dead man. They left my brother in the mountains."

"Dead?"

"No. Lost. He went out alone to hunt one morning. A grizzly took the camp by surprise. They scattered like sheep without even looking for Aiden. Not one would go back."

Intah fell silent. The bluster she'd shown at Rose Ranch shadowed her in the open-air wild. A woman traveling with what most called a savage was more than madness. Yet here she was. The coming question rolled toward him like a hot summer storm during a dry harvest. Welcome relief —and misgiving.

"Will you take me into the mountains?"

He ran a hand through his long hair and considered the task. "A mountain is more than just a way to get to the next valley. The Bighorn is an obstacle that tests. Few pass its scrutiny in winter. A bedroll won't keep you alive against a hard snow. There's no pump for a simple drink of water or shelter from ravening wolves. No comfort of a neighbor arriving with aid. The mountains have a way of showing a person hidden things about themselves."

"If you won't help me I'll find another way." Eden turned away.

He took her arm and turned her to him. "I am the way. I have not said no. But you need to look me in the eye so I can see that you understand what that means."

Eden looked at Intah. Her face, determined beauty. Her eyes, green as the belly of a glacier. "I've already seen hidden things about myself. Some I'd just as soon forget. But what I want this moment more than anything is to find Aiden."

She turned toward the Bighorn. "Most would say you're the last person I should trust. I have set aside their opinions. I trust you. And I understand well what it means."

The Root of It All

A horse lay bloated at the river's high-water mark. Flies buzzed around its overcast eyes.

"It's him, alright," said Maddie, "can see the branded double R from here."

As fast as the soft ground allowed, Maddie followed Jenny through the trees to the Powder. Though its level had returned to near normal, the earth, from flood line to flow, lay a soggy mess littered with branches and debris. Before the bank dipped down, still a good distance from the water's edge, the two came to a stop over Eden's dead horse.

"Decided to see how far the river'd gone down on my way back home this mornin'," said Jenny, "or I'd never come 'cross it."

Eyes glued to the animal, Maddie tried to shun the obvious conclusion forming in her mind. "You feed afore you left?"

"Yes, ma'am. And the goats was there, too. Milked 'em 'fore I set off. Didn't give but a drip."

Maddie nodded as she scanned the shore on both sides of the river, trying to dissuade the rising emotion in her heart. "Don't give much with the drought. But don't do a body no good if they dry up roamin' the prairie."

Downstream the water lay smooth and slate-colored. Hard to imagine the river such a rage the day before. If Eden had swept downstream she could be clear to Montana, alive or not. Maddie's eyes overflowed with tears.

Jenny moved closer. "Ma, maybe she made land. She's smarter than an old horse. She'd know not to swim against the flow."

"Could be, missy, could be. But ever heard of horse-sense?" Maddie checked her tears but her spirit would not be lightened. She looked at the hills beyond, a bone-dry columbine.

A land with death on its mind.

Not a patch of green existed. No rain was traded for the disaster around them, only runoff keeping to its own course. Even though it meant hardship, she yearned for snow to kill the notion of fire on the desiccated prairie.

"Ain't no way to know. Just pray," said Maddie. "You follow the river all the way from Eden's place?"

"Yes, ma'am."

"Odds are she'd go a far piece more than a heavy horse." Maddie headed off down river, calling behind her. "Tell Papaw I'll be back by dark. Tell him I'm takin' that letter to Eden if you want. Do the milkin', then git yourself back to Rose Ranch. Told him last night you was helpin' her shoe the ponies. Tell him Missus Rose needs the two of us for shoein' that wild colt of her'n."

Maddie walked the shore beneath the cliffs lining the west bank of the river. Sandbars fell off along the way, still spongy with runoff. She searched the midstream beaches, looking for any sign of movement. The Powder roamed sluggish again. Occasional pools and riffles remained.

Though the morning broke with a crisp chill, the sun was hot. Maddie was thirsty. But the water roiled muddy as ever, too thick to drink, and sporting carcasses to boot.

The burned-out barn Cleve told her about was an ash heap a little distance away from the bend of the river. Its ruin sent a shiver through her. Barns didn't burn themselves. Maddie scanned the sparse cottonwoods around her for any sign of the renegade, but an Indian with his reputation as a scout would move through the wood with no trail.

She gazed downriver, fearing what horror her eyes might greet. Maddie wished to find Eden alive or not at all. She walked farther on but stopped short of town. If anyone saw her seeming to search for something, Cleve would hear. She'd not betray Eden's secret until she knew for certain she was lost for good.

She sat in the shade of a cottonwood on the riverbank, resting ahead of the trek home. The day warmed, but a harsh edge to the air suggested another change in the weather. She'd not eaten since breakfast. To think of Eden without the stores she'd packed made her belly even tighter. The dead horse was still strapped by the saddle and bags. Eden would be hungry, too—if she was alive. Maddie's mind wandered over a dozen pictures of her best friend's ruin until she shook the images from her head.

Instead, in her mind's eye she saw Eden making the shore, drying her clothes and camping for the night. Her fiction delivered Eden to Intah, and Maddie's mind eased thinking it must be so.

She skirted the river again, hoping to see something she'd missed before. A lump caught in her throat for miles, but she couldn't bring herself to cry it out. Bawling allowed little hope, and she had no mind for that. Where there was no hope there was no God, and she believed in both.

The sun slipped behind the Bighorn as she reached her porch.

"Musta been a devil," said Ezra.

"What's that?"

"A devil—that young colt. Takin' you hours to put a set of shoes on a horse. I'd cut him if he was mine."

Her father's words stole the pain of thinking on Eden.

"Was a devil alright," said Maddie.

She opened the door to the smell of beef frying in the pan and potatoes roasting in the oven. Cleve stood at the stove with a crowd of small heads around him, all looking up at their mother.

"Came fer those pigs," said Cleve. "Early enough to cook."

"Glory." After the day she'd had, Maddie could think of nothing more welcome than a meal she had no hand in.

They all sat down to supper around the big kitchen table and devoured the treat of fresh beef. The one thing Maddie didn't raise for eating. She left that to the cattlemen. Maddie put a forkful of potatoes into her mouth. They were better than anything she'd ever tasted, cooked with little bits of bitter greens and onion.

"Cleve, where'd you learn to cook like this?"

"Best way to soothe the soul is to feed it, my ma used to say. Comes in handy when you're a mortician. Feeding the bereaved. When I took up butcherin' it was only natural to use some of the bounty on my own table. A man can't eat at the dining hall forever."

"Lan, Cleve. I had no idea."

"Woman's work," said Ezra.

The children giggled.

Cleve looked at Ezra. "Well, I ain't no woman." He fixed his eyes on Maddie. "But it gives a man the freedom to court because he wants to, not because he needs to."

Maddie felt her face color. "A woman who can tend her own don't court because she needs to, either."

Cleve raised a bowl of roasted turnips, winking to Maddie as he passed it. "Sometimes you find you need things you never gave a mind to before."

* * *

When supper was over, the children cleared the table and Ezra wandered off to his room in the back of the farmhouse. Cleve and Maddie went out front. She sat in the metal rocker, and he, on the top step of the porch.

"Didn't want to say nothing at the table, but you got stock missin'."

"How do you know?" asked Maddie.

"Well, I come for twelve pigs and all you got is eleven. Goat's missing, too."

Cleve followed as Maddie pushed up out of the rocker and made her way to the paddock near the barn. "You told me to turn 'em out, so I did. Have you checked the fences?"

"Yep. Reckon they been stole—for food."

"Who would come way out here to pinch food on the hoof?"

"A hungry Indian?"

It was as though someone hit her in the chest. Excuses made the best poultice. "Maybe the wolves are back. Or maybe they wiggled out 'neath the fence. Stock gits loose all the time."

Cleve reached a hand out to touch Maddie's shoe and smiled. "Or maybe they run off together."

"Not funny, Cleve," said Maddie.

"Ain't tryin' to be funny, Maddie, but you gotta be the stubbornest woman I know if you see no danger in it."

"I been seein' danger all week, Cleve."

Maddie was sure she'd be squashed under the burden of her knowledge if she didn't lay it all down right then. She told Cleve of Eden, the Indian at her door, and the trek undertaken to fetch Aiden.

When she finished, Cleve let a long breath slip between his lips. "All on account of her brother."

"Yep," said Maddie.

Aiden was the root of it all.

Cross the Heavens

Two nights passed after Ink left him. Temperatures kind, but the food disappeared and then the weather changed its mind again. As soon as the sun set, a small icicle formed out of the gentle drip of snowmelt from a tree above. Aiden pulled the canvas tight around him as well as he could with one arm, existence hewn down to a frigid sliver between the star-strewn sky and a spiteful cold.

As the night wore on, and his remaining strength ebbed, he pictured Ink's fingers fondling the beloved golden timepiece, holding it to the moonlight like poor Yorick's skull.

Alas, he knew that watch so well. How well did he know Ink?

He had to trust that Ink would return. Rage was ill-afforded. Yes, Ink would come for him, and warn Eden about the renegade's threat to leave the Powder River settlers freezing in their own fluids come winter.

Aiden's teeth chattered in the silence, and the Big Dipper shimmered low across the black velvet night. The vision of his sister sitting by the fire in the sod cabin warmed him, and though the tremors were slow to recede, when they did, Aiden floated among those fiery stars, warmed in their glow, the Powder lurking below just around the bend.

He pulled the small bag of homeland heather from his pocket and pushed the bundle to his nose. Dry again, its scent faint, a fleeting heartbeat. In it, Aiden conjured the marshy bog, broad stream, a wide tear across the valley, and barren escarpments of the Scottish mountains weeping North Sea storms into the river below.

He struggled to stay awake, enjoying the company of an old memory. When the aurora came up to the north, his eyes were half-open and, at first, he thought they were a dream. He'd seen the lights plenty in the Highlands, rising up late out of the vast ocean, glittering on a broken mirror of ruffled water. But in the wild of Wyoming, the phenomenon was different. With no water to reflect the rays, they seemed ungrounded, beckoning upward and away from earthly realms—alpenglow to a darkened forest.

The sight, as lovely a thing as Aiden had ever seen, brought tears to his eyes. Streaming down his face on one side, they froze in a tiny fold of one ear, and the skin ached with a cold knocking at his brain. Yet each ripple across the sky lifted Aiden from his mortal pain, leaving him unfettered by loss or abandonment or the threat to his sister. Strangely, the aurora warmed him. His brow beaded with sweat. He threw off the canvas to lie exposed, expecting the color to lift him into the stars. The brisk air nothing less than a tender embrace of summer.

The atmosphere lay a strange hushed crackle under vague ruffles of magenta crossing the heavens. When sound joined the rustle of a gentle wind through the leaves of a nearby aspen, the ether came alive with a jig of light across the sky.

So mesmerized was Aiden that the snap of underbrush nearby lost all meaning. The light above grew more intense as the noise prospered, enveloping as a leap into a warm lake fills every sense. The earth no longer beneath him nor the phantom fingers on his missing hand nor the tears on his cheek. Each breath he blew fanned away in long streams evaporating into the frosty air. His eyes were bound to the display overhead. No quarter was given to the steady huff approaching from the dense undergrowth.

By the time he saw the grizzly, the mammoth towered above him, cloudy breath mingling with Aiden's, a thick, bloody mat of hair across its massive shoulder blocking Aiden's view of the beckoning sky. Even at the crush of hot jowls Aiden tilted his head to see around the creature —as though the animal were nothing but another constellation overhead.

Northern Dancers

Intah helped Eden up the steep slope as she favored one ankle. His horse grazed nearby. As soon as it saw him, the animal walked to his side.

Breathless, she put her hand on the animal's flank. "I've never had a horse walk to me so. How do you break an animal to do it?"

"Not break. Show." Intah scratched the horse's neck under its mane until the animal's lips curled in pleasure. "When he comes I *show* him I am pleased."

As Eden's lips turned to a wry smile, he lifted her onto the horse. Intah swung up behind her, urging the animal in the direction of the Face of Arrows at the base of the Bighorn.

It was some time before either of them spoke. Eden suspected they were both thinking on the words that decided the trip. Each understood well what it meant to travel together. Though riding tandem with the Indian was as foreign to her as the bear claw about her neck, the duplet was less fearsome than she'd expected; an invitation to try all things new. A quickening.

Intah's breath bathed her neck as he said, "Snow's coming."

The Bighorn stood tall along the western horizon, dusted white at their peaks. "I have a little money. I can buy warmer clothes in Buffalo."

"If the snow falls deep, I may not be able to bring you off the mountain."

"Aiden will do that."

"You're extremely sure of this brother."

"Blood is thick. Have you no kin?"

"Kin often go their own way."

The notion of being at odds with Aiden was impossible for Eden to grasp. She could think of no reason that might cause such a thing.

Intah looked to the peaks beyond, then nodded. "We'll camp at the base of the mountains. A trip to Buffalo will cost a day, but you'll need the warmer clothes. I'll wait."

Eden knew that Intah was not about to show his face in a town full of settlers looking for a renegade to hang. "Fair enough."

The heat of Intah's body seeped through Eden's jacket to warm her as he coaxed the horse back down a short hill into a long, shallow ravine drawing west toward the Bighorn. A cool breeze followed their course, and his long hair rustled on the linen at his shoulders. He smelled of sage and wood smoke.

A long time had passed since she'd been held in such a safe and gentle fashion. As weariness overtook her, she fought the desire to lean against him and rest. So she sat upon the horse with her back straight, trying her best to keep to herself.

They covered the route in silence except to acknowledge needed stops for relief along the way. Few suitable places granted privacy on the open range. Intah managed to discover them: a cottonwood, a clump of sagebrush. Eden was grateful for his thoughtfulness about the matter. She imagined Indians to be immodest at best, yet Intah honored her wish to be private about such things, on both their accounts.

When surprised at the top of each draw, pronghorn antelope, a hundred arrows shot from a single bow, raced away in all directions. After a time they reached a narrow valley split by a meager stream. Smoke flagged from distant chimneys in the direction of Buffalo. White curls twined up and vanished into the parched air. Intah pulled the horse to a stop, scanned the creek in both directions, and dropped down the slope to water the horse.

"We've met the Crazy Woman, again," said Eden.

It was the same glassy creek flowing through Rose Ranch, only upstream some miles. The rough track of a buggy wound its way along the water. Following the creek was the quickest way between Buffalo and Suggs, and largely unpopulated.

Intah pointed to the ridge above the creek. "We'll follow the rim of the valley to the base of the mountains from now on."

He let the horse roam free, and it wandered away to the privacy of some dense vegetation. Eden took off her boots, pulled the legs of her pants up to her knees, and waded into the cool water. She dipped a cupped palm into the creek and drank until hoofbeats came up downstream. She turned to see Ruth and Boss Williams driving a surrey up the creek valley. Little to do but stand her ground in the middle of the gentle water.

The buggy pulled up on the bank near Eden.

"I declare," said Ruth. "What on earth are you doing out this way?"

Boss stared at Eden's bare ankles with an expression of a lion come upon a pronghorn carcass.

Eden yanked her pant legs down as well as she could. She was up to her knees in the water. Even though they'd come upon her in surprise, Ruth would think it the highest impropriety that Eden presented a bare leg.

Boss's tone hit hard. "In trouble?" He pulled a long rifle from the well between the dash and the cushion fall.

As Eden stood back up, Intah walked from the brush.

Boss handed Ruth the harness traces and pointed the rifle. "Trouble."

A single shot rang out. Eden jumped and turned. The bushes behind Intah shook with the reverberation of a bullet.

Intah froze.

Boss held him in his sights. "Didn't hit that brush by mistake."

Eden picked her way from the rocky creek. "No trouble, Boss."

"Convince me," Boss said, unwavering in his aim.

Eden didn't know where to start. If she told them how Intah arrived at her door a few days before, the query would be why she hadn't told them that at tea. And to hide such a thing, at least in the mind of Ruth Williams, suggested another soaring impropriety.

Boss kept the rifle pointed at Intah. "Well?"

Eden looked at Intah, hoping him to take her cue. "He knows Aiden. He guided for him last spring. News traveled fast about your boy, Boss. The man came to take me into the mountains to find my brother."

"Damn genial of him, I say." The rifle didn't move. Boss called in Intah's direction. "That true?"

Intah was silent.

Ruth's tone, irritated. "Boss, if it weren't true, do you think he'd tell you? Why would she be out here with such a man if it wasn't so? This is Eden we're talking about. Let her go on and find her brother. God forbid another of the clan be buried."

"You say you know Aiden," said Boss. "What do you know of him?"

Intah spoke. "That he's as willful and copper-headed as his sister."

Boss lowered the rifle. "Well then, know this, if harm comes to the woman it'll be on *your* scalp."

Eden looked at Ruth. "I'm not afraid."

The revelation set Eden to tingle. For the first time in a long time, she wasn't frightened.

Ruth nodded. "I can see that."

"Indeed," said Boss, scrutinizing Intah as though measuring with a stick. He slipped his rifle into the bottom of the buggy and took back the traces.

Ruth leaned in Eden's direction when they passed by. "We're going to pick out a coffin for Jack. They're finer in Buffalo than in Suggs, you know?"

Eden sat on the side of the creek, a shamed dog. Soon the entire Powder would know that she was in the company of an Indian.

Intah waded to her side. "You have a quick mind."

Eden granted him a deadpan stare. "Willful is it?"

"If you weren't you wouldn't be here."

"And just how do you know Aiden has my color hair?"

"A guess."

Eden tossed her head in a nod. "Lucky."

Intah chuckled, and Eden joined him. She put her socks and boots on and they were back on the trail, riding the higher western ridge of the creek, keeping an eye to other travelers.

Two hours passed. To the right of a narrow rift carving its way through the mountain ahead was a broad, rocky face strewn with dozens of arrow-shaped outcroppings, as Intah described. The Face of Arrows. She'd been this way before, seen the cliffs. The settlers called them the Bighorn Spires. She'd never perceived the sight as suggesting the arrows until Intah described it so. Yet she was certain she could never see them any other way again.

They left the creek and rode straight for the cliffs, passing under a small orchard of spent apple trees. Plenty of rotten fruit graced the dry grass. The scent of hard cider permeated the air.

"There." Intah reached for several small apples yet on a low branch and handed them to Eden.

She placed all but one in the fold of her linen shirt. "Want one?"

Intah took a piece of fruit from her and ate it in four bites, core and all. He slipped from the back of the horse picking as much fruit as he could reach on the trees and placing them in a large doeskin bag he wore over his shoulder. He pulled at the fruit with care as though not wishing to harm the tree. When the bag was full, he squashed a rotten apple under his hide boot.

"Too late to make good juice. These will make you drunk as that bear."

"Might keep you warmer in winter," said Eden. "There's no harm in a little nip to a Brit. You *are* part English."

Intah looked at her as though she were trying to talk him into poison. "How do you know I have England in me?"

"It's in your words, a touch here and there. Enough to recognize."

"Didn't know that." Intah slid behind her.

"You couldn't learn English from an Englishwoman and be without it." She bit into her apple, chewing through her compliment. "It's a fine lilt, you have."

They rode under the cliff to the base of a ravine. From the chasm flowed the slip of a stream, and as soon as they entered the protection of the rift walls, a rushing symphony surrounded them. Eden looked to the cottonwoods flanking the creek, thinking the sound was wind through the trees. But the leaves were still. The water alone rustled beside them.

Enchanting.

Intah slid from the horse and Eden followed. She stood by the stream watching its water spill down a slender canyon.

"Look familiar?" asked Intah.

Eden cocked her head in question.

"It's the same water running the creek by your home," said Intah.

"The Crazy Woman again?" Eden stiffened. No escaping its hold.

"The light will soon be gone. We'll overnight here. The morning will take you to town."

Eden nodded, wrapping her arms around herself for warmth. Sunlight was absent in the gap. Cold seeped from the meltwater running off the mountain.

Intah took the elk skins from the horse's side and unrolled them. "They're not yet cured but these will keep you warm." He laid them out in a clearing near the stream.

Eden bent to run her hand over the thick fur and stopped. "They smell a fright."

"You'll be warm enough to sleep. And so will your grumbling nose." Intah took the bridle off his horse, hung the leather on a low branch, and flung his bear robe under a tree. "Heat will help drive the stench away. Gather up some dry windfall. I'll find firewood."

Eden soon had a fair pile of tinder waiting as Intah pulled dry wood from the banks that had tumbled down the ravine with the highest waters of last spring. By dusk a hearty fire blazed, its heat toasting the elk skins and cooking an undersized rabbit Intah managed to kill.

"This rabbit's no bigger than a rat." Eden pulled the last bit of meager meat off one of the fragile bones and licked a finger.

"Better small than not at all."

"Clever. But I'm afraid it's not enough to satisfy."

He shook his head a little, threw a piece of wood into the fire. "Have an apple and tell me what you see up the canyon."

Eden pulled an apple from the burlap laying next to them, put a hand on the elk skin behind her and leaned back, looking up the narrow canyon as she ate the apple, crisp and sour-sweet. "A devil of a climb."

"That's all?" He chewed a last bit of rabbit.

She'd not tell him of the vision that often took her in the darkest nights—the blood, the fever of escape, the terror. Clear, as though she merely stared at the horror through a clean window, and nothing but thin glass stood between her and the threat.

She took another bite of fruit, swallowing a rising panic. "What do you see?"

"A gift of water, and a protected path into the Bighorn."

"And a devil of a climb," Eden repeated, as though focusing on that tangible logic might forestall danger brooding in her mind. Besides, she didn't care for being mocked. She wasn't looking forward to the rigors of the slope, even from the back of a horse.

Words she knew would lead to bitter memory spilled like milk across her tongue. "I've done the same before."

Too late to sop them up.

Intah only granted an odd, slow nod seeming to look through her.

"Eight years gone. My husband engaged a guide to take us into the mountains to hunt. We were just married and newly arrived."

Intah tossed the rabbit bones into the fire. "Husband?"

For the first time she grasped that Intah had no idea she was a married woman. A piece of apple stuck in her throat. She coughed, hoping to delay a response.

Intah reached for an apple. "Where is he?"

"Gone. To Britain." An uncomfortable admission. Why?

"Britain." He bit into the apple.

"Surely, your mother talked of it. It's another country, like America, but smaller. The size of a gem to compare. In spring, green as an emerald—if you know what that is. It's where I'm from. Scotland to be exact."

"You're not American?"

"Is anyone, really?"

The notion occurred to her that she hadn't given up her British papers because, in the back of her mind, she counted on going back someday. Like Hugh. She shook her head. Eden had judged him harsh for it, yet she wasn't so far different in her thinking. "Couldn't you tell that from my accent?"

"I don't speak to enough people for it to make a difference to me." Intah threw the spent apple into the fire. "My father was native to this place."

"I think you are whatever your mother was, personally. Same with breeding horses. The mare carries the importance of the pedigree."

"So, if my mother was English," said Intah with a glint in his eye. "That makes me so?"

"Aye, it does indeed in my eyes, though I say there's never been the likes of you in Britain. You said your grandmother was white as well?"

"I don't know more than that she came from the Dakotas. My grandfather stole her on the way back from a vision quest."

"Vision quest?"

"A journey, alone, to the sacred land beyond what you call the Belle Fourche. I was coming from there when I found your horses."

"And did you have a vision?"

Intah nodded. "That I might find pleasure in my days."

"And what be the pleasure in this day?"

"To live through it, I'd say."

Perhaps survival was the common bond of mankind.

"That I know," she said.

Neither of them spoke more until Intah walked to the creek and back. Firelight flickered across the rift walls.

"Too bright. We need no visitors." He squelched the flames with water from the stream. Eden laid her canvas coat beneath her and wrapped herself in one of the animal hides.

The skin was drier and the odor of elk diminished in the open air. Sweet as a fresh cut side of pork. They stretched out on the lush, spongy grass flanking the stream. The stars glittered across the strip of sky above the ravine. A quarter moon slipped beyond the highest peak, leaving a night so black Eden couldn't see her hand before her face except where it denied the twinkle of starlight.

Though the night was darker than the deepest ocean, she sensed Intah's gaze. "What is it you want to know?"

"What kind of husband leaves a woman with winter coming?"

"How long do you have?"

Silence fell between them like an eclipse.

Eden let a long breath slip through her nose and looked into the night. "Desperation drives a hard bargain and he's had years of it. He'd been a soldier most of his life. He was well-to-do and wanted a wife. He found one, retired from service, took her to Wyoming, and planted her there." Eden raised herself up on one elbow. "We found out as we stood on the platform in Cheyenne to begin our travels back to Scotland, that the Bank of Glasgow had failed. Hugh had nothing left. Not even change to make the ocean crossing home. What started as a season away from Britain, ended in a permanent move. The house was sold in Scotland to pay debts, and to buy land here, and here we stayed."

"And the horses?"

"A blacksmith in Buffalo told him that a thousand mustangs littered the plains, untamed, unowned, and free for the taking."

"Sell them for profit."

Eden chuckled. "Indeed."

"I don't understand."

"Hugh's plan was to round up the mustangs, train them for polo, and ship them back to Britain where a man will pay for one good pony what a homesteader pays for a barren stretch of dry land."

"Polo?"

"It's a game on horseback, as old as the pyramids, some say. Mallets are used to chase a ball across an open field."

"Sounds like a good way to teach the game of war." Intah breathed a long sigh.

"Aye. It was used by the ancients to practice maneuvers. Takes wild men and quick, agile horses. The West holds both."

"And he's in Britain now?"

"To beg the bank to loan against a boney herd of horses so I can spend another bleak year as a crazy woman on the creek."

The silence was long and still until a lone coyote called out against the darkness. Eden wondered if Intah had drifted off to sleep under the weight of her broken dreams. She sat up, trying to see his outline beside her.

Intah's voice was a murmur. "Will he come back?"

Her reply spilled abruptly. "No."

"Not what you want."

Eden let the ambiguity of his sentence hang in the air. No need for him to know her truth. She didn't want Hugh back.

"Never wanted any of it. Life seems to be less about what is wanted, and more about what is lost."

"It's of your choosing. It's always of your choosing."

For so long she wanted things that never came, or arrived only to slip away—the last pennies in a money jar, a final crop of undersized potatoes...the fragile life of a child in the night. Wanting no longer came to her mind with confidence. More and more yearning arrived with a pit of dread reaching to her toes. She lay back down and turned her head toward the stream.

"The mountains scare you," said Intah.

Eden lay still. She tried to bury her fear with conversation, but panic had grown along with the mountains on the horizon. She hadn't wanted Intah to know. She wanted to keep the memory buried.

"If you are to pass through safely, you must not fear them."

"A healthy respect then," said Eden.

"Call it what you like, but if fear is behind the name, fear will come."

"So many things you say, I can't grasp." She turned in the direction of Intah's voice.

He lay invisible, his deep soothing tone floating in the ether, "If you pay attention, you will see things anew."

Eden turned her eyes to the stars and considered his words. More riddle than counsel.

They lay quiet in the grass for some time until Intah's breath changed to gentle slumber. Despite the tug of sleep, she gathered in the splendor of the stars. She didn't often sit beneath them. It was a luxury to be fresh enough at the end of a day to consider the heavens.

"The Great Bear." Intah pointed low in the sky.

Eden tensed at the description, then looked in the direction of his extended arm. "I see it."

"Do you know its meaning?"

"I'm sure you'll tell me."

"The bowl of the Big Dipper is a giant bear. The stars of the handle are three warriors chasing it. Low in the sky at autumn, it's bear blood that turns the leaves to red."

"So it's killed."

"No champions among those warriors. The Great Bear can only be slain by a hero." At the lip of the ravine soft light rippled in and out of sight. The glimmer became brighter and brighter with each swell, and soon the Aurora Borealis filled the sky. She reached out to prod Intah's side and he jerked awake.

"The aurora."

Intah's delivery was soft, as though sound might drive off the spectacle. "Northern Dancers."

"Why do you call it such?"

"When a new spirit enters the heavens, the Dancers gather in welcome. The light you see is the light of a great fire they surround."

Eden's mind went to Aiden even though, to her, the pretense of an aurora as the bearer of bad news was impossible. "Death?"

"More—a changing. One energy to another." Intah held Eden's arm to the lights. "See the color there? Red is the color of strength. Hot. A soul of strong mind and will is being welcomed. The ripples come in random beats, showing passion. See? The light is strong and quick to move."

Intah's face was illuminated in the lights. His eyes were black in the night, his expression striking and earnest.

"What of other colors?"

"Orange is a soul of courage and joy. The dance, a steadier rhythm across the sky. Yellow, the color of wisdom, is pale and slow, sometimes a single sheath of broad light, like the glow of a sunset." Intah raised his arm and swept his hand across the stars in a slow motion. "Blue and green are holy men or healers, and the light is calm across the sky, long waves in a clear lake. Purple is one who is searching."

"Are there more?"

"Many. But the rarest, gold—someone who finds their greatest power in the heavens."

"You believe this."

"I know it. As surely as you stated it without a question in your voice. That makes all the difference."

"You have a fine way of speaking."

Intah pulled the hide over his shoulders and turned over. "For an Indian."

For anyone.

Useful Gifts

A sleek grey sky moving in from the west delayed the morning. Sun peaked underneath the cover, pinking up the eastern rangeland and the western peaks, before disappearing to the rest of the day under thick clouds. Intah laid the fish he caught on the grass. Eden's back was to the prairie as she slept. The brief sunlight never touched her eyes. Her short curls lay strewn around her head, cheeks the ruddy mottle of a duck egg against the charcoal tips of the elk hair. Summer had tanned her face well.

She was as fair a woman as he'd seen. Difficult to understand why she was alone. If she were an Indian woman abandoned by her man, she'd be fair game to another. But she was a white. Her man, even if he didn't want her, would kill before allowing his woman the company of a Native. Intah did his best to banish the spirit moving him toward the woman. He would take her into the mountains, find her brother, and then leave the memory behind.

Intah regarded Eden in the lush grass near the stream until she blinked awake.

She propped up on an elbow, perched her head upon one palm, and rubbed a hand through her hair. "Every time you look at me you look surprised."

Intah walked to the campfire. "You remind me of someone I once saw."

"Must have startled you to see my face at the door that first time."

"It was a start when first I saw you crossing the pasture." He looked down, shy to admit the infraction.

Eden's voice was indignant. "You'd been watching me?"

Intah nodded.

"And for how long?"

"For as long as it took you to mend the fence and gather water from the well."

Eden stared hard at Intah. "Did you free my mares only to gather them up again?"

"No."

"Well, then, it was a fair piece of fortune for you, wasn't it?"

Intah smiled, pushing the embers of the fire with a small stick.

"Tell me," said Eden, as she rolled onto her back. "How'd you get to be so distant from your kin?"

"You're fixed on that, aren't you?"

"Well, it's just that I love my brother so, I can't imagine a thing coming between us in so deep a way."

"I had something he wanted." Intah threw the stick into the fire, and looked out across the prairie. "He was promised as the next holy man of our tribe. Our father took another wife. I was born, blue-eyed son of a holy man. It was said to be the doing of the spirit world, to mark me with such a thing. And the first vision I ever had was finding water for our people. Blue eyes, blue water. My brother lost his place."

"So he hated you for that?"

"Not yet. He resolved to rise as chief instead. Many games are played by a young warrior to train for such things. As holy man, it was not my place to join in, but he taunted me to try. I beat him each time. I think it was because I cared nothing for the outcome."

"So, he never became important in the way he wanted."

"The hatred drove him to Crazy Horse."

"He was with him?"

"Until he stole a scalp that Crazy Horse had taken in a raid, and presented it as his own prize. The truth came out. He left the tribe, disgraced."

"What became of him?"

"He began to hate whites from the inside as a scout for the army. He led Custer to Crazy Horse. I still don't know who he

200

wished to betray. Perhaps he didn't either. He was promised freedom for his help in rounding up the tribes. But he was assigned to a reservation. He ran again."

"They say the renegade rode with Crazy Horse and with Custer. I don't suppose too many did both."

Intah threw another piece of wood on the fire.

"You know it, don't you?" asked Eden. "It was he who killed the trapper."

"He has a cruel heart. Cruel hearts often go unchanged."

"That can't be all to drive his rage."

Intah stood up and drew an arm across the distant horizon toward the Powder River. The sweep of beauty in the fresh light caught the speech in his throat. "The curse of lost land drives some men to ruin."

Eden followed Intah's gaze out across the prairie. "I know."

Tears welled in Eden's eyes. Intah remembered the disrepair of her barn and fences, the string of little graves by her door. He thought about all dreams lost between two souls, worlds apart, who sat on the same mountain, together in their loneliness.

Intah walked back to the creek bank to clean the fish. "Breakfast," he said holding out the speckled trout. His horse was out of sight, so he whistled once. The animal trotted up the hill, coming to a stop short of Eden.

"So, show a creature pleasure and he comes to you, you say." She stood to pat the horse. "What, may I ask, did you do to make that bear retreat?"

"What I intended." If she insisted on trying to know his ways, he would insist on telling her straight on what they were, even if his words perplexed. "I thanked him for leaving."

Frustration laced Eden's voice. "After he walked away."

"No. Before. Like throwing a rock. Know where it is going before you throw it, and it goes where you intend."

"Then you willed him away."

"Power comes from knowledge, force comes from fear. In fear there is no power—and in power there is no fear. Which drives your mind?" Intah walked up to the creek, fish in hand, and cleaned their meal in a stream of water falling from a wide clear pool.

Eden followed him to the water's edge, standing above as he worked. "I don't understand you."

"It's mutual."

A cool breeze moved down the ravine and rustled the amber leaves lacing the aspens on other side of the creek. He laid the cleaned fish on the grass, washed his hands in the running stream, shook them dry, and offered his hand.

Eden looked at the hand as though once she took it she might be bound forever. But when Intah began to pull away, she grabbed his fingers and they walked up the creek a short distance.

When Intah found what he sought he stopped, pointing to the narrow space between two aspens. "What do you see?"

Eden leaned forward, squinting in the flat light, then straightened. "A spider, big as a walnut."

"And?"

"That's all."

"He's floating?"

"On a web, I'm sure."

Intah lead her straight toward the bug. "You didn't see it, yet you knew the truth."

"That'll be far enough." Eden stopped. "I don't fancy spiders."

Intah pulled her a few feet closer anyway. Dew lined an outer portion of the intricate pattern hidden by the brush. He touched a finger to the back of the spider.

"Don't be touching it."

The spider slipped, smooth and straight to earth, then gathered itself to ride an invisible silken cord on return.

"We believe a lie when we see *with*, not *through*, the eye," said Intah.

"Blake, again."

"Aye," said Intah with a smile, mocking her language. "There is much to the man beyond his words, only seen if you recognize and understand your third sight."

"You mean second sight?"

"I do not mean seeing the future. I mean understanding the now. We do not see with our eyes alone. Look beyond. Use the third sight. Much lies in the invisible."

He led Eden back to the stream, picked up the trout and handed it to her. "Breakfast."

Eden took the fish by the gills. "Not before you tell me how looking beyond to see a thing that doesn't exist fits into intending that bear away."

A rusty teacher. Perhaps that was the point. Only proof holds easy understanding, and there'd be none of that to show. Just faith. And faith took courage. "Invisibility doesn't mean nonexistent. Learn to see through your eyes, not with them, and you will know."

Eden's tone was sharp and impatient. "It's all a riddle to you."

"No, it's practice. You tend to see holes in the road and not the road itself." Frustration rose in Intah's throat.

Eden's face flushed. Her jaw squared to show the fine bones of her face and the resolve that followed. "And you're so perfect?"

"I try, that's all, to keep my eyes on the road. No judgment, only observation."

Too late.

"That's the second time in as many days you've *observed* that about me. And neither time did I like it." Eden threw the fish at Intah's feet and stormed toward the sputtering fire. "I'll be on my way to Buffalo for a horse, unless you think you can intend me up one before I go."

He hadn't been the brunt of a woman's fury for a long time. In an odd way, her anger lightened his spirits. Sweet memories were often bound to sour notes. Intah smiled. As soon as he did so he knew he'd made another turn wide of the mark.

Eden pulled on her jacket when she reached the fire then turned to him, set her hands on her hips, and cocked her head as if waiting for a response. Intah stooped to pick up the trout. A man rode toward them in the near distance and Intah stood tall against the sight. Eden turned to see the approaching visitor as well. Intah moved to Eden's side. The black man rode into camp, a tethered horse in tow. Eden cast both Intah and the extra horse an awestruck glance.

The man came to a stop, and drew his rifle. His breath was silver in the morning air. "Ya'll need help?"

"Is that the way you greet a person?" asked Eden.

"Not too many white women travelin' with Indians these days," said the man.

"I've not seen a black man travel at all. And I need no help, thank you."

The parallels between the black and red man struck Intah as ironic. In the eyes of a white, neither of them was worthy to garner Eden's attention. Yet, here they both were.

The man sat back on his horse and tipped his hat, but made no move to lower his rifle. "Fair enough."

"He's my guide. We're bound for the mountains."

The man looked at Eden then again at Intah. "Ya'll sure about that?"

"Yes, I'm sure, now put that thing away. Do I look like I'm under duress, man?"

"Beg your pardon, ma'am. But your cheeks was colored up like you was scared. Cain't be too careful."

"I appreciate your concern, but all's well," said Eden.

Intah pushed the fish onto a long sharp willow stick, put more wood on the fire and set the trout over a flame. "There's enough for three."

The morning breeze was ice on the back of his neck, and the sky's ceiling dropped. Snow was on its way. Intah intended to talk the man out of his extra horse. If Eden could buy one here a whole day they couldn't afford to lose would be saved.

"Mind if I do. Name's Ink." The man swung a leg over his horse, tied the animal to a tree and squatted by the fire.

"I'm Eden Rose and this man is Intah."

"Pleased," said Ink, rubbing his gloved hands together close to the low flames. "Colder'n moonlight on a tombstone."

"Aye, and it's getting colder. You wouldn't happen to have a spare coat to be bought in that bundle over there?" Eden pointed to the broad pack on his extra horse.

"Might have something ya'll can use." Ink went to the horse and rummaged around the pack, returning with a long oilcloth coat. "This'll keep the wind off you, at least. Afraid I cain't spare the rest."

"How much?" asked Eden.

"Two bits'll do."

"Glad to pay it." Pulling two coins from her coat, Eden passed them to Ink who pushed them into his vest. When his hand returned from the deed, a golden watch fell on its chain from the pocket.

She pointed to the dangling watch. Her voice dropped to a murmur, "What'd that be?"

Ink stood, tucking the timepiece back into place.

"I think it's I to be pointing the gun now, sir," she said as she reached for the buffalo gun Adam insisted she take.

Intah turned the fish over the fire and stood. He had no idea what had happened, but by Eden's tone and Ink's reaction, it was nothing good.

205

"What do you mean?" asked Ink.

"That's my brother's watch, as sure as I'm standing here. I saw the crest at the top of the face. Where'd you get it, now?"

"That's a big weapon for a small target," said Intah. "Use that and there'll be no watch left."

"A man give it to me," said Ink, hands over his head.

"Blazes he did. That was my father's watch, given to him by his father, and his before that. My brother'd die before he'd give it up."

"Well, he is dyin', unless I get to him first. Found him on the mountain, in bad shape."

Eden flinched.

"I come down yesterday light. He can't travel on foot. Took me a whole day to find two good horses for loan because I ain't got no money for such. Ain't no pleasure ride. You shoot me that'll be the last of your brother."

"Enough." Intah stepped to Eden's side, and put a hand on the rifle barrel. Eden lowered the weapon. "You know where he is?"

"Sure do," said Ink. "Might be there by nightfall if we get a move on."

Eden eyed the extra mount. "I need a horse."

"Ride the spare. I brung him for your brother."

Minutes later, camp was broken and they were headed up the slip of a canyon, following the steep creek along a path no wider than a horse.

Eden spoke to Ink who followed her. "How did you ever manage to borrow two horses?"

"Used to work for the livery in Buffalo. They knowed me. I didn't steal that watch from your brother. I took it to trade.'

"But it's in your pocket."

"The blacksmith has a taste for Kentucky whiskey. Stole it back before I left after he passed out."

Intah listened to Ink as he related the story to Eden. The man was forthright in his tale and his face gentle in the telling. A good man. The horse, the coat, the watch, and the way to camp—useful gifts. Yet, Ink watched Intah's every step, as though he'd seen him before but couldn't place him. Impossible, for he had never seen a man as black.

"Thank you," said Eden.

"Ain't mine to sell." Ink pushed his horse forward at a slender widening on the trail and handed the watch to Eden across the space between their two horses.

The land became steeper and the way narrower as they climbed. The horses kept to the open trail along the creek, scaling the rocks, but the ascent was hard going. The horses would need to blow for a few minutes before continuing. Intah stopped at the front of the line and turned his mount across the hill. Water fell hard against the rocks above.

Ink raised his voice over the din of reverberation, "Cross here."

"No, up above." Intah pointed to a ledge five hundred feet up canyon.

"But it's shorter this way," Ink said. "Get across without gettin' wet."

The falls ended a short way up and the water slid from beneath a mound of boulders heaped up across the stream.

Intah shouted over the noise of the spray from the falls up the ravine. "The rocks fall from above, look solid. But they're loose. They'll move if we put a horse on them."

Ink looked up the mountain. The man was agitated at the prospect of crossing the ledge. Eden looked as though she measured both men and their ideas, unsure where to settle.

"I've crossed that ledge many times under the falls," said Intah. "It's strong and safe."

"Come on," said Eden to Ink. "He hasn't yet steered me wrong."

"'N how long's that been?"

Eden regarded Ink, then the crossing above, her gaze landing on Intah. She spurred her horse past Ink, overtook Intah, and continued toward the ledge beyond, calling behind her as she traveled. "Long enough."

A Clear Conscience

At the beginning of the stony ledge, Ink insisted on taking a place between Intah and Eden. Halfway across the shelf, Ink's mount held up. Eden's horse stopped behind it. With no direction, the animal stood still on the precipice awaiting a cue. The man seemed paralyzed by the height, staring down the sheer cliff to the fog of water vapor below.

"Push your horse across," she said. "I've no mind to be here all day."

Ink sat motionless, back straight as a stick. "Cain't."

"Have to. There's no way around you, and no way back. Forward is your ticket if you be looking for your health." Eden leaned in toward the cliffside and looked at Intah who had already crossed the threshold to safety.

Intah dismounted and walked back across the ledge. Ink's eyes were glued to the other side, but when he dropped his gaze to the falls below, he wobbled in his saddle.

Eden held her breath. So slim was the passage that if he fell, his horse could go as well. That might spook her own mount clear off the shelf. She eyed what little room lay between her and the inner cliffside. Too little to jump in safety. She eased her thighs around the horse and sat deep in the saddle, relaxing the reins to hold him still. Eden focused on the other end of the crossing, where the rocks disappeared into a thick carpet of grass. On the other end of the journey, reunited with the one person who understood her enough to bring true joy. Without Aiden, she might as well turn her horse out over the falls and push the beast to jump.

Intah took the reins of Ink's horse in one hand and gave a gentle tug. The procession inched across the shelf, shale falling from under the horses' feet, until they all made the bank of the opposite side in one piece.

Ink's shoulders relaxed, and he slid off the horse and knelt down in the grass on all fours. "Don't cotton to height."

"Well, you didn't tell us, did you? You could have kilt us both," said Eden.

"Sorry ma'am, but if it has feet, it can fall. A horse don't seem stuck enough to the ground for guarantees."

Intah shook his head. "How much farther is the camp?"

His tone suggested displeasure. A comment on the aptitude of his charges she guessed. A woman not smart enough to understand the hidden meaning of his words, and a black man without the fortitude to brave a height.

Ink sat back and looked around. "From here, I guess six more hours' ride."

"We better move if we want to make it by dark." Intah mounted and turned his horse up the hill.

It occurred to Eden, as they rode onward, that she and Ink shared the common ground of literal translation. Intah seemed to find his answers in the unseen. Plain fact was, every inch of the West was more often exactly as it seemed than not. She didn't care that Blake encouraged her to see through, not with, the eye. Blake had never seen Wyoming.

They passed through great copses of lodgepole pine bordering wide meadows turned pale by an aging year. Trees stood devoid of any birdsong save the occasional scolding of a crow. At the top of the first hill the mountain opened up to a smooth roll and they were greeted by the slap of a brisk wind. Intah was well ahead, and Ink and Eden were bunched up together at the ridge.

"Hold up," said Eden.

Intah turned around and rode back to join them. She slipped from her horse and untied the oilcloth coat she'd bought from Ink. As she pulled it on over her jacket, her inner sleeve rode up inside the arm. She pushed her hand inside to retrieve it and her bracelet was revealed.

"I seen that before," said Ink.

Eden nodded. "On Aiden."

"Tried to get him to let me cut it off. The wrist was swole up from a fall and the thing was cutting into him something bad. But he'd have none of it."

Eden's throat closed at the thought of Aiden sacrificing his comfort for the sake of the bracelet. She tended to her sleeve, stepped up onto a stirrup and swung her leg over the horse. They turned upslope again, riding close by until Eden found the words she wanted. It was torture to speak of the bracelet, let alone Aiden, for imagination always took her to the place where her heart ended in pieces. Yet her mind was full of questions. She pulled the watch from her pocket and checked the time.

"Sure glad I run into you," said Ink. "Gives me a clear conscience returning that watch."

"A clear conscience is a sure sign of a bad memory." Eden pushed the timepiece back into place. She looked over at Ink who rode close to her side then up to the peaks ahead. "Tell me. Do you know why my brother left camp alone?"

Intah, who rode ahead of them, cocked his head and turned an ear.

"Your brother has a bit of a boy in him, ma'am. Was bound for a bear. Went higher on the mountain thinking, I suppose, the herds were yet near the peaks and a bear might be on their tail. But that's not the way this country works. Turns cold, things move down-mountain, not up. Like we shoulda."

"How'd you find him?"

"Found me. I took to a tree when a bear came through. Couldn't find no good way down until he come along. He was hurtin', but whole."

"What do you mean, whole?" The biting air gnawed at her core.

"Seems he saw the same bear—grizzly the size of Tennessee. Scared his horse into pulling his wrist and shoulder apart. Gashed hisself with a hunting knife—bad."

Eden put a hand to her mouth.

"Gangrene. Did some mending in the army. When blood takes poison, only one way saves a life."

Eden's palms grew moist, and her head, light. "You cut off his arm."

"Done it plenty in the war. Leastways, watched. But he came through fine. Just couldn't get him off the mountain without a horse."

"Where's his own?" asked Intah.

"Says some Indian stole it," said Ink.

Eden and Intah exchanged a glance.

"And I guess it's true because I saw his big bay walk under me with an Indian on top when I was in that tree." Ink gave Intah a hard look. "Fact is, looked a lot like you."

Intah straightened, giving no question mark to his words. "Did he."

"The renegade?" asked Eden.

Intah nodded. "He'll keep to the mountains until spring. No better place to leave the law behind. He has a horse, and two mules to get him through the winter. One to ride, one to eat."

"Well, he plans to ride that one down to the Powder soon as the snow's deep and kill every white man he can," said Ink.

"What makes you think so?" asked Intah.

"'Cause mister Aiden told me the red man told him that. Made me promise to pass it on—to you ma'am. He mighty scared for you."

Eden looked at Intah. "Could he do this?"

"He's done worse."

A chilling unease filled the air. All three pulled their wraps close against its threat as they moved on up the mountain. Gaze ever scanning the hills, the sun dropped over the highest ridge before they spoke again. Eden spurred her horse to a quicker step and sidled up next to Intah.

Worry for all that could be, drove deep within her. "What's ahead do you think?"

"A cold night."

"No, I mean, with that renegade on the loose up here. What will happen?"

Intah's voice was stoic. "What will happen."

Eden was at the end of her patience. "Why do you speak in tongues when I need the comfort of an answer?"

"I can only tell you what I know. Intentions have consequences. The quicker you find that to be true, the sooner you will learn to choose your path, not fall onto it. You cut your own way. You're doing nothing to grasp that."

Eden struggled to line up the facts. "A bad thing, having that Indian in the wood. Doesn't sound to me like he's the kind to spare you just because you're blood."

"Could be. I prefer to think upon what it should be and, for me, him being on the mountain should be no problem."

"Well, if we all cut our own path, then why are you here?"

Intah spoke without looking at her as he passed, continuing up the slope. "It's your journey. And I stepped upon your coach, Madame."

By Silks and Fine Array

Intah had never been so confounded by a woman. He rode well ahead of Ink and Eden, annoyed with himself. Yet, simply laying eyes on Eden brightened his spirit. His inability to convey his faith to her made him wonder what he believed at all. If he couldn't teach, did he really understand? Certain things were truth, for he witnessed them. True riches, though invisible to the eye, lay at the hand of man if he only allowed them. As Blake said, "the countless gold of a merry heart, the rubies and pearls of a loving eye" — Intah had seen such jewels.

Yet, he was sure that the woman defined the circumstances of their travel by those fears she used to define herself. Though he didn't harbor the same concerns, they infected him by association. He couldn't seem to shake them off. Intah was at a loss when it came to showing her meaning, and it nettled him.

Daylight faded as they came upon a meadow of spongy moss. A shallow berm flanked a small stream running through the middle, and a lone moose grazed in the marsh grass at the far end of the field. Intah stopped to watch the animal as it looked up at him, unperturbed. Graceful antlers, as wide as a man is tall, balanced the beast's enormity. Ink and Eden pulled up short behind.

"How much farther?" asked Intah.

"Another two, three hours. Been slower going up than it was coming down, with stopping to blow the horses now and then. Gotta get over the pass, then drop down to Ten Sleep Lake."

"A long way to go to hunt. Why not track on the east side?" asked Eden.

"Lake's long and comes straight down from Cloud Peak. Game's thicker than ticks on a squirrel along a string of water, ma'am," said Ink. "Moose, elk...bear."

Intah looked at the sky. "Won't make that by nightfall. There's a shepherd's cabin close to the top of the pass. We can't travel at night with no moon."

Eden's voice leapt an octave. "We can't leave Aiden another night on the mountain."

"I ain't going another step past that shelter until dawn," said Ink.

Eden straightened. "But you know he has a better chance the sooner we reach him."

"You've forgotten the bear on this mountain. They don't usually hunt at night, but a wounded animal is hard to read." A bear preparing for winter would feed its hunger twenty-four hours a day, but Intah saw no need to relay the information. What he said instead was the truth of it. "If the bear has its way with us, there'll be no one left to find your brother."

Eden's voice approached a whisper. "And if he has his way with Aiden?"

"Aiden will no longer need us at all."

The men were silent.

"Well—I won't be going alone, then," said Eden.

"If he's made it alive this long, chances are he'll be the same in the morning," said Intah. No use putting them all in danger. He would get them settled in the cabin, and go on alone in the darkness. The mountains were his home. Ink was not necessary to finding the camp.

The cabin was dilapidated pine plank, but sound. What little snow remained from the latest fall slipped its way down the roof and dripped into a puddle at the front door. A generous pile of wood lay stacked nearby, left by the last shepherd to pass through as payment forward to the next occupant, who'd not pass by again until late spring. They walked through the door as the hinges creaked.

Inside stood a cot, a wood stove, and a smooth stone fireplace. Two chairs sat at the hearth, and a window to one side allowed the last of the afternoon light to wash one wall of the room. The air hung tart with creosote used to keep the fleas and ticks at bay. Black stains coated a mattress standing in the corner. Intah walked to the fireplace and set one hand above the embers. Warm.

"Keep the door open as we make the fire," said Eden, "to shoo the stench away."

"I'll fetch wood," said Ink.

Intah scooped up a handful of tepid ash with his palm and with it came a flood of memories. He pulled a finger through the cinders, yearning to heal. So long since that day, yet the wound was still a hot brand to his flesh. And in the blur of pain he still saw the face of the scout on the hill above the ruin—and his blood ran hot.

Intah brushed the ash from his hands. He'd not raise the question of who had been in the cabin last. Intah tended to the animals outside with one eye to the woods behind him. He was sure with the horses grazing near the cabin the thief would be warned away. His horse would not be coaxed to the hand of another. The others would follow that cue. The search party would all be gone by morning, and wouldn't be back.

Ink carried load after load of firewood into the cabin as Intah unpacked the horses. With the pulling of a last log, Ink yelled.

Eden came running from the shelter. "What's happened?"

"Curse of a splinter, that's all." Ink cradled his hand.

"Let me see." Eden took his hand in hers. "Deep, too. Come in. I'll tend to it."

Soon the smoke of a blazing fire masked the stink of creosote and the door was closed to garner the heat. Intah brought the bag of apples in from the cold as Eden used a needle to dig for the imbedded shard.

Intah placed the fruit on a table. "Where did you find the needle?"

Eden spoke without looking up. "The cupboard."

"Shepherds leave all sorts of stores for predicaments and what. Sometimes, a secret squirreled away, too—a bottle of some sort—tonic or whiskey." Ink raised an eyebrow as though he might look.

"Best left for the shepherds," said Intah.

Eden continued to tend Ink's hand. She hadn't hesitated to help the man, though she didn't know much about him. His color didn't sway the aid she offered. Intah knew no white women beyond those who had been taken into his tribe, but the ones he'd heard of were reluctant to take the hand of anyone but a white man. Yet Eden had done it twice in one day. She may have a stubborn streak, but she had compassion in her, as well. That would make all the difference if she were genuine in wanting to learn his ways.

They dined on the crisp fruit and slices of grilled salt pork that Ink packed for the trip. By the time they finished, the cabin smelled of bacon, and their bellies were full.

Eden stood to peel off the oilcloth coat and the short jacket beneath. Her form, golden in the firelight.

"Never supposed I'd be warm again." Eden set about unbuttoning her flannel shirt.

Underneath she wore another blouse. When she stepped in front of the blaze, the outline of her skin and undergarments behind its fine linen weave stood against the flickering light. Her hair matched the fire, swirling in reddish flames about her head, beckoning something deep within him. Eden pointed to the large bundle Ink had brought in from the horse.

"Would there be a pot in that pack?"

"Yes, ma'am," said Ink.

"Well, if you bring it I can make some tea."

"Don't have none of that."

Eden pulled a fist full of sage from a pocket in the oilcloth coat.

"But I do. Picked it along the way straight from the horse's back. Just the thing to fortify us for the coming day. I mean to be out that door at dawn."

Ink fetched a small tin pot and she looked at Intah as she poured some water from a canteen into the pot and scattered the sage on top, stirring the brew with her index finger.

"Wise to pick it. It grows no higher on the mountain." Impressed by her resourcefulness, Intah gave her more credit for the day.

Eden leaned over, setting the pot inside the fireplace where the flames would heat the water. "I'm not good for nothing after all, is that it?" She turned to face Intah with a crooked smile.

The braid and bear claw slipped from beneath her blouse to lie outside the garment as she straightened. Eden placed her hand around it and returned Intah's stare as he nodded but said nothing.

"It's gotten me this far, hasn't it?" said Eden.

"What's that?" Ink asked.

"Bear medicine," Intah said. He was pleased that she had taken the luck from the door latch. No doubt, the talisman had kept her safe.

"Guardian in the wild," said Eden.

"And much more," said Intah.

"Indeed," said Eden. "As fine a braid I've never seen. Even the raw side is flat. Can you show me how to do it?"

"No," said Intah. "But I know one who can."

Ink gawked at the great claw beneath the braid. "Never seen a bigger nail from a beast. You see him?"

"Didn't have the pleasure," said Intah.

"How did it come to you?" Eden reached for the pot of steaming water, poured some into three tin cups, and served them around.

"It is passed from holy man to holy man in my tribe. Dreams of the people are told by the etching at the top." Intah reached his fingers to the rim of the claw. "Bear is the keeper of dreams. It collects the teachings until the dreamer awakens to them. That was my charge."

"Holy man?" asked Ink.

"Shaman," said Eden.

"A white word, but you know of such things?" Intah asked.

"When you move to a foreign land, you read all you can about its people. Indians included." Eden sipped her tea.

What she might have read, Intah wondered. His own mother came with odd ideas about the ways of the western tribes. For her part, she had been quick to learn otherwise.

"How has bear come to be guardian of the wild?" Eden asked.

"Her strength is the power of introspection. Bear does not force. She is not lightning in the face of a threat. Quick action is often wrong, especially in the wild. Bear collects information, takes it to her cave, thinks upon it, and then decides. She tells us that dreams are realized by going within, and the wilderness of the spirit understood by looking beyond what we see."

Eden gazed at Intah. "Through the eye and not with it?"

"Yes." Perhaps the woman learned after all. "Amulets can be important medicine."

"How so?" asked Ink.

"My brother, of a different mother, was given many amulets before he was born, to invite warrior spirits to him. He has always been a warrior. My white mother bestowed no amulets to call the spirits to me. The conqueror was never invited in. A gentler spirit coaxes me down the stream instead of headlong into the current."

"I wish I'd had the bear claw when I last came to the Bighorn," said Eden.

"When was that?" Ink asked.

"Eight years ago. My husband brought us up the hill to hunt. But all we found was the rage of a grizzly. Maybe the same one who treed you," said Eden, looking at Ink. "Was a giant. Killed three horses and a man. I vowed then the mountains weren't for me."

"Figured you'd die?" asked Ink.

"Not then," Eden said, shaking her head. "Scared as I was." She looked into the fire. "I've had a picture in my mind of how I'll die, and it wasn't by the fury of a great bear."

Intah stared at Eden. "How then?"

"I see myself on a mountain perch—the Highlands, I think. An old withered woman, fading away to sleep."

"I see myself too high to get down in one piece," said Ink. "Have dreams of the same—falling. Guess that's why the prospect of a roost runs me cold."

"And you?" Eden asked Intah. "How do you see your end?"

Intah's face warmed in the firelight. "By silks and fine array."

Eden shook her head. "Have you memorized the whole of Blake, sir?"

He looked into her green eyes and smiled. "Only the parts that matter." He stood and wrapped the bear robe around his shoulders.

Eden cocked her head as if waiting for him to tell her what those parts were. "Where are you going?"

"Over the pass. I can find the way."

"Straight west, I figure," said Ink.

"In the black of dark?" Certain that their success was bound to Intah, Eden added, "Why can we not go together?"

"I know how to travel the Bighorn at night. And you're right. The quicker your brother is reached the better his chances. One horse can pass without the interest of as many night creatures than would three tramping up the mountain." He opened the cabin door. "Bolt the door, then come along at daylight. And keep the rifle close. There's no way to know who is on the mountain—or why."

There was no question in Eden's voice. "You think he's here."

"My advice is to shoot first. A red-headed scalp used to be quite a prize."

Intah couldn't depend on the other horses to raise the alarm if a stranger approached. He fingered the heavy deadbolt. It would do to hold them in safety if someone tried to break through. The one window in the cabin was too tiny to admit anything larger than a bobcat. The door was the only way in.

Eden followed him outside to stand under the overhang of a tiny porch. Intah mounted his horse. He glanced at her, the curls of her warm breath setting a halo about her head in the wicked cold, and his heart beat a little quicker.

He found the North Star, then turned the horse west, riding straight up the mountainside into the dark of a savage night.

The warmth of Eden's gaze was on him until well after he was certain she could see him no more.

Telling a Tale

The buckled carcasses of possum and ground squirrels washed out of their dens littered the banks of the receding river. The second day the air was putrid with rotting flesh heaved up at water's edge, but as the week wore on, an array of critters arrived to scour the carnage. Each dawn brought the riverside closer to its usual dreary dress of brittle grass and brown dust. But the air was sweet and cold.

Maddie walked the river from where the Crazy Woman fed the Powder at Eden's ranch. She kept a pistol in the pocket of her sheepskin coat and rested her hand on its cold handle as she paced the shore. In the other pocket was a small package for Eden with a foreign address. Cleve delivered it to the farm. Maddie reckoned it held the eyeglasses Eden had ordered months ago. A thing her friend might never have the chance to wear.

When she reached the Crazy Woman, she followed its frenzied way up through the cottonwoods. The creek weaved a foolish path. Its various arteries carved into the soil, telling a tale of its frantic searchings for the river below, as though the stream lost its mind year to year.

"Crazy, indeed." Maddie picked her way up the trail and across the wooden bridge to Eden's house.

No smoke escaped from the chimney atop the sod roof. Jenny was sure to be up. Maddie scanned the pastures hoping to see her daughter bouncing behind the small herd of mares, urging them to the paddock for hay. But the mares stood in a scattered bunch at the end of the field. The door of the cabin was open, not a thing she cottoned seeing after impressing on Jenny the importance of bolting the door behind her every time she entered. The vision quickened her pace and, by the time she reached the house, she was breathless. She kept to the side of the structure, out of sight until she reached the entry, then pushed the squeaky door full open.

Maddie leaned in the same moment a hand laid upon her shoulder. She jumped and turned. "Good God, child."

Jenny stood before her, a goat on each side. "Just comin' in. Been tryin' to gather those chickens. They's as wild as can be. Cold's comin'. Should be in the henhouse."

"Well, mind you leave the door closed."

Jenny walked over the threshold, goats behind her. "What's the difference, Ma? If harm's comin' my way, it'll just as soon come inside as out."

She was right, but the habit of closing the door was a good one no matter what. "Make me feel better, Jen, and do as I say. What in blazes is those goats doin' inside?"

Jenny scratched one of the goats. "Tame. Ain't they cute?"

"First time they leave a pile for you, I reckon you won't find them so. As much as Missus Rose likes 'em, I don't expect she invites 'em in her house." Maddie stepped into the cabin.

"But, the floor's already got plenty of dirt on it."

"Dirt comes from the sod, not the goats. Why ain't you swept up?"

"Had enough to do outside. Plum tired after it all."

"Get used to it, girl. Age doesn't make it any easier. Eden likes things in their place. Mind you, keep it that way."

Maddie eyed the china dishes stacked in neat rows on the cabinet, and the bowl half full of apples, dead center of the table. Everything as particular as could be in a sod shanty. Except for the mass of Eden's curls on the floor. The breath went out of her and thoughts crackled in her head. Had Eden come to her senses and doubled back only to have her uncommon scalp taken as a heathen's gewgaw?

Maddie pointed at the hair. "What's that?" She searched the floor for traces of blood.

"Expect Missus Rose's hair. Scissors on the table got hair in 'em."

Maddie swore in relief. "God almighty."

"Yes, ma'am." Jenny pushed the she-goats through the door. "Don't know why she'd have a mind to cut that handsome hair."

An odd sensation came over Maddie as though the curls were all that remained of a cocoon, its butterfly broken free.

Jenny opened the door. "Got to bring that colt in from the pasture. Shoulda been done a few weeks ago, I reckon. He's botherin' those mares. Since he's the one stallion Missus Rose got left, can't afford to git him kicked in the wrong place. Wanna help?"

"You know 'bout such things, missy?" Maddie grinned at her daughter. She pulled Eden's package from a pocket and placed it on the table.

"Any fool can see what he wants and what they don't. Think I'm too young to notice?"

She looked at Jenny. Her daughter's figure had started to round out from the boyish shape of youth. "You know I was married to yer pa 'bout your age?"

"Who's gonna marry me?" Jenny asked as though there couldn't be a man in all creation that would find her worth a husband.

"Oh, like that colt outside, there's some feller won't take no for an answer." Maddie smiled. "Off you'll go and leave me."

"Aw, Ma."

Maddie looked at the beauty her daughter had become. For the first time she understood her own mother's grief when Maddie rolled away westward. The one thing certain was change. One day her youngest would head down the road, her pa would be gone, and she'd be alone.

Maddie stepped back. "What would you really think if I married Cleve?"

Jenny gazed at the floor as though testing the notion in her mind before she spoke. "Be nice to have a sane man 'round, I guess." She looked up at her mother. "But the house'd get smaller."

"Guess we'll have to find you a husband, then, to make more room." Maddie winked. Time to start looking. Maybe get Jenny work in town. Maybe with Cleve.

Jenny looked stunned. "Never shoulda mentioned them horses."

Maddie headed for the door. "Let's get that colt outta the way of those mares."

The two walked out into the pasture in different directions, at first trying to cut the colt from the rest of the herd. Then they ran from opposite sides, pushing the horses toward the small paddock to be separated.

The Bighorn range loomed in the distance. The top half stood obscured in billowy clouds, a dusting of snow edging the trees below. The sight gripped Maddie. If Eden wasn't washed downriver, she sat on ice. Dead or alive, either prospect was cold and lonesome. Worry pushed Maddie's feet close behind the herd. With the last pony, she closed the gate.

"Can you cut him out from there?" she asked Jenny, who stood inside the paddock.

"Sure can," Jenny said as she raised her arms to shoo the mares aside.

The mares shuffled away, but the colt turned and lunged, missing her hip by an inch. Maddie shrieked and Jenny turned as the colt took another pass. He grabbed fast to Jenny's arm. She was a rag doll between his teeth.

Maddie pulled the gun from her pocket and pointed it, her hand trembling, daughter being tossed in the air. When Jenny fell back to earth, Maddie took aim and shot. The colt collapsed in a heap as the panicked mares scattered around him. Jenny hit the ground with a thud, got to her feet and ran to the fence. She was up and over in one motion, but her upper arm missed a lump of flesh, and blood rolled down over her elbow to the dirt.

The colt convulsed and was still.

Jenny wailed, "You kilt him." She stood at her mother's shoulder, pulling at the air in long huffs.

"I did. And you're alive." Tears clouded her eyes. The last time she'd been as scared was when the boar pig chased baby Oran into the barn.

Maddie pulled the girl to her and hugged her hard. She sometimes wanted to take a rest from motherhood. The duty was nothing but fret.

She took Jenny by her good arm and led her to the cabin, sat at the table and washed her wound. A good chunk of the arm was torn away, but not enough to reveal bone. There'd be a scar, and Jenny'd be off milking for a while for the pain of it, but that was all. She dressed the arm with strips of linen from an old tablecloth, grateful the damage wasn't worse.

Jenny's voice was a whisper. "Ma, you kilt the colt."

"Ain't nothin' I wouldn't kill to protect you, child. Don't you know that?"

"But Missus Rose's yer best friend. What she gonna do without a stallion?"

Maddie looked at her daughter, hard. "We all has choices, Jen. Sometimes a thing needs killin'. She'd have done the same in my shoes. And you'll do the same for yer young'uns. That's what a ma does."

Jenny winced, tears streaming down her cheeks. "Hurts somethin' bad, ma."

Maddie looked through the open door to the paddock across the creek. "I'm gonna let them mares back out to pasture, then take some oil and catch fire to that carcass."

"Why?"

"So critters don't bother it none. Wolves would be on it by dark. With a taste for horseflesh there'd be nothing but hooves in the pasture come sunup." Maddie inspected Jenny's dressing. "And you're comin' back with me. I got medicine to put on that arm. Let the chickens be damned. Horses, too. Get rid of that fresh meat in the yard, reckon the mares can fend for theirselves if they're left alone."

Maddie noted the dry grass in the pasture beyond as she crossed the yard. Lucky the colt was dropped in the dirt of the paddock; otherwise, there'd be no way she'd start a fire. But the wind was calm. Without a breeze, it was safe.

Maddie directed her daughter with a pointed finger toward the barn. "Find me a shovel."

She followed Jenny, located a small drum of lamp oil and carried it to the paddock. She collected a pile of dry wood and laid the fodder up well around the fallen horse. As she poured all of the oil over the whole mess, Maddie noticed the barrel of the colt rise once. She set the drum down and leaned over the carcass with care. The colt's head reared up at her, teeth bared, and the animal screeched as a convulsion took its body and it collapsed. Maddie screamed as she leapt back and, with shaking hands, struck several matches and flung them the way of the colt. The flame burst up easy and bright, even in the daylight, following the course of the oil. The smoke was thick and black, and a pungent odor of burning hair and sweet, roasted flesh invaded the afternoon. Jenny ran from the barn with a shovel in her hand.

"Give it here," said Maddie.

She set about scooping a trough around the colt to stop the fire from spreading. When she finished, Jenny stood at her side. The fire raged hot and strong against Maddie's face even as her anger cooled. She'd torched the one thing that might have saved her friend from giving up the ranch and returning to Britain. Yet, nothing to be done different. She had no choice but to shoot the nasty stallion. If it hadn't done her daughter in, the demon would take the opportunity with Eden. She was doing a favor. If Eden returned she'd see it the same. Surely, she would.

The hard work of the flames did little to dent the carcass. The colt was big for his age. It was clear Eden had given him extra feed to bulk him up in preparation for the freeze and anticipation of breeding a slew of outside mares next spring.

Maddie was eager to get Jenny home and it was a long walk. She turned her gaze back to the fire. It was an uneasy feeling to leave it burning, but the blaze would smolder through the night given the hide on the animal. No time to watch it more. Jenny's wound needed tending before infection laid in. She wouldn't see the girl lose an arm to such. She took the shovel that Jenny fetched, and dug a second shallow trench in the hardpan around the fire. She reckoned it would have to do.

She returned to the cabin, gathered up her daughter, and they started off, the pair of she-goats bouncing behind them as they beat a dusty path toward home.

Chance Will Come

Dawn's tinge had reached the perimeter of the ruined camp when Intah arrived. The warm glow of an oil lamp gave his heart a leap as he expected Eden's brother yet alive. He pulled his horse up short when he spotted the silhouette of a tall, heavy-coated man.

The figure was still, stooped over a pile of canvas, snow, a drifting swarm of whiteflies. Two mules and a bay horse stood to one side, switching at the frost with their thick tails. Intah believed the stranger to be Aiden, standing, uninjured in the middle of the camp. Yet, something was familiar to him beyond what Intah imagined might be a resemblance to Eden. A certain turn of the man's chin, and the way he tossed his head as he threw back a ground cloth left Intah unsettled.

The big bay nickered at the sight of Intah's horse at the rise of the slope. The man turned in one revolution, widening his eyes as if to bring the full vision before him into view. He uttered a short, contemptuous snicker. Intah pushed his horse forward.

"So, this is where you ran to," said the man.

"I could say the same."

"Brother, running is all we've done for as long as I can remember. No more."

"Hear you plan to clear the Powder."

Black Fist was an apparition in the faint light. The man had filled out some with time. Though he was several years older than Intah, he had the strong look of a man half his age. He wore a buckskin coat and wool trousers—bounty from the dead trapper.

"News travels." Black Fist turned his back to Intah and pawed through the canned goods and packs of dried beef laying under the canvas.

All the years, and the man hadn't lost the edge to his voice nor his brutal spirit. "I'd think your fury would have burned out by now. What feeds it?"

"This will do till spring," said Black Fist as he hoisted up a sack of flour.

"And then?"

"No business of yours. You made your choice to keep your head hidden."

Intah's tone sharpened. "The choice was to hold on to what I had left."

"In retreat."

"Freedom."

"Then, brother, we are of the same mind. Only I choose freedom on the Powder."

"Our minds have never held a single similar thought. It's a futile path you take."

"I don't question yours."

Anger nibbled at Intah. "No, you curse it."

His brother picked over the stores left abandoned by the hunters and packed them into saddlebags on the stolen trapper's mount. Intah considered the dead man in the valley below, throat slashed for the luck of two mules.

"You do not remember who you are."

Black Fist turned to Intah, eyes of coal, words hot tar. "Because I never knew who I was."

Intah had always known that the man burned in a rage fed by fear, but he'd dreamt, as well, that a time might come when his brother no longer shook his fist at the wind. The man would never allow a better feeling to cross his mind. And in that, he was lost.

"Was a man left in this camp, alive?" said Intah.

"Empty when I got here. Except for a cold fire and a set of warm tracks. Big ones." He pointed to broad, deep tracks yet visible beneath the fresh snow. "Same grizzly I put a bullet in last week, I wager. Why do you care?"

Intah weighed the wisdom of letting Black Fist know of the others on the mountain. If he came across them, he was certain to bring them to ruin whether Intah was with them or not. He could not bank on even one small bone of mercy in the man.

Intah stared at the man he once called brother. "Where are you headed?"

"Lake below Cloud Peak to set some snares before sunup. You won't see me, if that's what you're wondering."

Top of the mountain, the direction away from Ink and Eden. Intah drew a long breath of wintry air. The two stood still for a moment as a gentle snow dusted their shoulders and ebony hair. Both considering the same thing: what next might come.

Intah mused about killing Black Fist right there. Both the man's weapons were in their saddle scabbards. If he hit him square, it would be quick and done with.

Black Fist seemed to read his brother's mind. "Don't want to take the chance of crossing paths again?" He spread his arms out at each side. "Shoot me now."

"What you've done is no concern of mine anymore." Intah tried to chase away the fury rising at the face of the man who erased the lives of so many. Killing him would bring no one back. Intah stopped taking human lives long ago. Murder was a fleeting satisfaction.

Black Fist laughed, then spoke without remorse. "Well, I'm sure the chance will come again." The man cinched up the saddle on one of the horses. "Look where chance has brought you. From ashes to a mountaintop. You never thought you'd lay eyes on me again."

He walked to Intah and offered him a package of jerky. "For your trip, whereever it's taking you."

Intah kept his hands on the reins, turned his horse, and followed the tracks of the bear toward the river.

The hooves of his brother's horse and mules echoed against the granite as they clamored up the mountain.

The Heart Makes No Promise

Eden slept hard but woke early. Her breath blew white against the dark timber walls as dawn came up. The fire lay dead and Ink snored softly inside his bedroll. She wriggled from beneath the elk skins, slid open the bolt, and cracked the door. Long icicles had formed from the snowmelt overnight. The freeze was slow coming, but took full hold.

Daylight arrived tentative and pale behind a thick cover of clouds. The horses lay at close hand by the shelter, back-to-back, exchanging warmth in the harsh cold, respiration steaming overhead. Eden closed the door and pulled on her canvas coat against the chill. She poked the fire for embers, fed a small spark with dry tinder, and placed a piece of wood on top.

Ink stirred beneath his cover. "Wager by the nip there be snow."

"Aye. We'll have a cup of hot tea and be off. I've no wish to be snowbound on this mountain."

Ink slipped out of the bedroll, took two apples from the hearth and offered one to Eden. "Got bacon, too."

"Fry it then. I'll take no time to eat again today. As soon as I reach Aiden, we'll be turning for home."

When the water boiled and tea steeped in their cups, Ink used the same pot to fry some thick pieces of pork. Eden sat quietly, not speaking her angst at the road ahead. When they finished the meal, they packed up and readied their horses. At mounting, Ink turned to the cabin, stood his horse still for a moment and glowered.

"What are you doing?" asked Eden.

"All the time I spent on the mountain, I ain't never seen this lost cabin 'fore."

"Many things on this trip I've not seen before, and many things I hope I'll not soon see again." She turned her horse up the slope and Ink followed.

Wilderness was an ulcer, eating at her will to move forward. Every hour Aiden spent alone decreased life's favor. She damned the weather. The penetrating cold was an ice-wall slowing her resolve.

She and Ink rode up through a wide, golden meadow into lodgepole pines strewn across the slope in a lanky swath, dotted with the spark of late-leaved aspens. Ink took the lead, and at the edge of the wood where trees opened up once again to a wide glen, he stopped.

Ink pointed to a pine standing close by. "See there?"

Eden pulled up behind him. Her horse nibbled at the rump of Ink's mount. She set her sight on the aim of Ink's finger. Long scratches laid deep into the pine as if someone had whittled a series of perfect stripes into the tree. The butternut color of fresh wood lay exposed next to the rough grey bark.

"Bear," said Ink.

Eden said nothing. Ink moved his horse into the glen and Eden followed.

The first gesture of the storm was snow in sporadic tiny flecks as they crossed the field. A meager stream split the sweep of meadow, mounds of grass skirting its trail, and the ground nearby the hard, bumpy surface of bog gone to freeze under the horses' feet. Broad prints pressed deep into the sandy bank. Eden pointed them out to Ink. Forefoot claws were a clutch of arrows pointing toward the mountaintop.

Ink nodded. "Grizzly."

They pushed through the steam. On the other side Ink paused again, looking down.

"That's as big a pone of scat I seen," he said. "Recent."

The large pile of shiny black dung mounded in the stiff grass was topped by a dusting of powdery snow.

236

"Black with blood. Bear's been eatin' meat."

Eden looked to Ink's eyes for a sign of hope. "Like an elk or such."

Ink returned her gaze, then looked away. "Or such."

They continued up the slope, through row after row of pines and palomino aspen, beneath the mounting snowfall. As the sun reached its highest point on the other side of the clouds, they reached the perimeter of the modest camp where Ink had left Eden's brother. Trees stood etched against the luminous winter sky and snow accumulation allowed horse hooves to blot a trail behind them. The air hung thick with dry flakes, driven to and fro by an indecisive breeze. The tracks of Intah's unshod horse lay muted but recognizable, as was the sepia ash of a once blazing fire that sat protected from the snow by an adjacent pine. No sign of Intah, nor Aiden.

Ink leaned over the horn of his saddle. "This is where I left him."

Eden slipped off her horse and knelt by the ashes, feeling for any heat still living beneath. The remains lay as bleak as the air. She scanned the camp around her. A canvas tarp, blood-stained and rumpled to one side of the exhausted fire called the past, and up Eden's agonizing vision came, like an eaten meal, spewing across the camp: the blood, the fever of escape, the terror.

She squeezed shut her eyes, but the specter lay clear. Was it memory? Or had it been a second sight? Had she seen this moment, felt this hour? She fell on the idea as hard as she yearned that a third sight might spring forth allowing her to see beyond and grasp a meaning from it all.

Eden opened her eyes, hoping the slate before her be cleansed with the pure snowfall. Instead her eye caught a familiar brindle peeking from the bloodied tarp—a book. She walked to the canvas, throwing it back to find an assortment of canned goods and a leather-bound book—Aiden's journal. She stooped to pick it up and held the book to her breast.

"Wrote every day in that thing," said Ink. "And when he couldn't no more, had me do the same."

Eden nodded. Aiden made a daily entry since he'd joined her some months ago. She'd longed to know what he'd written, his true thoughts about the West and the hardship he'd found upon arriving at the calamity of Rose Ranch. She looked to the ground as she rubbed her mouth with a frosty hand.

Huge bear prints traced in the snow and dirt led away from the fire pit. Ink and Eden let their gazes follow the tracks and in their stead stood Intah at some distance, watching them with deliberate eyes. Eden regarded the journal in her hand. She'd not broken her brother's trust. But as long as he lived he'd never leave it behind—unless he'd left a clue inside to his whereabouts.

She drew a quick breath and thumbed to the last sentence of the final entry written in Aiden's hand: *All I've come to know in this desolate wilderness is that life holds no guarantee, and the heart makes no promise.*

The truest feelings of an unhappy man. From the moment he'd joined her, she'd known the West hadn't suited him. He'd masked his angst well enough, but his voice took an edge every time a wolf howled or the prints of a mountain lion graced the riverbank. The land might be as familiar a landscape as Scotland, but it was stagnant water in his stomach. Eden hoped he would become used to the ranch in time. Yet, underneath it all, he wanted to purge himself of the whole misguided visit.

And he had. Her eyes burned under the weight of concession. The heart makes no promise. The same way she'd crossed an ocean into a life turned to hell—just as her heart had forsaken its promise to Hugh.

"Told him I'd keep to the stream to find my way down to where the pass cuts through," said Ink. "Maybe he tried to follow, ma'am."

Eden nodded, but the wind was kicked from her lungs. Aiden's final entry amounted to the musings of a man resigned to death. When Intah reached her side, he placed a heavy hand on her shoulder.

Ink pointed. "Follow the water."

"Yes," said Intah. "I rode upstream but found nothing."

Eden pushed the journal into her coat, and the three mounted, riding to the edge of the lake then turning downstream. Snow raced ahead of them, pushed sideways by a furious gale falling fast from the peaks above. A howling to rival wolves sang through the woods. They followed the shore a good distance until the lake escaped into a wide stream. Intah dismounted and stooped to fill their canteens.

His gaze scoured the water's edge. The horses waded in for a drink. Intah was a mere outline in snow falling so thick, the opposite bank faded behind its curtain. He turned his head upstream, then down, and froze as though turned to marble.

Eden was quick to follow his line of sight to a fragment of sand outstretched above the water, midstream, a few yards away, shielded from the falling snow by a broad tree. On the bar— shreds of clothing. Below, shrouded by thin snow at the edge of the water, but undeniable in its form, lay an arm. A faint, copper-colored cord traced the wrist of the dismembered limb.

Eden's head lightened as blood drained from her cheeks. In the gale, no one but she bore witness to her solitary word. "No."

Not mindful of the water below, she slipped from the saddle. In despair, her knees gave away. She crumpled into the gelid stream. The cold burned her skin as it soaked her clothes through to her waist and wicked up her shirt. Her mind allowed nothing. Tears would not come. Too horrified to cry, her body was the fragile half of a shell, empty of all but the memory of being whole.

Intah called over the howling wind and pulled her to him with one arm. "You'll freeze." Eden clung to Intah's legs as he shouted, "We can't stay here."

She wailed, "I can't leave him."

Intah held her tight against him. "That is no longer your brother."

She wept, the rush of glacial water numbing her legs. Pellet snow pummeled her cheeks in the biting wind. As though God himself demanded her surrender.

Eden pushed from Intah's arms and raised her wavering voice over the wind. "He deserves burial."

"And he shall have it. But get up now. If you don't warm up we'll be burying you both."

She gazed to the bar at the last of her brother, then up at Intah. She searched his eyes for some sense of what had happened. In the reflection, she recognized a kindred soul, alone. All hearts broke the same way. In his eyes was something she couldn't refuse. As much as she wanted to curl up on the bank and give herself to the cold, in him was the desire to go on, though she didn't know why.

With Intah's help she stood, leading her horse to the rocky shore to join Ink.

Intah mounted his horse and forded the broad stream to retrieve what was left of Aiden.

Eden looked at Ink. Perhaps he was confused when he told her of the one he'd amputated. Her voice rang out over the wind at the chance it was true. "Could it be the one you buried?"

Ink shook his head, staring across the river at the braid around the wrist of the dismembered limb. His voice shook as he removed his hat. "That weren't the one I took."

The truth erased all hope, just as the mountain had erased her brother. She straightened. "Put your hat on, Ink. No use us both dying of the cold."

Intah splashed back through the river and dismounted. "I'll wrap what's left and put it in a tree."

Eden stared at him in disbelief. "That's far from proper."

"Ground's too hard to dig," said Intah. He pulled his bearskin around her body.

Eden looked at the ice-covered limb, tears freezing to her cheek as they fell. From her coat, she pulled the blue baby blanket she'd been using as a pillow. "Use this to wrap him, will you? And I want the bracelet."

Intah took the blanket and walked into the pines. Eden watched. He unhooked the fine gold clasp, put the bracelet in his pocket, and wrapped the limb in blue, knotting two ends around the middle. Hurtling one end of a rope over a high pine bow, he tied the other end to the funerary and hoisted it into the branches out of sight, tying the rope end off on the slender trunk.

Ink studied the limb lifting through the gloom of the blizzard. His voice wavered in the gale as he shook his head. "Like an enemy flag bein' raised on a taken hill. Didn't win this one. Tried."

Eden said nothing. She pulled the bearskin tight around her. Ink whimpered beneath the shouting gale. She looked at him. The man risked his life to be on the mountain with them. Without him Aiden might have been among the flock of those disappeared on the Bighorn, with no end to their story. Eden's heart could never have rested with that unknown. Trembling under the shock of cold and heartbreak, she pulled Aiden's watch from her soggy pocket. She turned the gold over and over in her palm to memorize the fine engraving on its rim and the blush of its case.

"You did the right thing," said Eden. "Twice."

Ink stopped his sniffling. "Ma'am?"

"You took the watch to buy a horse for Aiden, and then stole it back for return." Eden pushed her horse next to Ink's. Reaching for his gloved hand, she placed the timepiece in his palm. Her voice quaked. "Aiden was a good man. He would have given it to you for your trouble."

Ink closed his hand around the watch without saying a word, but the look in his eyes told Eden he had never received such a fine thing.

"You're a good man, too, Ink."

"You're the first to say it, ma'am." He looked up into the canopy of pines overhead, his voice a whisper. "Don't know how I can be so good if it all turned out so bad."

Intah rejoined them, barking to Ink above the wind. "Follow me. We can't see to get off the mountain today. No telling how long the snow will last. My shelter is nearby. We can wait it out."

Eden shouted, quaking under her wet clothing despite the heavy fur around her shoulders. "We can't see through the snow."

"My horse can find the way," said Intah. "You're freezing. Get off and ride with me for warmth."

Eden slid off her horse and Intah pushed her onto his mount, joined her, and drew up the reins.

"Ain't spendin' another minute than I have to on this mountain," yelled Ink. "No thanks. I'll take my chances. Follow the water like I did 'fore."

"What about the horse you lent me?" Eden asked. "I'll need it to come home."

Ink shouted through the wind. "Take him. Was meant for your brother, anyways. If you ever get back to Buffalo, you can settle up with the man who owns him."

"You can't see well enough, and your horse doesn't know these mountains," Intah called to Ink. "Don't be foolish."

"That bear has a taste for man, and I'll wager he cottons to the flavor. I'm gettin' outta this wood."

"Mind the ledges at the base of the mountain, and what you learned about the loose rock," said Intah. "There's deceit beneath fresh snow."

Ink pointed his horse down the slope. The storm consumed him, leaving large snowflakes, a swirl of ivory buzzards in his wake.

Above the Wind Somewhere

Intah turned his horse up the mountain and gave him his head. The horse spent his life on the Bighorn, running loose when not carrying a man. The way home was as certain as a salmon knows its way to the crystal water of its birth. Intah held fast to the reins of Eden's following horse. Less sure of the course, it pulled against the lead and Intah's arm ached at the strain. But the horse wouldn't bolt. Herd animals preferred company.

The snow went from thick, soft flakes to small, dry barb in the falling temperature and biting wind. Sandpaper on his cheeks, they stung as sure as they'd been slapped. A wolf howled above the wind somewhere ahead. He closed his eyes to the ferocity of the storm. He needn't watch the path. The more he trusted the horse, the better the horse would guide him home.

Eden leaned into his chest. Her drenched clothing soaked through his shirt, making him feel as though they were skin to skin. Her hair smelled fresh from the mountain stream. Though tragic, he gave thanks for the moment that brought her to him, as he did for the fur around them that had changed hands long ago, and the bear that gave it up.

Eden rested against Intah without the stiffness she'd shown him on that first ride. She said nothing. At first a steady shiver suggested she was both cold and overwhelmed by tears. After a while her body calmed as though unconscious in her grief. It occurred to Intah that her voice was too feeble to be heard above the turmoil of the forest rising against the gale. Little else was in his ears but the scream of the wind.

Though his hands were gloved, they were senseless with cold. His feet, hanging well below the bearskin, were ice. Doeskin boots were little salvation from the freeze. He leaned to one side. Eden's feet were also exposed—and her wet boots, shrouded in ice, looked as though they were made of wax. If they didn't reach the cave soon, they both would be short some toes by morning.

He held Eden tight against him and relaxed. The warmth rising from her smelled of salt and tallow from beneath the bearskin, but sweeter than both. The heady scent took him back to the camp long ago on a riverbank west of the mountains—not to his wife, but to his small son, lying beneath a raccoon skin, asleep at his side in the shelter. Every breath returned him to that moment when life lay simple and charmed.

When the prairie was black with buffalo, before the blue-coated soldiers and men who killed for nothing but sport turned the land to blood. The blinding snow surrounding him was a blank slate, written with another chance at something of which he'd been robbed.

Eden's hand fell clear of the bearskin for a moment and Intah looked at the braid on her wrist. He had not understood its significance until he'd seen the same on what was left of Aiden. A strong bond, siblings, whether in love or in hate. The pain of leaving a home, to abandon everything and cling to one person for strength and reason, all clear. The old woman in the cave was that to Intah. Though Eden might offer something more, he knew he could never leave the old woman—and the old woman would never leave Ten Sleep Canyon.

One way to satisfy his appetite for Eden, and the odds did not favor the result he craved. Best to push the hunger from his mind. After all, she had a man to keep her on the plains. He concentrated instead on the movement of the horse and the pleasure of the moment with Eden close against him.

Intah opened his eyes when the wind seemed to whip from below. The horse reached the crest of the pass into Ten Sleep and whinnied into the shifting air. As they descended, the wind abated. With darkness full around him, the inviting glow of a fire was a beacon ahead. The horse picked its way along a lean path skirting the canyon wall until the cave entrance welcomed them, tall flames burning at its edge.

An old woman sat close by the warmth. "Heard your horse."

"We have a visitor."

"Yes?"

Intah opened the bearskin. "A white woman from the Powder. Needs warmth and rest, and no questions tonight."

The old woman nodded, but the scowl on her face was not lost on Intah. He braced a semiconscious Eden as he slipped from the horse. The bearskin plopped to the ground as Intah took her into his arms. Grabbing the fur with one hand, he carried her inside the cave. He laid Eden atop a thick, dry pelt and pulled another well over her, then returned to the horse.

"I have a good clutch of apples from the trip and an elk hide, but nothing else," said Intah. The cavern was warm and dry. Firewood Intah had stacked before last leaving lay dwindled to a few pieces. Replenishing the pile would be his first task of the morning.

The old woman's voice was laced with sarcasm. "Woman's not nothing."

Intah ignored her. "I'll be doing the rest of the hunting as soon as the snow melts. Winter hasn't yet pulled on its coat. There's still game in the mountains. Probably have enough put up by now anyway to last us till spring."

Intah pulled the bridle from the horse and the animal moved with the other to one side of the cave entrance, reluctant to join the falling snow.

The old woman spoke again. "And a woman."

Intah put a hand on the old woman's shoulder. "No questions tonight."

The woman had little time for white people. No commingling had come to her tribe as it had to Intah's. He peered into a large clay pot standing at the entrance of the cave. Near empty of the water he'd left. Another chore for the coming day.

The old woman sat down beside the fire, taking up a long, unfinished braid to work, as Intah uncovered Eden's feet and pulled off her stiff, iced-up boots. Her toes were white. Intah took them into his hands and rubbed each foot hard to bring back some color. Soon they were pink, yet still cold to the touch.

He threw off the skin covering Eden. She opened her eyes, gaze unfocused in the direction of the old woman. Intah hesitated a moment, examining her still-damp clothing. He knew what he must do as well as he knew she would chide him for it tomorrow. Wet clothing was an obstacle to warming her.

When Eden closed her eyes, Intah was quick to strip her clothes. He couldn't help but notice everything revealed. The color of her arms and face, browned by the sun, gave way to creamy skin strewn with a thousand speckles; stars, matching the tone of her fiery hair. And his bear claw against her naked breast—as though marking her as his. His. The picture stirred his desire and sparked him to thinking. But as soon as Eden was naked, he covered her again with a dry fur warmed by the fire. She wasn't his to think on.

He pulled Aiden's bracelet from a pocket. Intah placed it on Eden's wrist, above its mate, and then sat at her feet, rubbing their color back until his eyes begged for sleep. The old woman shuffled off, far inside the cavern. Intah took off the muslin shirt dampened by Eden's clothes and walked to the edge of the cave to check the horses. The cold air and wet flakes braced his bare skin even as exhaustion took his mind to improbable places. The wind was dead but the snow fell fast and thick. He supposed several feet by dawn, and the mountain, impassable. Far too early for winter to lay its icy grip on the Bighorn. Yet snow bought him time—and hope.

Though he'd been grateful every day for his life in the canyon, little glimmer of anticipation ever took him, save for the approaching seasons. An unsure grip of expectation tested him. Man waiting on the prairie or not, he mused, if the snow locked her in, there'd be nothing to do but stay. Snow sticking early made for a long, lean season. An even trade.

The horses lay at the entrance to the cavern, out of the falling snow. Intah's nickered as he passed by and the man gave a warm rub to its neck, looking over at Eden burrowed deep into the bearskin at the far end of the cave.

"Well done."

Heaven Rising from Hell

Wind raced around her. Pushed down the canyon, harsh through the pines, drowning out all thought. Over and over. Eden cried out—and awakened on a dense heap of animal skins.

Empty and wrung out, but warm, with no idea to where she was, the obscurity of despair was her shroud. Intah stood at her side.

"It was no dream."

He knelt, touching a warm hand to her forehead. "No."

She closed her eyes, deadened to the world. Aiden's loss no longer raised anything but a brief and hollow question—why? As after every child's death and Hugh's leaving. Protection from disappointment assured by abandoning emotion.

Solace there.

Dreamless sleep came upon her again. From time to time, when she came conscious, she squeezed her eyes shut tight, willing herself back into slumber. But the sun had its own notions, and the fur against her skin warmed her into a sweat. Eyes preferring dark were slow to open.

Bright daylight beamed through the cave entrance. Eden threw back the fur for relief. At once she realized she lay naked, and replaced it. She'd rather have clothing—to seek comfort from the skin of a bear seemed all wrong—but her garments were nowhere in sight. She raised the fur under her chin and sat up to the startle of an old woman sitting at a nearby fire.

How long had she been nude before her?

"Morning," the woman said without turning her eyes from the flames.

Eden's cheeks burned. "Where did you come from?"

"Same place we all do." She threw a stick into the fire.

"Who are you?"

"Blood and bone." She picked up a braid. "Wiconi."

The words set Eden at sea.

As though reading her confusion, Wiconi spoke. "Life."

Still, the description made no sense.

Eden studied the cave's interior. Sparse but efficient, the space held burlaps of apples, baskets and clay lidded jars in neat rows. The space was ripe with the odor of tallow, bear, elk, and boar emanating from salt-speckled meats dry-curing on a far wall. One mound of furred skins—the one on which she lain. She stared at Wiconi. Did Intah and the old woman share more than shelter?

"Where do you sleep?"

The old woman looked Eden's way. "Where do you?"

The discomforting answer prompted Eden to slip out of the covers and rise. "And Intah?"

"River." Wiconi's hands worked the weave.

The old woman's answer fell short of addressing the root of Eden's question. With a knot in her throat, Eden scanned the cave for proof that she'd not shared her bed. A second stack of skins laid up against an opposite wall beyond the fire. Two beds, three people. The knot tightened.

"How long have I slept?"

"Two suns." The old woman tossed a bundle of small leaves onto the fire and white smoke crawled through the air to touch the cavern overhang.

"And my clothing?"

The woman's voice was unconcerned. "Missing?"

Eden pulled the fur up to her neck. "They were wet."

A sweet scent of burning sage reminded Eden of high church service on a fair Scottish Sunday. Eden shoved away the memory. She had nothing to offer God nor man, and at present, memory was a wicked plaything.

"I expect they dry." Wiconi pointed to the entrance of the cave. "Sun will do."

Eden grasped the heavy bearskin around her, and walked to the entrance. Her legs, weak under the weight of the fur.

She stepped outside onto a wide, flat shelf above a deep canyon. Red stone cliffs ascended in layered rock along the crevasse, one enormous Scottish cairn. Pines ice-bound by the heavy snow dotted the rim, and a sterling curl of river sparkled in the gorge under billowy clouds crossing the sun. A pleasant surprise. But the light blinded her, plucking nerves already frayed. The crystalline air sharpened her sense of loss, a reminder of a dismal life on the prairie below. The cave was easier. Eden turned back.

On its outer wall, under a broad overhead lip, her clothes, still wilted with moisture. Her pale long johns stretched across the rock face, the shedding of a snake basking in the intermittent sunshine.

Reentering the cave, she passed the old woman. Her face, worn by the years, cracked with deep lines, like the surface of a dry lake in summer—a once beautiful body of water, still framed by supple shores—the woman, stunning, even under the weight of age. But her manner didn't solicit conversation. Good. The notion of recounting the mountain trek terrified Eden. She clutched the bearskin to borrow its strength.

Go on—the unwanted refrain of life.

Unlike Intah. His words, *Look beyond.* But she didn't want to look beyond. Life's meaning was fearsome.

She fingered the bracelet on her wrist, and found two. Aiden's journal laid beside the bearskin where she'd slept. That and the bracelet, all she had left of him. Even her tears failed. As the rising sun shifted rays across the cave, color caught her eye. On the opposite side of the cavern stretched a painting, high as summer wheat, standing vivid against its backdrop. Eden raised the edge of the fur at her ankles and walked to the stone canvas. She touched the wall. Smooth and sparse, as though the color was rationed, the characters were few and delicate.

"This mural. Yours?"

Wiconi gestured to the braid in her hands. "This is my work."

"Intah?" Eden rubbed her hand across the images. Changing scenes suggested a story. "Do you know what it means?"

The old woman gave no answer as she worked the braid. Then laying down her work, Wiconi put a finger to one eye and shook her head.

"You're blind?" A wave of relief washed over Eden. Wiconi had not seen her in the raw. "So you don't know this painting across the wall of the cave?"

"What do you see?"

"A green meadow. A river. Tan triangles—shelters, I think. A large brown bear." But not a cold-eyed grizzly—Eden's heart skipped. She leaned closer to the image—the doe-eyes of innocence. "Like no bear I've seen."

Wiconi's voice echoed in the cave. "Bear medicine."

Eden touched the bear claw hanging at her neck. She stepped sideways, following the direction of the mural, putting a hand to the cool wall. "A woman with long, black hair. Bees about her head. A babe playing in the grass at her feet—"

Wiconi's tone was certain. "The bear by her side."

Eden stared at Wiconi in disbelief. "How—"

"One does not need eyes to see."

Eden turned back to the painting, the notion of looking beyond calling her forward. "Now a meadow white with snow. Campfires billowing smoke into the sky, the river, ice. The bear, on a distant hill, overlooks it all."

"And the snow turns to soot."

"And the river burns." Eden eyed Wiconi who sat like a statue, firelight catching the crags of her neck, then continued. "On the hill beyond is a blue-coated man on horseback—"

"Long braids, a rifle. No bear." The old woman sat mute, brow furrowed.

The next section of the mural took Eden's breath away. "And from the smoke, the canyon, from black to umber to the crimson rock of the cliffs." The beauty of intermingling colors was unlike anything Eden had seen. The gore of birth, the splendor and awe of creation itself.

What horror had gentle Intah experienced to inspire such a scene? She struggled with the notion that such loveliness could erupt through the crust of despair, yet the image struck a chord of truth. "Heaven rising from hell."

"And?"

She took another step. "Tangled gullies like the ones of Dakota. An elk, a lion, vivid hues of seasons coming and going—and always the bear." The fire lay too dim to cast good light on the rest and the painting stretched off into the darkness. Eden turned to the old woman. "What's the sum of it?"

Wiconi spoke as though Eden should have landed the conclusion on her own. "A man's life."

Intah appeared at the cave entrance with a spear full of trout. He raised the prize high above his head in triumph. "We eat."

Eden looked at her self-satisfied provider in a new light. She had seen the lashings of his soul and the skill of the artist who'd expressed them, in much the same way he had seen the whole of her the night before.

Eden granted him a shy smile. "You think my clothes might dry by spring?"

"I think plenty exists to keep you warm if they're not." Intah reflected her smile. "You have a little more life in you this morning than when last we spoke." The fresh wood he laid on the fire, spit and flared. He separated the fish on the spear and set it near the hot coals. His voice softened. "What are you thinking today?"

"I'd rather not wear the skin of a bear."

"Kept you from freezing. You may thank that skin you're wearing for the skin you have."

An indentation between Wiconi's eyes deepened. "She's hot now."

For the first time Eden noted that her bare feet were bright red and warm. She looked up at Intah in surprise. "The earth's warm."

Intah turned the fish, already brown on one side. "Underground springs. Only one or two left in the canyon."

"Like us," said Wiconi.

"Hot springs?" The term, relief itself. For her all things were vanquished in water: waste, want—life.

"I have spent most of the last two nights letting them take the chill from my bones. You were not the only one near frozen."

The admission led Eden's gaze to the bed she'd occupied, then to the second pile of skins behind the fire. Intah's eyes were on her when she looked back at him.

He granted her an understanding smile. "Eat and I'll take you to the place."

Eden looked into the fire. "I'm not—"

"No food, no springs. You'll not come this far to starve." Intah pulled a piece of fish from the skewer and handed the morsel to Eden. "Eat."

Eden took the fish and picked at the crackling skin. The white flesh was sweet and good. She couldn't remember the last time she'd eaten. The moist trout was a pleasure on her tongue. Though it failed to pique her appetite, she was grateful for the indulgence. "Is this all you have in winter?"

"A rabbit or two from time to time. Enough preserved elk to last the snow," said Intah. "Much can be found if you know where to look. Dried rose hips, wild plums and onions, pine nuts, and a thing you call purslane. We store all these, and wild oats, over the summer."

"Eggs in spring." The old woman beamed through two missing teeth.

Eden turned her attention to Intah. "Your painting...a lovely puzzle."

Intah looked startled, his face darkening. He looked out to the bluffs. "It has meaning for me."

Eden couldn't bear to see his sadness, so she said, "It's good work. You used fine oils. I know."

Intah stared at her. "You know?"

"Aye. Where did you get them?" As the words left her lips a sharp wind surged through the cave. The fire flared up and ashes blew in small twisters across the cavern. It snowed again, inside and out.

Eden studied the flakes. "Will we be snowbound?"

"There's blue to the west. This will pass."

"And I'll get home." The last time she'd considered it, her mind was to never return.

"If you wish," said Intah.

A dozen reasons could be found to remain far from Rose Ranch. The loneliness alone would kill her before any blizzard had the chance. But she had pined for the return to gentile life in Scotland so long the goal had legs of its own. And without Aiden, who would remind her who she really was? God knew, she'd forgotten.

Intah looked at Wiconi as though he wished the old woman to say something. But Wiconi was still, fish dangling from the end of a toasted skewer, faint smile on her lips.

"It's a hard winter alone," said Intah.

He wasn't just talking about himself. Eden's mind landed on the remaining ponies, and her beloved goats. The horses could make do on a white range, but the goats would only feed the wolves.

Odd to be thinking on the survival of goats.

Eden shook her head. "I have stock to care for."

She couldn't rely on Maddie through a long freeze. She had her own farm to tend. If anything would beckon her return, it would be loyalty to her friend, a woman who'd writhe in disbelief if she discovered where Eden had landed, and how she was dressed.

Eden continued. "And, no offense, if I'm found to have wintered with the likes of an Indian I won't be much welcome at home. If you won't be taking me back, I can find my own way."

The old woman's voice was firm and humorless. "I will take you back."

Intah gave the old Wiconi a startled glance.

"That's a joke," said Eden.

Intah rose, took up a long piece of thick, woven broadcloth and offered it to Eden. "To dry yourself."

Eden followed him through a narrow passage at one side of the cavern that led to the outside. A slender fall of water slipped over the cliff in a rush and arrived in a small pool edged by smooth river rock. Water streamed out the opposite end of the steamy pond making its way on down into the canyon, joining the river a thousand feet below.

"Hot water rises beneath the pool. Too hot without the cold water from the falls. I brought stones to guide it along. Temperature's near same as the body."

Eden dipped a hand below the surface. The water was soft and warm in the crisp air. A fine haze wafted in swirls at its surface. She looked at Intah.

"Go on." He made no move to leave her.

"I know my clothes didn't take themselves off last night, but I can now handle that part alone."

Intah smiled, turned around, and disappeared inside the cave.

Eden let the bearskin drop to her feet. She groped for a foothold in the deep pool, then slipped into the tepid water and out of time.

Part Three

To See What Comes

"Take her home—now." Wiconi worked her hands through long, fine strands of horsehair.

"Don't be so hard," said Intah. "She's been through a war."

The fire burned a shallow flicker and smoke lingered at the cavern ceiling, creeping along into the outside air.

"And we have not?"

Intah loved many things about the woman he'd met in the canyon so many years ago. They had much in common. Both ran for their freedom; both lost much along the way. But Intah found the similarities paled when compared to the degree of intolerance Wiconi mustered. The old woman came from a tribe that had never taken in a white. She believed it tragic that Intah carried anything other than Native blood. But Intah knew that the old woman blamed no one for the union of Intah's parents, save the settlers presenting themselves as novelty.

"Best to let her alone." Intah walked to the edge of the cliff and looked down onto the river below. Sun broke through clouds again.

Wiconi raised her voice. "White. She has no place here."

"I'd think your lack of sight would blind you to the color of her skin."

"Different skin, different heart."

"There's but one difference between her heart and yours. Hers is open."

"Why? Because she came with you? What was her choice?"

"She's a strong woman. She could have found her way."

"Then, why did you not leave her to it?"

Silence.

Wiconi snorted, widening her cloudy eyes. "You want to keep her."

Intah looked up, grateful for Wiconi's blindness, for the old woman would have seen acknowledgment in his eyes. As it was, the truth crystalized along with the breath Intah blew into the freezing air. No denying the idea took hold of him as hard as the snow lay deep, but he lacked the courage to admit the notion.

"You have attended too many deaths, old woman, and not enough births."

"Done my share of both. My medicine's as good as yours. I may be blind but I can see. Your sight does not grant you the same pleasure."

Oh, it does. It does.

And Wiconi did see a thing Intah had not. In all the years they'd spent together in the cave, through the ice of winters and the calls of spring, he was the blind one. The grief he'd held for a decade, a curtain he'd drawn upon the world. Himself. And her.

Intah turned to Wiconi now wishing she also saw the smile on his face. "You are jealous."

Cold words. "And you, proud."

The edge to her voice begged the facts to stand in silence between them.

"Take her home," said Wiconi.

It was not her proclamation that surprised him but the tone, expressionless yet full of purpose, as were Intah's musing of Eden. The way to her was to bid his heart feel what his mind wanted most.

To let go.

"Sun will melt the snow in time," said Intah, warm light on his back. "Enough to cross the pass."

"Time to change her mind?"

Intah looked out over the canyon. "To see what comes."

Eden could not be captured. Wiconi was right. The improving weather would offer a choice. And the choice must be Eden's.

She appeared in the neck of the cavern, bright-colored broadcloth peaking from the rim of the bearskin wrapping her body. Her face was rosy and her eyes scarlet, as though she had wept her way through the waters of the spring.

Intah dipped a wooden cup into a large bucket at the cave entrance, moved toward her and placed the cup in her hand. "Drink."

Delicate lips pulled at the water. Eden drank it down in one draw.

Intah took the vessel from her hand and led her to the thick pile of skins. "Sleep."

Eden melted onto the furs. Intah sat with her until her breath was steady, then slipped the bearskin off her. The broadcloth would be enough. The cave was comfortable above the heated earth. A gentle breeze from the cavern entrance refreshed the air, humid with the steamy springs.

Intah let his gaze follow the charming curve of Eden's body lying beneath the colorful cloth. Though he'd seen her work hard at the maintenance of her ranch, a tenderness about her suggested she'd not survive the rigors of life in a canyon cave. She was too fine a thing for these mountains. Born to fine furniture and the comfort of a feather bed. Yet she'd fared the mountain well until disaster struck. He'd seen her do the work of a homestead, alone. She could weather hardship.

He put a hand to her head, sweeping her damp hair away from her forehead. Tucking the material underneath her feet, he squeezed one of her toes with two fingers to check their warmth.

Perhaps—perhaps.

She was already fast asleep.

Intah turned to Wiconi, letting the bearskin drop next to Eden. The old woman reached for a piece of wood from the replenished pile behind her near the fire. She did well alone despite her blindness. Everything always lay in the same spot: stores of smoked venison and elk; corn they grew near the river; dried and ground for meal and bread; wood for the fire; drinking water collected in clay jars from the falls nearby; a cache of autumn fruit. Still, she'd not exist on her own.

"You'll need more wood before I go," Intah said.

Wiconi nodded.

Intah picked up a heavy axe leaning against the cavern wall, calling over his shoulder as he took his leave to the wooded hillside above the cave. "If the weather allows, we'll cross the mountain on the full moon."

Time enough for Eden's mind to change.

For Oh, So Long

Eden had no memory of walking from the hot spring to the pile of skins. She'd emptied her soul into the water. Sleep had been a drug, and the day gone when she opened her eyes to the flickering firelight.

Wiconi moved about the cave as though her eyes were young and clear, carrying wood from a stack of fresh timber to the fireside, and pulling dried meat from a woven basket. In the amber light, Eden marveled at her agility and the depth of memories possessed to find each thing in its place. Wiconi sat down by the fire and picked up the width of fine braid, loose hair hanging from its end, and worked by touch alone. Eden turned on her side and propped an elbow on the fur.

The old woman turned an ear her way and spoke with reproof. "The spell is broken."

"There's great repair in sleep—and the springs." Eden put one hand on Aiden's journal beside her. The water soothed her spirits, as she knew it would, but the book might as well be locked away. She couldn't bring herself to open its pages again. She pushed the journal under the bearskin.

Though Aiden wouldn't leave her mind, other thoughts kept his company. Reveries of stillness on the mountain and beauty in the canyon—the relief from tending her homestead. Her mind was not the usual rage of doubt, and she wanted to keep it so.

Her gaze settled on Wiconi's braid. "It's fine work you do."

Wiconi pointed. "Eat."

A round of bread domed above a wooden plate next to the fire. Wiconi set her work down, dipped water from the bucket, and drank. Eden's throat burned. She pulled the broadcloth around her and made her way to the bucket.

She reached for the dipper in the old woman's hand, cupping her hands for a moment around Wiconi's. "May I drink?"

The old woman jerked her hand away. The dipper clattered to the ground.

Eden stared at the old woman a moment. "I didn't mean to frighten you."

Wiconi looked Eden's way as though reading her face for intention, making Eden question just how blind she was.

Eden picked up the ladle, wiped its bowl on her wrap, and drew a long drink and replaced it at the bucket. She settled beside the fire next to Wiconi. "How do you do such a thing—blind?"

"Memory."

"And I can see it's a fine one, but the pattern. How do you make it so without sight?"

"Black horse hair is rough. Feel."

Eden reached out to touch the difference. To her, indiscernible from the white. "Can you teach me?"

Aiden was the braider in the family. Eden's fingers pulled a bow instead, but plenty of horsetail hair was available on the ranch. Perhaps if she learned the skill, she could sell fine bridles and reins to boost her income back home; teach Maddie, as well. They could share a business.

Wiconi fumbled for one of Eden's hands. She pulled it to her and rubbed the fingers as though testing the aptitude of her skin. "You work." The old woman seemed to approve of the fact. "Tough skin. But you have eyes."

Eden rubbed her fingertips together. Toughened from ranch work and the pressing of violin strings. Foolishness to think she could learn a skill as fine as the old woman's. Wiconi handed her a bundle of loose hair. Eden fashioned the top of the braid and watched as Wiconi continued her own work, trying to mimic the weave as well as she could.

"Did Intah teach you English?"

Wiconi's tone was resigned and flat. "Said it's the future."

Eden stared at her. That explained her demeanor. What red man could tolerate the white given the circumstance the Indian had been left? Eden expected these two natives might be the last outside the reservation. The last of their kind living free—but life held up in a canyon cave was no freedom.

Or was Wiconi's rancor something more?

Eden studied her. A stunning woman in youth, no doubt. Framing high cheekbones, steel grey hair glistened, breaking loosely about her shoulders, and slanting eyes tended to the exotic, transforming the force of age into ageless.

The idea that Wiconi and Intah had ever been more than friends lay uncomfortable in Eden's gullet, a seed of discontent sprouting a thing Eden had never felt: jealousy. "Are you kin to Intah?"

Wiconi laid her eyes on Eden as though the emerging seed was clear, but said nothing.

"How did you come to be here?"

"By smoke." The old woman nodded toward the mural as she repeated Eden's words from the morning. "We are the same."

"And that means?"

"We all have stories. Illusions we hold against our true nature." Wiconi's face was a beguiling collection of trails, a thousand smiles and furrowed brows. "Up here, it is easier to forget them. Better to listen to what serves you."

"And that is?"

"Hope. Promise."

Love?

The words rolled around Eden's brain, unsettled, constant. Green marbles deflecting inner truths. Eden couldn't lay her fingers on even one, yet she envied the wisdom as much as she did the old woman's relationship with Intah. But if Wiconi had been an intimate part of Intah's past, who was Eden to judge? What had Intah become to her that she even cared?

Eden pulled the strands of the braid hard as if tearing away the answer, and shook her head. "I expect I don't have the talent. It doesn't look at all like yours even a little bit."

"What you expect, comes."

"I don't understand."

The old woman turned to Eden looking straight into her, opaque eyes wide with a palpable reproach as though knowing every thought she'd ever conjured, and disapproved. "What fills your mind?"

The question took Eden aback. Survival had been her one worry for so long, little room remained for anything else. She looked out to the clear stars twinkling beyond, candlelight above the canyon walls. Eden listened to her heart beat double time in the quiet of the cave.

She wanted the comfort of clothing around her. "Do you think my clothes are dry?"

Wiconi nodded.

Eden stood, walking to the outer cave. The clothing lay cold as ice but dried out and smelling fresh. She pulled them from the rocks and slipped her long underwear on, followed by Hugh's baggy trousers and her linen shirt. The leather boots were still damp so she left them by the fire.

"Where's Intah?" asked Eden.

"Springs."

She walked barefoot down the long, cramped cave to the springs outside. Snow on the banks lay illuminated by a near full moon that outlined Intah in the steamy pool. Water rushed down the cliffside onto the adjacent rocks. The river below was a rushed whisper.

She stopped out of sight. Intah floated on his back without moving, at the water's surface. In the translucent mist and moonlight he hovered, a revenant in thin air. Eden stood spellbound.

She could float as well, but not without moving her arms to fight the water's pull. She'd never seen such a feat. Eden moved down the rocks to the edge of the pool and stopped. Intah was naked. As she turned in retreat, her foot kicked a small stone into the water.

He opened his eyes and his feet sank, head bobbing above the surface, wet hair onyx in the soft light. "Watching long?"

"I'm sorry." She crossed her arms and looked at him. "But how do you do that?"

"What?"

"Float without moving?"

"Balance." Intah moved to the rim of the pool and put both hands on its edge.

Eden was sure he was about to boost himself from the springs and she turned her back to grant him privacy.

"Balance and breath," said Intah.

Drops of water echoed off the rock walls and she waited until the rustle of broadcloth around Intah's waist bid she turn. "I want to try."

Intrigued enough by the chance to float unaided, dealing with wet underthings again was something she could bear. The cave was warm with the heat of the springs and plenty of skins were available as wraps. The long johns she sported were adequate cover as they ran from neck to feet. She'd make do with them alone, until they were dry again and needed to travel. Eden gave him a long gaze then shed the proprieties of home and dipped into the water.

Intah looked surprised as he watched her swim to the center of the pool.

"Tell me how," she said.

Intah pulled the broadcloth up tight between his legs, tied it, and made his way back into the spring. His advance, looking naked above the water, took Eden's breath. She'd not need a master in the pool. She was already floating. Afraid to give herself away, she fixed her gaze on a bright star in the black sky above as Intah waded toward her.

With only her long johns between them, he placed one hand on Eden's spine. "Lean back. Let your feet float up."

Eden tilted into his hand, apprehensive of trusting Intah to catch her before she dipped back too far. "Don't let go just yet."

His hand was strong and warm. A long time had passed since she'd been touched with such tenderness. But it was harder to relax than she anticipated. Propriety was not easily shaken. She'd clung to it since reaching the god-forsaken land of Wyoming. It kept her sane and rooted to her past. She stared at the star, Intah's gaze, a magnet.

"Now, close your eyes and shallow your breath enough to float."

Eden's eyes darted toward Intah's, self-conscious under his watch. She closed her eyes. She tried to find the balance between breathing in and out, but the thick cotton undergarment added too much weight to overcome. Every time Intah removed his hand she sank below the surface, coughing and sputtering in the sulfur-tainted water.

"Comes with practice." Intah smiled as though watching a child take its first steps. "But you'll have to shed your cover. Too heavy."

Eden opened her eyes. "In the altogether?"

"I'll leave you to it."

"How do I know you won't be looking?"

"You don't."

"I won't be able to focus on my breath if I think you're watching me."

"Then don't think." Intah moved to the edge of the pool, and climbed out of the water.

Eden turned her back and listened as the sound of his footsteps disappeared into the rush of falling water. When he was gone, she peeled the soaking undergarments from her body and pushed them onto the rocks at the side of the pool, moving back to the deeper center.

A gentle breeze blew swirls in the mist above her and when it parted, the moon and stars reflected as though she were afloat in the center of the universe. Eden leaned back into the soft water, closed her eyes, and let her feet float up. The spring's opalescent pearls clung to her body, as though she were bathing in a pool of champagne.

How Maddie would love the pleasure found in a wide, warm bath. Somehow, the idea made Eden lighter in the springs. When her ears dipped below the surface the sound of air rushing in and out of her lungs was all to fill her ears. It startled her and her head sank. She sputtered and came upright.

Catching her breath, she tried again. But each time, worried over sinking, she struggled and sank. Surely, the weight of Aiden's death kept her off-balance, dragging her beneath the surface. She pushed his image from her mind, replacing it with the pleasure of the pool, its warmth to her body, its gentle undercurrent a wisp of soft summer wind on her skin. Eden let her arms tread the water until the skin of her hands rippled prunes. She kept her mind on the bliss of the moment and, in her reverie, the water was her sole focus. Once time lost meaning the water buoyed her to balance. As if the answer was as simple as saying please.

She measured her breathing until she floated, mind empty. As her breath slowed, the barrier between her body and the water fell away in the even temperature. Though she hovered in the center of the springs, she was aware of the jagged, hard surface of the facing rocks, the water streaming from the canyon rim above, across the cliff face and the into the raw gorge beyond. In her breath the sound of her heartbeat dissolved into the burbling water.

No boundaries.

That single notion returned her to the limit of the pool. On only a flicker of disbelief, she was restored to herself. Eden opened her eyes to a moonless night. The orb slipped behind the western rim. What seemed moments must have been an hour. Or more. She grabbed at a deep breath, trying to hold the eerie pleasure retreating as the sensation of her body advanced. But something in her breast remained. She moved to the edge of the pool, folded her arms at the rim and laid her head on her hands.

Peace.

A thing neglected for oh, so long.

Meaning of the Word

Jenny's arm healed under a swath of clover honey and cotton, but Maddie suspected the flesh lay raw and sore under the bandage. She had but one hand to pull the cow. It made milking a long labor, and Jenny beat the sunrise to bring a full pail in by breakfast.

Hard to watch her work with a wound like that, but next in line was Rob. He'd never been good on any teat. Never even took to mother's milk. Maddie boiled cow's milk from the time he was born until he was weaned. Whether it was a cow or a goat he milked, he only managed to pull drips. The family was too big to live off a trickle of milk.

After breakfast, she told Jenny to keep her grandpa company on the porch while Maddie made her daily way to the river. Resting her arm awhile before they scrubbed laundry would do the girl good. The last washday had been well before Eden left. More than a week's worth of clothes were dirty enough to stand on their own.

"Gonna take a short mornin' walk, Pa," said Maddie.

"Be right here." Ezra gawked at Jenny as though Maddie was invisible.

"I'll believe that when I get back and find you in the same spot." Maddie studied her pa. "Make sure Jenny rests a bit afore we do that wash. Hear me?"

Ezra paid her no mind and raised his hand to pull his fingers through Jenny's hair. A strange smile crossed his face, the one he used to wear for her ma—gentle and compelling at once. The man seemed lost in the sight of his granddaughter. The image was a prune pit in her stomach, but she supposed the softness of Jenny's locks granted him a bit of calm. If Ezra was at peace, the rest of the family was as well.

"Well, mind you stay put till I git back, missy. If yer gonna be any help at all yer gonna have to rest that arm in-between," said Maddie.

She picked her way through the cottonwoods to the water. Scant use in the exercise. The river receded to a series of wisps again. There'd be nothing new along the shore. But from the Powder she could look back at the Bighorn. And the Bighorn held all her hope for Eden. Maddie clung to the idea of her friend being on the mountain and the optimism of a safe return. After all, if Eden washed up on some riverbank, she would have been found. If she caught up to the Indian, Maddie imagined he'd keep her alive—good or bad. As long as she was alive, hope remained.

She walked the shore up and down for some time, observing the tracks of river birds and small game coming and going from the water's edge. As lonesome as the river looked, activity swarmed when no human walked the bank.

Maddie swung up the low hillside above the stream and strolled back toward the house. She slowed her pace, granting more time before the scrubbing that lay ahead, and quieted her step to listen for the song of any late birds lagging behind the mountain snow. A crow sounded in the distance, and on its call came a cry…Jenny.

Maddie sprinted through the trees as fast as her legs would carry her, over fallen wood and trickles of runoff weaving through the desiccated soil. Jenny's shrieks grew louder until her mother broke through the tall grasses to the dirt road below the house where she pulled up short.

"Ma!" Jenny called.

Ezra made no move to acknowledge Jenny's cry. He had her pinned to the wall of the house backing the porch, hands on the girl's cheeks, pressing her small frame in rhythm against the planks with his belly. They were both fully clothed, her father merely going through the motions of something too dreadful for Maddie to consider.

She sprinted across the road and covered the two steps onto the porch in one leap. Grabbing the old man's shoulder, she braced herself against the house and used all her weight to push him away. When Ezra turned, his eyes were vacant, as though he'd been taken by a trance. He looked at Maddie's hands, pushed firm against his chest, blinked twice, and furrowed his brow. Jenny wept.

Maddie's promise was as cold and serious as a flood of mountain snow melt. "Pa, I love you, but if I ever find you doin' such again, as sure as I stand afore God, I'll kill you." Maddie drew a stuttered breath at the surprise of her intent.

"Don't know," said Ezra, shaking his head.

Maddie took her hands from Ezra and put them around Jenny's waist. "You all right?"

"Called me Genevieve." Jenny sniffled back her tears and pulled away to roost on the porch step.

Maddie's heart sank at hearing her mother's name. "This happen afore?"

Jenny shook her head. "Usually just pulls at my hair."

"Well, he ain't gonna do that no more." Maddie gave Ezra a poison stare.

Jenny was trying to protect him. The girl loved the old man despite himself. She prayed it was the first time he'd taken such liberties.

"I ain't gonna sit here." Jenny looked at Ezra, walked into the house, and closed the door.

Maddie turned to her father. "Pa, you understand me? This girl ain't Genevieve. Ma's dead and buried. You understand? Dead and buried."

Ezra nodded, walked to his chair on the porch, sat down, and gazed in the direction of the Powder. Maddie stared at the old man. Was he sleepwalking? Nothing registered. More and more. If he'd been a rabid old dog, she'd simply put him down.

No such mercy existed in the eyes of mankind. Humanity—where lay the true meaning of the word?

To Find Beauty

Eden walked to the edge of the cave. Sunlight devoured the mountain snow. Water poured from the red canyon rim above onto ledges around the cavern splashing crystal droplets into the abyss. The weather was summer again, though she gathered Intah believed otherwise. Each day, after he caught, cleaned, and cooked their main meal, he sat for long periods of time on the shelf beyond the cave, watching the sky.

She used the time to learn Wiconi's braid. The more she let the feel of the horsehair guide her hands, the better the result. Wiconi was right. Feeling was the best guide, whether working the braid or floating the springs. In either case, she was learning to understand which sensations gave her the finest result.

Evening was her favorite time in the pool. If she kept her thoughts confined to the details of the moment, far from the guilt of the past or the fear of what might come, she held her bliss longer and longer each time. A single minute of joy multiplied as soon as it was found. And even in the face of what she'd lost, hope was the common thread. Fate delivered an upward turn.

Relief came at her own bidding. How long would it last?

When Intah entered the springs, she would watch him from the cavern passageway, his breath so slow that she was sure it had stopped altogether. He remained so, eyes closed, oblivious to the world around him, then came conscious again with such ease and calm, it was as though he were rising from a night of deep and restful sleep. The gleam about him granted by something more than the water temperature.

One bright day, as the sun whittled away the snow and a cacophony of falling water splashed over the canyon rim, Eden left Intah to the springs and joined Wiconi. She picked up her length of braid. The old woman pulled a hand down the work.

Eden ran her hand over the same spot. "Not like yours."

"Think on now."

"How so?"

"I eat, I think about eating. I braid, I think braiding. Eyes on the moment, in silence, brings smooth work." Wiconi looked into the fire as though counting the tiny sparks rising their way toward the inner cavern.

True.

Since Eden had come to the canyon, time was just a string of nows. She glanced to the passageway leading to the springs, then to the cave mural shimmering in the low firelight.

"Are you lonely, the two of you?"

"Loneliness is nothing but yearning. I'm an old, blind woman." She laughed. "My yearning days are over."

"But you did?"

Wiconi's expression told Eden she very well understood the question.

"I suppose you are right. To end yearning, is to end life. And since I still breathe—"

"You know what I'm asking." A question coursing through Eden now as hot as the blood running her veins.

"Only the bed is shared." Wiconi stared back at her braid.

Ambiguity at best, the answer didn't get to the root of Eden's query.

Then Wiconi reached into Eden's thoughts and answered the one true thing that really mattered. "He does not share his heart."

Relief and disappointment began to go a first round somewhere behind Eden's heart. She swallowed hard. "Are you ever afraid here alone?"

"Afraid?" The old woman knit her brow as though deciphering the word. Then, she said, "Safe."

"And Intah?"

"For some, being alone is not penalty, but protection." Wiconi lowered her length of braid and looked Eden's way. "As I said, each has a story."

"And you know his, don't you?"

The old woman turned her head in the direction of the painted wall as though she saw it all and drew a long breath.

"Tell me," said Eden.

"Torch of bear medicine passes from the father, as his father took it from his. A son was born but his mother died. The holy man took another wife, a white woman. Came another boy. Blue eyes—a sign of great power. The torch passed over the first son." The old woman shook her head. "It was not forgotten."

Eden looked back at the beginning of the mural. "Intah told me this. But none of that is here."

Wiconi nodded. "It is all there, the way you told me. The bear is Intah."

"And the woman with the bees and the babe?"

"Bees are a mark of union. The woman and child were his."

Eden set down her braiding. Wiconi's admission lay a raw hand on her heart. "Were?"

"Bluecoat on the hill—brother. The burning, his work. From the ruin, Intah came to the mountain."

"His own brother burned the whole of the camp?"

"And a hundred white soldiers he brought along."

The story validated what the old woman thought of Eden—and why. Did the same feelings run deep in Intah?

"All because he couldn't be a holy man?"

Wiconi's voice reeked disdain. "He could be nothing."

"Why portray the past?"

"To find its beauty."

Eden couldn't understand that—she'd spent her life burying the past in the most literal sense—yet at the same time she understood its truth. She witnessed the beauty in Intah's painting. In his soul.

"It is said that you can't really live unless you've suffered. And *there* lies the beauty in pain."

Eden shook her head trying to grasp the old woman's meaning.

"Every step leads to the next, but only the next step is important."

"He's painted that, too," said Eden looking at the mural. "And it's a brighter picture than the first."

"The story he knows is painted in the beginning—the story he desires follows."

"So, everything after the fire is a yarn?"

"Everything after is life as he's made it."

"By painting what he wished for?"

Doubtful.

Wiconi smiled, raising her dark eyebrows.

Eden couldn't resist the irony. "I suppose he's lived happily ever after."

The concept that a life could be thought up into something real was delusion. Perhaps he suffered dementia of a sort. Compelled to check, Eden walked to the mural, for the first time following its farthest point. The images were faint in the low light, and the colors muted. Season after season greeted her along the passageway until she arrived to face the last scene—a broad, umber field embraced by low hills on one side and the slip of a stream on the other. Lone figure in the center—a woman with flaming hair.

Eden touched the wall then put her fingers to her lips. The oils were dry; drier than had Intah painted the scene in the time since they arrived at the cave. Her mind swam.

Wiconi's words echoed from the outer chamber as though she were seeing the same scene. "What you attend to, attends you."

The notion tugged at Eden's core. She recited them in her mind until something unspoken invited calm. Understanding flickered, then as fast as it had taken her, the knowing vanished, as a dream recedes the conscious mind in haste. "I can't see that."

"I can."

"You can see it? And what do you know about me?"

Her life, in two parts: the joy of her girlhood in Scotland, and the sorrow of her womanhood in the West. Regret lay as deep as the ocean between the two, welling in her as it had when she stood at the stern of the ship carrying her to America, watching Britain fade on the distant horizon. She walked back to Wiconi.

"Only fear drives a white woman into the mountains with an Indian," Wiconi said.

Intah's footsteps echoed in the passageway to the springs. He crossed the cave in one graceful motion, long, loose hair wet upon the back of his shirt. As graceful a man as she had ever seen. He dipped the ladle into the water bucket, drank down the fresh water, and tossed two pieces of wood on the fire before continuing out onto the wide ledge at the entrance to the cave. Eden followed.

Intah sat with his back against the cliff side, broadcloth around his shoulders, doeskin pants stained wet at the bottom, and muslin shirt loose at his waist. Steam from the heat of his body after the springs rose away into the cold, dry air of the late afternoon. The canyon sang a low chorus of creaks and moans.

"The rocks sing today."

"Bard ice," said Eden.

Intah looked at her, face a puzzle.

"My grandmother called it so. The thick ice of a freeze, expanding, contracting. The song of a bard."

"Bard?"

"A poet-singer of old."

"Your grandmother…"

"Aye." Eden sat beside him, thinking on the last image of the mural and Wiconi's words. "What makes the old woman so cross? Is she jealous?"

Intah chuckled.

"Are you and she—"

He chuckled again.

"And what's the joke?"

"Can a man and woman live together without—"

Eden raised her hand. "Don't say it."

"We do not know each other in that way." Intah stared at Eden. "She is nothing more or less than what her name implies."

"And that is?"

"Life. Physical procreation, spiritual birth. The woman does both. Men simply lend the tools."

"The tools?"

"The seeds of manifestation in either case for the bearing of a child, or the bearing of realization."

Baffled, Eden shook her head.

Again, Intah chuckled. "What woman has never felt vexed by a man and thereby brought to a deeper understanding of herself— and others?"

Eden stopped short of a smile, wanting to say, Amen.

"Some sense must come from the confusion, don't you think?" Intah asked.

"If I could make sense of the confusion, I wouldn't be asking. Wiconi seems to know what I'm thinking before I do."

"Your people call it the mystic. A seeing of truths beyond reason." Intah's gaze reached into hers.

Eden looked away. "And your name?"

"From my father. The meaning is in the sound. The 'ah' as it ends. Like water falling, wind blowing, rain beating the earth. He said it was all one sound. Voice of the Great Spirit." Intah looked at Eden. "And yours?"

She laughed. "I've never claimed it as any paradise."

"Perhaps you should."

Eden's gaze followed the trail that had brought them to the cave. The burned-out skeleton of a tall, two-top evergreen stood sentry adjacent the entrance. "Lightning, I expect. That happen while you were here?"

Intah looked at the tree and shook his head. "It waited for us."

"Waited?"

"Drew us to the cave. The two-headed pine. You know what they say about two heads?"

"Better than one?"

"Twice as many teeth." Intah smiled at Eden. "We figured this was home."

Noise from the tumbling river below filled the canyon. "I've been thinking that the whole of this trip has been fate, you know? The mares broke pasture just the time you passed. And—" Aiden's name stuck in her throat. "No good has happened since I met you but, for the first time in forever, and for no reason, I feel good. How can that be?"

"I don't believe in fate."

"That's no answer."

"I can only give you questions. The answers you must find alone."

"Then ask."

Intah scanned the opposite side of the ravine as if measuring the amount of water spilling from the cliffs. "Did you ever paint?"

Eden cocked her head at the out-of-place question. "Long ago."

"What stopped you?"

"This mountain."

She'd given up her effort to translate the dreadful beauty of Wyoming. She'd laid it all away to music instead; notes to soothe her soul.

"I told you I came up once before. My honeymoon. I brought a box full of oils with me, intent on capturing on canvas what Hugh caught with lead. I'm afraid it was all left behind to the bear that rolled through—" Eden stopped mid-sentence.

"What you left behind..." Intah rubbed his chin with one hand, drawing a knee up to rest his elbow. "The first autumn after I came to this place I rode the east side for game. Near Cloud Peak I came to a hunting camp similar to the one we saw, a mess of stores and bundles. Tracks of a great bear trampled through the site."

Eden's memory turned and, with it, the years between the two camps. Her voice was low, her wonder as deep as the chasm below. "And in the stores, a box of paints and a bag of brushes."

Intah nodded.

"My God." The idea was a wellspring inside her. Star-crossed paths. This man had found her paints, so long ago lost. And the two of them sat together on the same mountain, all because her brother had wanted to join a hunt. She shook her head and smiled. "Given to good use."

Intah walked into the cavern. He returned with a large flat book that he held with the gentle fingers of his broad hands. He rubbed a palm over the binding. "I had a fine teacher."

He handed her the book and knelt beside her as she leafed through its tattered pages. The leather binding was stained and faded, edges weathered. After all, the book had spent a year or two on the mountain before being rescued. The pages, watermarked along each edge, had been pulled apart with care.

She turned each one by one. Sketches of the mountain and the pines, the rugged canyons, the white water rivers springing down the hillsides, golden eagles and massive elk, various comrades of

286

that first hunting party, Hugh, and the last detail of a forgotten sketch near the middle of the book—a self-portrait.

The hopelessness she'd captured in her own eyes made her want to cry. She'd blamed everything on Hugh's failure, the deaths of her children, even the drought. All those things that happened after they homesteaded. The visage before her was of a woman yet to face any of that.

She'd unpacked that heartache in Wyoming.

Had she ever been happy?

"You looked familiar." He brushed the hair from Eden's cheek. "But I never imagined it was a self-portrait. Makes sense now. The depth of sorrow can never be captured by those on the outside, looking in."

"And you don't believe in fate?"

Intah's gaze reached into hers.

"This whole time, you knew me," she said.

"Knew *of* you."

"You found me." Synchronicity buoyed her above the canyon, and suddenly she was airborne looking down on the two of them.

"I simply came upon you."

"But when you saw me in the field for the first time—"

"I had seen copper hair once before."

"And you followed."

Intah studied the sky. A luminous evening star hung below the moon.

"Like following a star?"

Intah gazed at Eden. "Thou fair-haired angel."

Blake's poem rang in her ears. Perhaps the old woman was right—what Intah painted became real. Her head was a mix of pleasure and dismay at life's parallels, yet underneath it all was a sudden apprehension bringing her back to earth. Intah brought her this far, perhaps he had no intention of seeing her back home.

A rush of nerves forced her to speak. "Moon's near full and the days bright. The pass must be open. We should go."

Intah turned as if surprised.

Eden's mind was on Maddie. She was sure her friend had given her up, and Eden ached to think she'd be the cause of her anguish. "There's much to do before snow closes me in on the ranch. I can't be leaving my stock to starve. What will happen if I don't get back before winter sets in for good?"

Intah looked up at the sky and nodded. "What will happen."

"It's no question, is it?"

"Never."

"You'll take me?"

Intah's voice was disappointment. "If you intend to go, I'll see you there."

As soon as his pledge was delivered her trepidation turned to regret. She'd never been as content as she had the past few days. She feared if she left the canyon, her contentment would linger behind.

"I'll miss this," she said.

Intah studied at her for a long moment. For an instant Eden recognized that if he'd asked her to, she'd stay.

"Morning will see us over the mountain," he said.

"Back to the Powder." Desiccated and barren as the name. And as Wiconi implied, a thing that must be faced in order to be left behind.

She had to return.

Intah extended his arm to the beauty before him. "Think of this, not that."

She'd learned that how she considered the moment was important. The memory of the canyon, and Intah, would serve her well. Yet in some wee space just south of her heart, she understood that if any promise was left her, it lay in the arms of this man. Her longing was a strong current sweeping her to an unknown sea. Eden took a step toward him and stopped. Did he sense the same pull? She couldn't bear the loss if he turned away.

"It all seems so impossible," she said.

As if hearing Eden's thoughts, Intah stared at her, his voice, a whisper, "The impossible is the possible yet known. Go to the springs and dream of the possibilities."

Loneliness Had No Name

"I take her back tomorrow," said Intah. "Leave her."

Wiconi sat in her well-worn spot next to the fire in silence, tilting her head to and fro as Intah moved about the cave in preparation.

While Eden bathed, Intah gathered stores for the trip east as the fire burned brighter in the nightfall. Pemmican, elk fat, and cornmeal all went into a stout leather bag. He packed a large burlap sack as well, hoping to pick more apples on his return, and laid everything by the cave entrance, ready for daylight. The horses had roamed the cliff top for the last few days. They would be well rested for the time ahead. He would let them have one more night in the wood. A whistle would bring his mount to him in the morning. The other would follow.

Intah pulled a handful of dry wild mint from a small cloth bag, placed it in a clay cup, doused it with hot water and sat across from the old woman.

Wiconi nodded. "And your heart?"

"Small price to leave it, too," said Intah looking into his cup. "I never thought—"

Wiconi raised a hand, her voice soft as though delivering a secret. "Don't."

Intah drank the tea thinking on Wiconi's last word until an old sensation had him in its clutches. Soon she would be gone. He stood, trying to shake off the grip, but his agitation only grew stronger, quickening his heart—the primal beat of wolf paws in the wood.

It called him down the close passage to the split in the rocks leading to the springs. Eden floated in the center of the hazy pool, wet face glistening like a faint star. Intah moved outside the opening without a sound under the rush of a surging creek and its tumbling water.

She was more stunning than any sketch could ever convey. Even as the years hollowed her cheeks and the sun tanned her skin, her face was much more than that put to paper so long ago— a fire about her, a spark. Lightning in his veins. And it had set him aflame. Until he first laid eyes on Eden, his loneliness had no name. He didn't want to take her back.

She opened her eyes. Her shoulders bobbed from the surface of the water as she caught Intah's gaze. The two looked at each other for some moments as the water gossiped along the canyon walls behind them. Then Eden turned her back to Intah, moving to the far edge of the pool. She leaned into the rocky ledge and stretched her arms out along the lip of the springs. The invitation of a native wife—subtle and ambiguous as the lazy mists playing hide and seek with things lurking at the springs' surface. He took a step to the edge of the pool. Eden made no move.

Intah had been with no other but his wife. He had the right within the tribe to take more than one, but the Christian nature of his mother reasoned otherwise. He was content to focus his feeling on one woman. His hesitation at entering the springs surprised him. His Native wife would have expected him to take another woman—and yet, the idea was somehow disrespectful. No longer by his side, she never left his heart. A long breath slid between his lips. He'd traveled a prairie of despair for too long. Grief could be endless. The option was to attend it or not. The choice must forever reach in the direction of joy—and joy pushed him toward the springs.

With no knowledge of a woman for so long he was but half sure of Eden's signal, so he waited. She turned her head to meet his eyes once more, as if they held the answer to her feelings. She looked into the water for a moment then nodded to the mist. When she leaned forward against the water's edge, spirit seemed to nudge toward the lip of the pool, urging him to shed his solitude.

He let his clothing slip away and sank into the water.

It wasn't long before he was behind her in the dark, effervescent spring, broad hands on her bare hips. All at once, she turned. Eden slipped one arm behind his neck and laid her head upon his chest. A foreign grasp to Intah, for to his mind, things of carnal nature were not accomplished face-to-face. He put his hands under her arms and lifted her from him. Reached for her hair, bronzed by the water, which lay in wet curls about her head, and pulled his fingers through the strands. Eden paused, putting one hand against his shoulder as though she changed her mind. Intah froze. The sorrow would be unbearable if he'd mistaken her intention. He stepped back to read her expression. The bear claw below her neck swayed on its tether in the warm water above her breasts. She stared at the talisman as a tear escaped.

Intah pulled her to him and held her tight. "No."

He brushed back her curls with a sweep of his hand. Was she sorry they'd come this far? He wasn't. Whatever may happen beyond the moment was of no matter to what she'd made him feel. He didn't want her to fear the consequences of loving. He'd known well and for too long the shortcomings in that.

Eden looked at him, a faint smile crossing her lips.

The warmth of the water amplified in her arms. They held on as though each found in the other a missing part that would never again be lost. Intah's mind flooded with all that had vanished in the journey they'd each made toward the other, their lives emptied out to make room for something better.

Eden moved her hand up the middle of Intah's back to rest on his shoulder. She slipped her arm around his neck, fondling his hair with one hand. Their eyes met as she used one finger to trace the ridge of his brow. Drew her hand across his cheek to cup his chin. Brushed his lips, then pulled his head to hers.

His mother had kissed him many times on the cheek. A foreign custom to the rest of the tribe. He turned his head to receive it but Eden shunned his cheek, touching her firm, soft lips to his. Intah was taken by the surprise of it. He pulled away far enough to rub his nose against hers and push his face into her hair to smell its sweetness. But Eden would not be swayed. She took his head in her hands and again pressed her mouth to his.

His flesh took no time in responding to the call of novelty. He embraced her hair and returned the kiss, hard and deep, moving one hand down her neck to rest above the water on her cool shoulders. Eden wrapped her legs around his waist and took him in.

They floated together for a moment in the warm, sulfurous water, Intah afraid to move for fear any motion might break the spell of her. But, when his feet found bottom, he placed his hands on her hips and began to love her until, lost in her tenderness, he could think of it no more.

Those Who Search

They stayed in the springs until twilight commenced its slow rise to dawn. The pleasure of it all, sparkling waters, strong and gentle arms about her, and time after time, the warmth rising from her toes clear to the top of her head. Rapture, a gorgeous wreath.

At Intah's side, Eden slept straight through the night, something she seldom did. Contentment lay upon her as heavy and warm as the bearskin covering the two of them. Never was she loved so tenderly or sweetly or completely.

The taking of him surprised her. Eden had not supposed she would ever be as forward with a man. Modesty and station always held a firm grip, and in its grasp, to behave in any other way would be her downfall. But she'd left her rank in Scotland, propriety dissolving into stark survival in a foreign land. Little was left of the woman who crossed the Atlantic. She'd seen it in that full-length mirror. Her behavior in the springs confirmed it. She was all West—wild and appropriate to the present moment, changing as leaves turn along the seasons. At winter's rise, spring is just around the bend.

When she opened her eyes, Intah's breath moved in the slow, rhythmic rise and fall of sleep. Her cheek nestled in his long, damp hair. The faint smell of sulfur returned her mind to the water. She wanted nothing more than to stay by his side.

Intah opened his eyes and looked at her, as though he'd read her mind. "We go today."

"And then?"

"I'll see you to the Powder, then I come back."

"Just like that?"

Intah gazed at Eden.

Her Scottish temper raised its head, and Eden's voice rose. "As though nothing has happened between us?"

He looked at the cave ceiling.

Eden propped an elbow next to him, trying to calm her anger with logic. "All this time you've been telling me to live my life in the moment, not in sadness of the past, or worry of the future."

Intah stared at the entrance.

"Well, I think it's you who keep yourself chained to the past," Eden said, ire taking control.

He rolled over and stood, wrapping one of the skins around him, and walked to the cave opening.

"It's you who won't let yourself move beyond this hole in the wall. I guess the frailties of life show no preference, do they?"

"You and I have no place together in the valley below." Intah dropped the bearskin and pulled on his doeskin shirt and pants. "You know that."

"Aye." Eden paused a moment to be certain of the words she was about to speak. "But I know, too, that love shouldn't be deserted."

Intah froze, his tone startled. "Love?"

"An Indian loves but once, is it?"

Intah stared at her as though she'd uttered a secret. His tone, firm. "What do you know of that?"

"Enough to know that this place is not simply an escape from the roll of the white man west." She sat up, pulling the heavy animal skin up around her shoulders. "You know loss and fear, just as I do. If it must be faced to be overcome, there's no facing it in this place. We're both afraid, aren't we? You, of the past, I, of the future."

Intah broke her gaze.

"At least I admit it. You've run from it as long as I have, and that's the truth. Now, for a reason I don't know, we've found each other in that race. Does it mean nothing to you?"

Intah looked into the waning fire, sparks drifting up through a ray of morning light.

"I see. Well, I'll not be taken back by you. I can find my own way. You've taught me to move on, so I'll go it alone. You stay here and hide."

Eden stood. Intah glanced her way but not into her eyes. She gathered up the animal skin around her ankles and crossed the cave in front of Intah to fetch her clothing. Intah reached out when she passed by, taking her arm.

Eden regarded his hand, then challenged his eyes. "Heed your own words, man, and look beyond. What do you see?"

Intah gave her a long look, released her and walked through the cave entrance into the clear day beyond.

Tears rolled down Eden's cheeks. She hadn't meant to be bitter. She'd awakened as happy as she'd ever been, and in an instant, on the hinge of a single term, the feeling swung away.

Love.

Perhaps she didn't really know its meaning. She had no notion of how it happened, or why it didn't. Like faith, no hard proof of love existed, only implication. And, as with anything implied, room was always made for misinterpretation. Eden shivered.

She closed her eyes, trying to conjure up the dream of the springs the night before. Intah, so sweet and gentle. She couldn't imagine any man, let alone another human being, acting as lovely and not feeling love. Maybe the sentiment was a woman's lot, for she never remembered a time when Hugh had been so tender. Even her own father never returned the affection that her mother offered. Perhaps love was nothing more than a certain misunderstanding between two people.

She sniffled, as the sound of steps came up behind her. The fingers on her arm were warm. She turned to the shoulder of the old woman, and cried. Wiconi let her be for some time, stroking her hair with a sturdy hand.

"I'm lost," said Eden.

Wiconi straightened her up, blind eyes looking straight into Eden's as though seeing them for the first time. "There is no reason to find yourself unless you're lost."

The notion swept a tingle up the back of Eden's neck and across her face. Was Wiconi privy to what had occurred the night before—what would she think if she were? The woman spoke as though she'd been present for the entire conversation between them.

"He denies his feelings by pushing them away, but pain has a way of jumping from one to another. Grief is a swarm of locusts through wild oats, eating at everything it touches."

"I don't understand."

"He does. He has spent years being content in the now, casting the past away because it brings him sorrow. He painted it, yes, and it brought him some comfort. But he's forgotten fortune exists in every step. And those steps brought him to you. The happiness of his every day took form." Wiconi raised her hand to find Eden's cheek and rubbed two cracked fingers across her face.

"But it can't work, can it?"

She smiled. "You both need to stop seeing things as they are, and see them as you want them to be. Living in the now is fine, if you keep your eye on what makes you happy. The world is nothing but a reflection of how you feel about it. That's how pain multiplies. Love, as well."

"I don't know where to start."

"Start by seeing what you want to see." Wiconi turned back to the fire, knelt by a stack of wood against the cave wall, and fed the flames a handful of small pine branches.

Eden pulled the bearskin tight around her and walked out onto the precipice beyond the cave entrance to breathe the fresh air. The cliffs across the canyon were full of light, and snowmelt tumbled from every crevice. The morning sun was still well below the rim of the canyon but the air had lost its nip. Intah was nowhere in sight.

She wiped her face with one hand as she stood before the beauty of the gorge.

See what you want to see.

She walked the narrow trail at the edge of the cliff winding around and up a short hill to a place thick with pines and spongy grass, still wet by the melted snow. Intah stood under a tall lodgepole checking the hooves of his horse. The animal whinnied as Eden came over the rise but Intah did not turn. She walked to him, put a hand on his shoulder and laid her head against the doeskin covering his back.

Intah stood still. "You said I don't look beyond. Maybe it's true."

"But you can. You've shown me how."

"I can't. The past is who I am. The present is who I am." Intah looked out over the ravine. "The future doesn't want to know me. It's easier to simply look around, find those things pleasing me now."

"And what are those things?"

"This moment." Intah let the horse's hoof fall from his hand, and slipped his hands under the bearskin and around Eden's waist. "You."

Intah kissed her hard. He picked Eden up and pulled the animal skin free to lay it fur side up on the soft grass. The horse nickered, making its way up the slope beyond a stand of trees. Intah laid Eden into the deep pile of bedding and knelt beside her. He found her mouth and kissed her hungrily. Eden closed her eyes, letting herself be carried away by the warmth of his breath on her cheek and the depth of his kiss. When she opened her eyes Intah was naked. He slipped to her side and they were flesh to flesh atop the thick fur.

Eden whispered, "This solves nothing." The fresh air turned her skin to gooseflesh.

Intah rolled atop her and cupped her head with his hands. "I don't mean to solve it."

His words were so mild and tender that Eden's heart sank under the weight of reality. He was right. A solution was unseen. Only one thing clear. The moment, stopped, as two lovers love. Intah raised himself on his arms and lowered his face to hers, catching her lips again. Though new to the art, Eden found him a quick study. He kissed deep and long as though his breath depended on it. He put his chin on Eden's shoulder and rested his cheek on hers as he lifted himself and found his way. No longer tentative. Greedy. Eden arched her back and reveled in the taking. His arms were ropes around her, binding her to him. They bathed in sweat and tears until it seemed the only end to it would be sheer exhaustion.

In the aftermath, Intah clung to her as though she were a single boulder in the middle of a raging stream. A soft breeze lifted from the canyon, drawing across them like a current of cool water. Sunlight fell across the opposite side of the gorge. The day grew.

Home.

The idea daunted. She could lie forever cradled by a man who lifted her heart out of the dust and washed it clean. Perhaps life *was* as simple as moving her mind from heartache. She'd reached for peace since arriving at the cave and, at last, held it in her arms.

Intah opened his eyes. He watched her, lips suggesting a smile toward a home glimpsed for the first time after a long trek. Eden grinned.

Intah tugged the short curls on her head. "I never asked you why?"

"The woman with the long hair never would have come to these mountains."

"Then I like it so."

"Was it I who brought you to me, or you?"

Intah traced the curve of her lips with the edge of his thumb. "Does it matter?"

The two rose, making their way back to the cave as Wiconi shuffled in from the long path to the springs. Wrapped in broadcloth, her long braids dripped gems of water in a trail of light behind her. Wiconi touched the cave wall near the fire to take a bearing, then slid to the ground. She ran her hand along the base of the wall to find a flute, held it to her lips and delivered a slow and steady loft of notes into the still cavern air.

How strange it would be if the flute sound the trapper spoke of, and that windy melody so long ago on the mountain, emanated from the cave. Eden imagined pulling a tight bow across her crafted violin in accompaniment. A strange duet, the breath of the flute and the hewn of the fiddle. Yet, in her mind, the tunes married well.

She sat with Intah by the warm blaze, listening to the strange melody, until the old woman's song ended and she placed the instrument in her lap. The cave lay silent as though Eden's ears were dipped again beneath the springs, and the world fell away to somehow make things clearer. Much more was granted by music than the soothing of the soul. The order to the notes gave the melody meaning. The order of one's life. How and when events occurred. The pace and tone of living were nothing more than a piece of music.

"So," said Wiconi, "there is fortune in the ash."

"Is that what the water tells you this morning?" said Intah.

Wiconi turned her face to the cave entrance. "Tells me you leave."

Eden stood and walked to the mouth of the cavern, looking up the narrow path that delivered them, willing the trail to crumble.

"The sun's up over the canyon rim," she said.

The old woman looked Intah's way. "Best get on."

Intah raised his brow as though surprised, and stood. "Yes."

He worked quietly, gathering the horse and supplies, until they were packed and ready. Eden tucked Aiden's journal into her coat pocket and turned to the old woman who stood at the cave entrance in a wash of magenta light.

She walked to her side. "I never finished my braid."

"You never do. Only the hair grows too short to work." The old woman turned toward the noise of Intah adjusting the pack on one of the horses. "And the painting? Is it finished?"

Intah looked at the old woman without speaking.

Wiconi frowned, shook her head a little, and rolled the wooden flute between her gnarled hands.

"I play an instrument, too, you know," said Eden.

The old woman raised her eyebrows and smiled. "Pan's flute?"

Eden looked at Intah.

"My mother told me many tales. She's heard a few," said Intah.

"Maybe next time, I'll bring my strings and the white woman can play in the canyon with Life herself." Eden grinned.

Wiconi was gruff but Eden had come to understand her. Eden reached for her hand, and this time Wiconi didn't pull away.

"I'll see you again," Eden said, wanting more to convince herself than anyone else.

Wiconi squeezed her hand in return. "The heart makes no promise."

Eden drew in a quick breath of surprise. Aiden's words. How had Wiconi came to know them? The journal was hidden away the whole time she'd been in the cave, safe from blind eyes anyway, unless Intah took the liberty. She looked at his face: expressionless. Wiconi's sentence had to be one glorious proclamation: Aiden was yet with her. She gave the old woman a long embrace before parting, as though it were her brother she held, then turned and mounted.

"Seven days," said Intah. He gave Wiconi a long look, then let his gaze fall off along the walls of the lower gorge, across the flats to the west, as though burning the scene to memory. Turning his horse up the path toward the mountaintop, he headed away from the cavern.

"Listen to him," said Wiconi, with a nod toward Intah's voice. "He's your compass."

The old woman stood, moist eyes sparkling in the sun. Eden looked at the two-headed pine as they passed, and behind her twice, before the trail made a blind turn wiping it all from sight.

The ledge along the cliff side skirted the canyon high above the swath of river below. Eden was thankful for the blizzard that drove them to the cave. All she could do was focus on Intah riding ahead of her on the path, for every time she looked down into the valley, her head spun from the height.

At the crest of the mountain, the land opened up and Eden and Intah rode side by side. He was strangely silent, given what had transpired between them. As though nothing more had occurred than the ride up and down the Bighorn. Eden was uncomfortable as she reran the interaction between them. Sifting through everything said over the last few days, wondering if she'd displeased him. Perhaps his silence was the way of a native man in such matters. Her mind came to Hugh.

Few were the words between them, as well, yet her bond with Intah had no rival. The touch of spirit made all the difference. Nothing but flesh had passed between her and Hugh. The press of want, not desire. Eden learned the difference between the two. One expressed lack, the other, fulfillment.

A few lonesome trees scattered between broken rocks at the summit. Eden had seen none of it before. She understood at once why the wind had been so strong. Nothing stood along the backbone of the Bighorn to hinder its course. The granite under the horses and the infrequent trees implied eons of unchecked weather blistering the ridge. Their arrival to the cave had been a miracle.

Eden thought of Wiconi. "What if the weather closes in again and you can't get back into the canyon?"

Intah spoke without sentiment. "To spend the winter alone would kill her."

Eden stared straight ahead, dwelling on her own desperate season she faced. "Aye. Winters can kill." She remembered the morning and the old woman's first words that day. "What did she mean, there's fortune in the ash?"

Intah gave Eden the pleasure of his eyes for the first time since leaving Ten Sleep. "If your ranch weren't failing, your husband would not have left you alone. If he hadn't, your brother would not have come, not been lost on the mountain. We never would have made this journey. Tell me which part is good and which is bad."

He rode on until they were off the slippery expanse of rock covering the pass through the peaks. The wind was absent, and any birds enjoying the mountain before the storm had vanished to the south. The air was void of sound save the slop of hooves across a boggy meadow.

Intah's tone was certain when he broke the silence. "Your man will return."

"Maybe." As good an answer as she could give. Hugh's letter sounded firm, but if she refused to join him he might find his way back.

Intah nodded a few moments as if thinking all options through. "Shall we share you then?"

"Certainly not. I'll be sharing nothing."

She hadn't thought beyond the last night. The situation seemed insoluble. The one place she didn't want to go was home, the last person she wanted to face, Hugh.

Rather than think it through, she preferred to cast it out of her mind altogether. Not being honest with Intah had protected that right. The privilege was gone.

"Seems to me you've not much feeling for him. How'd it happen?"

"It's a long, long story."

"It'll be two days to the Powder." Intah kept his eyes on the trail.

Eden wanted to shorten the whole sordid description of the last decade she'd spent in purgatory, but she'd been privy to Intah's story. He deserved hers in all its rotten detail, though she'd never told another soul the whole truth of it. Little would make sense to the man beside her, but she would tell him everything.

A heaviness in her voice weighted each syllable. "My father was a Lord in Scotland, a high station man of substantial wealth. Our home was Lilybank on the Isle of Arran off the west coast of Scotland. The Panic of seventy-three ruined him. My father lost most everything, except our home. The strain of it all killed him.

"My mother, brother and I lived on in the house, but it was rough going. What little money we had left, eaten by the upkeep of Lilybank. Aiden was a boy, years away from a proper avocation that might contribute to the family funds. Over the years, mother became ill in mind and body. By the time Aiden left for university in Glasgow, she was a shell really and I, at twenty-three— spinsterhood spread before me like an empty larder." Eden shook her head, gaze fixed on the far horizon.

"Then came Hugh Rose, a moneyed colonel in Her Majesty's army who wished to marry, and set his mind to me. In my mother's eyes, a savior to us all." She looked at Intah from the corner of her eye. "Not an unattractive man, mind you, but mother's age. I had no interest, but mother, desperate, pushed it like wheat against a millstone."

Memories flooded back, daring her to keep her head above the waterline of grief and the stench of death. The horror of a night so long ago it turned her feverish.

* * *

305

Winter's edge was on. Lilybank stood taciturn and dim at the edge of the Scottish sea, waves beating the shore, wind threatening more snow. Eden and her mother sat in the parlor sipping cups of tea, talking of a future Eden couldn't fathom.

Her mother's voice was a rumor against the gale at the window. "I'm old and sick and I'll not have us all die penniless. The house will be lost soon. We'll have nothing. Do you understand what I'm saying? You must marry him."

"I'll not marry a man I don't love. You didn't."

The frail woman pointed a hen-bone finger at her daughter, glaring with the vacant eyes of despair. "I had more choices than you."

Eden's cheeks burned. Her mother, as frank as Charlemagne, and colder than the North Sea.

"You may not have another offer. You're handsome, not young. You have status but no wealth." Her mother beat a hand on the parlor table. "Are you daft? Will you wither into nothing as I have? Is that what you want?"

"You don't care what I want." Eden fled up the wide curving staircase to her bedroom. She slammed the door, chandelier crystals rattling above.

* * *

"So you traded love for money."

Intah's curt words brought Eden back to the mountain. If he believed her heartless for marrying Hugh, he'd certainly think her godless for the rest of the story. She couldn't do it.

Eden used his scornful conclusion to end her tale. "And ended up with neither."

Intah kept his eyes on the mountain ahead, his delivery, flat. "Really?"

The two rode on, up and over the pass, down the smooth, rock slope to the east, through a copse of pine and across broad meadows. Eden thought on Hugh until her mind made nothing else out but the disgust in his eyes and the contempt he'd have for her if he were ever to discover what happened in the cave at Ten Sleep. The simple explanation of being swept by the sorrow of Aiden's death would hold no water for her actions.

She pushed away the shame. To hide behind such an excuse would be folly, for the truth was that she'd found someone who had shown her the way to herself. But what was Intah thinking now?

Change your mind. Look beyond.

It seemed impossible to outrun the penance that would surely come at the pain and disappointment she'd caused so many. She expected it, the way she expected dusk.

They rode out onto a flat bluff jutting out above a broad, deep stream tossing with snowmelt fifteen feet below. Water noise rushed with a fresh breeze over falls below them and lodgepole skirted a patch of barren earth near the lip.

"Sun's well over the peak," said Intah. "We'll night here."

Coyotes yipped from somewhere up-mountain.

Eden shivered. "What about the shepherd's cabin?"

Intah slipped from his horse. "Miles behind," he said without looking up, as though there would be no debate.

Eden scanned the campsite. It didn't seem to her they had come that far until she recognized the place where they all crossed the stream a few days before. The slim ledge they traveled under the fall of the then-small stream was a torrent of whitewater.

She dismounted and unrolled two elk skins Intah had packed. Intah laid the thick bearskin well away from the ledge and placed the saddlebags and buffalo gun at its side. Eden made her way down the embankment to the edge of the water to freshen up beyond his sight, while Intah gathered wood from loose undergrowth around the base of trees. Soon a fire burned hot, and dusk bled into night.

She returned to sit close by Intah in the soft light of the flames. They nibbled pungent dried elk, watching sparks roll up into a down-valley breeze rising in balance to the setting sun.

Intah was quiet since they arrived, and Eden lost in thinking of the coming days. The silence vexed. What bound them in the last twenty-four hours seemed undone, too fragile yet to bear honesty. Regret filled her at telling him anything. The truth he'd heard was only a portion, but its weight had pushed him beyond reach.

"I shouldn't have told you about Hugh."

Intah extended a hand and she took it. Still, he didn't look at her.

Eden used her sleeve to wipe her tears. "I'm not what you thought I was, is that it?"

Intah's eyes met hers. "You're every detail of what I thought you'd be. And there's no shame in any of it."

"Then what is it? What's changed."

Intah looked back to the fire, releasing her hand. "It makes no difference to me that you have a man. The difference has been you. I found something I never believed to find again."

Eden put her hand to his cheek then dropped it into her lap. "I haven't had that man for a long, long time. And he's set on staying put in England." Eden paused considering the choices she faced. "He wants me to join him."

Intah looked long and hard at Eden, then stirred the embers with a long stick. "For me, there is no leaving the canyon."

"For me there is no leaving—period. I have neither the money nor the will to return to Britain. But I know what I want."

"It's good to know what you want." Intah drew his hand over her forehead and smoothed back her hair. "But learn to ask for that, or better. Let spirit decide."

"Thing is, I can't see Hugh in my life anymore. But I don't see you in it either. I've tried all afternoon—to feel it. Nothing comes."

"Perhaps you don't know the feeling you're looking for."

"And what's that?"

He looked up mountain. "A bluebird in autumn."

"Beg your pardon?"

"If you saw that, what would you feel?"

"Amazement. There's not a bird save the crow on the whole mountain this time of year."

"A miracle?"

Eden looked up at Intah. "Aye."

"Feel that."

Eden sat still.

"Go ahead," said Intah.

Eden stretched her mind around the bluebird. To see it fly through camp would be a feat on the tail of a snowstorm. She closed her eyes and pictured its brilliant azure feathers against the patches of stark white snow, bright as the blue of a summer day showing through pale clouds.

The awe coming with the vision startled her. Then, the bird was gone. "I can't keep it in my mind long enough to feel it so."

Intah nodded, staring off into the distance as though looking for the same offhand miracle with no luck.

"And you, too, then?" asked Eden. "What does it mean?"

"Bear medicine tells us to possess our dreams. Perhaps some can't be owned."

Brush snapped at the edge of camp and both Eden and Intah jumped. An elk bounced across the small clearing and leapt into the opposite thicket full of serviceberry and rabbit brush.

Intah scanned the sky through the treetops and stood. "Ahead of time tonight."

The fire burned low burnishing his ruddy face, yet Eden could make out Intah's silhouette in the heavens beyond laced in a faint glow. The aurora. She stood next to Intah and raised her face to the skyward flush. An easy shine at first, then as flickering candlelight against satin water until every iridescent ray joined in a rippled sheet of indigo across the night.

"Purple. Those who search."

"Then we mustn't stop." Eden cupped his cheek with her palm. "We have a long ride tomorrow—come."

As she took his hand and led him to the bearskin, Intah took a turn toward the bluff letting her hand slip away.

"Where're you going?"

"To feed the stream."

The horses nickered and danced as Intah stood at the edge of the precipice. A fine low purple light bathed his back. Ethereal. As she lay back upon the thick hide, her body tingled in anticipation of his touch, her soul yearning for one more night of peace in his arms. But relief would never be complete until she told him the rest of her story. Fierce talons of resolve gripped her.

She'd confess it all.

The wood across the camp snapped again. By the time she sat up to look, a great bear pounced stiff-legged from the brush, its back arched high as the mountain behind them.

The ground trembled. Its paws were an iron mallet against the earth. The horses raced into the woods. Terror pushed Eden to her feet then paralyzed her. The bear reared up. Wailed a roar that filled the slip of a canyon even above the rush of water. It fell upon Intah before he turned to face it. Man and beast rolled back short of the cliff. When Intah managed to slide away the grizzly crushed him down again in a fury. The struggle broke Eden's fear into action.

The rifle.

Eden took it up. Aimed. The light was nil and neither man nor beast lay in clear sight. They were balled up together, eight legs, fur and skin, reeling back and forth on the precipice.

If she shot she might hit Intah. If she didn't, the bear would kill him for sure. She cocked the rifle. Intah made it to his feet. The bear held fast to his shoulder. Eden fired. Intah and the bear vanished in the boom and flash, a gruesome trick of magic.

Eden raced to the edge of the bluff. With the rifle still in hand, she searched the furious water as far downstream as darkness allowed. All that existed was the glitter of whitewater in the basin below. In it, the violet shine of the heavens.

Widow's Veil

Eden sat at the lip of the bluff waiting for the world to come into focus. Whitewater rushed over falls. Coyotes yipped in staccato time until the night turned to dawn and the calls grew fainter and fainter under daylight's burden. Cold spray wet her face. Thick fog blanketed the mountain, a widow's veil draped along the murderous stream.

The horses, scattered by the bear, returned to her company. They stood, heads down, at the side of the camp, as in mourning. Her shirt lay damp against her from a night full of tears. She stood, rolled the skins, packed the horses, and mounted. Nothing else to do than quit the mountains. The beguiling, bedeviled Bighorn.

She made her way down a slick rocky bank to the water's edge, noting every shady reach of lodgepole pine, each boulder large enough to hide a predator. The torrent broke hard at great rocks strewn across the stream, swirling in black arcs and eddies. Picking her way over the uneven shore was slow going. She followed the water's course short of the valley below, searching for Intah. Eden wouldn't believe he'd been lost.

Gone like lightning—was it that for Aiden in the end?

She scanned every bank and crevice for evidence of clothing or hair. Nothing but the rip of tumbling water down the Crazy Woman, rocks worn out smooth by its raging course. The same water to pass by her sod house. She entertained the notion of simply floating home, taking Maddie by surprise, emerging from the creek to take up where she'd left off, alone.

The late afternoon heat seared. Eden pulled up near a broad deep pool above a simple creek adding to the torrent. Even in the balmy air, swirls of steam danced on its surface. Springs. Despite her grief they were welcome, if only to dip a tired hand and beckon yesterday. She slid from her horse and plunged her fingers into the hot water. Her palm ached from holding the reins tight, and the warmth soothed her skin.

The furious stream behind her filled the rift with the sound of a tempest—wind, rain, and thunder all wrapped into the rush of violent water. Drowning out all other sound, until a hand on her shoulder pushed her under the hot springs. She fought to turn, sulphur burning her throat, and through the blur of the clear water she made out a buckskin shirt and long braids.

Kin Enough

A feeble call whispered through the pines. "Hey."

Intah pulled himself up on all fours and listened. The angry creek had stripped him naked using her awful, roiling waters and rocky spurs. His body was covered with broad scrapes and deep scratches, the palms of his hands raw from grasping at low branches on his way down the torrent. Blood trickled from his calves, but his skin was numbed by the frigid water. His injuries were no worse than those he'd suffered before. The bear had never managed to sink its teeth, but claws had done their work. Intah placed his fingertips over skin scraped thin across his chest. His warm hand burned the wound. The feeble call came again and Intah stood. He held his breath and focused.

Another weak sound. "Help."

Intah walked to the edge of the pines to find Ink flat in the brush, his lower leg bloody and swollen around the jagged chops of a trap.

"Didn't have the strength to open the thing." Ink winced. "Was blind in that blizzard. Gave up and dug in. Let the horse go for itself. Snow broke five days later, but the horse was gone. I walked back down the way we come up. Never saw the leg-hold under the snow."

The man had been trapped for a week. Intah knelt. "I'll free you."

"Won't be the first time." The men's eyes met and Ink smiled through sweat streaming from his forehead. He shook his head. "Won't do no good now."

Intah ripped his trousers from the trap, revealing Ink's thigh. His flesh was the color of moss and tinged purple at the highest edge.

Ink shivered. "Got the blood poisonin'."

Intah picked up a small hunting knife lying by Ink's side.

"No problem taking someone else's off—didn't have the belly to do it to myself. Got water?"

The trap lay tethered to a tree, locking Ink in place, though the stream was only a few yards away. Any water available had melted with the snow. He walked to the bank and cupped his hands to hold a gulp of water. By the mounting puddle of blood, and the fever taking Ink's body, it was clear the man would soon be out of pain. He walked back to Ink and dripped water into the man's mouth.

Ink coughed. "Cain't say as you look any better than me."

"A rough trip down the meltwater."

"Well, you're alive to walk outta this hell. Something I won't be doin'." He pulled his rolled-up coat from beneath his head, pushed it toward Intah and nodded to a canvas bag beside him. "Have trousers in my pack, too. Ain't too good, but they'll do you. And my shirt's whole." He flinched and let out a long gasp. "Won't be doing me no favors."

Intah buttoned the coat around him and sat down. "I don't need them just now." He raised Ink's head into his lap, put an arm across the man's shoulders. "You sleep."

Ink closed his eyes and wheezed. "Spent all my life thinking Indians was odd. But a man's a man, I guess. Expect we both spent a fair amount of time running from whites." Ink opened his eyes and looked at Intah. "Suppose that makes us kin?"

Intah smiled. "Kin enough."

"Good, because I always wanted to die in my mama's arms." He took a deep breath. "You'll do."

"I'll do fine."

As Intah's legs warmed, the wounds on his chest and calves sizzled. Intah focused on the stream as the indifferent water raged by, and in time Ink's arm went cold.

A Good Hide

For an instant, Eden believed Intah was by her side. But when the man lifted her to the surface, relief was demolished by the pool's wake. He was as tall as Intah, the features of his ruddy face familiar, and his shoulders broad and square. Yet she'd not laid eyes on him before.

His voice was curt and low as he pushed the barrel of the buffalo gun he'd taken from her saddle deep into her ribs. "Git on your horse."

Eden coughed up a puddle of water and stared. Her body quaked, weak with sleeplessness and horror. Though logic and fright bid she struggle, the man didn't have the look of one who might barter her freedom. His stony face said all or nothing. If she was to die, she'd rather have it be later. Time may present a better opportunity to flee than down a slender, rocky canyon.

She'd keep her tongue.

He made no move to boost her onto her horse. She pulled herself onto the saddle. He tied her hands together with a wide, bristled cord, then tight to the saddle horn. Granting a long look at Intah's buckskin, he ran his hands down each of its legs, then gazed at Eden. Her arms were gooseflesh as she looked at the man's horse behind him.

Aiden's big bay.

He mounted and led the prize of stolen horses downstream, Eden riding drag behind them.

They were well down the ravine when one of the horses whinnied. Cleve's words came clear in her mind: *a murderer, and done some worse.* The renegade had not looked back at her since the springs, as though she were just another animal. Eden wished that's the only way he saw her, and her heart bled hope with every beat.

317

She imagined she was yet sitting on the bluff watching the water in the black night, dazed and tired from the chore. Her chin dipped twice under the sun's heat reflected off the chasm walls and her eyes closed against what lay ahead.

Her horse halted and she opened her eyes. In the sky above, a circle of crows made wide slow turns. On the bank rested the great bear, washed up and lifeless, skull, a blown-open melon. On its flank was an open wound, washed clean by the ripping stream, but still showing raw with infection and the ashen hue of decay.

"I put that shell in him," said the man, pointing to the bear's hip. "And he picked up a few more somewhere, too." He gestured to the animal's head then looked at Eden. "But only buffalo guns do that."

Eden gave no reply.

"Good thing I took you before you could get a hand on your rifle. You got good aim."

She granted the man a hard look. He wore an odd pale necklace around his neck, clicking together as he dismounted. He tied the tether to a large rock and skinned out the bear as Eden sat, mute, in the saddle above him.

"A good hide." He looked at the bearskin rolled on Intah's horse. "Now we'll have two for the winter."

He intended to keep her.

A chill ran through her spine even in the heat. She sweat beneath her coat under the warm sun. By the time he carved the hide away, rolled it tight, and remounted, she regretted not asking to drink from the stream. She'd had no water since the night before. Her tongue was dry and her throat ached. There'd be no stopping. The tumbling flow beside them teased her all the way along the water's edge until she thought she might beg to drink. Her throat cracked with thirst but she feared what could happen if they stopped.

The sun rose hot and clear until pushing over the ravine's westward wall. Eden considered the erratic Wyoming weather, knowing a cloudless night sky would bring an autumn freeze. She reveled in the cool sweat against her back, but in no time it would bring a chill. She looked ahead at the water, churning with her own hope and dread.

Stream spray caused a rainbow in the slanted light, a ray of hope that Eden yearned to tether to her soul. She recognized it as the place where Ink wanted to cross.

The renegade pushed his horse around a narrow path and stopped, looking down the spillway. "The Crazy Woman takes no prisoners."

A body lay heaped up where the trees lined the stream. Eden's heart leapt into her throat. But the corpse was too far from the water to have been Intah's, its skin more like the bits of obsidian littering the chasm.

The renegade dismounted and kicked at some loose stones. "Gotta watch what you do with yourself in these parts."

The renegade walked to the body. He cocked his head as if listening to the woods and the rushing stream, deciding which merited his attention more. He scanned the trees, then straightened.

"Singular for a man to be in his long johns out here, don't you think?" The renegade studied Eden as though she held a key.

Had Intah been there first? She looked at the stream instead, as much to wet her mouth with the sight of it as to hide any recognition.

He pulled a canteen from his saddle. "Drink."

He touched the water to her lips and she drank until it ran across her chin, down her shirt. Heaven on her skin, but would turn her cold as evening came.

Appreciation came to her as habit. "Thank you."

His smile was grim. He narrowed his eyes in contempt. "You're no good to me all dried up."

319

The man pulled the horse's tether from beneath the rock that held it and remounted. Eden was struck by a difference. Intah never tied a horse. Gentleness brought obedience. Only the dominated need be bound.

Their pace was quick following an uneven trail back and forth. Wither-shins the creek. Up the mountain.

She dropped her chin and closed her eyes as darkness overcame them. The pitch black offered nothing, but Aiden's big bay somehow recognized the way—as Intah's horse sensed the way to the cave. The big bay had been wherever they were headed before. How long had Aiden's horse carried this man? Eden's wet shirt clung to her skin as the temperature dropped. She shivered. Her hands grew heavy. By the time her toes were numb, the horses stopped.

She looked up to see the shepherd's cabin and remembered Intah feeling heat from the ashes inside. He knew someone had been there. Had he known who?

The renegade slid off his horse to light an oil lamp hanging at the front door. Two mules lay nearby, tethered to the limb of a tree. He released Eden's hands from the saddle and pulled her down. She steadied herself on the horse's shoulder, tingling hands still tied, and stretched her back until her legs came to life.

"Three horses, two mules, and a woman. Not bad for two weeks' work." The man lifted the lamp to her face and reached a hand to her hair. "And fire-headed scalp used to be quite a prize. Don't see 'em much."

He led her into the cabin, sat her on a wooden chair and pulled a pair of leg irons across the floor. "These'll do you as good as they did me." He clicked them into place around her ankles. "I picked 'em off. Bet you can't do the same."

The iron lay cold and heavy. She'd not make it far in their company. The man ferried the skins inside.

"Wood's woman's work." He nodded toward the open door. "Git the fire going. You're hobbled, not hurt."

Eden shuffled out the door to a stout pile of wood that hadn't been there the week before. She carried in several loads, lay them beside the fireplace. Found a tin of sulfur matches on the mantle and struck up a fire. She sat on the hearth in the heat of the flames. The renegade brought in a jug of water from a barrel outside and pushed a slop jar into Eden's hands.

"Better go now." He sat on a chair across the room, watching her, as though he took pleasure in seeing her embarrassed.

"I'll go outside. Can't go far with these." She gestured to the irons.

"Here'll do." The man didn't move, a dark grin tingeing his face.

She'd held her water since morning and though she'd not had much to drink, she felt she'd soon burst. But overlooking the opportunity was foolish. She turned her back to the man.

"Won't be no one else on the mountain till spring. You can turn 'round all you want, but best git used to my company."

Eden slipped the jar on the floor under her coat and undid her trousers with her tied hands. She squatted and the water came. Relief, audience or not. Once the deed was done she rebuttoned her pants and turned. The man still watched.

"Slop your own," he said jerking his head toward the door.

She picked up the jar and delivered its contents to the bushes outside, some distance from the front door. Brittle air hung beneath a sky full of sparkling stars. She stood a few minutes, wondering if Intah had eyes to see them, recalling the warm water of the spring, Intah's arms around her, his soft voice in her ear whispering, *wait*. By the time she returned to the cabin, tears had streamed trails on her cheeks and dried.

"Thought you'd run off," said the renegade, sounding as though he gave no particular care to whether she tried. "Didja know wolves like white meat? One will go for your throat while the other shreds your breast. Pull your innards out before you're even dead. A boar bear would just as soon use a red-head than a sow, and his pickle won't bring much satisfaction. Makes me prettier, don't it?"

He unrolled a sheepskin, shook it out once, and laid fleece across a cot in the cabin.

Aiden's coat.

Blood rose to her face. "That's not yours."

The man looked at the lambskin, then back at Eden. "Mine now."

"And how'd it come to you."

"From a man up-mountain." He looked at her hair again.

"You have his horse, as well."

"Guess he weren't so good at keeping his things together. Least he knows where they got to."

"Did you kill him?"

"Hell, no. Didn't have to."

"You took his horse, and his gun and coat, on a mountain that holds no candle to your frigid heart. And you say you didn't kill him."

"He was a big boy. Mountains either make you stronger or suck you dry." The crackling fire drew in his stare.

Eden parsed her words, fearing she'd come apart. "He was my brother."

"You care."

The voice was hers, though she scarcely recognized it. "Wouldn't you?"

"I got me kin. Don't much like him, but I reckon I'd leave him be if—"

"Lucky man."

Their eyes locked for a moment. He pulled pemmican from a canvas bag and threw her a piece. It bounced twice, and landed at her feet. Eden picked up the meat with her tied hands and nibbled at its end. She had no hunger but ate what was given, not knowing if or when the offer might come again.

The man stared at her in the hellish firelight, but not at her eyes. He kept his attention on the bear claw around her neck, gaze lingering long after Eden stopped feeding, and until she could keep her eyes open no more.

"I know who you belong to," the man said.

Eden opened her eyes. The admission confirmed what she'd not wanted to admit the first time she'd seen him. As if keeping the truth at bay might prevent the horror of it.

The man was Intah's brother.

The renegade advanced, kneeling on one knee beside the hearth. He fingered the bear claw and snorted. "His line has a habit for white women."

As he toyed with the claw, his necklace rustled again. The pemmican rose in her throat. The string was not of shells, but fingernails.

He spoke without emotion. "All the sweeter."

He slipped his hand behind her neck and pulled her to the floor on top of him. Eden struggled, screaming in his ear and kicking at his groin. He rolled over her, pinning her with his body, and pushed his nose into her cheek. The smell of sweat and wood smoke took her back to the woman she was on Rose Ranch. The pemmican on his breath mixed with the rank odor of his mouth...the sick smell of Hugh after a drink of scotch and long smoke. The paradise she'd found in the last week crumbled in the parallels.

She thrashed her body against his, arms pinned at her back until he held both wrists in one great hand and yanked her head back by the hair, covering her mouth with his. Eden bit his lip until she tasted blood. When he cried out in pain she turned away from the sour smell and spat. He released her wrists, taking the back of his hand to her face. She scrambled toward the fireplace but he was on her again, yanking at her breeches, pulling her undergarments to her knees. He flipped her on her stomach, avoiding the difficulty of the irons and their close hold on her legs. He drove her face to the floorboards. Her head was a spike and he, an iron mallet. Her spine agonized at the pain of his weight, the chains holding her ankles to the planks beneath her. She couldn't move.

He'd just as soon kill her as use her.

And the many labors she'd been through had taught her that to fight against the pain only made it greater. So she lay limp as a corpse, giving him a taste of that prospect—the way she'd done when Hugh had a mind to take her too soon after the birth of a child. A similar agony: the burn of penetration, revulsion—loathing.

Wait. If she could accomplish it, there'd be some ration of gratification in the killing of him. Then notion of it was an hourglass crashing to the floor of her mind, razor shards stinging her better judgment. But the glass could not be mended. Eden considered nothing but murder as the Indian used her over and over. After forever, as the sun came up he moved to the heap of skins to sleep.

The fire flickered and waned. Eden, sore and weak and sickened—at one with the floor—feeling that she'd never rise again.

Remember

Eden expected death's rescue, would have even welcomed it, but she was still alive. Her body ached from two nights spent between the rough floor and the hard man. Her skin burned at her wrists where he held her down and pain seared the parts he used over and over. She'd bit her tongue till it bled—she'd not give him the pleasure of hearing her cry out.

She couldn't imagine the winter should she survive. At least the man had reason to leave the cabin from time to time, hunting, cutting wood and pulling water from a rain barrel near the cabin. She used those times to rest and nurse her wounded parts, bathing their tenderness in fresh water and using a can of rancid elk grease she found to quell the pain.

She contemplated laying a trap for him when he returned, but nothing of any great weight was in the cabin with which to bring him harm, and he made sure every weapon went with him when he left, though he said he lost the buffalo gun while racing an elk to its death somewhere down-mountain. She relished the fresh meat for his effort, but he was furious about losing the gun and used her harder when he returned. She considered locking him out the next time he left but he pulled the latch from the door so that it couldn't be bolted. When the wind came up, the door rattled and banged as though a stranger were standing outside offering rescue. She was quick in learning not to leap every time a breeze blew.

She reckoned the man didn't think she'd try to escape with the leg irons intact, and he was right. She'd make no headway in their charge, and if confronted by anything wild, she'd have no chance to run. A cruel joke, the door unlocked, yet a prisoner of her own belief in the shortcomings of capture. She tried her best to think beyond, as Intah had said. She yearned to do so. But the moment was etched in lusterless dread. Her thoughts were a circle of vultures around the wretched horror of Black Fist's last use.

Once when he finished with her and rolled to the comfort of the thick hides, she caught the waning moon beyond the tiny window. The light winked between scattered clouds as if to say, *remember*. She focused on the sphere, fishing for anything to pull her into the daylight, reeling Intah's spirit her way. Just as she'd hooked the feeling, the closer it came to grasp, the darker it became, golden edges turned to flames. All she'd capture would be the devilfish himself—the renegade.

Had it been only a few days ago that the moon waxed on the west side of the mountain, when in Intah's presence life seemed fuller? The moon's light bounced from the canyon walls, flickering like a thousand candles, its splendor multiplied a million times more than when it shone above a flattened prairie. The same orb's slant seemed to pour out its heart—soon it would be dark and empty.

The man had still not offered his name, as though knowing she understood who he was, and all it implied. If she was awake, he merely stood above her with a lustful look conveying his intention. When she was asleep, he would introduce himself with a short, broad knife at her throat until she awoke to the pain of the blade. He took her with such force each time, she was certain she'd either rip in two or be flattened into nothing against the cold floor. She'd never encountered a soul angrier than his. She seemed to be his one consolation and, after the deed was done, he lay upon her, heavy and quiet.

Last night had been different. His fire extinguished, he sat on the cot, rummaging through his saddlebags. A hoof pick, a pair of gloves, a soiled cloth the length of a neck scarf, and a handful of candies wrapped in paper. He slipped one from its cover, and pushed it into his mouth, the brittle confection, a hollow bone between his teeth.

He looked up at Eden as he chewed. "Horehound. Good for the digestion."

Eden was silent, though her last meal of cornmeal and bear fat was a stone her belly.

He picked another sweet from the top of the cot and leaned in her direction. "Want one?"

She reached his way expecting him to jerk back the offer, but her fingers touched the crackling paper without a tease. She unwrapped the candy and let the treat linger on her tongue. The man's gaze was riveted to her mouth as she rolled the sugar between her cheeks. A faint smile came to his lips. His expression was the point of cold steel. She bit the candy hard and it splintered into pieces.

* * *

The next morning, he was gone early and all day. Eden slept as long as she could before stoking the fire. The cabin froze again and she pulled on her oilcloth coat. Sitting as close to the fire as she could, she put her hands in her pockets for warmth.

Aiden's journal.

She pulled it out and held it in her hands, feeling the supple leather of its binding and thick, rough-edged pages. She was drawn most to the last entry, hoping to learn something new, something deeper than peripheral details. She opened the book, thumbing to the last few pages. The writing was a scrawl and she assumed it was the part Ink had written for him. Sounding out the letters was the only way she made sense of it. The reading was slow going. She paused at the word, *truth*.

Eden looked into the fire. She'd not read the journal before because she could stand no more pain. But there could be no worse agony than that of the past few days. Her brother's thoughts would be a comfort. She drew in a long-determined breath, exhaling a curl of steam in the arctic cabin air. Ready to bear anything, she pieced together misspelled words, Aiden's voice, vivid.

> *And now, dearest Eden, I must tell you the*
> *truth of a thing that's built up as tall and weighed as*

heavy on my soul as a Highlands cairn. It is the truth of a night that I carry with me to this mountain, in part to toss into a deep crevice, an oblivion that I know now does not exist. A truth that should have been shared long ago, for I know you to be forgiving, yet I could bear not the admission of cowardice nor deny my pride, a pair of traits that do humanity no good. Fitting, somehow, that the hand of another finally does it as I most certainly face death. Choice often brings such a dichotomy. Truth is, Eden dear, that I killed Mother as sure as if I'd taken a gun to her. I spent near an hour that hellish night lying in bed, listening to the gale outside, wrestling with mother's calls. At first, I believed her to be crying out from her bedroom, as she often did in the night. The illness she bore had made it a habit to which we'd all become accustomed. Too accustomed. Even after I realized the calling came from outside, I cowered at facing the storm in the black of night. I waited, you see, to answer the call to courage. I turned my back on duty because of fear. I am to blame for the hardship you suffered in her care, for having to watch her die a slow and horrible death. I am the cause of your feeling you must marry Hugh. I am the one who planted you here. I came to Wyoming with a mind to remedy all that. You see, if I could beat this mountain, and that bear, I'd be the man you believe I am. But life is disparate. I am soon to be free of the West. Not by return trip to Britain as I'd hoped, nor even in a box, but seeped into her ruddy soil like the water she craves. A great irony, for though I will be free of her, she will hold my bones forever. Small comfort, death. All I've come to know in this desolate wilderness is that life holds no guarantee, and the heart makes no promise.

Atonement. And they had reached it together, as surely as if they had climbed the mountain side-by-side—for it was all a certain hell.

Eden closed the book and shut her eyes against the shame of never having told Aiden *her* truth. Because of it, he was dead. Destroyed bit-by-bit under the wrath of a mountain that cared nothing for his ego or his courage or his yearning to be the man he believed she saw. She'd killed him as sure as if she'd been the bear.

Yet, deadened by her ordeal, no tears came at the conclusion. Instead, the old familiar ache of enduring loss that drives the outermost edge of one's soul to reach for absolution: Love.

The door banged open, jarring Eden as if the sound had shaken the cabin. In its frame stood the man, like the blood-being of a hungry lion, a full string of fish in one hand. Eden pushed the journal into her pocket.

He threw the fish in the bucket of clean water she'd drawn from the stream, and removed the heavy fleece. "I'm hungry." He leered at her as he pulled off his gloves. "And half froze. Expect you can help me with both." He lunged forward.

Eden jumped up out of his reach. "I can't."

The man lunged again and caught both her arms. She struggled one hand free to scratch the side of his face and he threw her to the floor.

Eden screamed. "You'll rip me open."

He sneered, holding her arms hard against the floor. "Then you'll know what I feel. Laid open by people like you, a gash that never heals. Your kind brought us the horse that carried us out of our farmland, made us who we are. Gave us more tools to kill, chased us from our homes, treated us worse than the buffalo you slaughtered. For what reason?"

"I did this?"

"You and your father, and your father's father. And each time my people were hungry fish at the lure, eager to leave behind the peace. Blame's manure all across this land. And the blame's called Greed."

"So I must take your revenge?"

The man pushed to his feet and fastened his trousers as though disgust had deflated his ambition. His gaze burned. "I fought the whites with Crazy Horse, then I led Custer to him on the banks of the Little Bighorn. You're *all* my revenge."

Eden spoke with as much contempt as she could muster. "Reward's for those who give."

It was the last time she planned to speak. She toyed with the idea of moving him to such rage he'd kill her then. She felt he'd do it anyway, come a spring thaw making the mountain passable.

"I've given plenty—and what I didn't give, was taken." He slammed the door behind him.

The sun was going down and a long time passed before he returned. Eden slept until he came through the door. She didn't move, waiting for the blade at her throat, but it never came. Soon, behind the darkness of her closed eyes, the man snored. Relief came over her as a sound sleep.

* * *

Before dawn broke she was awakened by the faint tip of his boot to her side. "More wood."

Eden rustled to her feet and made her way to the door. By the time she'd replenished the stack of fodder near the hearth, the sky had pearled up to dawn. She built a fire and made sure it took, then turned her back to the man in order to make water. She had moved past the shame. He'd seen much more of her than a short squat on a cracked ceramic jar.

She shuffled out the door to shake the pot dry into the underbrush near the cabin. The horses and mules grazed at the outer edge of the meadow. She'd hate having to eat one over the winter. She contemplated the long, snowbound season ahead— one more bleak than anything endured at Rose Ranch—as the tint of the sky drew her gaze upward.

The heavens were bathed in the deep pink of the coming sun. High, sheer clouds rippled and shone silver in a preview of morning. The beauty pierced her with something that hadn't crept to mind for days: a promise.

A vision of the cave at Ten Sleep overtook her and Intah filled her mind, flooded her heart. Intah's words in her head: *The impossible is only the possible yet realized.* But it was not Intah's voice in her mind. It was hers. Promise overtook her. She was alive. And in that living anything *was* possible. A love she'd never known before, and choice—a truth she'd never understood. Her face was wet with traces of hope, and the appreciation that she was alive to *feel* it.

Atonement, no.

Reparation—to make ready again.

In the distance came the creak of the cabin door and faint footsteps somewhere beyond her thoughts.

"Iced up, or what?" the renegade asked from the front door of the cabin. He saddled a horse. "Goin' up the mountain to check traps. Restack the wood. I'll be bringing in more this afternoon." He looked at Eden.

She turned her face toward him, tears sliding over the faint smile on her lips, managing to find a thread of joy. Something she'd not let slip from her again.

Black Fist walked to Eden, staring into her eyes, expressionless.

She stood still, waiting for him to strike her, but the hand he raised cupped her cheek instead.

His eyes softened for a moment, his voice low. "I…"

Eden was mute. A strange warmth ran through her where his fingers touched—an empathy reserved for injured dogs or a crying child. The wounded. She stared hard at him, with the only thing left in her heart—compassion. Who on the earth was not wounded?

His gaze traveled over her face, as though the same thought passed between them. He dropped his hand, walked back to the horse, mounted, and disappeared into the morning shadows.

Eden had a fleeting notion to analyze his action more, but settled instead into the solace at being left alone. She returned to the cabin spirits lifted, her mind turning another day of captivity into one day closer to freedom. For the first time, she was sure of it. She slipped on her coat and headed to the woodpile.

Pulling a few pieces from the top, she worked her way down to the base that rested on the narrow wooden porch. She removed the bottom log to reveal a small, square trap door. Eden dropped the log on the porch and knelt. Using her fingernails, she pried the loose door up. Laid out inside was a pistol and a small box of shells.

Eden's heart raced. Ink's voice echoed: *Usually a secret squirreled away.*

The good shepherd giveth his life for the sheep.

This shepherd gave her a chance.

She searched the perimeter of the woods for Black Fist. The glade was still under the threat of snow. The trees were silent. She reached a hand around the handle of the gun and removed it to her coat pocket, pushing the box of bullets behind it.

Replacing the door, she restacked the wood in a long, double row above it, ready to receive the fresh wood of the coming afternoon.

Inside, she pulled the gun from her pocket. Her hands shook at the meaning of it. She checked its load; ready to be fired.

Bullets enough to use on herself if she missed the first target.

The making of final amends for unspeakable actions in either case. An ultimate reconciliation. The whole of her trembled. She pushed the gun back into her pocket and built a fire.

Sunlight streamed in the eastern window. Eden sat by the fire, feeding the flames as it shrank, watching the ray of sun creep across the cabin floor and disappear. Her throat was cotton but she made no move for water. If she were to succeed, she must be ready to act at any moment. Failure would be her doom. Nothing would take her from the opportunity at freedom.

Early evening, her eyes were heavy and dry from staring at the door. She blinked several times and yawned for comfort. Shifting her weight on the hearth, a creak on the porch brought her attention to the entrance. She straightened her back, pulled the gun from her pocket, yanked the hammer back and pointed it at the entry. Her hand wavered. Harder than shooting chickens from a tree, the pistol was no shotgun. Her aim would have to be perfect. She brought her other hand up as a brace, pushing her back against the stone hearth for stability, wedging her heels between a wide crack in the floor planks.

The latch clanked. The door swung open. Black Fist stood in the entry, a lighted lantern in his hand. A whistle came from beyond the entrance and he turned to look across the meadow.

A faraway voice cried out in the distance. "Chance comes again."

Blaze of Glory

"Git yourself to Rose Ranch this mornin'," Maddie said. "I got other things to do today. But I don't want you stayin'. Feed and come back like I been doin'. In and out, and that's that."

Maddie made the daily trek to Eden's to tend the stock ever since Jenny had been laid up with the bad arm, but the wound was on the mend, and Maddie couldn't put off pulling the last batch of piglets off the sow another day.

"Yes, ma'am," said Jenny, and she trotted the red mule down the road toward Eden's.

It took Maddie the better part of the morning to swipe the baby pigs from the rank old sow. She put them one by one in a small pen, but two or three times the runts squirmed through the lattice fence, racing back to their mother. Once, the sow trapped Maddie and she had to climb right over the boards to stay clear of a yellow-tooth mark to her ankle. She hated weaning, especially her own babes. Just meant one more mouth to cook for.

"You all go on like you're gonna be kilt," said Maddie as she let the last pig slip from her hands into the weaning pen. She muttered under her breath as she threw the bunch a basket of corncobs. "Course that's what yer bound for, ain't it?" Maddie reckoned the whole brood saw their future.

She looked over at her pa rocking on the porch in the late morning light. "Maybe down deep we all know what we're in fer."

She picked up a rake she'd used to push the sow away and headed for the house. The children were at the river hunting frogs that would soon take to hibernation with the turn of fall. She'd promised them a pan full of legs for dinner and they were intent on filling it, granting a change from the monotony of farm meat. They squealed in the distance, no doubt on the heels of some poor toad. She rubbed her brow for the pain it gave her that morning and patted the pistol in her skirt pocket. She'd kept it close by ever since Cleve brought news of the renegade.

Ezra stirred as she approached. "Frost in the mornin', flames in the afternoon. What your ma used to say about this country."

"Amen to that. Wind's hotter than a fresh peach pie. Goin' down to the river," she said to Ezra. "Sit on the bank a while and see if I cain't shake this poundin' head. I'll look forward to finding you here when I get back."

Ezra nodded, jutting out his chin in agreement to her plan.

She leaned the rake against the house and headed for the cottonwoods lacing the river. The day was hot again. It was no wonder they didn't all have the ague, she reckoned, given the swing of the autumn temperature.

Maddie found a soft spot in some long dry grass above the riverbank and lay down. The clouds were sheer curtains against the blue. A team of storm clouds built in the south, and a roll of thunder echoed far away. She wondered if Eden heard the same.

Soon the cottonwoods rustled and a few golden leaves swayed north with a fresh breeze. Maddie smelled rain on the wind, clean and earthy, and considered how nice it would be to feel it on her aching temples. She closed her eyes and imagined Eden riding down the road in the distance. Eden seldom left her mind as sleep was hard coming each night. Maddie dozed under the whisper of the trees and the smell of water. Soon the children's wails and chatter were nothing more than background to a deep sleep that was long needed.

She awoke to hooves beating a path up the bank from the river, and Jenny's high voice beside her.

Jenny shouted. "Fire!"

Maddie sat bolt upright. "Where?"

"Missus Eden's." Jenny was breathless. Her horse stood blowing hard at her shoulder. Jenny bent over, resting her hands on her knees in exhaustion.

"Lightnin'?" Maddie looked at the sky trying to get her bearing after a deep sleep. Storm clouds were still well to the south.

Jenny hesitated, eyes big as fists. "No."

Maddie knew then exactly how the fire happened. "Jen." She grabbed the girl's shoulders.

Jenny sobbed. "Colt never burnt up like you figured. Half of it was left and rottin'. Was coyotes all over trying to eat him, so I set him off again to take care of the rest." Jenny's hands pulled at her dress as though wringing her message from the cloth.

"Get hold of yourself. There's no time for bawlin'." Thick smoke billowed up in the distance.

"Wind came up quick, took all the sparks. Grass just took off. Was an accident..." Jenny's voice trailed off.

Maddie got to her feet and turned her face to the wind. Straight from the south. Right from Eden's. And gusting. The trees no longer whispered, but leaned well away from the wind's call. Above the cottonwoods to the south, the sky was bronze, its bottom edges streaming sparks into the mounting smoke. "Git to the house."

By the time they reached the porch, the smell of grass smoke was strong, even though the air was still clear.

"Fire," Maddie cried.

The word brought Ezra straight out of his chair to look upwind.

The few trees at the perimeter of the property near the house were dry as a bone. Leaves, ready for autumn, were a dingy brown. Maddie looked up at the live oak in front of the house. Its leaves were green, but it was deception. The tree was old and two of its hollow branches had exploded in past summer heat. Nothing more than tinder.

Wind pushed dust around the yard, and white smoke billowed high above the far-off trees, a second storm rising against marbled grey rain clouds in the distance. Maddie raced to the barn and opened the massive doors, shooing the horses from their stalls.

She threw back the pasture gate and yelled to the children. "Git in here and flush out them cows. Then open those pig pens and run 'em all out."

The children scattered to open all the paddocks, and Ezra filled every bucket he found in the barn with water from the well. Maddie turned at the vibration of hooves coming up behind her.

"Godsake, Maddie." Cleve sat on his horse, gaping at the flames lapping beyond the trees to the south.

"Ain't got no time to curse the work of the Lord, Cleve. If you want anything left to roast yourself, better git down and help me drive the stock ahead of those flames."

Cleve slid from the saddle. His horse pranced, unsettled at the smell of smoke and the whipping wind. When Cleve let go of the reins the animal took no time in running back the way it came. Cleve and Maddie raced around the farm until every animal was flushed out. They then turned their attention to the house, hoisting each full bucket of water to the structure and splashing the contents across its wooden sides. They carried bucket after bucket as Ezra worked to refill them.

"Injuns," yelled Ezra, as he pulled water from the well.

"No Indians, Pa. Fire!"

Her chest heaved against the smoke and her eyes brimmed with tears. She railed against the prospect of having to deal with his disjointed rambling. If he looked into the face of fire and saw Indians, he would never see clearly again. He quit the well and crossed the yard to the house.

Cleve yelled as he pointed to the southern perimeter on the farm. "Ain't no use."

Fencing at the corner took flame, burning a fuse in the direction of the barn. The wind came up, seeming to be driven by the fire behind it. Maddie's hair was damp with sweat and blowing into her eyes, smoke thickening. A shift in wind direction stopped and turned her. As quickly as the gusts came up from the south, the gale changed its mind to blow from the north. The fire turned itself into a great whirlwind of smoke and dust, sparks swirling along its edges. A devil rising from the middle of scorched earth, it bent a crooked path across the flats in the direction of her farm.

"Fire's eatin' up the air," yelled Cleve. "We gotta git."

Maddie pointed toward the blaze. "No time."

The blaze had covered a few miles in the blink of an eye. A bellow from the inferno burned in Maddie's ears and the sight of the flaming tornado struck more fear in her than she'd ever known. She stood, spellbound for a moment before Cleve took hard hold of her arm. His fingers bit into her flesh. He was as frightened as she. Yet, in his touch, even with an infernal wrath at hand, for the first time she needed him.

"The well," he shouted. "Water's low enough. Cain't do nothin' else."

She turned to look at Cleve. If he was wrong about the safety of the well it would be their tomb. No man had been much right in her eyes, she reckoned, and she hadn't cottoned to advice from any of them. The conclusions she'd always drawn were her choosing. But she found an odd comfort in Cleve's recommendation.

Maddie called for her children and they came from all directions.

Cleve yelled, "Where's your pa?"

"Lord, no time to wander away now." Maddie's gaze searched the cottonwoods.

"Saw him go into the house," Jenny said.

Cleve ran for the porch. The wood roof flared near the back of the house where Ezra's room was. Cleve disappeared inside as the first flame sprung out of a shingle.

Maddie shouted, "Cleve." The door slammed behind him. Maddie shouted to the children. "Stay put, y'hear? Jenny, you get yourselves into that well if I'm not back by the time that fire reaches the chimney." Maddie raced for the house and pulled open the door. "It's burning."

Cleve and Ezra wrestled in the hallway.

"He's got his Springfield," yelled Cleve. "And he's ranting words I don't understand."

Maddie ran to the two men and pulled at the rifle in Ezra's hand. "Pa, you don't need that thing. Fire's gonna kill you before anybody else will."

The last thing she wanted in her demented father's hands in any calamity was a weapon. Ezra was old but he was substantial. It would take more than Cleve's help to wrestle the weapon away. Maddie helped pull at the rifle.

The fire's heat blazed in Maddie's face. Her eyes stung. No time left to argue about the gun. "Oh, just let him have it. Good God, we're all gonna be dead anyway."

Ezra bolted for the door, Cleve and Maddie on his heel. At the base of the porch steps he hesitated, letting his two pursuers pass him by. Ezra turned and stood to look at the house, in flames, before him. Maddie reached the well before noting that her father remained behind. She opened her mouth to call him as he fell to his knees. He put his face in his hands, rifle barrel resting along one cheek.

Maddie ran back to his side. She knelt beside him and put a firm arm around his shoulders. "Pa," she said into his ear, "It ain't Dakota. Ain't then—it's now. Ain't no Indians to cause this. They cain't hurt us no more. But if we don't get in that well, the fire will."

Ezra looked up into Maddie's eyes. She'd never seen a face take the expression of such pain, except a dog she'd had once that went rabid and near begged her, in its agony, to take its life.

"Pa. Come on."

The old man got to his feet and Maddie supported him. The air was hot as an August day but black as night in the midafternoon. Flames licked the base of the barn, beginning to feed on the straw inside. Dense, beige smoke billowed out the broad, open doors.

Tears streamed down Maddie's cheeks as the leaves of the oak at her front door sparkled flames, a bundle of silken threads going up in smoke. When the fire died—and if she was spared —there'd be nothing left to show for how hard she'd worked for so many years. She reached the children and looked down at their faces. Their eyes shined bright in the firelight.

Maddie looked at Cleve as she choked out a sentence. "May as well have never started."

"Maddie, don't you know that the best thing is to start?" He put his hand at the back of her neck then drew his fingers across her cheek. "We'll start again. Now, git."

Maddie went first to receive each child, every one in tears as they reached the bottom. Little Oran held one of the young rabbits from the hutch under his arm as he was delivered. She couldn't help thinking it might be the one creature left them.

Cleve threw Maddie the rope when he'd lowered Ezra and she snaked Cleve down as slowly as she could. Cleve's bulk took most of the weight off her feet and Jenny lent her strength to give him a gentle landing. They were shoulder-to-shoulder by the time they arrived in the well. The water was two feet high and cold. Soon they were all shivering with chill and fear. Ezra mumbled, his wide eyes glazed and befuddled. He clutched the rifle as though he'd never give it up, careful to keep it dry. He rocked to and fro, standing with his back against the cold stone of the well. Maddie didn't figure her pa was even aware that he moved so—the thing fueling the motion, fear.

The smoke shone bright orange in the low sky above them. Though the air inside the well seemed clear, Maddie couldn't catch her breath, as though her nose were covered with a thick scarf. The air, consumed as a candle flame is in a down-turned jar. She'd loved that trick as a child. Standing in the middle of a seething fire, she'd rather never seen such a thing.

Maddie looked around at the youngsters standing in silent awe of the flames licking at the rim of the well. She didn't want to know that the air thinned. The last picture she wanted to be in her mind was not of a soggy heap of bodies at the bottom of a shallow well, but rather, a blaze of glory—everything good her life had been. She looked around at her children. If they stood any chance at all it was because of Cleve's quick thinking. Maddie looked up at Cleve, who through no fault of his own was sharing in the hardship he tried to save them from. She leaned into him, laying her head on his shoulder. Maybe that was what it was to have a man in your life. Not just dividing the labor, but to share life in its completion and all that came between.

She rested her mind on that.

More to the Lord above than to any one in particular, she spoke. "Ain't gonna let it take us."

She squeezed Cleve's hand and looked up as the rope above, linking their bucket to freedom, burst into flames.

There God Is Dwelling

Intah held a steady bead on his last kin.

"Chance comes again, all right. Like the fortune of your women." Black Fist stuttered a laugh. "If you were going to shoot me you would have done it last time we met. No point in it now." The man reeled back toward the cabin door. "Can't stop me from doing something already done."

Intah called across the meadow from his position in the wood. "You're finished doing."

Black Fist froze. "And I thought you were done killing."

In an eerie way his brother looked the same as he did the day he'd brought the cavalry into Intah's village. From a distance he resembled a smooth-skinned man and, turned to the east, his stature took a youthful slant. Intah recalled the few times they'd hunted squirrels together as children—before the decision was made to pass Black Fist over for holy man. Before the rage was born. There had been a time...

"Comes a point when an animal needs to be put out of its misery." Intah focused his eyes on the tips of his fingers as they curled around the barrel of the rifle.

"Your misery, not mine. You're the one who turned your back on the agony of our people. Ran. Hid."

The trigger was ice, begging Intah to squeeze it into his warm palm, yet Black Fist still saw fit to goad him. Intah always expected the white man to finally wipe his kind from the earth, now his own hand was poised to do the same. He sensed no boundary occurred between anger, fear, and sadness. The emotion was one long word—hopelessness. As long as the distance between the two of them.

"Our people? I had no people left. You saw to that."

"And so, finally, you became nothing. How did that feel?" Black Fist asked. "Let me tell you. Pain is a hungry dog looking for food, isn't it? Relentless and mean. It never gives up."

Intah cocked the gun. "It follows as long as it's fed. Starve it and it dies."

"Is that what you think you've been doing all these years? Ignoring your pain?" Black Fist looked into the cabin, then at Intah again. "Pleasure can do that for a man. That may be enough satisfaction for you. I need more. I could have killed you on the mountain in that hunter's camp. I aimed at your back as you rode away. Cocked the rifle. Tasted your blood. But I wanted more. I want more. And I'm due another dose."

Black Fist looked back into the cabin and raised the burning lantern, seeming to speak to no one. "Care to play with fire?"

He tossed the lamp into the cabin and lunged at the doorway as Intah aimed and shot. In the thunder, Black Fist vanished inside.

Intah ran toward the cabin, three shots ringing through the air. Arriving at the threshold, he found Eden pinned under his brother's body, as mute as the pistol she held tight in one hand. The man was dead without a moment to spare for regret. A feeling took Intah to a place he'd only witnessed in the company of his wife, his son, the cave springs—his surrender to Eden.

Satisfaction.

Finding the buffalo gun lying near a hunting trail on his way up the mountain was no accident. But the good fortune was a hollow grave. Acting against anything was nothing more than acting against the self. Intah knew that as well as he knew the action would haunt him. All deaths, lingering ghosts.

Intah rolled Black Fist away from Eden under the clank of chains. Eden stared at Intah, the pistol falling from her shaking hand. He gathered her into his arms, and the two held each other in silence, save for Eden's soft weeping.

Intah stared at the corpse. "Won't need a doctor."

"I—I had to kill him."

"No." He'd not tell her that the first thing he'd seen was a wound at Black Fist's temple. He couldn't argue with a shot at point blank, but she'd suffered enough without taking on the guilt of killing a man.

Eden gazed up at Intah.

Intah pointed to the great bleeding hole in his brother's side. "No pistol makes a wound like that. I did it."

Eden regarded the buffalo gun at Intah's side in a way that told him she would trust his answer. She put a hand to Intah's neck and traced a deep gash with one finger until it disappeared beneath his shirt. She shook her head and blinked as though she'd gone mute.

Then, "I looked for you."

"The river delivered me," said Intah. "I don't know how long I laid at her side. I returned to the last camp we made, then figured you'd followed the creek, so I did the same. When I found the bear carcass stripped clean, I knew where you were—and with who." He laid his hand on the side of Eden's head. "I was too long coming."

She pulled at the collar of the shirt Intah wore, blue plaid flannel. "You found Ink."

Intah nodded, looking back across the glade. "He wasn't alive long after. I stayed until the last. Ground was too hard to bury him." He reached into the pocket of Ink's trousers and pulled out Aiden's watch. He pressed it into Eden's hand.

Another tear fell from her chin. "What you let go comes back."

Intah nodded, looking at the body laid open before him. He swept his hair back to take an honest look at his actions.

Eden put a hand on his arm. "Your brother."

"We shared but one word. Our definitions were different. Freedom does not fight against. True freedom is fearless."

Eden took Intah's hand. He put a hand to her cheek. Soft and warm in the morning light. The fear was gone.

He knelt beside her and touched the chain running between her ankles. "Is there a key?"

"I think not."

"I don't know how to get them off, but I can break the chain." Intah retrieved an axe from the woodpile outside the cabin. He walked Eden to a place on the ground where the granite shown through. "Sit and be still."

Eden pulled her ankles apart as far as the chain allowed and closed her eyes. With one fall of the axe and a sharp clink, the chain was broken.

"The rest will have to wait for one who knows locks." He pulled Eden to her feet and looked back at the body of his brother.

"What are you going to do?" asked Eden.

Intah went into the cabin and returned with a threadbare woolen blanket. Then he walked to the body, heaved it over his good shoulder and walked away from Eden a good distance into the woods. He undressed the dead man, trading his pants for his brother's. They were dirtier than Ink's but a better fit. Intah swaddled Black Fist in the blanket, bound him with a rope at four points, and used the same line to raise him into a lodgepole. He stood a moment, looking up at the bundle hanging in the tree. A cocoon of a gypsy moth, the metamorphosis of a tortured man from birth to death. Blood seeped from the bottom of the blanket.

Intah assembled and packed the four horses. Eden donned Aiden's sheepskin coat and attempted to mount, wincing as she swung a leg over the saddle, eyes misting as she settled into the seat. Intah closed his eyes for a moment. A sudden understanding of her abuse was too clear to bear with them open.

Eden gazed straight ahead. "I came into the wild, now I want to go home."

As soon as they started to ride, she pulled the coat tight around her and cried.

They rode down the mountain without a word. Intah dropped behind to watch her. She wobbled on her horse as though she might fall. He feared she'd slip. Wanted to offer comfort. But she showed no interest in sharing his horse.

Used hard.

The idea made his eyes well. He couldn't bear the horror that Black Fist wedged between them, and sought to diminish it as best he could.

He rode up beside her. "They say he was born in fury. His mother died being delivered of him. When he was five he put his fist through a dead oak in anger. Turned his hand the color of a ripe plum for two moons, so they called him Black Fist."

Eden continued to look straight down the trail without acknowledgment.

"Much has been ended at his hands. I never dreamed his end would be at mine." A deep, familiar sorrow wrapped its arms around Intah's neck.

Eden's voice was ice. "Sounds as though there's mercy in you for him."

Intah let the opinion hang on the autumn air for a few minutes, giving credence to her hatred. It was not without reason. But hatred caused her calamity. She'd have to rise above it or be consumed.

"Do you know the original 'The Divine Image'?"

"Blake?"

"Our first meal together in your shelter."

Eden was slow to nod in recognition.

"'For mercy has a human heart, Pity, a human face, And Love, the human form divine, And Peace, the human dress.'"

Intah offered his hand to Eden as they rode along and she took it. "All these things man is meant to be. Do you know how the poem ends?"

Eden was silent.

"'Where Mercy, Love and Pity dwell, There God is dwelling too,'" said Intah.

"Words," said Eden.

"My father said it a different way. If you don't let a mad horse go, it will drag you to death." He let her hand slip away and trotted his horse on ahead to let Eden think on that.

If she dwelled on the past few days, bitterness might pull her apart. Guilt had already had its way with her over the years. She'd come far in her beliefs since reaching the cave at Ten Sleep. He couldn't bear thinking of her slipping back into the fear that once ruled her.

An hour later, Eden rode up behind him, keeping her eyes on the landscape ahead. "There's a prologue to the story I told you of Hugh." She hesitated, her words matching the rhythm of the horse's gait. "Like the horse your father spoke of, I've meant to let it go before now."

"You needn't tell anything about your time in the shepherds' cabin."

They rode on a few paces, hoofbeats echoing off the granite beneath them. In her mind, Eden counted the steps until she reached one hundred.

"I killed my mother."

Intah pulled his mount to a halt.

Eden stopped her horse. "Not like you think."

"You don't know what I think."

She pushed on and Intah followed.

She didn't look at him while telling the tale. "We had a dreadful argument. I told her that nothing could drive me to marry a man I didn't love. She went to bed sobbing. I sat up that night waiting for Aiden to make the ferry crossing from Glasgow as he did every Saturday after school. When he arrived, I told him nothing of the quarrel except to say that mother suffered a peak in her depression. She had spells that left her crying through the night at times, hallucinations that frightened her. Aiden and I were used to them.

"After midnight, she ran out of the house into a harsh snowstorm. I suspect she was driven by my obstinance, not delusion. She broke through an icy pond. Her screaming brought Aiden to the rescue, but she was half-frozen. The gangrene was quick."

"It killed her."

Eden raised a hand. "The rot lingered, turning the flesh on her legs and arms from red to brown to black, God-awful in the pain it caused. The fetor of death itself. And nothing, nothing to be done to stop it. The wailing, the stench—horror. Two weeks." Eden looked at Intah. "I put a pillow to her face."

"Is there no kindness in that?"

"Is there kindness in driving someone to their death in desperation?" The question pushed tears to her eyes.

They rode down the slope of the Bighorn in peace, through broad stands of pine and across granite crags, until they reached the place of their first campsite near the apple trees at the base of Crazy Woman Canyon. The genesis of a storm boiled up far to the south and velvet booms of thunder rolled across the prairie that fell from the Bighorn's shoulders. The wind was gentle in their faces at first, then roared, an off-key horn blowing from the heavens, stripping aspens naked at the base of the gorge.

Intah built a fire while Eden removed her clothes, and carried them with her into the river. Little whitecaps frayed the water as tiny white threads. She beat her clothing against a large, smooth rock by the water's edge, until Intah was sure they would end in scraps. Then she laid them on the bank and rubbed her skin so hard she was bright red when she emerged. Her nudity didn't seem to bother her as she hung the garments to dry in the swaying brush. Shyness, driven from her by indifference, as though she had nothing private left.

By the time Eden walked back across the clearing and into their camp, treetops bent to the gale. She turned her back to him as she reached for her oilcloth coat, revealing a depth of sorrow to Intah he'd never experienced. Bite marks across her shoulders, some scabbed over, some fresh. Visible scars of a soul shredded. Tears filled his eyes at seeing the damage. Not as deep as the destruction inside — in spirit and in flesh.

The howling wind whined across the mountain. As Eden slipped on the coat, Intah moved to her side. She seemed reluctant to look at him.

When her gaze met his, tears were warm trails down his cheeks.

Mercy. Love. Pity.

Meaningless.

He had no words to quell his own heart. Why did he fathom words existed to mend hers?

Ever since he'd first seen her portrait he'd been haunted by the pain held within her beauty. A reflection of his own. His heartache mingled with the grace of having shared it.

A fierce bond.

They cried together for all their wounds. Around them the gale raged. Eden shuddered in his arms. Murdering his own was a poignant consequence for losing his heart again. The burden, ravaging. An avalanche of grief and regret had waited a decade for the right moment.

When the rain came, the salt of their tears melted into the passing storm. They stood in each other's arms, showers drenching them. If they melted away, he expected they would do it together.

The flames turned to embers under the sudden deluge. Its smoke curled into rays of sunlight bidding farewell to the cloudburst. A short trill pulled his vision upward. Something blue caught his eye.

"Look." He pointed to the low branch of a fallen tree at the river's edge. A mountain bluebird used the perch to pull a drink of water.

Eden looked unmoved at the sight. "It's a few days late."

"By whose calendar?" He drew his fingers across her wet hair. The bird was a reminder.

Fortune in the ashes.

Eden produced a faint smile, nodding.

Intah set the cinders to flame again and the two of them sat, arm in arm, watching the fire spit and crackle into the deepening dusk. They huddled close, saying no more. Her breast nestled against his arm, slow and measured with her breath, and soon she was asleep. Intah laid her down with care and unrolled the bearskin. He lifted her onto it, stroking her forehead with his hand before setting about to find something to eat. By the time he fashioned a spear from an aspen branch and cleaned a fish, the fierce deluge crossed the plain.

Intah looked at Eden across the blaze. She lay motionless on the fur, eyes reflecting the firelight, her face expressionless. He let his gaze follow the sweep of darkened prairie behind her to the north. A point of light in the distance straightened him, bringing him to his feet. She watched him without moving.

He walked a short distance up the hill for a better view. The horizon to the northeast radiated aurora-soft, the distant edge of the prairie gilded along one ridge. The Powder flowed beyond the drop where the Crazy Woman joined its northern travel, and the crest lay etched in flames. The fire was a medusa holding his gaze.

Eden arrived warm against his shoulder. Panic tinged her voice. "Saints, I'm no good with direction."

Intah pointed to a place on the horizon where a notch lay on a hilltop in front of the fiery glow. "That's the cut of Crazy Woman, but distance is hard to judge on the flat. No way to tell just where the fire is. Could be well beyond the river to the east." But he knew the fire was close to her home.

"If we ride now, I can be back by the end of the day tomorrow."

"If it's lost, you can't save it by reaching it sooner."

The moon set, and the prairie was black save the burnished smolder far to the east. An easy beacon to follow, but they would be blind to any uneven or boggy soil in-between. Yet, Eden was right. If they didn't leave right away, they'd either overnight again on the prairie tomorrow, or arrive in the dead of dark the next evening. Besides, the blaze had energized her, a sight he feared he'd wait a long time to see again.

Eden started back to the camp. "Then I'll go alone."

Intah grabbed her arm as she passed. The two looked at each other for a moment.

He let her go. "There is no alone."

This, or Better

Eden had little idea how to travel in the black of night, but she trusted Intah and his sure-footed horse to find the way. When he offered her to ride double with him, she accepted. The temptation of a man's touch was distant, but as soon as he delivered her home, Intah would travel back to the canyon. Their time left together was a matter of hours.

The prairie lay cold after the strong blow from the south. The wind left behind the fresh smell of rain in the air, though Eden suspected it a fickle tease. Rain spent months passing by well to the north or south, leaving the Powder just that. Intah pulled the bearskin around them as they rode on. She leaned back into the warmth of his body, her heart certain this man meant her no suffering. The rhythm of the horse became hers. She stared at the bronze plains ahead. Amber smoke billowed and curled into the sky.

The Crazy Woman, littered with few settlers, had sparse cover along its banks. Intah chose to return the way he'd come, keeping out of sight of ranchers along the way, using the less settled floodplain of the Powder. By dawn they reached the river. At sunrise, they turned north toward home, beating a straight line as the water, an eager serpent through scattered cottonwood, slithered along the basin. They said little, but Intah always kept a hand at her rib cage, underneath her breasts, a reminder of the security of his arms and the intimacy they had shared.

She covered his hand with hers. All that need be conveyed. His simple caress was the most important thing she'd come to know. She felt safer than she had in forever, unburdened by her heart and at last, her rueful spirit. In it, she'd found the jewels of truth and hope—and Intah. She never wanted to let any of the riches go.

A red sun was well to the west when they crossed the river at a wide shallow point in its flow. Ahead was a small farm, and Intah had no mind to meet those tending the dusty fields in the distance. The air was warm and dry. Intah had long since slipped the bearskin over the rump of his mount. Crossing the Powder, the horses splashed cool water across Eden's legs. She let her feet drag in the flow until they reached the other side. They both dismounted to drink. The water was tart and alkaline, sharp against Eden's chapped lips.

Intah pulled an apple from the saddlebags on Eden's horse and offered her the fruit, which she ate. They both looked downriver toward Suggs. No sign of burn lay beyond the smoke, clear view of the broad ribbon of water and trees, obscured by a silk sheer of oppressive haze.

Intah glanced at the sun. "You'll see home by dusk."

Eden fed the unfinished apple to her horse. She had no appetite. "But will I know it?"

Sunset pinked up the prairie through the veil of smoke. It was all a blush. Even the river ran red under the fading light. The last bend before Rose Ranch, Eden sat forward to see what remained. They forded the Crazy Woman Creek, again swollen wide with meltwater from the recent snow. But Eden focused ahead. The cottonwoods from the river's edge north of the creek were nothing more than black spikes flanked by the dark shadow of a smoldering barn. The fences were charred bones against the pasture, clear to the tumbling stream. The sod shanty stood tinged green in stark contrast to the burned-over country beyond.

The cabin was saved by the Crazy Woman. But not an animal to be seen. Chickens, goats and horses were absent. The only remnant of her stock, a roasted piece of horseflesh in the burned-out paddock. The fire had taken up close by and headed straight north through the cottonwoods of the Powder—toward Maddie's.

Eden bounced from her horse and ran into the sod cabin, hoping to find Maddie and her brood. The house was empty and stale smelling, waning light filtering through the smoke-filled air hanging at the window. As she turned to leave, an envelope on the cupboard caught her eye. A note from Maddie, she figured, before she remembered that her friend had no skill to write. Eden tore the letter open.

Eden,

> *Forgive the last correspondence. My mind was full of medications and I fear I was not thinking clearly. It is inconceivable that I leave you to find your own way back to Britain. I will return come spring. Rose Ranch will rise again. We will begin anew, together.*

> *Hugh*

The message stuck in her throat. Eden didn't know whether Hugh's decision or her worry for Maddie set her heart sinking.

She left the letter on the table, rushing from the cabin to mount her horse. "We have to go on."

The Greatest Power

Intah and Eden galloped into a yard of embers fronting what used to be a fine, small house. A rocker stood unscathed amid burnt and broken boards of the porch, rocked to and fro by a gentle breeze. Intah thought it odd that it was all that remained of the farm, until he determined the chair was metal.

He made out the remains of a good-sized animal shelter, one wall still standing; heaps of smoldering wood left in misshapen lines hinted at paddocks and pens. The one thing standing other than the chair was a well between the house rubble and the ruins of the barn. Everything was silent save two pigs grunting along a gully below the farm.

Eden said nothing as she rode across the remains.

"They could have gone ahead of the fire." Intah pulled the bearskin up around his shoulders. The air, though smoke-filled, was frosty.

Eden pointed to a pile of black wood and partial spokes of a wagon wheel. "If they did, they went on foot."

A voice rolled up in the dusk. "Hey!"

Eden and Intah looked at each other.

The voice, again. "Hey, ya'll."

Eden turned her head in the direction of the call. "The well?"

They slipped from their horses and ran across the yard to peer over its rim. A flock of eyes stared up.

"Good God," said Maddie. "You're alive."

"I could say the same," Eden said. "Are you all there?"

"We are. And Cleve, too."

Eden held one end of a frayed rope. "The line's burned through, Maddie. We'll get another."

The man next to Maddie spoke. His mumble echoed up the well. "That an Indian?"

Maddie's tone was curt. "Yes, Cleve, and *he* has the rope."

Cleve called out. "Bucket's down here."

Intah fetched a rope from Eden's saddle, and another from Aiden's big bay. He tied them together and lowered one end into the well. The old man's eyes narrowed to fix on the dim light, a rifle, tight in his hands.

Cleve secured the bucket.

Intah watched Eden as the two of them pulled the survivors from their refuge. Love, desperation, and the desire to see her dearest friend's face lent Eden strength. Maddie came out first and she and Eden fell into each other's arms.

Maddie cried, "My God yer a pretty sight."

She released Eden and gathered each child as they arrived at the lip of the well. They were all drenched and shivering. Intah took time in-between passengers to fetch the hides he had packed. One by one, the children were wrapped and warmed.

The oldest boy stood as tall as his shoulder. Intah estimated him to be near the same age his own son would have been if he'd lived. He stared at the sky, remembering the last time he'd seen his boy. He smiled as the heavens cleared of smoke and the first few stars of twilight broke through the shroud of sunset.

When Cleve cleared the well, he turned to Maddie. "Girl, I know you wanted me to wrest that rifle away, but yer pa ain't giv'n it up for blood or money. And I weren't gonna start a tussle with him down there in the dark."

"Then watch him, Cleve. I got my eyes on other things." Maddie looked at her brood.

As Intah glanced back at the well, he saw the toddler. The youngster weaved his way with faulty steps toward the remaining wall of the barn where the marvel of a few hens had made their way back from the safety of the river. Seeing the baby tugged at a never-ending ache. A light breeze whistled through the rickety, charred barn wall. The boards squeaked and the little boy laughed. Chickens scattered as the child trotted their way. But when the wall cracked and bent the baby's direction, instinct took over.

Intah sprinted across the ashen yard, scooping him up with one arm. Intah turned as an old man emerged from the well and the barn wall collapsed. The old man, wild-eyed and silent in the clatter, clung to a rifle as though it were a raft in high waters. When his eyes met Intah's, they locked.

He ambled toward Intah, stooping to draw his hand through the ash, hold it to his cheek for a moment, then let the cinders fall through his fingers. Intah understood the man's pain. But for every story ending in ash, one emerged. Intah held the toddler close and started toward the old man who was rambling on, but fear in his voice made the hair on the back of Intah's neck rise and his stride, shorten.

The old man raised his rifle. Setting his sight on Intah he shouted, "Indian."

Maddie's voice was the staccato-high of a blue jay calling danger. "Pa!"

Footsteps came up behind him. Eden stood at his side. No question lingered in Intah's mind that the man was crazy. No logic in his eyes. Close as he was, he saw insanity plain as signal smoke. Intah stepped back. Eden stuck to him, shoulder-to-shoulder. The baby giggled. The old man yowled curses in such a stream, Intah had difficulty keeping up with the words.

Eden's voice was steady. "Ezra Caine, this man is my friend."

Maddie called from behind, near the well where the children assembled. "Ain't the man you think, Pa."

The old man screamed, "I know a heathen's face. Ain't gonna let him take nothin' else. Put that child down."

Intah spoke in a flat tone. "I have no weapon."

Ezra's eyes were dead focused on him. So much so, that the old man didn't flinch when Maddie moved behind him.

"Pa, you don't need no rifle."

Intah slipped the child from his arms. Maddie made her way to her father, feet light upon the ashes. The toddler scuffled away to the other children. Intah lifted his hand, putting it on Eden's arm to turn her back.

He whispered, "Go. Now."

Eden spun away to free herself, all the while looking at him as though he was the crazy one for wanting her to step aside. But he'd not have her come this far to be killed. He gave her arm a firm push.

"No," was all he heard before the crack of the rifle and a blink of light took him from the strength of Eden's word.

The earth beneath him, still warm from the fire that had passed, was an odd comfort until a shriek filled his ear. He had a clear view of his assailant, but the old man looked clear of mind, a stricken look on his face as though he'd awakened from a dream with a weapon in his hand and a victim before him. Intah closed his eyes for a moment. Eden's breath was sunshine on his cheek.

They had both fallen together in advance of the bullet.

Intah's muscles relaxed in that notion. The baby cried. A sound of scuffling and grunting as if an old pig were being tied down and stuck with a hot iron poker. He opened his eyes. Maddie's arms encircled her father as she struggled to pull the rifle from his hands. Wrestling it from his fingers, she threw the weapon toward the burned-out house.

Ezra looked at the dim horizon and cried. "Look at them Indians, child. Place is crawlin' with 'em. Shoot. Shoot." The old man's hands trembled, eyes wide like a cornered wolf. His lips glistened in the low light of remaining embers.

Intah turned his attention on the well where Maddie's children huddled underneath the great bearskin, then back to Maddie. She stood before her father, moving a slow hand into the folds of her skirt as the man continued to rant. Pulling a pistol from her pocket, she lifted it to his head. The barrel was inches from his skull, but he paid it no mind and prattled on. She shook her head, disbelief and grief filling her face so full that Intah saw only heartbreak.

Her eyes closed. A single shot rang out.

The picture faded into the thumping of boots across the yard.

Cleve's voice. "Dead."

Intah wanted to tell the man that he wasn't dead, but his mouth was numb.

Children wailed.

A young girl shrieked, "Ma, you kilt him."

Intah managed to turn his head toward the words. The children stood in an arc around the body of their grandfather, mouths open and sniffling, their mother bent over the heap, her head upon the dead man's shoulder, whimpering.

Eden's voice. "Get me a wrap."

Her hand lay atop a dull pressure above Intah's hip. As she pushed herself away, the front of her coat wore crimson. He raised a hand to touch it, thinking she'd been hit. When his arm refused to go the distance, he finally understood that it was he who bled. Eden's hands moved across his body as if searching.

The feeling faded.

Cleve covered Intah with the bearskin.

Great tears flooded down Maddie's slate-pale cheeks. "My God." She put a hand to her mouth as though the frenzy had happened with such haste it couldn't be stored for memory.

Eden didn't take her eyes from Intah's. "Take our horses and get on to my place. You can all put up in the house."

"You can't stay here alone," said Cleve.

Eden looked at Maddie. "Why not?" Her voice was tight, devoid of emotion as though she were reading an edict meant for the dead. "That's the way I'll be leaving".

Intah turned his head. He was aware of the children filing by and then understood the reason for Eden's tone. She'd not add her own fear to the traumatized brood.

Her voice was velvet. "Go and let us be."

The beat of the horse's hooves fell away until a forgiving hush of air through a half-burned oak in the yard exhaled as though the whole group had sprouted wings and taken flight. Eden lifted the bear hide. The stricken look on her face and the paralysis crossing his body told him he would die on that spot, under the great skin of the bear and a million stars.

The cave emerged in his mind. The mountain.

Eden whispered, "You were my hope." She cupped his face with a warm hand and sobbed.

Intah summoned as much effort as he could. "Now, faith."

"Change has no mercy."

"It's what you do next."

He wanted to tell her to go to Wiconi. The old woman could never winter alone. But what he considered to be done next might not be what was in Eden's mind. If she were to go, she alone would have to choose the path.

Eden nestled beside him under the bearskin, folding one arm across his shoulders, holding a hand to his cheek. Her touch was the one thing rooting him as he looked skyward. The stars enamored him, growing larger in his eyes until he was uncertain whether they fell toward him or he rose their way. A pale flush tinged the northern horizon. Starting as a ripple, the light played white on the rim of the prairie. It was slow to cast great rays out to the south, but they came, coloring up to shimmer gold overhead.

Eden gasped at the sight.

Intah struggled to turn his head toward Eden and looked into her eyes. "The rarest."

She stroked his forehead as lovers do lying under the heavens, resting her hand upon his heart. Intah wanted to say more but his mouth was frozen. He'd not look upon Eden's face much longer, and hoped his eyes reflected his soul. She had returned to him. In that moment, he was as happy as he'd ever been. A feeling for which he had long ago given up the hunt.

The air came harder. Intah lay helpless to catch it, but power rested in each breath, too. Each lifted him higher until he looked down upon himself, beneath a great bear, across fallow earth readied for renewal. Eden was a vine curled around him, his heart, a fading drum. He didn't feel the ground, nor the fur of the bear against his skin, nor Eden's breath upon his neck. Intah regarded a wholly other being, untouched by pain, unmoved by the scene at all. Blood ran from under the edge of the hide, but he paid it no mind.

The only thing remaining in his sight, Eden. The one thing that mattered—his desire.

To love.

All That Remained

Eden lay at Intah's side until his body grew cold and she shivered. The aurora played out near dawn. She wasn't sure whether its light simply returned beyond the northern horizon or sunrise chased the dancers into retreat. Either way, little doubt remained in her mind that Intah had fled the world on their rays.

Faith. All that remained.

She kissed his pallid cheek, covered him with the hide, and sat alongside in her memories. Eden mused at their strange and gorgeous union, a dream—or incantation. Running her hand under the bearskin, she pulled the top button from Intah's shirt. She stood, looking at the bee carved into the shiny, black stone, and closed her hand around it tight.

Fortune among the ashes, Wiconi had said. In some odd way, she'd seen the future.

She gave Ezra's bloodied scalp a last look and headed for home. She stopped once, a good distance down the road, to look back. Her procession left a whitish trail in the dark ash, ending at the heap that was once Intah. The footsteps mimicked the pattern of her travel since they'd met—toward him, then away. Her experience on the Bighorn occupied the emptiness between—the invisible, intangible, indescribable—yet so real its veil blocked the advance of desolation across her heart. Instead, the design, a braided weave, finally connecting every disjointed point of her life.

When she reached her home, a sliver of smoke gestured from the chimney, but all was calm. The silence lead Maddie to her thoughts—and the killing of her father.

Ezra's mind was a burden, and Eden, never aware of how deep the load weighed upon her friend, bent too low under her own troubles to look up. A sudden remorse struck her for not ever taking the time to consider Maddie's woes. An intermission from her own tragedies might have made all the difference.

The three horses and two mules that had come off the mountain stood tied to one of the willows near the front door. The few she'd left in the pasture had probably fled the fire through the old weakened portion of the fence. She scanned the hills surrounding her ranch for any telltale of them grazing across the Crazy Woman or standing in the shade of a sparse oak on the unscathed hillside to the south. Nothing.

As she neared the door of the cabin, the two she-goats came around the corner of the shelter. They butted her legs in tandem and raced on across the bridge to the burned-out barn. Eden untied the horses at the willow and let them walk free. She knew they'd not go far. She turned toward the cabin again.

Maddie abided in the doorway. "Gone?"

Eden stood a moment before she could answer. "Aye."

"I—"

"We've both lost. I know what you're feeling."

"I kilt my pa." Maddie's face was granite.

The notion came as easily as if Intah were whispering in Eden's ear. "You put him out of his misery, Maddie. There's kindness in that."

Eden told Maddie the story of her own mother; the rest of the tale coming piecemeal, as if they made a sentence it might be her last. "And Aiden—dead, too."

With that the tears were stemmed no longer. The two women fell together and cried until Cleve joined them in the yard. He put an arm around Maddie and pulled her to him. Both gazed at the leg irons on Eden's ankles.

"Lan," said Maddie.

"I haven't the strength at the moment to tell you. And haven't the skill to get them off."

"I do," said Cleve.

He walked back into the house, returning a moment later with a long ice pick. With more ease than she ever imagined, she was free of both irons. Her legs were gloriously light even under the freight of her sorrow.

Cleve tossed the shackles in the direction of the creek. "Best git them both in the ground. I'll go."

"No." Maddie took a step back and sniffed. "Me and Eden'll do it."

Cleve looked at both woman. "Ground's hard."

"Not as hard as burying someone you love," said Maddie looking over at Eden. "It's our work. We's had practice."

Eden followed Cleve into the sod house. Strewn with sleeping children, bedding lay from wall to wall, and furniture was out of place. What would have sent her into a spin a few days ago, mattered not. Eden went straight to the carved chest at the foot of her bed. She pulled two white, embroidered linens from inside, put them under an arm, took a sewing box from her bureau, and picked her way through the sleepers past the kitchen table. Hugh's letter still lay open where she'd left it. A tremor took her at its contents, but her mind held too many things to think on what might come. A long season lay ahead to consider them— alone. She continued out the door.

Maddie had two of the horses and lifted a saddle onto one as Eden walked across the bridge to the remains of the barn. One wall still stood, and on it hung the miracle of a few tools. She grabbed a shovel and pick and met Maddie at the bridge. Eden chose Intah's horse, running her hand beneath its coarse mane before riding down the sallow road.

Steps from the ruined farm they pulled up next to a burned heap of bones and burnished hair.

"Red mule, I 'spect," said Maddie. "Lord didn't leave me much."

"Alive," said Eden, looking at Maddie. She'd learned as long as she could breathe, hope could be rallied.

The women each took a sheet to bind their dead. Eden wrapped Intah as tight as she could. Reaching his chin, the notion took her mind to the scissors in her sewing box. She used them to cut a good length of his hair, wrapped the mass in a curl and pushed it into her pocket for another braid she'd make—someday. She finished up, lacing each end of the burial sheet with her finest stitch. Then she and Maddie set about digging graves. Cleve was right. The ground was slate. The work was slow and in no time their hands were blistered.

"Should we jist dig one?" Maddie leaned against her shovel.

Eden thought a moment. She looked at the two bundles laid before her. "Eternal reconciliation to be hashed out, you think?"

Maddie gazed at Eden. "Would Intah mind?"

"I don't think he would have faulted your father if he'd known all he'd been through. They shared the commonality of loss. Humanity's bond, I suppose. We don't all love, but we all lose."

"Guess it don't matter no more. Maybe I'll crawl in, too."

Eden put a hand on Maddie's shoulder. The woman trembled. "You're right, Maddie. Doesn't matter now."

They laid the men side by side in one deep hole, and stood next to the grave.

"I don't know what to say."

Maddie pointed at the bundle that was her father. Her voice wavered. "Stay put, you hear?"

Eden granted Maddie a half-smile. She stared at the bearskin laying by the excavation for a long time. She'd meant to lay the hide over the top of the bodies, but her legs wouldn't allow the mission.

"Should I leave it with him?"

"That skin? Yer crazy. Ain't gonna do him no good. Winter's too cold in this holler to put a prize like that in a hole."

Maddie was right, but that wasn't the reason she picked it up and bundled it on her horse. She didn't know what drove her.

They rode back to Rose Ranch in the same silence they'd occupied on their way to revisit the dead. Neither wanted to speak much of recent times. They all burned too bright. But returning home, with Intah so present in her heart, made her think of Wiconi—alone on the mountain.

She studied Maddie, who knew nothing of the journey so far. Eden hadn't the stamina to recount it all. The story could wait, but could the old woman?

When they reached the house the children buzzed around the yard in the long slant of late afternoon light, trying to catch a few chickens that had found their way home. The women unsaddled and turned the horses out. Cleve picked through the barn looking for anything worth saving. A pitchfork with no handle and a metal saw laid out on the blackened ground. A crumpled tin of penny nails stood guard. Eden entered the cabin on the close heels of Maddie, who was already intent on straightening up.

"Don't take a lot of time to take a place over," said Maddie. "Know you like things just so." She rolled up the bedding and righted a fallen chair.

"Things," Eden said, waving her hand at the room. None of the valuables gave her pause.

"Reminds me." Maddie walked to the dresser and picked up Eden's wedding band. "You're missing somethin'."

She handed the ring to Eden, who said nothing.

Maddie looked at the note on the kitchen table. By her tone, she'd been dying to know what Hugh had written. "I see you read the letter come fer you."

"He'll be back come spring."

"Told you so," said Maddie. "Ya'll see? Things are gonna be good again."

Eden sat down at the mahogany table and rested her head on her hands.

Maddie walked to her side and laid a hand on her shoulder before pulling her fingers through Eden's short curls. "Walked in here the first time to find the rest of this on the floor. Gave me a fright. Thought you'd been scalped. Why ever did you cut those good-lookin' locks?"

One reason. "Change," said Eden.

Maddie tried to cheer her. She had no way of knowing all Eden had been through and what Intah meant to her—nor that within that meaning was no place for Hugh. Eden needed to think. Maybe she'd find direction in her brother's words.

She walked to her coat resting over a chair back and pulled Aiden's journal from the pocket. "I'm going to the river for a while."

Maddie nodded as Eden pulled on the coat, left the cabin and crossed the yard. Jenny sat by the Crazy Woman, working a long stick into the muddy bank, changing a wisp of water from its course.

"I'm sorry about your grandfather, Jen," said Eden.

Jenny looked as though she was touched that Eden might say so. "Sure." She went back to digging her hole, as though lost in a struggle between guilt and heartache.

The contest Eden knew all to well. A deathmatch best left behind.

Eden expected minding a crazy old man was a painful thing, and let it all slip from her mind as she walked to the Powder. Suffering was nothing new to any of them. She searched out a soft spot in the unburned grass south of the creek and sat above a smooth, quiet stretch of Powder water. The river rolled and dipped in places, betraying boulders along the bottom.

As she opened the cover of the journal, a loose folded paper fell away. Eden picked it up, opening it flat. A page from a book of Shakespeare—Prospero's speech from *The Tempest*—four lines from the middle of the discourse circled in ink: *But release me from my bands With the help of your good hands. Gentle breath of yours my sails Must fill, or else my project fails, Which was to please.* The last word blurred through a salty lens.

To please her.

True Love Doth Pass

A week later Eden lay next to Maddie on the feather bed in the pewter light of dawn, still burdened by Aiden's diary. She'd have lost him either to the mountain or upon a ship sailing home.

She fingered the braids on her wrist and remembered the fine piece hanging unfinished in the cave at Ten Sleep. Intah's last words to the old woman, "seven days." Well beyond that. Soon the snow would lock Wiconi in a dark and barren grave.

Eden craned her neck to the first ray of sunlight coming through the dirty pane. A crow called somewhere beyond, and the sound returned her to that place on the mountain, when the bluebird happened across the path. An absurd notion to see such a thing after a hard snow, but there the bird had been. As unthinkable as finding hot springs in a canyon—or one's heart with an Indian. She no longer believed in the impossible.

Eden arose, picking her way over the brood of sleeping children. Violin and bagpipes propped each other up in the corner. The joy they had given her over the years was a blessing, but neither had the power to vanquish all she'd seen. On the cupboard, still lay Hugh's last letter. She pulled the envelope from the shelf and stepped out the cabin door. The air was crisp for the first morning that week. A bright star rose to the east even as the sun glowed below the horizon.

Venus.

The irony was not lost on her. She turned to face the mountains standing behind the low rise as the Crazy Woman bent away from the Powder. She yearned to see them, smell the pine— lose herself in the healing of the springs.

Eden closed her eyes to enter the vision of the red rock of Ten Sleep, a thread of smoke rising from the cave, hearing the music of the old woman's flute cherishing the canyon. She rubbed the rumpled linen paper in her hand until her gaze settled on the last line.

We will begin anew, together.

Whether sitting in Scottish parlors sipping tea and nibbling shortbread or continuing the folly of the ranch, both made her nauseous. She drew deep breaths to quell the rising in her throat, then ran down to the creek and retched. She sat beside a stream grown quiet over the past week and dipped a bare foot in its cool water. Her parts were no longer raw from the use they'd had by Black Fist. No sign was left save deep bruises on both ankles that took their time to heal.

She hadn't told Maddie of the misuse and didn't think she would. Every time its horror came to mind, anger took her. Intah's voice rippled through the stream: *If you don't let a mad horse go, it will drag you to death.* Weary of being dragged, she'd let the horse go.

Eden pushed herself up the bank toward the cabin, her stomach unsettled. It had been so the past few days. And her head, light as though drunk with a full glass of spirits. Another stray horse sauntered its return down an old cow path along the draw. Cleve had rounded up three before he beat a trail back to Suggs for lumber and supplies to rebuild the barn. The rest had come back a few at a time over the week. Nine, and the foals to boot. One of the colts was already interested in an open mare that was in season, tail wagging over her back as she turned her rump to him. The sight dampened Eden's palms and stopped her cold. She counted the days from her last bleed. With a hand on her belly the landscape swayed again. The sign was star bright and bold across her mind's eye.

It always took her quick—like the flu.

As the possibility formed, a hundred tiny birds swirled overhead, reaching for the tallest willow flanking the house. The air burst into song, a wellspring of a thousand crickets on a summer night. Then, as swiftly as they came, they took flight, vanishing into the dusk of the southern sky. Eden's heart darkened under the weight of her rolling stomach. There'd be no knowing whose seed had taken her. The shared features of the two brothers would betray neither in any resemblance the child might have.

She looked through the cottonwoods to the Powder River, a run of water impervious to its wicked ways of drought and flood, unconcerned by the eons of humanity laid in graves along its shore, aloof to any effort not its own. Like so many of those who settled the country—men who were wedded to their struggle.

A lone horseman splashed through the river, the horse's hooves raising billows of ash in its wake as the pair traveled toward Suggs. Eden drew in a long breath to steady her stomach. Staying at Rose Ranch under the eyes of the prim settlers was out of the question. She'd be one more canker on a land already cursed. She crumpled the letter in her hand as she walked to the cabin. Even if she wanted to, she couldn't wait for Hugh. At Intah's side, hearing him draw his last breath, she believed her soul could reach no deeper well. Be it in love or in grief, the wellspring of the heart is bottomless. And deep within its cavity the rim seems impassable.

A voice startled Eden to present. "I wanna know if your brother wrote 'bout me." Maddie stood in the doorway of the cabin with the journal in one hand.

Eden walked to her friend, watching her for a moment, then pulled the book from her hand.

She turned to a page written soon after Aiden's arrival at the Crazy Woman and read. "Down the road lies a small shanty farm that is as dismal as its maid is fair. Madeline is her name and she has the sparkle of a cool stream in this godforsaken dry." Eden looked up at Maddie who wore a giddy smile at the information, then continued. "The only snag to her is a raft of children fixed to her like glue. It's a greater piece of cake than I wish to eat, though I'm sure quite sweet. But I have no plan to remain in this land beyond my duty to see Eden through the winter. Spring will find me in Glasgow. The drab of Wyoming carries little more attraction than the gem down the road. And taking a shine to a woman who shines to this wasteland invites ruin."

Maddie's expression turned sour. "He hadn't no stomach for these parts. Not much whitewash to that."

"He'd have left me, too."

The truth of it was that her brother's hatred for the land was what had killed him. And in an irony that would have made Aiden laugh, Hugh's love of the same had been his savior. He'd risked everything to earn the prize of return, only to be saved by failure. Eden wouldn't read the part of the journal speaking Aiden's change of heart. Would do no good but give Maddie something to pine after. The future in such things was futile.

"Gonna marry Cleve, anyway."

"Thought you didn't need a man."

Maddie had come a long way since Eden had left her.

"Don't. I want one. Though with a passel of mouths to feed, I suppose he ain't gonna have two pennies to buy me a ring."

Eden shook her head. "I can't see you living in town."

"Well, there'd be economy in that. Besides, ain't no place else to go." Maddie crossed her arms and looked down the road toward her ruined farm.

"A good man once told me there be always choices." Eden regarded Maddie and, as she did, great love welled within for the friend who had never asked for anything but friendship. Love made sense of mismatched intentions.

Eden considered the sweep of land she called home. The ranch, purchased with her own money. She held the deed. Maddie mused to her more than once about what she'd do with a fine piece of land.

With water by its door.

Eden smiled to think that Maddie's dreams had arrived. "You have this ranch."

With the wash of the delivery came an updraft to Eden's heart, her spirit lifting as so many leaves on a westward breeze, a final push in one direction—Ten Sleep Canyon. And the babe, no matter the sire, carried Intah's blood. The notion, a bath of morning light.

Maddie's expression was a question mark. Eden took her friend's hand and walked her to the Crazy Woman, where they both sat, the melancholy sound of the dwindling stream nearby, until Eden delivered the essentials of her journey into the Bighorn—and her decision to return. She'd included the warm springs in all their detail, and the splendor of the bond between her and Intah.

The words came, bullion flowing from her lips, forever banishing the prim patrician woman she'd been. Rose Ranch was no longer her home, the clan of Brits, no longer her people. Those things that had bound her to the place were the same things releasing her. Freedom was her closest ally. Locked arm-in-arm, Eden flew with deliverance, somewhere just above the real world––the realm of faith.

Eden's final say on the matter came easy. "There's treasure in truth."

Maddie's eyes sparkled in the afternoon light. "Them words of yours, beautiful as you. What happened on that mountain, in the end, I reckon happened for good."

Eden nodded, well understanding that other truth.

Maddie was still a long time after, hands resting in her lap. She shook her head. "What'll I tell Hugh?"

Eden was quick to answer. "Tell him I never had with him what you have with Cleve. One look at the two of you and he'll know it's true." She smiled, putting her hand on Maddie's. "Tell him I have someone new in my life."

"And what makes you feel this babe will live? It's not been yer luck." Maddie placed her other hand over Eden's, her gentle voice conveying her compassion.

Eden dipped a toe in the stream, watching the water bunch up on one side to ripple on the other in its wake. "Faith."

Maddie wiped tears from her cheek and looked at the sod house. Her stoic face suggested only one thing be done. "It's a fine place. Cleve can add a room or two. And there'll be another barn."

The squeal of children brought the women's attention to the cabin door as Maddie's family emerged fully immersed in a loud game of tag, little Oran taking up the rear, laughing as he toddled along in pursuit.

Maddie stood and waved her arms. "We got things to do. Ya'll start cleaning up the mess of that paddock."

The children ran across the yard and over the bridge, taking their game of the moment to the residue. In the distance, a wagon rounded a bend in the road with Boss and Ruth Williams.

Eden left the journal on the bank of the stream as though leaving its weight behind her, and walked to the house, looking behind her once to see Maddie pick up the book and follow.

Boss pulled the wagon up to the door and stopped. "Glad to see your home still stands. Near everything from here north, just short of Suggs, is coal."

"Well to the east, too. We lost a hundred head of cattle. Thought for sure you'd be burned all the way out." Ruth looked at Maddie. "A passerby told us of your home, Madeline. We're awfully sorry."

"Thank you, kindly." Maddie looked at Eden.

Ruth stepped down from the wagon. "I hope these will get you all through the winter." She reached over the rim of the wagon bed and raised a burlap bag up and over the side. "Clothing for the children—and you."

Maddie beamed shock. "Oh, my lan. What a blessin'." She walked to Ruth's side and peered into the wagon. "But where you'd you ever get all this?"

Boss spoke. "News got out. People want to help."

"Me?" Maddie scowled.

"You." Ruth placed her hand on Maddie's shoulder.

"Don't know what to say." Maddie turned toward Ruth with the expression of a woman seeing a newborn, awe and gratitude and dismay passing her face like so many clouds across the moon.

"Say thank you," said Eden.

"Yes," Maddie said. "Yes."

Boss turned his attention across the yard. "I'll send some hands over to help with barn, Eden. They'll have it back up before snowfall." He jumped off the wagon and unloaded several gunny sacks and two crates. "We'll set this all next to the cabin and be on our way. Men will come tomorrow morning." He extended his hand to Maddie. "And we'll have you put back together enough to bare the winter, Mrs. True. Good as new by next summer."

Maddie shook his hand. "Thank you, sir."

Eden gave Ruth a long hug, and the two Williams climbed back in the wagon and disappeared down the sooty road.

"Never would'a figured." Maddie's face was scripture: Revelations.

Aiden's comments over the years threaded through Eden's mind as an apt beginning to the saga: *Ever notice when things get bad, they tend to worsen?*

Dear one, it only gets better by choice.

She gave Maddie's hand a squeeze, then let go. "An open heart can make magic."

Eden gave the sod roof a long look and entered the cabin. Her gaze landed on the violin. She lifted the case, bagpipes slipping to the floor, and took her instrument from its safety. Holding its wood to her chin for a moment, she enjoyed the comfort of the fine grain between her fingers and a faint sharp smell in the marrying of maple and spruce. She let the violin slip to her side as she walked to the bank of shelves by the fireplace. She rubbed a hand over the frayed bindings. They'd all been read—a hundred times. Two would make the trip to Ten Sleep—Blake and the Bible.

Eden's mind returned to that first night in the shepherd's cabin when she, Intah and Ink had all spoken of how they imagined their own end. Ink feared a height and the notion had brought him to tragedy. And Intah's words had made no sense to Eden: *By silks and fine array.* A poem long since forgotten. She set the violin on a chair and pulled Blake's book to her, thumbing through its pages until she found what she sought.

> *My silks and fine array,*
> *My smiles and languish'd air,*
> *By love are driv'n away;*
> *And mournful lean Despair*
> *Brings me yew to deck my grave:*
> *Such end true lovers have.*
> *His face is fair as heav'n,*
> *When springing buds unfold;*
> *O why to him was't giv'n,*
> *Whose heart is wintry cold?*
> *His breast is love's all worship'd tomb,*
> *Where all love's pilgrims come.*
> *Bring me an axe and spade,*
> *Bring me a winding sheet;*
> *When I my grave have made,*
> *Let winds and tempests beat:*
> *Then down I'll lie, as cold as clay,*
> *True love doth pass away!*

Eden's flesh tingled. The words ran together as though dissolving into the two mattering most. True love.

Tenderness took her in its arms as Intah had, and a vision swelled beneath closed eyes: a great outstretched hand hovering over a red rock canyon, bright water spilling over pine-strewn cliffs—an old woman and a child. And the sight was warm and safe. More than anything she'd ever felt. Past heartache. The far side of every cross word she'd uttered and barren thought she'd had. She saw beyond it all.

Beyond.

She closed the book. She'd read the final chapter. Yet her heart told her the full story was more than a single volume. Eden wiped her eyes, resting her hands about her neck as she made a mental list. She collected a few clothes, some infant things she'd kept over the years, packed the saddle bags with food, scissors to keep her hair tamed, and the small hand mirror. She secured the violin in its case. With pen in hand, she scribbled out a rough deed to her land, signed her name, and placed the paper underneath an empty fruit bowl on her cherished dining table.

Eden stood perfectly still to hear the Crazy Woman's whispery dance through the creekbed stones nearby. Soon winter would grip the stream, lidding it over in bard ice and memories, secret water flowing under the season's frigid hand. Then, only the imagination would see liquid running beneath a purposeful opaque cover so frequently drawn, as well, across the eyes, shielding hidden truths even in spring.

One last look at the tintype of Hugh, Eden by his side. The photo had faded, as though Eden herself stood stoic and resigned, fading at last from a picture that would remain vivid in another realm—not hers.

She pushed her arms through Aiden's sheepskin, lifted the ornamental birdcage he'd sent in jest so many years ago and carried it to the yard. In no time the cage held a cockerel and a banty hen that Jenny had returned to the henhouse. There'd be fresh eggs before spring. Eden smiled to think of Wiconi's face at the news.

She saddled Intah's horse, for it knew the way, and turned her face into the breeze. The wind beckoned with a wicked finger from the mountains beyond.

Winter marched on.

But the threat raised no fear. She focused on the trail back to Ten Sleep, and the wise old woman who would help see them through the season. Eden fetched what she'd packed from the cabin and headed back to her horse where Maddie stood solemn-faced.

She put a hand on Eden's shoulder and the two women embraced. "You left this." Maddie held out Aiden's journal.

"I want to see no more of it."

"Well, I don't want Cleve to see none of it." She tore the pages out, shredding them to the wind. The pieces, confetti dancing across the yard.

Maddie disappeared into the cabin, as Eden watched her past scatter in bits that might as well have been of fool's gold and diamonds. Tender heartaches and morsels of joy. Then she packed Aiden's bay with essentials: a burlap bag for apples she aimed to pick on her way, the animal skins that had come down the mountain with her, the great bear hide belonging to Intah. Maddie emerged from the house and ran to the horse's side.

She handed the small twine and brown paper package to Eden. "Almost forgot. Yer spectacles come."

Eden tore open the paper and pulled the glasses free. She put them on and looked around. "Think I've learned to see better without them."

She slipped them off and into her pocket, fingers touching the cool gold band still resting there. Her hand lingered a moment as her mind retreated into a past as cold and heartless as the metal. She rolled the ring into her palm and pulled it from the pocket, holding her hand out to Maddie, who stepped forward with a quizzical expression, hand extended.

"Give this to Cleve." Eden dropped the ring into Maddie's palm, the awful weight of the scant gold and all its anguish, dropping away, as well. She needed no token to remind her of love save a gift received from Intah, the compass of her heart.

"I declare." Maddie took it in her fingers and held it up. "What if he don't give it to me?"

Eden chuckled. "Who else might he be giving it to?"

The goats trotted up to Eden, bleating for a kind hand. She kneeled to scratch their chins. "You're safe here, girls."

"Ain't that right," said Maddie as she scrunched her nose. "No goat on my table."

Eden looked up. "They're good friends."

"The best." Maddie's eyes were round, bright pools.

"Even better." Eden stood.

"Know I told you to start looking ahead, but it ain't right. Livin' with an old Indian, alone."

"You think it's wrong. She'll think it's right. Who gets to choose the answer?"

"There are boundaries, girl, to what you're planning."

"Can you tell me, Maddie, where the borders lay between her life and mine, between mine and yours? Between us and anyone else on this earth?"

Maddie stood on one foot then the other, as though straddling a broad silence between her thoughts and the answer.

"The lines are self-made, my friend. We imprison ourselves. No one does it for us." Eden smiled in relief. The independence she had craved laid before her. In some grand scheme, all things were right. It finally made sense. Only now mattered.

Eden swung up onto the horse and looked around her ranch. The willows had avoided the fire. They rocked in the wind, the loveliness of their fair-haired leaves twirling into clouds of glitter. The two she-goats ran across the yard. Happy to play with the children in what remained of the barn, they paid no more mind to Eden's departure. Jenny sat near the cabin content to fashion the long, pale curls of her younger sister's hair with an ivory comb, a girlhood gift from Eden's father. Cleve angled the fine mahogany table through the door and pulled it into the yard. A cabin designed for two needed the extra space. The thought lifted her spirits in a way that once only Aiden had.

Eden bent down to kiss Maddie's cheek and held her hand tight.

Large tears plopped into the dust at Maddie's feet. "What will happen?"

"What will happen." Eden grinned at the children skipping through the remnants of the barn. "May you find fortune in the ashes, my friend."

Though the air nipped her cheeks, Eden was snug in Aiden's fleece coat. She let her friend's hand slip away and turned toward the bloodstained rim of Ten Sleep Canyon, her heart but one desire.

"Still don't know what it's all about." Maddie's voice faded in the wind.

Eden called behind her, the single word glistened her lips, as if bubbling to the top of a thermal spring. "Joy."

About the Author

Robin F. Gainey partnered in the creation of California's Gainey Vineyard; presided over winery culinary programs; and, with Julia Child and others, founded Santa Barbara's American Institute of Wine and Food. She also oversaw the breeding and showing of champion Arabian Horses begun by the Gainey Family in 1939. Over the years, she's lived in Arizona, California, Colorado, Washington, and Rome, Italy. She returned to her hometown, Seattle, to find her heart in writing. Active trustee of the acclaimed Pacific Northwest Ballet, she enjoys reading, cooking, horseback riding, skiing any mountain, and spending three months every year cruising British Columbia's Inside Passage by boat—mostly alone. *Light of the Northern Dancers* is her second novel. You can learn about Robin and her writing at www.robinfgainey.com.

CPSIA information can be obtained
at www.ICGtesting.com
Printed in the USA
FFOW05n1420181017

9 781945 447495